YESTERDAY'S WIND

YESTERDAY'S WIND

A LBERT B ARTLETT

authorHOUSE®

AuthorHouse™
1663 Liberty Drive
Bloomington, IN 47403
www.authorhouse.com
Phone: 1 (800) 839-8640

Published by AuthorHouse 10/05/2015

ISBN: 978-1-5049-5378-8 (sc)
ISBN: 978-1-5049-5379-5 (e)

Print information available on the last page.

Any people depicted in stock imagery provided by Thinkstock are models, and such images are being used for illustrative purposes only. Certain stock imagery © Thinkstock.

This book is printed on acid-free paper.

Because of the dynamic nature of the Internet, any web addresses or links contained in this book may have changed since publication and may no longer be valid. The views expressed in this work are solely those of the author and do not necessarily reflect the views of the publisher, and the publisher hereby disclaims any responsibility for them.

Part I

The tanned farmer stood under the windmill in the hot cloudless July afternoon. His soiled blue cotton shirt was buttoned to the collar. Before him, his nineteen-year-old son, ramrod straight in his immaculate Marine dress blues lamented, "Dad, if only I could turn back just a few months, then I wouldn't be in this predicament." The father, his jaw set, gazing up at the windmill vanes, quiet in the summer calm, uttered softly, "You can't pump water with yesterday's wind."

CHAPTER 1

October, 1922

It reminded him of an anthill—dozens of people moving endlessly in disorganized, yet patterned directions. The hollow echo from the thick heels of the nurse's shoes striking the marble floor had the effect of a metronome out of sync. He thought the silly white hats the nurses wore looked like leghorn chickens with their white rounded rump feathers. Their scurrying about reminded him of farmyard goings on. The pungent chloroform odor of methylal pervaded the cavernous room. In the center of the admissions lobby, a rangy man and his curious-looking wife waited. They were a forlorn pair; he, a blond, deeply- tanned fellow in his tan suitcoat over blue denim overalls that had been washed so often that they were faded to a pale blue. He was a poor farmer, and looked the part. His wife, in her print dress and frayed wool coat, stood beside him. Her hair was straight and black. Her prominent cheekbones suggested Native American genealogy. It was said that the woman's great-grandmother was an Iroquois squaw, although there was no documentation to support the claim. She had a tin-type of her grandmother that would lend a convincing argument.

The farmer shifted his weight impatiently from one foot to the other gazing up and down the endless hall. His woman stood motionless, occasionally taking her eyes away from the baby she held in her arms.

Presently, a heavy balding man in a dark suit approached. From the pallor of his skin, it was apparent he spent his time indoors. His thick round glasses made his eyes look big. He carried a thin sheaf of papers which he placed on a desk top before taking a seat. He motioned the two to approach. Adjusting his glasses, he asked. "Walter and Mildred Hubbard?"

Simultaneously the two responded, "Yes."

"Okay, Walter. Repeat after me. I—."

The two began as one.

"Just you, Walter," he pointed to the farmer with his pen. Mildred bit her lower lip.

"I, Walter Hubbard," the man began again, "declare my position of indigence."

"I Walter Hubbard, "he choked on the words, "declare my position of—of"

"Indigence," the man seated at the desk prompted.

"Indigence."

"And am unable to satisfy the sum of this expense, nor any portion of it."

Hubbard repeated the words.

"And I swear before the people and the governor of the state of Colorado that this is my present financial situation, so help me God."

Again, the man of simple means repeated the words.

"You are aware," the official cautioned, "that any misstatement as to the accuracy of this document may lead to penalties or fines as adjudicated by a court of law, are you not?"

"Yes," Hubbard answered in an obedient whisper.

"Sign here," the administrator instructed, sliding the paper across handing Hubbard the pen.

The muscular farmer bent down appraising the flaccid official, relieved his own life involved healthy hard work and visible results. He was happy he didn't have to do what that fellow did. The officer, glancing at Hubbard's threadbare overhauls and his gnarled, weathered hands came to the same conclusion. He was content with his safe, comfortable sinecure.

The new father signed on a line. Below, the words read, "Sworn before me at 2:12 p.m., October 19, 1922, at Colorado General Hospital, Denver, Colorado, Robert R. DeCamp, Administrative Director, Hospital Charges and Remittances." The official then witnessed the document by adding his signature.

"Okay, Mr. Hubbard, you're free to go. Good luck to the three of you."

Walter and Mildred Hubbard walked out of the hospital with their new son, Andrew Walter Hubbard. By his father's action of taking the pauper's oath, the boy entered the world free of charge.

"It's kind of painful that I got to beg to get my kid out of that joint," Walter complained passing through the lobby. His wife, careful of her child, didn't respond, joining him to the short trek where their worn Chevy truck waited in the parking lot. It would be a long tedious drive back to their farm in Cottonwood.

The Hubbards, a family now, had accomplished what many fledgling young couples had not, surviving in an environment that defeated so many. They had come a long way from the time the two met in the rolling hills of Missouri.

Mildred Franklin was a teacher in a small country school when she met Walter who moved into a nearby town. Hubbard and his first wife were renting a farm in Oklahoma when his wayward spouse abandoned him. From there, he began wandering. He found a job working in a grocery store not far from the school. Mildred, living by herself in the school, would come into the store to stock up on provisions. Tall, gangly and unattractive, the twenty-year-old school marm was pleased to be courted by the dashing blond man who was on the lam. In a short time, they would marry.

Mildred's parents were strict Baptists who refused to take in a man that had been married before. Unable to convince her to denounce her love for Walter, she was disowned. There was compensation, however. Mildred's father would not to turn the daughter out without something. Hence, he awarded her $500 going away money—hardly a fortune, but enough to give the two a start if they watched their pennies.

Their plan was to homestead a farm. Knowing available lands from the east into the Midwest were already spoken for, they would go further to the unsettled west. Walter studied the homestead laws. It was the first serious attempt at book learning in his existence.

He found that if he had a chance at all getting a piece of un-claimed land, he would have to go west—far west. That was okay with him, and Mildred wanted to get as far away from her family as possible.

Properties originally homesteaded in the eastern portion of the country in the 1860's were 160 acres in size. Those were prime acquisitions, but by now, were all settled.

As the land grab craze and the push west spread further into the arid regions, the size of the homesteads were increased to 320 acres. When expansion shifted into the less fertile lands of western Nebraska, Kansas, and Colorado and beyond, the size was broadened to 640 acres; the conclusion being a larger farm or ranch was needed in order to scratch out a living. By the turn of the century, precious few parcels remained, and those bordered on being worthless.

Walter would go first to find a place. As soon as that step was accomplished, he would send for Mildred. In the meantime, she intended to work and scrimp until she received word from him. The grocery store had a telephone, and Walter's friend, Clem, who also worked there, would relay any call. She checked her telephone messages daily. Once the call came, she would pick up and leave. Clem would take her into Kansas City, and for six dollars and some change, she could ride a passenger train to Denver.

Leaving immediately had two disadvantages: the first was that her abrupt abdication would most likely result in a forfeiture of any further compensation, and two, leaving her post would leave a blemish on her record, as well as an embarrassment to her parents. That's how it had to be. She had already disappointed them and would not be coming back for a job.

Walter was damaged by his unfaithful wife's desertion. All this changed when he met Mildred. Her encouragement was sincere and comforting. Mildred would be faithful, strong and caring for him. She was all those things— but he hadn't come to appreciate it yet.

Since money was tight, Walter boarded an empty freight out of the stockyards of Kansas City. This was not the first time he rode a train. When leaving Oklahoma, broke and discouraged, he traveled in box cars, living the life of a hobo.

Hopping on a train west, he discovered, was much more troublesome than riding the slow leisurely conveyances that wound through the river country of mid-America. He was on a cattle train this time. Cattle trains were subject to hijacking by rustlers. Railroad police— "bulls," they were called, regularly inspected the box cars and checked the rails—sections under the cars where, of necessity, vagrants rode. The only safe place was atop the cars on the wooden catwalk, where Walter would hunker down to keep from being discovered. After an hour, the train stopped in Salina, Kansas. Walter had enough of the catwalk that November afternoon. He found an angry-looking railroad marshal and begged him to let him ride in a box car. To his utter surprise the cop consented. His passage would be inside all the way to Denver! He took this piece of good luck as an omen. After four days of discomfort, he arrived, fittingly enough, at the stockyards in Denver. In his boot was $200 of Mildred's dowry.

November, 1921

Walter hitched a ride and found his way to the Bureau of Land Management at the Civic Center in downtown Denver. Unable to decipher the convoluted application, he appealed to a well-dressed man at the court to help him with the process. After the train ride, Walter's appearance was a notch above a tramp's, but his wasn't significantly lower than any poor farmer who regularly wandered into the agency.

To his dismay, he was informed homestead land was no longer available in Colorado; just like Missouri, there was nothing for him here, either. The man related a desperate tale; not only were there no more parcels available, but a significant number of homesteaders were starved out, and their lands were absorbed by larger operators. Disappointed, but not defeated, he pressed the agent for information. If it were so difficult to make a go of it, he reasoned, why couldn't he find a homesteader who was in trouble? Shouldn't there be an opportunity available? Wouldn't they have any names of people in that predicament? If that man had to rid himself of a farm, Walter reasoned, he himself might be able to make a deal with him. Walter convinced the man that he was no quitter and would make it where others wouldn't.

His persistence paid off. The land man smiled, rattling change in his trouser pocket, gazing across the large room. Leaning against a wall near a window, a person who looked to be an older farmer was speaking to another man behind a desk sitting in a large wooden swivel chair.

The well-dressed man looked Hubbard in the eye extending his hand. "I'm Sam Armling. I'm the boss around here. You want a farm. How do you expect to get it? Do you have any money?"

Impulsively Hubbard gushed, "I have two hundred dollars."

Armling shook his head. "That won't do any good."

"But I can get more —"

The man turned, showing small interest. "How much more?"

"I can get three hundred more."

He paused, studying the floor. "That might do it. Do you have it on you?"

Hubbard scratched his head. He knew he had spoken too soon. "What I meant to say is—we have five hundred, but we'd still have to buy a car, I think, and some cattle and a span of mules—there's also the planting this spring."

Armling looked over to the man at the window, then back at Hubbard, shaking his head compassionately. "It takes money, son."

"But I do have five hundred—it's just that I need some of it for other things. Can't you do anything for me?"

Again, Armling jingled coins in his pocket. "What can you raise?"

Hubbard's mind was racing. Finally, he replied, "I can raise three hundred."

"That's it?"

"That's all. I still have to farm."

"Do you think you would want this man's farm?" Armling asked pointing to the man standing against the window.

Hubbard's spirits leaped. "He has a farm?"

"He does, and he intends to sell it."

"Sure—er—what does he want for it?"

Armling turned. "Let's find out."

Armling knew the man standing was a bachelor farmer named Abner Harper. He knew Harper well. Armling respected the good farmers, and was admired by those he represented. Harper was one of those. He motioned to Hubbard, shepherding Harper, into a small conference room. Introductions were made and the three sat.

Armling began, eyeing Harper, a crusty-looking man with gray flowing eyebrows. "Abner, this young fellow wants so buy your farm."

The grizzled man turned to Armling. "Tell him to give me five hundred dollars, and it's his."

Armling turned to Hubbard. "There you are, young fella. You want a farm. Here's your opportunity."

Hubbard felt betrayed, turning to the old farmer. "I do want a farm, but I don't know anything about your farm—what it's like—-where it is, and the five hundred dollars I have, but I need to keep some back to get started."

"Then I guess we don't have a deal," Harper uttered.

"You've already been offered five hundred in cash," Armling put in.

Harper tossed his head in anger. "Don't bring that up. I won't have anything to do with any son of a bitch who's too proud to get off his horse."

Armling smiled. The two knew something Hubbard didn't.

"I wish I could think about your farm, Mr. Harper, but I guess I can't," the raw- boned young man offered.

"Wish in one hand—shit in the other," Harper groused.

A secretary stepped through the door, announcing, "You have a telephone call from Washington, Mr. Armling. You can use Mr. Scott's office."

Armling excused himself rising. "You two sit here for a minute. This shouldn't take too long." He left the room. The agent followed.

An awkward silence followed.

"Why are you leaving the farm?" Hubbard asked, in an effort to break the silence.

"Just had enough—that's all."

"I bet it's your wife's who's had enough."

Harper looked up gloomily. His blue eyes and gray brows seemed to grow. "No. That's not it. I never had a wife."

"Never wanted a wife?"

"Oh, I did. It's just she didn't show up."

"What do you mean, 'She didn't show up?'"

The farmer turned in his chair facing Walter. He drew a long breath. "I was to meet her in Denver. She was a mail-order bride. We spent over a year writin' back and forth—sendin' each other pictures, and the like. I got to where thought I knew her. We had it all planned when we'd hook up. She woulda' come sooner, but I felt I had to get the farm in order first. By the time I did, and I sent for her, she was to be on the train at the Union Station in Denver. She never showed. I drove a God damned horse and buggy over sixty miles to pick her up—and she never showed. I stayed out another day thinking I got it wrong, but I didn't. I wrote to find out what the hell had happened to her. A month or so later, I get a letter from her God damned husband! Can you beat that?"

Hubbard fixed a stare at the table surface, pausing. "I don't know which is worse - having them leave you before, or have them leave you after..."

"What are you gettin' at?" Harper asked. Walter told the farmer his story.

Much later, Armling entered the room. He sat. "Sorry about the delay. Where were we?"

Harper looked at the director, motioning to Walter. "This young feller's buying my farm, Sam."

Armling glanced at Hubbard, then at Harper, scowling, "He what—? What about the financing?"

Harper waved a gnarled hand. "It's all done Sam. Get the girl to get the papers ready."

"You have the proof document—" Armling cautioned.

"'He knows."

"You have to register the patent release—"

"I'll do that."

"And the mineral rights file—?"

"Oh hell, I forgot about that, Sam." Harper said rising from his chair. "You know all that stuff—you take care of it. I thought we had it all hashed out while you were on the telephone. Can you get your girl? This young man and I have other fish to fry."

Armling also rose. "We'll use this office, Abner." He motioned to Walter. "You stay right here."

After a short period, the secretary stepped to the door, signaling for Walter to follow her. He noticed Abner Harper standing near the exit. Giving the secretary a silent wave, Walter walked over to the farmer.

"I appreciate what you've done for me, Mr. Harper."

"Call me Abner. Mr. Harper makes me feel old."

"Is there anything you need to tell me before I go in there?" Walter asked motioning to the woman standing in the doorway.

"No. They got it all," the farmer answered, fumbling with his hat, indicating impatience.

"I'll get you paid. You can depend on that," Walter promised.

Harper placed his worn felt hat on his head, turning to the heavy door. "Spect you will, son." The plain farmer disappeared down the hall.

Walter sat down across from Armling. The secretary was off to the side with a set of papers. The director wore an expression that was a mixture of surprise and humor.

"Do you mind telling me how you pulled that off? He's one of the tightest guys north of the equator, and he's letting you move onto that farm free of charge. Are you aware of that?"

"I am."

"What went on in there? You two must have something in common for Abner to do something like that. Want to tell me about it?"

"No."

"That's just how Abner reacted when I asked him. Okay," he exhaled, turning to the secretary. "Let's get a couple of signatures."

Walter didn't have much to sign beyond the contract for deed and promissory note to Harper. But one was a very necessary affidavit as Armling explained.

"There's a water source on your property that has to be filed on. You don't want that to get away."

"Mr. Harper—Abner, mentioned a spring, but I don't know anything about it."

"Well, it's a mineral right, and an important one. Since your farm is not on railroad property, you want to have those water rights in your name."

"What do you mean, 'It's not a railroad property'?"

"It means you get the mineral rights if you file on them." He nodded to the secretary who passed an official-looking document over to him and pointed to a line.

Walter signed on it.

She took it back, attesting his signature and clamping her notary stamp on it.

"What's that thing?" Walter asked.

"It has to be notarized," Armling replied, smiling fatherly.

Walter decided he wouldn't ask any more questions.

The secretary passed a crude map that Harper drew to get to the farm.

Stepping out of his chair, Armling began, "Did you know what sort of property you are getting?"

"Not at first—I still don't, really."

"Well, it's a good spot."

"I understand it is."

"You're aware you make your payments to us?"

"Yes sir—to the Federal Land Bank in this building."

"You understand if you default, Abner takes the loss—not us?"

Walter bit lip. "Yes. I know that."

"Okay. That covers the land transfer." Armling laid a manual on the desk, facing Walter. "You said you were thinking about getting a car."

"I am."

"Maybe you should think about getting a truck."

Hubbard shifted his weight unsurely. He squinted, "I don't know what to get. I have to have something."

"How would you like to look at a truck?"

"Do you guys sell trucks, too?"

Armling chuckled. "No. We're not in that business—not yet anyway. This vehicle belongs to the Welfare Department. It's a delivery truck—we call it the 'commodity' truck."

"Why are you selling it?"

"All official vehicles are retired after a certain number of miles—10,000 in this case."

"That's a lot of miles."

"They're not the kind of miles a farmer would put on them. This truck's never been off the pavement. The only cargo its hauled is packages; nothing like grain, farm animals or dirty heavy things. It's serviced regularly."

"When can I look at it?"

"It's down in the motor pool. We can see it right now if you like."

Walter was agog at the number of vehicles parked in the semi-darkness of the parking garage. The two stopped alongside a truck. It was larger than Walter imagined or could afford.

"What do you think of that wagon?" Armling asked, loosely swinging his arm in the direction of the vehicle.

"Oh, that's a nice one. It's big."

"It's unusual. Most factory models don't have the side doors and roll-up windows like this one. It even has a manifold heater. That makes it nice this time of the year."

Walter had no idea what a manifold heater was. "It looks brand new to me. What kind is it?"

"It's a Chevrolet. This truck has a transmission—three gears forward that you won't find in a Ford," Armling said. "The 490 four-cylinder engine in this thing has lots of power. This is a real work truck. It can haul 2,000 pounds."

Walter was beginning to sense that there was something special about it.

The vehicle was large; not something so imposing that Walter would have looked at twice. Its blue paint glistened, as did the black fenders and blue spoke wheels with their yellow pinstripes. Stepping around the back, he looked at the hardwood bed of the truck. There wasn't a mark on it. That would soon change if he had a truck like that. Walking around the front, he saw that the cab and glass were in mint condition; as was the entire truck.

"It doesn't even look like it's been used!" Walter marveled.

"Keeping them clean and under roof helps."

"What year is it?"

"It's a '20. This model came out two years ago. It's called a T model."

"I thought a T was a Ford." Walter put in.

"T stands for ton in this case. It'll be two years old in a couple of months."

"Well, it sure doesn't look two years old."

Armling, as was his habit, jingled his pocket change. "Nope, it doesn't. That thing cost nearly thirteen hundred dollars new—"

Hubbard cut him off. "Thirteen hundred! I couldn't begin to afford something like that!"

"Would you like to have the truck?"

"This one?"

Armling caught Walter's eye and nodded affirmatively.

"Sure. Who wouldn't? This isn't the truck you were talking about is it?" The director was enjoying the banter. "It's the one."

Walter exhaled noisily, "Well, I can't afford anything like this."

"How about a hundred dollars? Don't tell me you don't have it."

Walter was aghast. "Are you kidding? One hundred dollars for this T?"

"That's it," Armling replied easily.

Walter's mind spun. He still had the two hundred that he expected to have spent by now. Gazing at the vehicle, he bent over removing a boot. Quickly, he retrieved two one hundred dollar bills, peeling one off, handing it to the chief. Grinning broadly, he exclaimed, "It smells like my feet, but it's worth a hundred."

Armling took the certificate, placing it in his lapel. "You have your truck. Now, suppose we get your title, so I can get back to work."

Hubbard had his farm, and although he hadn't seen it, he knew it was a bargain. Homesteads were free—when you could get one, but fences, wells, barns, and buildings weren't. And he had a new truck. What a day it had been!

He was lucky again. Mildred was in the store when he called. His good fortune made him uneasy. His experience had been that bad luck replaces good luck twofold. He prayed it wouldn't happen again.

His call put Mildred in a happy mood. In fact, she'd never been so giddy. "You bought us a farm that you haven't seen?" she baited good naturedly.

"Well, we'll see it together. Can you get Clem to take you to Kansas City in the morning?"

"Just a minute. I'll ask him." Shortly, she returned. "He says he could take me this afternoon."

"Could you be packed and ready?"

"I already considered it. I'll take all I can. Clem and his wife will keep the rest of my things, and what I have of yours, and send them once we get where we're going."

"Then you get on a train. I'll just hang around in the train station until you show up." The instant he said "show up" he thought of Abner Harper.

14

"One thing—how are you going to get to the station?" she asked.

"Oh, I forgot to tell you. I bought a truck."

Walter signed the truck title that afternoon, and would be on his way. He felt fortunate that so many of his needs could be attended to in the same complex. Before Walter left, Armling advised he break the one hundred dollar bill.

"Most places can't change a bill of that size. You'd be smart to reduce that into smaller denominations."

Walter complied, stacking his boot with smaller bills. Armling shook his hand, wished him well and suggested he look in the bed of his truck before he pulled out. Earlier in the afternoon, Armling saw to it that an extra mounted tire was placed in Walter's truck. The director knew something about un-paved roads too.

Walter did inspect the bed of his truck. A mounted tire lay in the box. "Why the extra wheel?" He wondered. He guessed the truck didn't come with a spare, but crawling under the frame, there was a spare that never been out of its hanger. He didn't understand why Armling would throw in an extra spare. He would find out.

In a rare splurge Walter bought two heavy wool blankets at a dry-goods store. He knew they would be needed. This night, they would be his bed on the long padded bench seat of the truck. Late in the afternoon, sitting along a bank of the Platte River, he dined on bread and bologna. Off to the west, he gazed at the white alabaster lining the foothills, wondering how much snow would cover the ground at his new home. While waiting, he decided to take his truck for a drive. The headlights worked fine, the engine was quiet, and the heater worked. He was proud of it, awarding it a name — "Abner." Arriving at the train station, he checked the departures out of Kansas City. He saw that the Rock Island Company had a passenger-freight leaving that evening at seven, getting into Denver at noon. Hopefully, Mildred was on that train. Making his bed in the parking lot at the train station, he readied for the next day— and, his wife.

Bread and bologna was the menu for breakfast. He found free coffee in the train terminal.

Noon came and no train. Walter had another serving of bread and bologna. At three in the afternoon, he was getting worried.

Twenty minutes later, the announcement was made. The train from Kansas City was pulling in.

He saw her. She was carrying a bag that resembled an oversize pillow slip, and an enormous black cardboard suitcase. She dropped them both when she saw Walter.

Mildred explained that one of the wheels on the freight had a hot box and that was the reason for the delay.

Although later than expected, the trip began without incident. They made a quick stop on the edge of town to stock up on groceries and essentials. Then, two headed east through the bite of the November cold. The roads were dry, except for an occasional patch of snow here and there. The truck ran beautifully—Mildred thought it was new. The ride was smooth and pleasant. After an hour and a half, they averaged thirty miles an hour. At this rate, they could expect to be at the farm by sundown.

As Walter predicted, the good luck could last only so long. The oil road turned into a rocky, rutted course. The uniform thirty mile an hour drive was now a jarring side-by-side rough jostle reduced to ten miles an hour.

"I knew this was bound to play out," Walter mused.

"This is how it's going to be," Mildred responded softly. "There will be difficulties. We have to expect them."

An hour later, Walter felt the shudder of a tire going flat. He brought the truck to a stop, and searched for the tire tool. He located it under a seat. The jack and wrenches had never been used. In a matter of minutes, the spare Armling had placed in the back was in use and the two were again on their way. Dusk was settling in, and Walter was becoming concerned. He still had the spare that came with the truck, but what if he had to use that? He would have no way to continue. In addition, there was the pang of doubt of not knowing for sure, where they were. He kept on, hoping for the best.

It was dark now. Across the prostrate expanse of land, dim lights twinkled on a black flat horizon. At the same time, he felt the truck vibrate with another flat tire, but it happened conveniently in view of what must be Cottonwood. Walter fumbled again for the tire tools. Fortunately, earlier he'd located the spare that came with the truck. Working in the dark, he unbolted the remaining wheel, mounted it, and started up the road again. He was grateful for the truck's heater—and headlights. Never had the two experienced such total blackness. The flickering lights in the distance were the lone beacon in the void.

As though a rite of passage had been satisfied, the road became smooth. The two entered the tiny settlement. Motoring in, they saw the buildings all located on one side of the road. The opposite side was vacant prairie, as though nothing could survive on the other side. Continuing along the maze of buildings in total darkness, save for an occasional dim glow emitting from lamp light, Walter spied a gas station with its painted Sinclair sign in front. The lights were on inside the simple white stucco shop. He pulled to a stop under the canopy.

A stocky man wearing a worn pinch cap and greasy herring-bone coveralls came to the doorway. He switched on a light flooding the small gravel driveway in a yellow glow, baring paint-chipped front windows stuffed with automotive advertisements. Walter hopped out of the truck, taking notice of the man, who approached the driver's side. A crookneck pipe protruded from beneath a bushy moustache. Walter guessed the man to be in his mid-fifties, and the owner of the station. The man glanced through the wooden stakes of the truck box at the spare wheels.

"'Looks like you found some of our obstacles," he commented.

"Boy, I sure did," Walter answered. "That last thirty miles was a buggar."

"Well," he began, exhaling a miasma of blue smoke, "They're putting in a new road, and if they ever get done with it, it'll be a favor to all of us. I just think they could keep it in a little better shape while they're at it."

"Any chance of getting one of these fixed?" Walter asked. "I imagine it's about closing time for you."

"Naw," the older man replied easily. "That's my business. Let's get at it."

Walter jumped up in the back, taking one of the heavy wheels. "I'll fix the other one, if you have some patchin."

The man mechanically caught the spare, commenting, "I got that," adding, "this looks like a nice truck." He then glanced at the flat. "This is a good tire. I hope you didn't ruin it."

"I sure hope so, too. I stopped as soon as I felt it go down," Walter quickly explained.

Mildred was out of the truck, now. She felt the bite of the late November chill, watching a tumble weed roll lazily down the gravel main street in obedience to the ever-present prairie wind.

The town, located on highway US 40 was accountably built singularly on the leeward side of the road. Square front buildings strung along like soldiers standing enfilade confronted the gale that blew year-round in orderly discipline out of the northwest. Presumably, somebody started a business along one side and those coming later, followed suit.

The station owner rolled the flat through a door behind the counter into a cluttered room. Walter and Mildred trailed. Mechanically, he reached up in the dark pulling a chain attached to the single light bulb on to a braided cord hanging from the plaster ceiling. The swinging bulb provided dancing illusions on the greasy panel walls reflecting tires and various paraphernalia stacked around the dingy room.

"Passin' through?" the station owner asked mechanically as he began tearing the tire down in the dim light of his shop.

"No. We're stoppin' here," Walter said.

He halted, glancing up. "You are?" was the surprised response. "Where?"

"Know where the Harper place is?"

"Sure. You bought it?"

"That's what they tell me," Walter answered lightly.

"Be damned. I heard he was wantin' out. I didn't know he already sold," The man said, pulling the tube out of the tire, giving it a close inspection.

"Looks like the tube just got pinched— tire seems okay."

He looked up shortly, "That old Abner. He never got a wife. Funny how some folks get by never needin' a woman."

Walter merely nodded, knowing he had information that the long-time resident didn't.

"By the way," the station man said, extending his hand, "I'm Jim Thurston."

Walter shook his hand, introducing himself and his wife, asking, "Lived here long?"

"Over twenty years. I know I look smarter'n that. I started farmin' just like you're about to. I came to town so's to make a living. That's what everybody does if they don't leave the country entirely."

"*Everybody!*" Mildred asked painfully.

"Well," he said buffing the tube, not looking up, "this ain't exactly the best place to farm. Listen to the ranchers and they'll tell you that this sod never should have been busted up. But in your case, you've got a special problem."

"What problem?" Mildred asked cautiously.

"Oh, you'll find out."

"Not going to tell us, huh?" Walter asked.

"Well," Thurston drawled, "you got a neighbor who wants the whole state. And you know the more you get, the easier it is to get more. He'll try to buy you out right away, that I guarantee."

"That doesn't mean I got to sell right away, Walter said defensively.

"Doesn't mean that at all," he returned, focusing on the tube, "but maybe you'd be better off to make a buck or two. What'd you pay for it?"

The personal question took Walter aback. Caught by surprise, he hesitated.

"Sorry," Thurston apologized. "I've got no right askin' that. I guess I get a little nosy at times—at least I've been told that. But if you got it for a thousand you didn't get hurt, you can be sure."

Walter and Mildred's eyes met both with a satisfied look.

"There ain't nothin' left to homestead anymore, and that's the best place around you just got. Jack—er, your neighbor, will be plenty upset. He's been a tryin' to get that place off Harper for years. They never got along. Abner's a stubborn old guy—nobody pushed him around. Anyway, no one here has any money—only MacGregor. But," He hesitated, "'ol Abner always seemed to get by okay."

"Jack MacGregor. That's his name," Walter said.

"Yeah. I guess that one'd give you the most trouble," Thurston admitted, as he reached for a tire pump, and started pumping.

Over Walter's offer to help, Thurston continued filling the tire until he was satisfied with the pressure. He then handed Walter a round tin container with the logo of a camel on its side. Inside, were rubber patches, a buffer and glue needed to repair a puncture. The kit would prove invaluable—the primitive condition of the roads would see to that.

"How much?" Walter asked.

"Thirty-five cents, if it's handy," Thurston returned, with "Keep me in mind when you come back to town."

"You can be sure we will," Walter promised, producing a small fat worn hinged leather pocket purse from his bib overhauls, fingering out the proper change. "How much for fixin' the tire?"

Thurston began rolling the wheel toward the door. "This one's on the house. I'll catch you the next time. By the way, I guess you know how to get to your place."

"I have a map. What are the roads like out that way?"

"Bettern' what you just come through." Thurston threw the tire in the truck. "Look up Marshall Reiss. He'll be your neighbor—lives just south. You'll like him. He's on the bottle pretty hard, but he's a good man."

"How do you know him?"

"I was his neighbor on the other side."

"And you sold out?"

"Yup."

"To MacGregor?"

Thurston chuckled. "Oh, he wanted it all right, but I sold it to Marshall."

"How big was it?"

"'Same as yours—a section." The "section" reference was 640 acres.

"Your man Reiss must have made some money if he could *buy your* farm."

Again Thurston chuckled. "I let him on for nothin'. He's still payin' me—most of the time."

"MacGregor must have been sore because you didn't sell to him."

"He was, but not so sore as he'll be when he finds out Abner's place is gone. He's been next in line for that for a long time—him and his dad, both."

Thurston wouldn't go into the subject of MacGregor's father.

"What about my place—what's so special about it?"

Thurston strode toward the door of his shop. "I can't give out all the secrets. You'll find out soon enough." He gave a final wave and stepped inside.

The orange moon rising in the clear evening sky began to illuminate the barren landscape as Walter and Mildred drove away from the garage.

There were sixteen miles to go. The two rode in silence when Mildred mentioned over the purr of the engine. "Well, I like him."

Walter knew she was referring to the owner of the filling station.

"So do I. He's a good guy, but it doesn't sound as though we're going to like everybody."

She answered philosophically, "There's only one place where it's that way, but we're not there yet."

"Thank God," he quipped.

Later on the road, he felt Mildred's reassuring pat on his thigh while he steered his prized truck for home. Mildred's physical appearance was no match for Walter's first wife, and though his marriage to Mildred was a rebound, he was quickly realizing the real value of being married to someone on whom he could depend. Her indelicate looks and large stature were surely giving way to her unfeigned character. Slowly and surely, he was gaining a strong bond for the good woman.

Walter, unlike Mildred, had little education, but possessed an innate ability to eke out a living where none seemed available. His blatant honesty was a natural gift. Gaining immediate trust from those he dealt with came natural to him. The favors granted him by Sam Armstrong and Abner Harper lent testimony. Walter harbored a deep contempt for those who would exaggerate or attempt to gain an advantage through deceit, wealth or station. He enjoyed a good joke and was quick to laugh. Unfortunately, he was equally quick to lose his temper and had a tendency to hold a grudge; so whatever redeeming benefits there were to his unbridled honesty, they were attenuated by his explosive demeanor.

CHAPTER 2

The Hubbards were not alone scratching out a living on that sterile existence. Several other families with a similar past were battling the environs in an effort to survive. Practically everybody living on that parched shard of earth faced the same problems—everybody, with the exception of the MacGregor family.

Liam MacGregor owned the largest cattle herd in the state. It wasn't that Liam was without his difficulties. He had endured as many, if not more, deprivations than anyone in the area.

Liam MacGregor was born to Padraic MacGregor, a farmer from Baldgdreen, West Erie, Ireland, in January, 1866. The economic disaster of the potato famine in the 1860's rendered the MacGregors destitute. In 1886, Liam broke from the family and immigrated to New York to escape the poverty and search for his own fortune. He was an aggressive young man, not content with the meager and mundane life that was his father's. Working as a brick layer in the city, he met Bonnie Chattman, whose father owned an apartment house. She was also Irish, having emigrated with her parents. Although the two were attracted to each other and joined by nationality and environment, Bonnie's father had other plans for his daughter. He wanted nothing to do with a simple laborer, unaware at the moment, an arrangement was being made.

In 1888, Liam caught a stage west through Indian country into Colorado. When it stopped for a change of horses in the mid-eastern part of the state, he hopped off. Although the broad expanse was vacant, he was enamored by it. Soon, he found work punching cattle and herding sheep for a struggling rancher. It was here on the plains of buffalo grass that Liam set his roots.

No fences existed, so sheep and cattle were free to graze wherever they could. The challenge was to control their migration, and a water source was the best cowboy of all. Animals never stray too far from a place to drink. Liam became an expert ranch hand, not taking money for his hire, but pay in the form of livestock when it was earned. In time, as his herd multiplied, he no longer worked for another; they worked for him. As his holdings expanded, so did his influence. The main water source, Spring Creek, came under Liam's control.

Stubbornness and conservatism were basics of his personality. Waste and squander were repugnant to him. He would hang on to the last thread before he would sell a single animal to buy the barest of necessities. He was also a disciple of self-denial. He lived for five of the last seven years in a dugout serving as a house burrowed into a hillside. The floor was dirt with a window positioned next to a door in the single room cave. Out of necessity, this simple dwelling faced to the east. A wood stove served as the heat source for the primitive hut. The dugout was uniquely suited to this lifestyle, since the morning sun offered light and warmth and the north winds were neutralized.

Life in a dugout wasn't where Liam McGregor intended to spend his life, but he was content to be there until he could return to New York and bring Bonnie back with him.

It had been five years since Liam and Bonnie had made their pledge. Now, he concluded his herd was adequate, and he would be able to plan a home and future for her. He did his homework well. His business practices were entrenched, and although his ethics were often considered ruthless, he was true to his word and paid his bills. MacGregor earned a grudging reputation of respect.

He rode the train to New York in the spring of 1893. Bonnie dutifully waited for him. The promise she fulfilled was the type of commitment necessary for survival that lay ahead. Not to rush into building a new house, the two lived in the dugout for another two years.

Careful and calculating, Liam MacGregor needed help to run his operation. He had six full-time ranch hands living in dugouts similar to his own, but he would be moving out, as Bonnie was pregnant. The time had come to give her a house. Liam preferred to put the house near a spot where an abundant spring ran year-round. He called the area "Spring Creek." It didn't belong to him; it belonged to the U.S. Government, but he always thought of it as his, since he used it as a water source from the beginning. Bonnie, however, selected a location on land he owned where a forest of pines on a plateau provided a breathtaking panorama of the plains to the west. That was okay, whatever Bonnie wanted was fine with him.

The blue jays were singing in the pines when Sean Padraic MacGregor came into the world. He was a robust ten-pound baby. Unfortunately, because of a womb complication, he would be Bonnie's only child. Sean was anglicized to John, that became "Jack", and he was, with the exception of his mother, never to be called Sean again. Jack MacGregor had traits of both of his mother and father. Bonnie wasn't considered large but she wasn't small either. Her father and brothers were large however, all standing six foot or more. Liam, on the other hand, was a slight man standing five foot eight. Bonnie was as tall as he. She was friendly, ebullient, and generous to a fault. Liam was quiet, calculating, and not taken to giving anything away and that included conversation. Both parents were driven and highly intelligent. Jack, as he grew older, would be as large as any of his uncles standing six foot two. Like his mother, he was outgoing and pleasant when he needed to be, and similar to both parents, he was intelligent. He inherited the indulgence for cunning and wealth like his father. But two traits unique to him were a love for gambling, and an insatiable desire to dominate. Jack grew into a ruggedly-handsome man and considering his affluence and ambition, he could be whatever he wanted to be.

In the years from 1895 to 1905 the MacGregors were a busy family. The ranch was flourishing, Bonnie was enjoying a sumptuous home and living a happy life. Liam was working around the clock intent on enlarging his operation. Two trips back to New York convinced Bonnie's father that she made the right choice. She had wealth and a handsome son.

However, in those frenzied times when Liam and Bonnie's focus was only on making money and running the family, a movement which would be a plague to the cattleman was beginning to invade the west—homesteaders.

Liam realized this threat all too late. He despised farming and farmers. He loved grass and hated dirt. His father went broke farming potatoes.

He could see what was happening miles east of him, and as the invasion crept nearer, he knew it could, very quickly, impact his lifestyle. When the government allowed designated BLM land available for private ownership, homesteaders swept in like locusts, and the barbed wire industry exploded. Immediately those on the open range did whatever they could to discourage this transgression, and seize those lands for themselves. At once, many abridgments of the law were employed, and McGregor was one of those who intended to get all this free land before an undeserving newcomer farmer did. After studying the law, he hired an unscrupulous federal agent to assist him in acquiring homesteads. The plot was to pay any person who was a bona fide citizen $25 to apply for a homestead with the proviso once the proof of application was recorded and the document was released, it would become the possession of Liam MacGregor. Finding dishonest persons who would take money for doing nothing was not the challenge: sneaking it past the government was. Each transaction took time, but once a signature was a matter of record and the transfer was made, all MacGregor had to do was wait three years and the land was his. He knew this unethical and illegal practice wouldn't get him all the property he normally enjoyed for running his cattle, but it would protect a large portion of it. As the homesteading process became more active, the illegal practices were exposed and eliminated.

He hadn't done too badly, however. In ten years, he had managed to grab twenty three homestead properties—over 15,000 acres. Although half of what he wanted got away, two that he desired the most and didn't get, soured in his gut. In 1900, Spring Creek which he considered his own, and the 640 adjacent to it, into which the runoff pooled, were claimed right under his agent's nose. Liam, in a fit of vengeance, saw to it that the agent was exposed and punished. The same agent who pulled so many illegal deals for Liam was sent to prison. It was unwise to mention these properties in Liam's presence. He never forgave himself for losing the land holding the element most critical to running cattle—water. The names Thurston and Harper were anathema to him. Concentrated efforts to buy them out had so far been unsuccessful. He had given up ever getting them, Jack hadn't.

In 1918, Bonnie's father died, and the family travelled back to New York to attend the funeral. Liam couldn't get out of going, as badly as he would have liked, and he couldn't ask Jack, now twenty three years old and very capable of running the business, to miss the ceremony honoring his beloved grandfather. He would have to trust Clete, his trusted foreman to take care of things.

For Jack, the trip wasn't a total somber experience. He met a nineteen year old Irish girl who was an acquaintance of the Chattman in-laws. Jack took an immediate fancy to Katherine Farnham and she was smitten by him. Her lush brown hair, blue eyes and splendid carriage hooked him. He would be coming back before the year was out.

The next June in 1919, Jack McGregor and Katherine Farnham were married in New York City. A brand new house awaited them one half mile from Liam and Bonnie's on the pine forested plateau. Liam frequently reminded Jack how much easier Kate had it than Bonnie.

"It would be good for Kate to live in a dugout for a couple of years," he would remark, often testing Jack's patience.

Katherine Farnham MacGregor was a serious young woman coming from a disciplined family. She made a commitment to learn the new way of life and fit the MacGregor mold.

CHAPTER 3

Walter's truck, "Abner," bounced down the pasture road in the moonlight following two paths carved evenly across the bare earthen table. The tracks, implacably weaving a disorganized path, bore evidence that the precise rhythm of the driver had to be exact if the truck were to continue. Walter nonchalantly fought control of his truck across a meadow covered with snow, then up a hill, past a barn, by a windmill and into a yard that confronted an unpainted house. The Hubbards were introduced to their new quarters. Braking the truck to a stop, Walter murmured, "Just like the map."

He shut off the engine and opened the driver door. A noisy silence greeted them as they looked at the weathered farmhouse.

"It ain't the Ritz," Walter mused.

"But it's ours," Mildred said softly.

"He said he left a few things in the house. Hope he left a lamp," Walter remarked, dismounting from the truck.

Walking up on the creaky porch, he opened the saggy screen door, tripping over an axe while twisting the porcelain door knob.

The door didn't budge. He twisted it again giving the door a spirited kick.

The door sprung open, covering him with a fine dust. He stepped in and lit a match. In the glow of the flame, he scanned the room, watching his breath condense in the chilly space. In luck! Sitting on a dusty table was a lamp half-full of kerosene. He lifted the smoky chimney, turned up the wick and lit the lamp. As the dim light began to grow, he glanced around the room. A thick layer of dust covered everything in sight. A round kitchen table, ringed by four stout wooden chairs, sat under a window. A huge iron cook stove with pots and pans on the surface squatted against a wall. An empty wood box sat next to the stove.

Walter thought the appearance of the place mirrored that of its subdued inhabitant.

When Mildred saw the dim light emitting from the old house, she walked into the kitchen joining Walter. He carried the lamp into the living room displaying an old potbelly stove, two worn wicker chairs and a tattered couch, all sitting on a gray cracked linoleum floor. The windows all had an abundance of dust and dead millers on the sills. Walter grunted as he walked into one of the two bedrooms. There was a bed with a dusty mattress; wallpaper hanging loosely from the walls and a broomstick fashioned for a closet rod.

"I didn't expect a mattress," he said walking into the next room. A mouse scurried across the floor as the light shone into the next dusty room which also had a bed and a mattress, but no closet. Obviously, the first room was Abner's bedroom.

"It's really not that bad," Walter said rubbing his stubby chin. "I expected worse."

"I did too," Mildred admitted.

"Well, I'll tell you," Walter began, "Maybe you can get some of the things in, dust the mattress and I'll go hunt for some wood."

As Walter went out to forage for firewood, he soon found out the supply was starkly different from what he was used to in Oklahoma or Missouri. There was no firewood. He spied a singular fence post, jerked it out of the obliging soil and brought it to the porch. He then chopped it with the axe he tripped on. Mildred busied herself making the bed. He took a newspaper out of the truck and started a fire in the cook stove. Mildred located another lamp so there was light in two rooms now. Walter warmed his hands over the open fire, replacing the lid on the stove.

"I'll go see if the pump works," he said to Mildred as she was making the bed. He noticed that she'd already hung some clothes in the closet.

"We could use some coffee," she said.

"I'll see if I can get some water."

Walter picked up a pail from atop the stove, removing the remaining empty utensils from the surface that was warming rapidly. The heat from the heavy stove was having its effect on the cold kitchen. He rattled around until he found a coffee pot. Seeing all this, Mildred automatically went to open a can of coffee she bought on their way out of Denver. Walter trudged off in the darkness towards the well, remarking, "Better not open that 'til I see I there's any water."

Three downward strokes of the pump, and to Walter's amazement, water gushed from its spout. "That's sure good news," he muttered to himself.

The guardedly-happy people sat in their kitchen talking about plans for their new home. Mildred put a new red and white checkered tablecloth on the round table and the old kitchen took on an instant lived-in appearance with the kitchen warm now.

"Well, Millie," Walter apologized, "It's not quite what you were used to in Missouri."

"What do you mean by that, Walter? I was living by myself in a cubicle at the school, and I was miserable. Here I have you and I have my own home. I'll be happy here, and nobody's going to throw me out."

Walter's face broke into a wide smile. "You just made the whole trip worthwhile, Millie!"

Mildred lay on the bed reflecting on the moments of her life during the past year. After getting her teacher's certificate from Kirksville Teacher's college, her first job was in a country school outside of the little farm town of Orrick, Missouri. In her second year, she had eight students in various grades. She had hoped to find employment in a larger school the second year, but she didn't, so she would work another year and try again—then she met Walter.

Inwardly, she was excited about her new lifestyle. She had a home, a husband, and the exhilarating prospect of raising her own family. She reflected upon her childhood. Her father owned a bank, and even though the family was large, she never wanted for material things. Mildred was endowed with a musical talent and played the piano and fiddle—especially the fiddle. She was good at it and played for square dance gatherings, so popular in the hillbilly environment. Although she enjoyed playing the instrument, she would have preferred to be dancing. That didn't happen often. The tall ungainly girl wasn't particularly popular with men. She had feelings like everyone else and longed for companionship, but such opportunities for her were seldom. Undeterred, she forged ahead with the positive attitude that was her makeup. She wasn't about to feel sorry for herself. The young girl who was the best bargain for any young suitor was avoided because of her appearance. Her mother continually reminded her of the adage, "pretty is as pretty does." Walter was finding that out firsthand.

Her new surroundings were a complete departure from the humid, verdant country she knew so well. The large house she grew up in was close to the Missouri River. As a young lady, she would sit on the upper deck of the large house watching the show boats, their large paddlewheels splashing through the night with the searchlights playing through the trees and their bands playing away. Often, she would take her fiddle and play along. She brought that fiddle to the farm, and tucked it safely under the bed. She snuggled happily against her husband who was fast asleep.

Mildred and Walter were up early, fresh from the night's rest. Walter chopped another post and built a fire in the big stove. The kitchen had gone through a metamorphosis, with the floors swept, window sills cleaned and the cupboards stacked with china and utensils. Mildred cooked breakfast, and steam boiled up from the hot water in the cook stove's reservoir. They would go exploring after she finished the dishes.

"Better bundle up, Millie," Walter warned. "The sun's out, but it's colder out there than it looks. We'll be out for a while."

The barn was in a state of disrepair, but functional. The stalls had the unmistakable pungent smell of a horse. Walter was immediately impressed by it. The farm just awarded Walter another unexpected gift. Three sets of harness hung on hooks in the feed room. Up in the hay loft, the sun pored through a few holes where shingles were missing. Walter would delight in fixing those. In the hen house, a dead Bufforfington carcass lay on the floor, and as in the horse barn, the odor of chicken manure claimed its own unique aroma. A forge, a vice, an anvil, several sets of tongs and hammers lay strewn about the shop. Completing the exploration of the menagerie, the pig pen was final.

"I don't know why pigs get all the reputation for their smell," Mildred commented. "I think chickens are worse."

Walter nodded in agreement.

The two turned toward the windmill, where the stock tank sat conveniently across hog fence. Walter knew it was there to provide water for the hogs to wallow.

To have a pump for domestic use as well as a windmill for livestock was unusual. It was an unexpected luxury. The windmill could run independently from household needs. Walter and Mildred stood under the wood tower. Walter decided to see if the windmill worked. Releasing the wheel brake, he looked skyward and watched the vanes starting to rotate, responding to the morning breeze. The sucker rod tugged and began its staccato churning up and down motion. Shortly, water began running through a pipe leading to the stock tank.

"We can make a living here, Millie. Harper left us a lot to work with," Walter said confidently.

It was time for Abner, the truck, to transport its owners around the homestead.

Fences were sagging, but they existed, and Walter would have them ready as soon he could gather a few cows. During this inspection, he discovered the prize of the homestead. Up ahead nestled in a sandy bank, a small forest of conifers appeared. Driving up to the oasis, Walter and Mildred stepped out of the truck and walked into the thicket. Coming up to a grove of juniper trees came the unmistakable sound of gurgling water. Walking closer, they discovered the spring. It produced a flow of fresh water running freely into a sandy ditch. He stepped across the ditch, shielding his eyes against the sun looking to the south—the direction the stream was flowing. Focusing in that direction, he identified a group of farm buildings.

Mildred, standing with him commented, "It's beautiful here."

Walter stood silently continuing his gaze. Finally, he spoke, "I think it's time to pay Marshall Reiss a visit."

Despite the farm's cluttered appearance, it looked friendly. Sheep were grazing next to the house. Toys, farm implement parts and almost any generic piece of trash could be found scattered between the house and barn.

Walter and Mildred stepped out of the truck. A brown and white spotted mutt barked, vigorously wagging his tail looking like he would bite if he *wasn't* patted.

A tall, gangly man of thirty years opened the door. His hair was light brown but his temples, moustache and sideburns had begun to turn gray. His face was friendly, unassuming, and honest. His blue eyes smiled. He tossed a loose jointed open-palm wave.

"Marshall Reiss?" Walter asked.

"'Fraid so," he replied.

"I'm Walt Hubbard. This is my missus Millie. We bought the Harper place. Jim Thurston said we should look you up."

The man's face broke into a broad grin.

"Ellie!" he called, looking back inside the house. "Come out here!" Reiss started toward the couple with his long arm extended.

"Glad to meet you Walt!" Reiss chirped offering an eager handshake. "You too...uh...Millie. I'm Marshall."

A tall gentle-appearing blonde stood in the doorway. A young child, with his thumb in his mouth, clutched her skirt.

Reiss led them toward the house as the tall woman with the timid child hanging to her stepped out of the house.

"Ellie, this is Walt Hubbard and his wife."

"Well, please come in," the soft-spoken woman said, motioning to the door.

As the three pressed through the door, Reiss looked back toward the yard. "Got a truck, I see."

"Yeah," Walter answered, "A guy named Armling set me up with it."

"Sam Armling?"

"You know him?"

"I know who he is. I've never met him."

"He's head of the homestead section—"

Reiss cut him off. "He's head of the whole shootin' match! I don't know how you ran into him!"

"I thought he was just another guy," Walter offered. "Anyway, I didn't plan on getting a truck, but he made me a deal on it."

Reiss hedged, "I won't ask you what you got it for, but you won't be sorry you got a truck. I sure wish I had one."

"Well, it's here if you need it."

Reiss grinned. "I've got to get coal. That trip into Cottonwood with a team and wagon is a bear. I'd sure make it worth your while, and fill your tank."

"I need coal too. What do you say we split the gas, and the coal?"

Reiss slapped Hubbard on the back. "I think you might make a good neighbor, Walt!"

"Can you get away tomorrow?" Hubbard asked.

"Sure! I'll come over in the morning or whenever's handy for you!"

"Why don't I come over here? We'll unload you first," Walter suggested.

Eleanor Reiss came back from the kitchen. "Why don't you two come in the kitchen and sit down with us? I've put the coffee on."

The living room was as cluttered as the outdoors, with clothes hanging everywhere, drying.

"Please excuse the mess," she said. "It's been so darned cold. I just didn't want to hang them outside."

The four sat down and started talking, seemingly all at once.

After a time, the little boy came and stood by with an anxious look, looking at Millie.

She turned to him. "What is it, honey?"

Shyly, he asked, "Do you have any kids?"

Millie, so aware what it felt to be avoided, merely smiled shaking her head no.

Eleanor Reiss broke the awkward quiet. "*We* aren't the only ones looking for company."

After two hours of animated conversation Millie said, "We really should be getting home. We just dropped in for a minute."

As the Hubbards were readying to leave, Walter asked, "Eight too early to be over?"

"That's perfect," Reiss answered, suggesting, "I'll be done with the milking by then." He added, "I don't want to tell you something that you probably already know, Walt, but park your truck on the south side of the barn."

"What for?"

"It'll stay warmer. The wind makes all the difference in the world out here when you have to start her up."

"Okay," Hubbard answered, leaving for the door. "Thanks for looking out for me."

Reiss smiled. "I'm looking out for me—you're draining the radiator?"

"I haven't."

"You'd better."

"Okay. You know the territory."

After closing the door, Eleanor admonished, "You're treating him like a child, Marshall."

"He's gotta' learn it gets cold out here, Ellie. He can't wait 'till somethin' breaks."

CHAPTER 4

The clouds were a heavy gray that morning. Walter steered Abner into Marshall Reiss's yard. The lanky farmer was waiting for him.

"Got time for a cup of coffee?" Reiss asked.

"Sure." Walter entered and sat. Eleanor, standing nearby, picked up a blue porcelain-chipped pot and poured him a cup of coffee. The boy came forward leaning against the table.

"Truck crank over okay?" Reiss began.

"Sure," Walter answered. "Why, shouldn't it?"

"Did you park it like I said?"

"I did."

"Do you know what 'wind chill' is?"

"I know what cold wind feels like, if that's what you mean."

"So does your truck. It can be twenty degrees out there, and if that wind blows, it becomes zero darned soon. If it gets that cold, nothing starts."

Walter nodded obediently.

Reiss shifted his body toward his neighbor. "Anyway, I wanted to talk to you about that spring that connects our places."

"I found it yesterday," Walter announced.

Reiss swallowed, taking the cup away from his lips. "That spring is what makes these two farms special."

"Why do you say that?"

A cow operation is essential to staying alive out here—that water is necessary not only for running cows but any other livestock."

"Okay, Marsh. What're you gettin' at?"

"That water runs onto my place and builds into a pond. It never freezes—not at the edges anyway."

"Why's that?"

"Water keeps runnin'," Reiss answered confidently.

"You must want to keep the water runnin'," Walter surmised.

"I do. Would that be a problem for you?"

"None whatsoever—why should it?"

Reiss issued a sigh of relief. "I paid Abner five dollars a year for it. Would you take that?"

"No. I won't take anything for what runs off my place."

"I'm used to paying it."

"I wouldn't feel right about that. If the water cost me, it would be different, but it doesn't, so don't even think about payin' for it."

"What will Millie have to say about it?" Eleanor asked.

Walter looked up smiling. "You folks want it in writin'?"

Marshall smiled back. "I guess we don't."

"Then, Marsh, why don't you tell me why I need cows, and I won't pay you for the information?"

Reiss leaned back in the chair with an air of importance. Not only had he resolved the question of water, he was accounting for it.

"You have to have animals to sell," he began. "You can't rely on crops out here. Drought, hail, windburn and the like makes it tough to farm. Your well at the house will take care of what you need around the place—hogs, chickens and the like—you got to keep them—you do have to eat, you know. But for range animals, you need a year-round water source—a source that won't freeze. That's what's good about artesian water."

"I understand McGregor wanted it pretty bad," Walter put in.

"You can see why," Reiss answered. He was careful not to mention that Jack MacGregor, still intent on acquiring both farms, and as recently as a month ago approached Reiss about buying his farm, and Reiss' refusal. Now that Hubbard moved in, he was glad he said no.

"Livestock," Reiss went on, "fills in for the down times. You have to include them in the works, Walt."

Walter calculated for a moment, mentioning, "That makes sense. Now, I'm beginning to understand why Armling insisted I sign that water deed."

Reiss straightened in his chair, expressing an immediate concern. "What's that about?"

"I signed this paper that transferred ownership of that spring from Abner Harper to me."

"Thank God you did!" Reiss burst.

"I'm guessing that was the thing to do."

Reiss motioned to his wife for another cup. She complied, filling Walter's cup, then her husband's. Hubbard's information settled him, and he returned to his easy gentle manner. "Damn right it was."

"Harper forgot all about it."

"What? That would have been a hell of an oversight! Who caught it?"

Walter was to come to learn if Reiss swore, it had to be for a reason.

"Armling did. Was it that serious?"

"It sure was. We both could have been without water if someone got wind that the file was vacant."

"How could that happen?"

"Anybody can file on an open claim. If that had happened, that spring would become theirs!"

"Impossible!"

"No it's not! This is water we're talking about, Walt. If it got in the hands of you know who, they could gain an easement and come after it!"

"I don't know how anyone could come on your place without your permission and take water," Walter protested.

Reiss eyed Walter warily. "Ask your man Armling about that the next time you see him."

"Okay. You seem to know what you're talkin' about," Walter surrendered. "We don't have to worry about it now."

Reiss chuckled. "You know what the Bible says..."

"About what?"

"'Says the meek will inherit the earth'—it's just they don't get the mineral rights."

Reiss's advice about running livestock did not go unheeded, but Walter wondered how a man so seemingly aware of what it took to carve out an adequate living could live in such cluttered circumstances. What he wasn't yet aware of was Reiss had a costly habit—alcoholism.

"I was thinking, Walt," Reiss went on, "that we unload your coal first, then after you unload me, I'll take you across my place."

"Good idea," Walter said rising, when a small voice interrupted them.

"Daddy?" the little boy asked.

"What is it, Augie?"

"Would you ask Mr. Walt if I could go along?"

"You ask him."

"Mr. Walt?" he began timidly, "Can I go with you and daddy?"

"Do you mind riding in the middle?"

He smiled, dashing out of the room, shouting, "I'll get my coat!"

The three hopped in the truck. The little boy stood on the floor peering expectantly out the windshield. Walter pulled out of the yard.

Reiss laid his hand on the boy's shoulder. "I'd think Mr. Walt would prefer that you sit, Augie".

The boy, crestfallen that his view of the road was just taken from him, dutifully sat.

Noticing this, Walter said, "He could hold onto the emergency brake lever, Marsh."

Immediately, the boy's face brightened.

"I don't care then," Reiss consented.

The boy sprang to his feet, clutching the metal lever sticking out of the floor. It was almost as long as he was tall.

"Just don't pull it, Augie," Walter cautioned. "That would stop us."

Reiss merely smiled. He knew the boy didn't have the strength.

"How old are you, Augie?" Walter asked.

The boy, suddenly feeling his importance, blurted above the accelerating engine "I'm four, Mr. Walt!"

In a short distance, the cab warmed from the heat of the engine. The heater was nothing more than a metal tube connected to the exhaust manifold of the engine. By opening a vent cover, heat, by convection, could enter the cab.

"You could become pretty popular in a short while with this rig," Reiss began.

"That so?" Walter responded, smugly steering the warm truck down the gravel road.

"We need a better way to get our milk into town," Reiss began explaining.

"Who's we? What milk?"

"Oh, some farmers around who sell milk. I'm one of them."

"They sell their milk?"

"Sure. We take turns carrying the milk in."

"When?"

"Every Monday."

"So what's the problem?"

"There are a few problems. The main one is that it takes too long to get it in, and the milk warms up."

"How do you keep it cold?"

"We can keep it cool, but we can't keep it cold. After it sets outside at night, it's cold. We pack it in straw. It stays cool, but during the trip into town it starts to get warm. We cover it with a tarp. That helps, but still it warms. Old Carl doesn't like warm milk."

"Who's Old Carl?"

"Carl Reichert. He owns the creamery. He bottles the milk, makes butter, cream, cheese—and buttermilk."

"It takes too long to truck the milk in?"

Reiss laughed. "You're the only one who has a truck. The milk is hauled in by team and wagon."

"Nobody has a truck?"

"Just you."

"What about McGregor? Doesn't he have a truck?"

"Nope, but that wouldn't matter. He doesn't raise milk, but he wouldn't help a farmer even if he did."

"Well," Walter said thoughtfully, "I'll help however I can."

Reiss glanced at him, smiling. "I thought you would. Why don't we get together with the other guys and see what we can work out? I can tell you, from just riding in this thing, it will beat the heck out of what we have at the moment. We're well on our way to town already, and this truck can carry a lot more than what you can get in a wagon. That would help everybody. They'll want to ship more, I know that. You'd be smart to get into the act."

It was two in the afternoon when the truck at the Reiss farm was empty of coal. The unmarked bed of the truck was no more. A tour of the Reiss farm revealed a thick grove of pine trees and a pond much larger than Walter anticipated.

In the coming months, Abner became a provident acquisition. The milk transfer was a vast improvement, and for compensation, Walter was awarded an occasional farm animal. Augie regularly rode with Walter, and came in handy occasionally serving as an errand boy. His weekly reward of a hamburger in town was well worth the indenture. Flat tires occurred regularly, but became a digestible part of the freight. All in all, it was a fortunate bonus for Walter, not only for starting his herd and his milk business, but for his friendship with the area farmers.

Abner, under Walter's caring hand, proved a valuable and dependable workhorse. Not only hauling milk into town, it served as a delivery truck bringing provisions back to the neighboring families. One duty, a distasteful one for Walter, but one he grudgingly accepted, was procuring a bottle of whiskey for Marshall after every trip into town.

CHAPTER 5

Liam MacGregor knocked once and entered Jack's house, a constant irritant to Kate, but one that she tolerated.

"Where's Jack?" he asked assuming his son was always at hand.

"He's back in one of the sheds," she said hiding her ire as she did so often. "Shall I go get him?"

"No, I'll go," Liam said as he walked through the house and out the back door.

Liam found his son working with some calves in one of the corrals behind the house.

"Guess what?" Liam said in his coarse voice.

"I dunno, what?" Jack asked without looking up.

"Abner Harper sold his place."

Jack stopped and looked up. "He what?"

"Yeah," the older man said. "I just found out from Royce Palmer."

"Were you in town?"

"I just come back."

"Wish I'd known that. I needed some stuff. When did he sell?"

"Hell! Two weeks ago!"

The younger MacGregor turned, hanging a rope on a nail next to the door of a shed. "I haven't noticed anything different over there—I guess I haven't paid much mind."

"Well," Liam griped, "He let some young homesteader by the name of Hubbard have it for five hundred bucks."

"How'd you know that?"

"Palmer said it was on the revenue stamp."

"What's a revenue stamp?"

"Damned if I know, but its public information—he told me that."

The son removed his gloves. "There's a chance this newcomer might let that spring water get past. I'll call to see if there has been anything filed."

"Save your breath. I already had Palmer call the reclamation department. It's been registered. Somebody's a lookin' out for that homesteader, I tell you that."

"Well, I told you we should have offered him more than that for it."

"I know you did. You go over and offer that new guy a thousand!"

"Okay, Dad," he said as he pulled out his watch and checked it. "I'll get back to you this afternoon."

His coat was slung over the rusty red pump handle off the corner of the house. Walter was hammering on the makeshift fence when Jack MacGregor rode up.

The specter of a tall cowboy replete with his ten-gallon hat and elegant sheepskin coat astride a magnificent buckskin stallion startled Walter.

The large collar of the coat was pulled up around the rider's neck. Foggy breath from the horse in the frigid afternoon resembled a knight astride a dragon exacting an ultimatum from a serf.

"Walter Hubbard?" MacGregor asked crisply.

"Yeah," Walter said straightening, placing the hammer in the loop of his overhauls.

"I'm Jack MacGregor," the horseman said forcing a smile. Walter expected McGregor to dismount. He didn't. "Understand you just moved out."

"You got it backwards. I just moved in."

"I think you know what I mean."

The conversation was not starting on the right track. McGregor waited for a response. There was none.

"It's a little rough makin' a go out here," Jack forced.

"We'll manage," Walter replied, reaching for his red handkerchief.

"We own the spread east of you," McGregor said with a grandiose sweep of his arm.

"I know," was Hubbard's reply.

"Pretty hard makin' a good livin' out here without a decent size piece of ground." His tone was solicitous.

Hubbard readied his handkerchief to his nose. "We're not used to a good livin' so I guess we don't need to be worryin' about that."

"I'd like to make you an offer on your land."

"Ain't interested in sellin," Walter said blowing his nose.

"Say a thousand—"

"No. That won't do it."

"What would?"

"Said I ain't interested."

"Come on. That's twice what you paid for it."

Walter would never have made a gambler. His quick temper clouded his reasoning. He recoiled. "How the hell would you know that?"

"Saw the revenue stamp," MacGregor bluffed.

"That ain't none of your damned business!" Walter snarled.

"It's public information," MacGregor continued.

"May be—I don't know anything about that, but it's none of your damn business what I paid for it!"

"Well," MacGregor retreated. "I didn't come here to upset anything."

"You already did," Walter snapped, stuffing the rag back in his hind pocket.

"I'll offer you two thousand dollars."

"'Spect you would, but it ain't for sale."

"You'll never get another offer like that," MacGregor spat angrily.

"Listen Mister! I wasn't run on here and I ain't gonna be run off!"

"Well, give it some thought. The offer still stands," he said turning his mount.

Walter glowered at MacGregor watching him ride away.

"Just like Abner said," Walter murmured to himself. "He wouldn't sell to any son of a bitch who wouldn't get down off his horse—well, neither will I! 'Sides, I like it here."

Walter continued to grumble while he hammered on his fence.

"He won't sell," Jack said to his father. "He wouldn't take a thousand! He wouldn't take two thousand."

"What! You offered him that!"

43

"I did."

"That's too damned much. I'm glad the dumb bastard wouldn't sell!"

"Well," the younger McGregor answered philosophically, "We'll get Reiss. I don't expect him to hold out much longer."

CHAPTER 6

Many thoughts flashed through Walter's mind as he and Millie drove the long road from Denver to Cottonwood with their new baby, Andy. Walter thought of the modest number of cattle he was able to accumulate through Marshall Reiss' guidance and the generosity of nearby farmers whose milk he hauled. He thought of the bitter winter days, bringing the calves in during blizzards, and chipping the ice in the stock tank so their mothers could drink, how the hens quit laying when it got cold, his stiff hands scraping hair off the hogs he and Marshall butchered one miserable December day.

There were the frigid nights when Millie and he played cards with Marshall and Ellie feeling the warmth from the hot stoves, while tolerating the wailing of their newborn daughter, Roberta.

It was late fall now, and the road to Cottonwood was a decent surface. It wasn't that way when the first trip was made. Abner didn't look new anymore, but he did his job without a hiccup or complaint. The 490 that had so many miles on it, purred the same as it did when Walter first drove it away. Like Marshall's appetite for liquor, Abner was learning the taste of oil. Walter was as gentle with machinery as he was with farm animals.

Expecting to farm with mules, he found that only horses were used in this country. He had worked them both, and while mules were better, he got along with horses. He got by with his horses and simple farm implements and looked forward to the day when he could retire the horses and farm with a tractor. That realization would wait.

Since so few farmers had automobiles, a good set of harness approached the value of a motor car. A fourth harness set was needed for the heavy plowing, and in his accommodating and diligent efforts to satisfy his fellow neighbors, he was readily compensated with the additional harness he needed.

There were other tools and implements that he needed and didn't have when he started farming. The farm implements he gathered were primitive, but with the forge and the shop, he kept them in repair.

The rundown farm was healing. The weeds were under control. The barn roof was patched. Sagging doors were squared. Broken window panes were replaced, and his fences allowed him to sleep at night.

There was much work to do before winter. The cane needed to be cut and shocked, the corn had to be picked, the beans threshed, and the hay wasn't yet in the barn loft. But he had Marshall—and Marshall had him. Together, they would get all that done—on both farms before the snows came.

They ate well, and he still held the trump card—his truck. Neighbors relied on him to haul milk, deliver coal, take their livestock to market and bring big things back from places where there were electric lights. Marshall Reiss was right. The truck made him popular. They were doing okay. Millie's parents would have to agree.

The light from the bouncing headlights splashed into the farmyard. Walter was jarred from his reverie.

Millie cradled her baby. Walter went on ahead and lit a lamp in the kitchen. He held the door open for her. She was tired from the eight-day hospital stay, the delivery, and the long road back. Smiling, she gazed around the room. Walter had kept the house as clean as she had. The living quarters bore little resemblance to the first time they had entered the house. The kitchen and living area boasted shiny linoleum floors; the walls were re-papered throughout; the windows and sills in every room were stingy-clean. In the kitchen, a new glass-front cupboard sat with stacked dishes visible inside. That was a surprise. Walter had sold a cow. She noticed it at once, handing the baby to Walter for a gleeful, excited inspection. All the rooms were clean; the chairs, the dressers and beds were in good condition. Those that weren't, had been thrown out and replaced. The $500 given to them had been well spent, but it was long gone. None of that would matter now, because they were happy.

Millie took her baby back from her husband to ready him for the night. She was prepared to begin her family.

CHAPTER 7

Fred Vogel was a destitute homesteader starving out of the grass country, but refused to leave. His land was of little farm value, but of particular interest to Jack MacGregor. Vogel realized this. The Union Pacific Railroad had a depot at the county line. The depot was placed at this juncture for the express purpose of allowing the engine to take on water. Railroads owned every other section in a checkerboard fashion for twenty miles on either side of the tracks. Fred Vogel's homestead straddled the railroad on a railroad-owned section, and bordered the McGregor property on the west. Jack MacGregor negotiated with the railroad, unsuccessfully, for the railroad to stop at some juncture on his land for the purpose of boarding his cattle. The railroad was unable to grant any loading privileges since they made but one stop and that was not on MacGregor property. Jack realized that if he owned lands bordering the stop, he could negotiate a loading arrangement. The outcome would be a substantial savings to the operation. Cattle, as was the custom, were driven twenty miles to Cottonwood, where the stockyards were located. The cattle would await the incoming freight train for transport. Hopefully, that would not be too long, because this exercise caused substantial weight loss, not considering the time and trouble involved in the drive itself. For many, this exercise was a loss of money. The arrangement that MacGregor and Fred Vogel made was to be most timely and profitable—not only in income, but in real estate as well.

MacGregor realized that food and supplies were a necessary commodity for the burgeoning influx of homesteaders. A general store could greatly benefit the growing community—and the ranch. He needed a wholesale outlet for his increasing crew and growing business. Jack offered to build such a store for Vogel, free and clear, at an even trade, for the title to his land. There was one stipulation, however: any and all products purchased by the MacGregor family would be purchased at Fred's cost. Also, the contract stated that such agreement would continue as long as the store existed. Should Fred sell, this covenant would remain with the business. Vogel accepted the offer. It was a good arrangement for both parties, since it was the first general store of its kind in the area. Because of its size, its nature of funding, and its diversification of products, it offered the convenience of one stop for all provisions. Vogel soon forgot about his trying times on the farm. He had what every businessman dreamed about. He had a monopoly.

The store turned out to be a better deal for Jack than he anticipated. Since a majority of poor farmers and small ranchers could not always pay cash for their food and supplies, Jack worked out an arrangement with Fred whereby Jack, behind the scenes, would finance credit for the borrower at the store. When the creditor got in so deep that he couldn't pay his bills, Jack would come out of the woodwork, offer to eliminate the encumbrance in exchange for the land, and perhaps enough funds to re-locate, preferably somewhere out of the county. It worked with regularity.

No rancher could survive without the knowledge of how to manage a drove of cattle. Jack's attention and expertise in running a herd came naturally, as it did for his father before him. He prided himself on his ability to save a baby calf when it was apparent the mother or animal itself, needed assistance.

This knack would come in handy that morning of December 4, 1922. Outside, a strong wind pounded the porch. A heavy chair slid across the railing, tumbling off into the white maelstrom. The raging blizzard brought a halt to all activity. Roads were impassible from winds and drifts. Visibility could best be measured in yards. Bonnie's contractions were coming every five minutes, and Jack was panicked. There were no telephones in that country and Jack was physically unable to summon help. He didn't dare venture out for assistance from his mother. In the howling gale and driving snow, there was little chance he could make it the half mile to her house, let alone, locate it. He had no choice but to employ the same expertise he would for a baby calf. That morning Chattman Liam

MacGregor was born. The kitchen was not optimum for the delivery, but Chattman was a fine, healthy eight pound boy. The MacGregor name would continue.

1923 began a prodigious era for Jack MacGregor. His land holdings were beginning to expand significantly. Several newcomers were leaving in a sad reversal to the expectant manner in which they arrived. Some ingenious, stubborn and determined homesteaders were persevering. A number of the same inhabitants were prospering because of hard work and good decisions. A few actually bought more land abandoned by those who, for lack of imagination or desire couldn't or wouldn't stick it out. Sometimes, failure was a result of the land's inability to produce. For them, it was just plain old bad luck. In any case, many of those who didn't make it belonged to Jack MacGregor. They were the unfortunate homesteaders who had no choice but have their debt retired, take the little bit of money offered to them and get out.

****

The ultimate test of friendship between Walter Hubbard and Marshall Reiss came at 2 a.m. January 17, 1925, when Eleanor Reiss knocked on the Hubbard's door. Marshall had gotten drunk this wintry night and must have gotten lost, she figured. She wasn't sure when or why he left the house. She searched in the barn, discovering the horses were missing. So was the wagon. Her assumption was that he drove away in the quest of liquor.

Earlier that fall, Marshall had prevailed on Walter, on his weekly trips to town, to buy him two bottles of whisky a week instead of the one. Walter compromised, buying one bottle that was a third larger. His ambivalence bothered him at the time, because Augie, who had ridden with him on the milk runs before, would occasionally mention his mother's concerns about Marshall's drinking. But Augie didn't ride with him anymore. He was in school now, so Walter was spared that compromise. Now his misguided compassion was paying a visit.

Walter bundled up as well as he knew know. He wasn't going to search for Marshall on foot, and he knew Eleanor needed to be home with her children. The truck would be of no use. He would harness a team of horses, hook up a wagon and take Eleanor Reiss home, in that order.

It was a miserable night, but visibility on the prairie country in a driving snowstorm was no less at night than it was in daytime. There were no landmarks for reference, and the hollow of the borrow pit of the road was the only proof that he wasn't in the ditch. There was nothing to do but to search—to try, in blind faith, to find a friend who vanished into a snowy faceless null.

Perhaps it was divined, but in Marshall Reiss' trek down the road, the wagon slid off the road. Whether he spooked the horses, or they bolted in the storm, it will never be known. The one thing Walter knew, the wheel of his wagon ran over something that shouldn't be on the road. He set the wagon brake and leaped off. Flailing the snow away, he discovered the tongue of a wagon! Quickly he glanced around for the horses. There were none. In the confusion, they broke loose and ran away.

Quickly digging the snow away from the wagon tongue, he saw that the wagon was in the ditch. He jumped into the snow-filled crevasse to discover that the wagon was upside down. The length of the wagon alone allowed him to burrow beneath the wagon box. Furiously, he began digging in the snow under the wagon. He felt an arm. With all his strength, he tugged the flaccid body that slid out from under the wooden frame. Marshall would have surely frozen to death but for the amount of alcohol in him.

By the time two approached the farm, Marshall, ashamed and sobbing, sat erect beside Walter. Hearing the dog bark, Eleanor rushed to the door. Entering the yard, the two men saw the loyal woman standing motionless in the light of the open farmhouse doorway. Marshall didn't need assistance coming into the house.

Walter stood in the kitchen for a short moment, wallowing in Eleanor's flood of gratitude.

"What are we going to do?" she asked, engulfed in tears. The despair in her voice was agonizing.

Walter set his jaw. His mind whirled. The vision of the times and experiences in the short time he arrived on the plain; the pain, the joy, the affection he learned from becoming a part of that family he had come to love. Suddenly, he realized he was a part of the problem. He looked into the woman's expectant brown eyes and with a somber resolve replied, "We won't buy him anymore whiskey."

"You're right about that," was Marshall's barely-audible concession.

CHAPTER 8

January, 1920

It all began in Cottonwood, Colorado, on a late blustery gray winter afternoon. A young man had been on the run from an angry Indiana father. He was driving a 1918 Cadillac he had stolen from his aunt. This particular fellow performed the second part of a nuptial obligation without bothering to attend to the first. The daughter was pregnant and still single. The father, believing that the hoodlum had forced himself upon her, was attempting to corral the swain in an effort to bring him to justice. Sometime later, the vagabond was holed up in a small western Kansas town when he met Margaret Stedman, a plain waitress in a highway 40 cafe. After a couple of days, he was living in her apartment. He told her of his dilemma involving the Hoosier girl, claiming the handy work he was accused of was not his, and she believed him, even though in the short time the two had met, he was handily working her.

Wary of being caught with a stolen car, he paid a junkyard employee two dollars to lift a pair of Kansas license plates from a recent wreck. Now, the police wouldn't be finding a Cadillac wearing Indiana plates.

It wasn't long before they packed up and moved further west. Fortunately for the sycophant, Margaret saved her money, so they would survive for the time being.

Well out of danger now, and low on gas, the two stopped at a tiny town, better referred to as a wide spot in the road. The wide spot was Cottonwood, Colorado.

Waiting to get his tank filled, he picked up on a conversation two farmers nearby were having. Ensconced in a resolute discussion while draped over the hood of a Model T Ford pickup, their problem, they concluded, was unsolvable.

He figured he knew something about the topic. Although it was none of his business, he realized that somebody wasn't being treated fairly, and with his convoluted set of ethics, he decided to intervene.

As Jim Thurston, the owner of the gas station, began filling the Cadillac, the fellow eavesdropped on the conversation. He understood it involved transgression of some kind.

One farmer was lamenting.

"He owns the damn ground between mine and his, and I can't get across his to get to mine. I never give it a minute's thought he'd keep me out when I bought the place!"

The intruder recalled a similar circumstance in Fort Wayne when he was a kid. His father worked in a laundry where patrons would drive across a vacant lot to pick up and deliver clothes, linen and the like. The lot offered the only way in and out. The parcel was sold and the new owner erected a barricade. A suit was filed and the result was that an entrance and exit had to be provided. The laundry was given an easement. The court ruled that the launderer must not be denied his right to make a living.

He sauntered up to the farmers asking, "You gents talking about ingress and egress?"

One pushed away from the hood, asking angrily, "About what?"

He smiled apologetically. "About getting across that property."

The farmer growled, "You musta' been nosin' in. Sure, that's exactly what we're talkin' about. What the hell's it to you?"

He avoided introducing himself, offering quietly, "You can't be denied access to your place of business."

One lanky farmer stood turning to the stranger. "You a lawyer?"

The impersonator massaged his chin. "You might say that."

The farmer, as did his friend, warmed to the traveler. "You sure about what you're sayin', mister?"

"Quite. He's bluffing." The man's tone was light, certain. "Don't let him get by with it," he added with a level coolness.

The farmer's indignation changed to humility. "Well—er, could we talk a little more about this?"

"We didn't intend to stop. We were just passing through."

"I'd sure make it worth your while—buy you supper? I'd pay you for what you have to say. I've got some money."

Off to the side, Jim Thurston waited patiently by the Cadillac, now full of gas. The vagabond noticed, and waved to his female companion. "Pay the man, Margaret!"

He turned back to the two farmers and cautioned, "Legal advice isn't free."

The farm owner paused, scratched the ground with the toe of his boot, and slowly glanced up at the traveler, "Do I have any choice?"

"Probably not, but I don't know where we could get together."

"How about the hotel?" the farmer suggested.

"Okay. I don't know where that is. You lead. I'll follow you."

Inside the coupe, Margaret commented unsurely, "I didn't know you're a lawyer."

"I didn't either," he returned, smirking.

A tall white clapboard structure sat perched on the edge of the prairie town. The English Tudor, with its high cylindrical doors, lofty ceilings and expansive red curtains hiding elegant lead-paned opaque windows appeared out of place in this austere semi-desert setting. From looking at it, one would conclude an oil boom was approaching or had just passed through.

The four sat at an oak table in the spacious dining area. Across the yellow maple hardwood floor, two cowboys sitting at the bar turned, taking note of the rare pre-evening activity.

A round of coffee was served.

The make-believe lawyer explained to the farmers there was no need to be concerned about crossing the land. The law would uphold a man's right to get to his livelihood.

The farmer leaned forward anxiously. "How do we know that? What do we do?"

"You start crossing the land as soon as you're ready—get it started."

"What part of the land?"

The wanderer was being challenged. He hoped the farmers wouldn't pin him down and ask too many specific questions. "It doesn't matter. Pick a spot."

"And what do we do when he comes up and starts raisin' hell?"

"You tell him that you talked to an attorney, and the law says you have the right to go on to your property; that you can't be legally kept off."

"What if he still gives us trouble?"

"You tell him that if he gives you anymore aggravation, the attorney told you to take him to court—sue him."

"We can't afford to do that."

"He doesn't know it. Take my word for it. When you say, *attorney*, and *sue*, he'll cave in. He knows he's wrong and won't want any part of the prospect of paying damages. It's a prima facie case." The masquerader remembered this reference from his father's confrontation.

The farmer squinted. "What the hell's that?"

"It means it's an open and shut plea."

"Man," the farmer cackled. "You know your stuff! And how you can remember them big words...!"

The pretender cut him off. "It's part of what I do."

Margaret, sitting to the side was awestruck. She was convinced he knew something about the law.

"Well," the farmer persisted, "You sound like you know this guy."

The heavy-set confidence man smirked knowingly, "I know his kind."

"Okay, you got me believin' it," the farmer breathed.

"He doesn't want you or your cattle wandering roughshod across his land, and he'll specify a lane, and I guarantee that's just what he'll do. It's his responsibility to provide you an access. Don't worry about it," he continued confidently, "You'll be granted your easement."

"I don't even know what that is or what it means," the farmer replied unsurely.

"You don't have to know. It's like a sore. Time alone will heal it for you."

"That part I understand."

The kangaroo lawyer was making the time thing up. Fortunately for the farmer, it was an accurate guess.

"Can we come back to you if none of this works and we get in a bind?"

At the un-anticipated prospect of a challenge, the man's eyes instantly became stony. Momentarily, he was a loss for words, straightening in his chair. He took a long thoughtful breath.

"Unfortunately, my wife and I are merely passing through. But don't let my absence soften your resolve," he said, regaining his confidence. "The law is still the law, whether I'm present or not."

One farmer remarked to the other, "I sure feel a lot better after talkin' to his feller."

The other nodded. "Now we just gotta' do what he tells us."

"So what's this gonna cost us?" the first farmer asked.

"I warned you legal counsel doesn't come cheap," the charlatan restated.

"I could tell that by the car you're drivin'," the farmer chuckled. "Anyway, what's the damage?"

"Ten dollars, I am afraid."

The farmer sat considering the charge, murmuring lightly, "That ain't so bad. Sort of like losin' a couple of steers," he calculated.

"Naw, that could be worse," the other farmer chipped in beginning to count his money in support.

Together the two came up with eight dollars and change. The farmer who owned the land promised to get the rest, if the arbiter would wait for him to get to the bank. The imposter waved him off conceding the payment was close enough.

"If I can cross my land it's sure as hell worth what we paid," the farmer allowed. "The way it was, that land wasn't worth a dime," turning again to the charmer, he probed, "I never got your name."

The slicker stammered for a moment caught in a confused mindset. He was too accustomed giving his real name. After an awkward pause, he answered, "My name is Palmer... Royce Palmer."

"Well, Mister Palmer," the farmer entreated, "Why don't you stick around a bit? You could get to likin' it here, and this country could sure use a man of your worth."

"Those are kind words," he breathed, glancing at his female friend. "We had no intention of stopping, but I suppose we could possibly give that some thought—maybe spend some time to test the water. Perhaps, I could be of assistance in your dilemma," he allowed, sensing another fee. He might have been eager to take the money and move on, rather than chance being discovered impersonating a legitimate lawyer. But he wasn't moving and he wasn't afraid. The euphoria of pulling off the ruse was taking over his psyche.

In addition, he was embarrassed and moved by the complement. Nobody that he could remember ever called him "Mister," or invited him to stay—at least when his name was Hinkle.

The pettifogger who "might give it some thought" moved in. He set up his office in the hotel, where the rent was $2 a week, until he could find an ante room, attic, anything that might serve as a better place to set up shop.

He moved out in less than a month, opening an office in a cubbyhole in the rear of the train station. The result was the farmer got his easement, and the new would-be barrister started a practice. Word spread. Cottonwood had legal representation.

Royce Palmer was a complicated man. Born Neil Hinkle, he was a womanizer, a master of pretense, an inviolable liar... and brilliant. He molded deception into an art form. His mother was unfaithful and his father was a Lothario, so the climate for him to learn what was proper and what wasn't—never existed. Sexual indulgence was his birthright. Affinity for the opposite sex was in his blood, and he had no ethics if they interfered with his desires. The one redeeming quality he possessed— and it was admirable, was his daring, no-fear aptitude. He would try anything, and normally succeeded at whatever it was. His shortfall was he wouldn't stick with it. He never finished high school and was seemingly unable to follow anything to completion. He needed encouragement, and received a precious small measure of it. Life in the poor section of his industrial Fort Wayne, Indiana home, offered little to steer him in a proper direction. Most of his neighborhood lacked education, and overall, was a disillusioned and immoral lot. Growing up, he was a fat kid, lazy and un athletic. He had few friends, but to the ones he had, he was loyal and generous. Although he was less than average physically, mentally he was tough as nails. Conducting business later in his life, this rigid inflexible disposition would make certain he wasn't going to be bullied. His main weakness was the opposite sex whom he diddled often, and he didn't care who they were or what they were like.

Hinkle had a spinster aunt living up in Auburn, who strenuously avoided him. The aunt was quite wealthy, having inherited a large sum of money from a lady friend who had been a close relative of the Leland family that started Cadillac. The rumor was this lady and Hinkle's aunt were lovers.

The aunt spoiled herself by driving Cadillacs, and exchanged one every two years. 1920 had arrived, and she would be trading her '18 in soon. Hinkle knew she never locked her garage, or removed the ignition key. The coupe she had was equipped with a heater, an all enclosed cab, an electric starter, and a big powerful, V8 engine. That would make an ideal getaway car for the cold west climate he intended to escape. The loss should matter little to her, he calculated.

He crept up the alley approaching the back door of her two-car garage. In fashionable sections, the common entrance to the garage was through the alley. That was fortunate, because he stood less chance of being detected there than on a front street. Cautiously, he lifted the counterbalanced door exposing the car. He acted quickly, noticing another car next to hers. It was a Rolls Royce. She was entertaining a rich friend, a woman no doubt. It was early dawn, Saturday morning, and the town was asleep, especially in this swanky section where people of means didn't have to get up. Quietly, he backed the car away, pulled the emergency brake, stepped out and carefully closed the door. He didn't want an open portal raising any red flags. Carefully, he idled the car out of the alley, then down a neighborhood street before entering Highway 69 taking him south to Indianapolis, then a straight shot out on highway 40 through Kansas and west. He didn't know how far. It depended on how his money held out. That wasn't his problem at the moment. He had to get rid of Hinkle. In a few days, that name would be plastered all over the Indiana papers. He was on the road for an hour thinking of an alias. He settled on the name Royce. When he saw the elegant car in his aunt's garage, he decided that. Now he needed another name. It didn't matter to him whether Royce came first or last. It would be used somewhere in his appellation. When he glanced up at a huge billboard showing a couple twirling on a ballroom floor, he had his answer. The caption read, *Join the Wonderful World of the Palmer Method of Dancing*!

That was it! Palmer! He was Royce Palmer!

After settling in Cottonwood, Palmer needed proof he was a lawyer. The word "attorney" was magic to him, and he was confident he could play the game. The jurist reference was a title that conveyed power, respect— even dread. After his first attempt to practice law, in which he was wildly successful, he paid a conspiring file clerk in the Denver City and County building to enter his name in the Colorado Law Register, listing Virginia as a previous address. The clerk also pilfered a blank certificate, replete with the embossed gold seal. That certificate bore three attesting signatures— all from the same calligrapher—very impressive. He considered which university would be the lucky recipient of his law degree. He decided it should be the University of Virginia, since that was where he supposedly lived. The plaque hung in his train office. Who could ever guess that he wasn't a lawyer? He could transfer titles, secure deeds, record land contracts, log the necessary entries for land assumption, issue marriage licenses, and even perform the ceremony. He could do all those things that only a bona fide lawyer could do—and more. If he needed a legal document, he would make a trip to the county records office in Denver, bounce it with his rubber stamp and it would appear original. Once his work was printed, it looked finished and proper. As an arbitrator, he would, for a charge, settle minor disputes with his phony claim that he was once a trial lawyer. He knew how to argue, as well he should. He'd done it all his life. Should someone need a legal interpretation, he would look it up. He did have a small library acquired from a deceased attorney. That's how he learned he could legitimately write wills. He was a notary public with property appraisal and real estate licenses—and he could fumigate houses. Bedbugs were a scourge and his was a guardedly-popular service.

The beguiling Royce Palmer was elected to the town council and the school board. In less than four years, the candidate for a double felony conviction, Neil Hinkle—the incriminated rapist and car thief—vaporized from the face of the earth and into thin air! In his place, a respected, much-in-demand citizen was living the life of prosperity, and anxious to move into a new building. It was a one-horse town and he was a one-man band.

Palmer inspected the construction on his new office, issuing orders to the two masons obediently bowing to his stream of demands. His action was an extravagant, pompous show of authority. The bank president and his secretary were looking on and Royce intended to make a statement— that he was in charge. The building was to be a two-story brick, with living quarters upstairs for him and his wife, Margaret. The ground floor would be used exclusively for office space while the basement would have a storage room for records, a bunk for emergencies, a dark room for him to practice his photography hobby, and a game room for him and his cronies to play poker. He struggled with the design of a sign on his building, which must be impressive and garish. It would bear his name "Royce Palmer," but there should be a middle name to add importance. What could he use for a middle name? He couldn't use Bernard, his real name which he hated. But he liked "Royce B." He concluded B was just an initial and that was all that was given. It would have to do.

He stood on the site, envisioning the sign which, upon completion, would soon appear on the front, emblazoned with the embossed lettering, ROYCE B. PALMER: ATTORNEY AT LAW.

****

In March of 1924, Mildred Hubbard gave birth to a second son, Samuel Franklin. Walter wanted to call him Samuel Armling, but Mildred objected, demanding that her family name be represented, rather than someone she hadn't met. After all, it was her family that gave them the start.

Walter again recited the pauper's oath, and he was again embarrassed— not because he couldn't afford the charge, but because he could. He and other farmers customarily benefited by taking advantage of welfare benefits. A prime example was receiving goods from the welfare truck that began coming down highway 40, now a paved road. The "commodity" truck, as it was called, came through quarterly, laden with clothes, coats, footwear and even script which could be redeemed for food products at grocery stores. A late model truck similar to Abner brought the largess. Walter referred to it as "Uncle Sam." People encircled the vehicle to claim whatever was given away. The exercise resembled the bidding frenzy seen on the Stock Exchange floor. Pride kept the wealthy away, but not the

Hubbards. Walter claimed a leather fleece-lined jacket that would compete with any expensive outer garment Jack McGregor would wear. Aside from accepting what was given, Walter's frugality placed him in good stead with people, because he paid his bills on time and his word was sacred.

CHAPTER 9

March, 1927

The Mitchell School was built in 1881 in honor of Helen Mitchell, the first school teacher in the area. In 1871, Miss Mitchell taught her first class of four students in a converted granary. She was passed around from household to household because the people in the area were responsible for providing her with food and shelter. Eventually, as the school grew and her salary increased, she moved into her own home and provided for herself. In 1894, Helen Mitchell retired and was replaced by Irene Pine, another single woman. The school board wouldn't hire a married woman considering that she may become pregnant and would have to be replaced. A teacherage with two bedrooms and a kitchen was constructed that year to accommodate the new instructress. Coal, wood and lamp oils were kept in supply by the school board. Miss Pine was self-sufficient, and served until February 1927 when she suffered a fatal heart attack. Finding a replacement in the desolate country that time of year would be difficult.

The community knew that Mildred Hubbard was a certified teacher, but there was one drawback; she was married. Although Millie was ambivalent about taking the job, Walter encouraged her, claiming their youngest Sammy would be no trouble at home. Walter had taken to the rambunctious towhead and encouraged Millie to take their oldest, Andy, now five, with her, reasoning, "He might learn something." The school board, having no alternative, hired her for the remainder of the year. Jack McGregor's "aye" vote was one he would later regret.

Mildred disliked being separated from her husband and younger son, but she could live in the billets provided, as was customary. She had the company of her son, and she forgot how much she enjoyed teaching. The school of eighteen students ranging from first to eighth grade was challenging for one person, but she was young and enthusiastic. The students appreciated her cheery disposition and she was popular with the parents as well. Andy was allowed to sit in wherever he pleased, and was able to interpret the basic reader nearing the end of the school year. The extra income was a relief, and Walter was taking the surplus and squirreling it away. With summer fast approaching, both Walter and Mildred, having become accustomed to the extra money, would have to get used to being without it.

Marshall Reiss honored Walter's admonition of no more booze. Determined to change his way of life, he noticed Millie's King James Bible on her table and asked her to allow him to take it for a while. His life was changed from the moment Walter dragged him out from under the wagon, but his introduction to the Bible was a transformation. His life as a farmer wouldn't continue much longer.

Dusk was approaching when Millie heard a knock at the door. She rose to answer it. Marshall and Eleanor Reiss had driven up. Marshall's Dodge car was parked behind them in the yard. When Marshall sold twenty of his cows and bought the car, his first, Walter knew the end of their farming relationship was near. Marshall had to have transportation to get to the church in Cottonwood, where he spent much of his time the past two months. Millie waved them in. They didn't look happy.

"I'll go make some coffee," Millie offered.

"Don't bother," Ellie answered. "We'll only be a little while." She turned to her husband, nodding. The two sat together on the couch. Millie sat nearby. Walter, at the dinner table, remained in the chair, but turned. His face showed concern.

"We came to tell you folks, we'll be moving out," Marshall began.

There was a somber pause. Walter broke the stillness.

"We expected it. How soon?"

"Pretty quick, I think Walt. We have a bunch of planning to do. We just wanted you to know first."

A tear ran down Millie's face, whereupon Ellie rose, embracing her. "We're just moving into town Millie. We're not moving away," she said softly. "We'll probably see you as often as we have living here."

Millie wasn't completely comforted. "It's just that we know you're there. It won't be the same for us. You were here when we moved in. I guess we've been relying on you."

"I think you've got that turned around," Marshall chuckled quietly.

"Any idea what you'll do when you move in?" Walter asked. He didn't want to see his neighbors go, but he wasn't quite as emotional about it as the women.

"I'll be running the creamery. Carl Reichert asked me at church." Reiss smiled, adding with a humorous admission, "He's a bible thumper too."

Walter noticed. "You always liked going in there."

"It's going to be fine—it's God's will, you know."

Walter rubbed his hands, embarrassed. "Yeah, you gotta' be right about that."

"Well, Walt. There's something else I came by for. If there's any way, I want you to have our farm."

"How much do you want for it?"

The room instantly became silent.

Reiss rubbed his nose. "We thought a thousand."

Walter didn't respond immediately.

"I think you might be able to get more than that, Marsh."

"Maybe I could, but think it over. I want you to have it."

Walter shook his head. "I don't see how I could."

Reiss rose, as his wife did upon his cue. "Well, see what you can do, Walt."

As the two headed for the door, Walter mentioned, "Maybe we ought to go in and see Royce Palmer."

Reiss stopped, turning, "Sure, when?" "How 'bout tomorrow mornin sometime?"

"Come on by when you're ready. I'll be waitin."

After they left, Millie lamented, "It's sad."

Walter brightened, "It wouldn't be so sad if we could buy the place."

"Would it make that much difference?"

"Sure—our place and his? We could make a real good livin' outa' both of them."

"You have trouble keeping up as it is."

"I know, but there's tractors a comin'—he looked around the room, and so are the boys."

She smiled, "Well, you'll figure it out."

"Yeah. That's the hard part."

The time was three in the morning. Walter shook his wife awake.

"What is it, Walter?" she asked, coming awake.

"I think I figured out how we can get Marshall's place."

"Can't wait 'til morning?"

"I don't think so, Millie."

She rubbed her eyes, sitting up. The moon was full, and a shaft of light bore through the room. She could make out her husband's expectant look. Taking a deep breath, she asked, "What is it?"

"Would you teach for a few years? I figure if you would, we could pay Marshall twenty five dollars a month, and at that rate, we'd have him paid off in less than five years."

She thought for a moment.

"I would—but I don't think they'd hire me back."

"Well, we're going to see the lawyer in the mornin' and I'd like to tell him somethin'."

"You can tell him I would if they'd let me. I'm going back to sleep."

Eleanor Reiss was hanging up clothes when Walter drove into the yard. Her hair, usually parted down the center was disheveled. She stood pinning clothes on the wire line, a clothespin protruding from her mouth.

Seeing him, she directed, "He's back in the barn, Walter."

Hubbard found him bent over, facing the wall arranging items in boxes. Upon hearing the footsteps, he turned.

"Marsh," Walter started, "if Millie keeps on teachin', I could buy your place. I mean sorta pay it off as we go along."

Reiss looked toward the open barn door, yelling to his wife, "Ellie! Could you come in here?"

Taking a clothespin from her mouth she yelled back, "Could you come out here? I can talk while I'm hanging up clothes."

The two walked up.

Marshall explained, "Walter wants to buy the place on time, Ellie."

She smoothed her hair with the back of her hand. "We'll need some money to get a house. How much will we get from the cattle and machinery?"

"Not much," Reiss answered.

Walter was uneasy standing between his friends while the two wrestled with the problem of how to allow him to acquire their land.

Walter offered, "Maybe you'd better sell it to MacGregor. He'll give you top dollar and in cash."

Unexpectedly, Eleanor cut in. "We've already discussed that, Walter. Unless you're unable to see your way clear, we could consider it, but our intention is that you buy our place."

Reiss adjusted his hat. "Let's get into town and talk to Royce Palmer. You haven't ridden in my Dodge, anyway Walt."

Walking toward the car, Walter recalled Palmer's being on the school board. This would be an ideal time to bring that up.

Fortunately, Palmer was in his office. The building was completed almost a year ago, and there were still things to do, such as gravelling the parking lot, planting trees and landscaping. The brick structure was a welcome and attractive addition to the little town. As Palmer envisioned, an imposing front sign announced his name and title.

The two farmers walked through the large glass-paneled door. Palmer was standing over his wife who was studying a typing manual. He was attempting to break his wife into being a secretary, and she was learning—slowly. Walter scanned the walls that were adorned with a spread of certificates. Glancing back on the glass frontage, he made out the painted advertising in reverse; Attorney-at-Law, Notary, Realtor, Will and Testament, Justice of the Peace, Photography. He also noted that there was no reference to decontamination. His profession had become too refined to advertising that ugly term... fumigating.

Neither farmer knew Palmer well. He came out to both farms three years ago to kill bed bugs.

Palmer straightened, turned, and offered his hand. "What can I do for you?" he asked, settling into his oak leather-bottomed swivel chair.

The two farmers, facing him waited unsurely. "Well, we..." Walter began.

"Sit down, Walter. Sit down, Marshall," he said, motioning toward two heavy wooden chairs.

Both men were impressed that Palmer remembered them, especially their first names.

Walter opened the conversation. "We're considering a business deal and we need your advice."

"Okay," he said, swiveling toward them. "I guess the last time we got together, I sanitized your homes. Did we get them all?"

"Every last one of them, Mr. Palmer," Walter announced.

"It's Royce," Palmer instructed.

"We never saw a bug in our house after that either," Reiss offered, referring to the process of covering and taping windows requiring an overnight stay in a barn or outbuilding providing time for the cyanide gas to take effect.

"Yeah, that's the only way to control those critters." Palmer again swiveled in his chair. "Now, fellows, what's on your mind?"

Royce Palmer was an unusual personality. To some people, he felt a natural aversion. To others, he was helpful and compassionate. With the poor and the homesteader, he was sympathetic to their cause. Palmer could identify with difficult beginnings—and he had the two farmer's respect which was important to him.

"Well," Walter said, "I don't know just how to begin. I want to buy Marshall's farm"— surprise flooded Palmer's face—"and we don't know if we can work it out. That's why we came to you."

"Have you arrived at a price?"

"We have," Reiss put in.

"How much did you decide?"

"A thousand dollars."

Palmer's eyebrows arched. Land was beginning to appreciate. He was aware of the water on Reiss's property. That gave it prime value. He knew Jack MacGregor's intention to buy the property and would pay more—but negotiating the price wasn't his duty or his service.

"So what's the arrangement?"

"Well," Walter began unsurely, "I'm gonna pay it off as I go."

"An installment purchase—is that it?"

"Yeah, I guess that's what it's called."

Palmer turned to Reiss. "Is that acceptable with you, Marshall?"

"That's what we agreed on."

"So how much do you have to put down, Walter?" Palmer asked.

"Well, I thought two hundred dollars," Walter answered confidently.

"That's a little less than the normal twenty-five percent. Would you go along with that, Marshall?"

"I would, but I've got another problem."

Palmer's face twisted, "What might that be?"

"Well," Reiss fidgeted, "that's just what I still owe Jim Thurston."

Walter was proud he had a down payment. He knew Mildred would be surprised that he saved half of the amount from her school teacher's salary. But the real surprise would come when she learned the other half came from her family's original gift. She thought her father's money was spent long ago. Walter hid it for unforeseen contingencies.

"Okay," Palmer sighed. "That takes care of the first deed of trust. What do you have for a down payment?"

Walter was confused. "I don't git what you're askin'?"

"I'm referring to funds to initiate the sale."

"Hell," Walter exploded, "that's what I just offered."

"You just committed to retire the debt Marshall owes to Jim Thurston. That's separate from the note you'll be indebted to Marshall. How much do you have to put down?"

"What I just offered is the down payment as far as I'm concerned."

Palmer looked to Reiss. "You know, Marshall. Jack MacGregor would like that property. And he would pay you in cash."

"If you don't want to work with us...!" Walter spat angrily.

Palmer cut him off. He was aware of Hubbard's quick temper.

"Don't get your dander up, Walt! I'll do as I damn please—a few years ago I wouldn't have said that, but in order to make this thing work—I'm not suggesting that Marshall sell to Jack MacGregor, but I'm representing both of you. If you can't get compensated, Marshall, and if you can't pay, Walt, then we're wasting everyone's time."

"Okay," Walter replied, appeased for the moment, "I'm sorry."

"What do you have for earnest money, Walter?"

"For what?" he asked, annoyed again with the prospect of further expense.

"Earnest money," Palmer continued, "is money to show good faith on your part. If the deal falls through, Marshall gets to keep it."

"Well," Walter confessed, re-arranging his thoughts. "I guess ten dollars."

Palmer broke into a laugh. "To hell with it. You trust him, don't you Marshall?"

"More or less," Reiss chuckled, smiling at Walter.

"Now, Walt. How do you intend to pay for it?"

"I'll be givin' him twenty-five dollars a month 'til it's paid for."

"Where do you intend to get the money for that?"

"Well, that's the sticky part. I don't know if you have found a teacher for Mitchell School," Walter began humbly, "and I don't know if Millie could be considered, but that's how we'd pay for it."

"Does she want to teach?"

"Yes."

"Has she applied?"

"No."

"Well, she had better do that right away."

"Do you think she has a chance to get the job?"

"Not until she applies. After that it's up to the school board, and I'm not at liberty to give you an opinion on that. At any rate, it all sounds a little iffy."

"Marshall understands that. If Millie doesn't get the job, we don't get the farm," Walter conceded.

"Okay, then," Palmer said. "If we all understand the risks, let's get this contract between you two put together."

When all the papers were signed, Palmer started to rise when Reiss announced, "I have another problem."

"What other problem?" Palmer asked, sitting back down.

"I've got to live somewhere."

Palmer brightened. "You're going to be running the creamery for Carl Reichert, I understand."

Reiss was taken aback. "'Guess news gets around fast… haven't told anyone, 'cept Walt. Anyway, somehow I got to have a house and I have to figure out how to get one."

"That won't be a problem," Palmer said easily.

"Why won't it? Walt doesn't have any more money, and I sure don't either."

"You go buy a house."

"With what?"

"You use the house itself for collateral and pay for it with your income from Walter. The money you get from the creamery would be for living expenses."

"Jesus! — I mean jeepers — that sounds easy! I can do that?"

"Yes you can."

"How? Where do I get the money?"

"Felton will loan it to you."

Palmer was referring to the Cottonwood bank president.

"You think he'll do that?"

"I guarantee he will. I'll co-sign for you, and I've got just the house," Palmer said magnanimously.

"You do? Where?"

"The Baker house."

"What's it like?"

"Great house—four bedrooms, two up, two down—indoor bathrooms, one upstairs and one downstairs. And, it has a full basement. You got a shop and a garage." Palmer spoke as though Reiss already bought it.

"That's sounds too good. What would something like that cost?"

Palmer hedged, answering, "You can get it for a thousand."

Palmer just picked it up on a foreclosure for five hundred. He would double his money, plus receive a commission.

"What would that run me?"

Palmer reached in his roll-top desk for an amortization book, started leafing through it, taking a pencil and a pad, he began: "Let's see, on a seven-year payment, it would be…" he licked his finger running it down the page mumbling, "my commission of two hundred, title insurance, recording the deed… total ten two thirty-five…," Palmer mumbled, finishing, "your payment would be...aah...twenty-one dollars, and thirty-eight cents a month."

"Well, swell," Reiss said. "That'd be just right—when can we look at it?"

"Can you bring Eleanor in tomorrow?"

"Sure." Again, Reiss and Walter, were impressed that Palmer remembered the wife's name.

Walter, sensing the need to end the negotiations remarked, "That's got it wrapped up, then, would you say?"

"Not quite, Walt," Palmer advised.

"What else?" Walter asked, his voice showing annoyance.

"I don't work for nothing," Palmer answered.

"That's right, Walt. Royce's gotta be paid," Reiss put in.

Walter shifted his weight unsurely, wondering what the next charge would be and how it would be resolved. He inhaled deeply. "Yeah—guess I forgot about that. This is beginning to sound to me like Tar Baby. What's it gonna run us?"

Palmer chuckled at the simile. "Well," Palmer answered, "The negotiation about the land transaction is your responsibility—not Marsh's."

"Why's that?" Walter reacted, visibly agitated. "I thought you're representin' the both of us."

"I am, but he's the seller, you're the buyer. That's how it works."

Walter scratched his head. "Well, I don't understand that either, but if that's it, how much is it gonna be?"

"I'm guessing around twenty-five dollars, but don't worry about it until we pin it all together. And you can take your time paying me if it becomes a problem. We've completed all the paperwork expecting that it'll all go through all right."

Walter smiled with ambivalence, relieved that he wouldn't have to come up with another immediate charge, but mindful of the possibility the deal could very easily fail.

"Yeah. I sure hope this'll go through," Walter breathed.

"And if it doesn't, I've got a real problem," Reiss breathed.

"Not really," Palmer said.

"Why do you say that?"

"If you get in a pickle, MacGregor will always buy it," Palmer replied.

Walter gritted his teeth.

"I sure hope Millie gets the job."

Palmer, standing now, patted him on the back. "She'll have my support, Walt. Have her get that application in."

Walter turned to shake Palmer's hand. "It was a good day when you moved in here, Mister... Royce."

Walking to Marshall's Dodge, Walter remarked, "He really knows his stuff."

"You were right, Walt. It was a good day when that guy rolled into Cottonwood."

CHAPTER 10

Marshall Reiss was arranging tools on a board when a tap on the wall caught his attention. With large wrenches still in his hands, he turned to see Jack MacGregor in the doorway.

Although the relationship between MacGregor and Reiss couldn't be described as amicable, it wasn't hostile, either. The two men would wave or speak when they passed, but in reality, they had nothing in common, so no friendship ever germinated.

"Looks like you're gettin' ready for a farm sale, Marsh," the large cowboy began. His felt hat created a shadow on the shop wall with the morning sun at his back.

Reiss turned, forcing a smile. "I guess that'd be pretty hard to hide, Jack."

"Understand you'll be running the creamery for Carl," MacGregor said, entering the cluttered dirt floor of the work place.

Reiss inhaled deeply, "Pretty hard to keep a secret in these parts."

MacGregor shook his head, silently agreeing, "Wouldn't want to get nosy, but how soon you plannin' on movin' out?"

"Right away, I've already bought a house in town. Ellie's in getting it ready right now."

The announcement was the word that MacGregor had hoped for.

He smiled, feeling comfortable, "Any chance of takin' this spread off your hands, Marsh? I could use the water, and I'm sure you'd have a use for the dough."

"I made a deal with Walt Hubbard," Reiss answered, turning to place the wrenches on the board. Swinging around, and without a reply, he saw the figure dart out the shop door, then the sound of an engine racing, followed by tires spinning out of the yard.

MacGregor's '28 Buick sedan slid to a stop in front of Royce Palmer's building. He wrenched open the door, stomping into the entryway.

"Where's Royce?" he barked at Margaret.

She turned in her chair. "Why, he's down in the dark room."

"Get him!"

"Just a minute," she obeyed, leaving the office. Jack could hear Palmer's unintelligible loud dialogue, then Palmer clambering up the wooden stairs.

MacGregor's breath came in short bursts.

Palmer rounded the corner into the entry room.

"Royce!" MacGregor snarled. What's this I hear about Walter Hubbard buying the Reiss place?"

"Didn't know it was public information, Jack," Palmer replied easily.

"Well is he?" he demanded.

Palmer drew in a deep breath, exhaling slowly. "There's something in the mill, I guess."

"You guess? How the hell could you do that, Royce? You know I'm after that place!"

"I know it," Palmer replied, retaining his composure. "I told Marshall it would be wiser to sell it to you."

"Where was Hubbard when you said that?"

"He was right here."

"How'd he take that?"

"Not well."

"Well, why didn't you let me know?" This last bit of information tended to placate MacGregor.

"Am I to let you know about everything I do? Do you let me know everything you do?"

"Look Royce. I've given you a lot —a *hell* of a lot of business!"

Margaret was frozen against the wall, apparently unable to move.

Palmer retained his composure, agreeing, "Yes Jack, you have given me a good deal of business."

"Well, I'm gonna tell you what, Royce. You stop that transaction, and you do it today!"

Palmer turned to his wife. "Margaret. I think you'd better let us discuss this privately."

It was as though a latch was released. She sprang from the wall dashing out of the room.

Palmer turned to the rancher. "Jack," he began evenly, "Those two men have a right to consummate a business deal. It's between them. It doesn't involve you."

"Right your ass! Don't you be telling me about what's right! You came into this town not ten years ago poorer than a God damned tramp. When I first met you, you were workin' in that dump along the tracks in the back of that train station—and you'd still be there! I've given you a ton of commission!"

Inwardly, Palmer felt a rush of mixed humor. His initial piece of business was not favorable to MacGregor's interests, although MacGregor never knew it.

"You helped me out a ton, Jack, and I appreciated the business you gave me at that time. I appreciate the business you still run my way. However, you wouldn't have paid me a significant amount of those commissions over the years if I hadn't made a number of parcels of land available to you. You had no idea those pieces could be bought," Palmer continued his quiet analytical tone.

MacGregor knew what Palmer was saying was true, but the rancher came to Palmer in anger, and he was still hot. "I'm telling you to stop the God damn deal, Royce!"

"You aren't telling me to do anything, Jack. I did come in here several years ago, and I didn't have anything—I admit it. But that was then—I was just getting started. Some of us do have to start our own businesses," he said in an obvious insult. Palmer was not about to let MacGregor take credit for what he himself had achieved on his own. "Maybe you run things out there," Palmer said, pointing to the large window, "but you don't run them in here."

"How much is the sale for?" MacGregor demanded, still angry.

"I can't tell you that, Jack."

"And why can't you?"

"First of all, it's a matter of professional ethics, but second, it privileged information."

"You and your big-ass words!" MacGregor cursed, biting his lower lip. "You want to talk about ethics, why in the hell don't I expose a little bit of ethics around town? How you been plunkin' Lois Babcock—." Palmer reflexively glanced to his rear fearing his wife could be within earshot, "Don Babcock would clean your clock if he knew about that!"

MacGregor knew but a few of Palmer's trysts, but enough to make it plenty warm for the philanderer.

Palmer could play MacGregor's game, too. Palmer was used to gambits, and was probably better at bluffing than MacGregor.

"Go ahead, Jack. You go ahead and you do that. You blast everything around town. Then, maybe I'll let it be known that the land Fred Vogel's store is on, is really owned by a lady in Philadelphia—not you, and if I make that public before the statute of limitations expire on that adverse possession, you and Vogel will both be out of a store. Or how about the time you bribed that meat inspector on that train load of cattle with Bang's disease? Or..."

"All right! All right! That's enough!" MacGregor shouted. He was beaten and knew it. Turning to leave, he uttered, "I'll read the damn revenue stamp. You can't keep me from findin' out how much Hubbard paid for it!"

Palmer smiled. "There'll be no public announcement of this transaction."

"What the hell does that mean?" The acid in MacGregor's voice still remained.

"It means there'll be no revenue stamp."

"Sure there will. There was one on his last deal."

"You know your cows, Jack, but you don't know real estate."

"Then you tell me why that won't be printed."

"His last purchase involved the Federal Land Bank. This one's between two private individuals. It's not public information."

Not appeased, MacGregor continued, "Well, you son of a bitch, I know how that dirt farmer is planning to pay for that place!"

Palmer glanced up expressionless.

"You know I know, don't you, Royce?"

A smile crept across Palmer's face. "Yes, Jack. I think I do."

"Well, she ain't gettin' that God damned teachin' job!"

With that, MacGregor wheeled and stomped out, with Palmer wondering how MacGregor knew about the plan to pay for the farm. It had to have been a guess.

Margaret Palmer stepped back into the office entryway. "That wasn't pleasant," she said. "I didn't know you were in there, Margaret. No, it wasn't friendly," Royce returned

"What was that thing he brought up about Lois Babcock?"

"Oh, MacGregor's a vindictive fellow. You don't think I would ever be unfaithful to you, do you?"

She slumped against the wall, folding her arms. "No. Of course you wouldn't, Royce."

As frustrated and angry Jack MacGregor was with Royce Palmer for negotiating the contract between Reiss and Hubbard, MacGregor began to reconsider; the agent was doing no more than what he had to do to scratch out a living. MacGregor, too, had performed necessary, yet distasteful chores with ambivalence; that's how things work, he concluded. He recalled Palmer said, "I told him he'd be better off selling to you." As weak as MacGregor considered it was, the statement represented a show of Palmer's loyalty. But he knew Palmer could no longer be taken as a pawn. With his angered feelings somewhat appeased, he would go back to the poker games he and his cronies enjoyed once a week night in the basement of Palmer's office building.

Mildred Hubbard's job application was received by the school board. MacGregor needed Palmer's cooperation.

It was midnight and all the players had gone home, except Jack MacGregor. Palmer sensed a confrontation when MacGregor half asked-half commanded, "You ain't voting for her—are you?"

Palmer merely stared back, not responding.

"Well, are you?"

"I'll vote my conscience, Jack."

"What the hell's that supposed to mean?"

"Jesus, Jack! Why don't you just campaign for a one-man school board? Why have a quorum at all? Let one guy make all the decisions. Is that what you want?"

Five members comprised the school board: Felton Caldwell, the bank president; Carl Reichert, who owned the creamery; Royce Palmer; Fred Vogel, who owned the town monopoly; and Jack MacGregor, school board president, who owned Vogel.

MacGregor knew Reichert would follow Felton Caldwell, and Caldwell would vote to retain Mildred. MacGregor and his lackey, Vogel, would vote against her, but MacGregor, by rule, could vote only in case of a tie.

"What I want, Royce, is your vote!"

"And I have told you my intention."

"Could your intention be negotiated?"

Palmer flashed an amused smile. "It probably could."

MacGregor eyed Palmer with repugnance. "Okay. What'll it take?"

"Oh, I don't know," Palmer responded lightly.

"How about fifty dollars?"

"Nah."

Palmer's tone was insulting, but MacGregor would hold his anger in check this time. "Okay, double it."

"No," Palmer answered softly. "That won't do it."

"Then two hundred!" MacGregor was starting to lose his temper.

"No, Jack."

"Why you son of a bitch! ...I ought to knock your teeth down your throat!"

"Go ahead and do that, Jack, and you'll be branding my cows."

MacGregor knew Palmer wasn't bluffing.

MacGregor's expression was grim. He expelled a huge breath. "Okay. What's it gonna take—three?"

"I guess," was Palmer's stoic reply.

MacGregor glowered at him, rising to his feet. "I'll have it in the morning, you bastard!"

Cottonwood School District 5 met quarterly as scheduled at the high school. Ethel Hoagland, secretary, dutifully unlocked the building, made coffee, readied the cups, condiments, silverware, and arranged the board members' chairs.

Jack MacGregor walked down the overly-lit hall. Pictures of graduated classes adorned the walls. Three of the four members of the board who arrived earlier, were in the superintendent's office sipping coffee. Royce Palmer was the lone member yet to show. His absence showed on MacGregor's face. The Cottonwood board held jurisdiction over both Cottonwood and Mitchell, twenty miles to the east. Mitchell remained because transportation difficulties necessitated its existence.

The meeting may run late if Palmer didn't show up soon. Felton Caldwell was talking to Carl Reichert in the room set aside for the meeting. Both men were on the board since it formed and Felton was the president since its inception. Just a year ago in June, he stepped down to allow somebody else to be president. Jack MacGregor, having served on the board but one year became that somebody. Caldwell, president of the local bank, moved in to Cottonwood twenty-one years earlier. His bank in Denver wanted to expand and sponsored his home along with a generous salary to relocate. The challenge for Caldwell, accustomed to the comforts of Denver, versus the stark primitive environs of Cottonwood, was a contrast that only a man of energy and purpose would be willing to attempt. Caldwell held every civic office, albeit small, from mayor to school board president, and elder of the Episcopal Church. He served as pastor for a short time years ago, when the standing minister died. Honest and ethical, this tall elegant gentleman with his trademark pencil-thin moustache and hair parted down the middle, was loved by all—except Jack MacGregor.

The meeting was scheduled to begin at seven-thirty; Eight o'clock had passed. Royce Palmer remained absent.

"We may have to start without him," Caldwell warned.

"We'll wait until he gets here," MacGregor returned.

Caldwell persisted, "The by-laws state—"

"I know damned well what the by-laws say, Felton!" MacGregor snapped, turning to the secretary. "Read the minutes, Ethel."

MacGregor in his anxious, hate-filled anxiety thought, if Palmer doesn't show, I'll personally feed him to the coyotes.

Back in his office, the counterfeit lawyer hesitated, finally switching off the lights of his office before leaving for the school. On his roll top desk, an envelope from Jack McGregor lay, unopened.

"March thirteen, nineteen hundred and twenty-eight," Ethel Hoagland began in her toneless droll, "the Cottonwood School District held its quarterly session. The mill levy for the coming year was approved four to nothing. The snows brought ample problems for the students..." she droned on. Felton Caldwell, bored, stared vacantly at the blackness of the office window. Carl Reichert was nodding off. "...The bazaar was held at the town hall to raise money for basketball uniforms. Nine dollars and twenty-six cents were raised and a good time was had by all..."

MacGregor was as bored as anyone, but the filibuster was saving his bacon, for the moment.

"We were very fortunate that Mildred Hubbard could fill in for our dear departed friend Irene Pine..."

Caldwell switched his attention to the secretary, who continued, "...and the board, in gratitude, unanimously agreed to buy her a sauce pan, which she greatly appreciated..."

The sound of footsteps up the stairs brought MacGregor out of his day dream. A somber Royce Palmer entered, and without a word or glance, sat down at the table focusing straight ahead. MacGregor flashed him a careful stare.

Ethel was wrapping it up. "Everett Davis finished varnishing the gym floor for the coming season and Superintendent Guy Burnett was satisfied with the results." She looked up from her papers, "respectfully submitted, Ethel Hoagland, secretary."

"I recommend we accept the minutes as read—do we have a second?" MacGregor responded, relieved that the ponderous treatise was over.

"Second," Vogel uttered.

It's been moved and seconded we accept the minutes. All in favor say aye."

The perfunctory utterances ushered in the meeting. For the next hour, the duties of running a school were hashed over, until the question everyone anticipated arose.

"The final item on our agenda is hiring a replacement for Irene Pine," MacGregor announced. "Who would like take on that responsibility?"

"We don't have to do that Jack," Felton Caldwell responded. "Mildred Hubbard has submitted her application."

"I know she has, Felton, but shouldn't we consider an unmarried person? Mildred may teach, have another baby next year, then where would we be? We'd have to go through the process all over again. She had a son livin' with her at the school and another one close behind. Really, she belongs at home."

"I think that's her choice, Jack. She has applied." Caldwell spoke in his soft, gentle voice.

"Well, if you think that, I suggest we put it to a vote."

"There is no need for a vote Jack," Caldwell continued, his voice raising an octave. "We have a fine qualified, enthusiastic person who is willing to teach. I don't think it's our responsibility to predict how long she is going to stay or interpret how she conducts her private life. It's simple. I move we hire her by acclamation."

"I second," Carl Reichert put in, then asked, "What do you think Royce? You've been awfully quiet."

"I have nothing to add." Palmer's answer was more of an utterance.

"What about you, Fred?" Caldwell asked, turning to the store owner. "You've been quiet too."

"I don't have anything," Vogel answered.

Caldwell realized neither Vogel, nor Palmer was voting his conscience.

"So moved and seconded," MacGregor announced nodding to the secretary. "Ethel, pass out the ballots, would you?"

"Oh, my goodness, Jack!" Caldwell protested. "We've been voting aye and nay since the beginning!"

"Not any more, Felton. It's better this way. If it didn't involve someone we know, it would be different."

"Okay," Caldwell surrendered, opening his hands. "You're the president and that's your prerogative."

Four ballots were passed out; the vote was made and collected by Ethel. Officiously, she opened them one by one, gathering them into a uniform packet.

"We'll, what's the verdict, Ethel?" Caldwell asked.

"Two four; two against," she said.

The venerable banker snorted, asking derisively, "Well, Jack—does it take a secret ballot for the tie breaker?"

Word that Mildred Hubbard was not rehired erupted like a dry grass prairie fire. The first flame was in Royce Palmer's office, when Walter Hubbard burst into it the following morning. Marshall Reiss was at Walter's house early. After driving into town to continue fixing the new home, he dropped Ellie off then stopped at the creamery to see Carl Reichert. Reichert gave Marshall the news. Reiss, intending to go back and assist his wife this day, had to give Hubbard the result of the vote. Reiss would go back and help his wife.

Walter found how fast Abner would run, racing into town. The engine rods were rattling when he careened into the parking lot.

Palmer was sitting at his desk, head in his hands awaiting Hubbard's arrival, which he knew would happen.

"You said you were in our corner!" Walter exploded.

Palmer looked up slowly. "I know I did."

"Then how in the hell could you do that?"

"I was wrong."

"You're damned right you were! Now Millie won't get the job, and I won't get the farm! I trusted you!"

"I know you trusted me," Palmer returned meekly, sliding the sealed envelope over to Walter.

Palmer's admitting to his error diffused Walter's anger. Looking down at the white enclosure, Walter inquired, "What's this?"

"Open it."

As if in protest, and with his thumbnail, Walter tore a jagged slit the length of the enclosure. Inspecting it, he pulled out six fifty dollar bills. "I don't get it."

"I want you to take it."

The blond farmer frowned at Palmer, confused. "Where'd this come from?"

"Jack MacGregor bribed me with it. I have to admit that to you. I'm as guilty as he is, and it shames me."

Walter crumpled the money in his fist. "I don't want any God damned MacGregor blood money!"

Palmer leaned back in his chair. "Believe me, Walt, he'd like to have it back, I can tell you that for sure. But if you think about it, that's a chunk of what Marshall's place is costing you. With that money, you wouldn't have to make payments for a year."

Walter fingered the money, drawing in a healthy volume of air, placing the cash on the desk top, sliding it back toward the lawyer, whose penitent eyes were fixed on the farmer.

"That's all and well and good, Royce, but with last night's vote I can't buy Marshall's place—not with one years' worth of payments I can't."

Palmer flashed a tired, yet confident look to the farmer. "Where's your faith, Walt?" he asked.

"Whaddya mean by that?" Hubbard grilled.

"I know the people in this county better than you do."

"What are you gettin' at?"

"They won't stand for it."

"Stand for what?"

Palmer exhaled deeply, pushing the money back across the roll top desk to Hubbard.

"This thing with your wife isn't over yet. Take my word for it."

Hubbard looked puzzled. "You don't think so?"

"No—I don't," Palmer answered grimly, motioning with his index finger to the crumpled wad of bills.

Walter again eyed the cash. "Well—I don't want anything that belongs to you."

After an awkward pause, Palmer breathed, "I'm not taking the money, Walt. I'm not giving it back to Jack, either—and," he smiled, shaking his head, "there's no sense in burning it." Hubbard, too, smiled for the first time, picking up the money. Palmer issued a huge sigh of relief.

"Take me over to Marshall's new house, Royce. I need a ride."

"You've got your truck," Palmer said, confused at the request.

"I just ruined it."

Inside Palmer's swanky new 1928 Cadillac convertible, Walter asked, "You always drive a Cadillac?"

"Always."

"I remember you had one when I first met you."

"I did," Palmer acknowledged, referring to the coupe he stole from his aunt.

"That's the one that got washed away in the flood of '24," Walter reflected.

"That's the one," Palmer mused.

"That was sure rotten luck," Walter answered.

"Well, Walt. Those things happen. You just put them behind you. Why am I telling you? You already know that."

The thing Walter didn't know was that in Palmer's budding knowledge of the law, he learned something about grand theft. The first thing he did was to forge a title. He couldn't be caught driving a stolen car. Securing ownership was simple enough. As his business began to grow and the 1918 model Cadillac was getting age on it, Palmer looked to upgrade. The next challenge was to collect on the insurance he arranged. The opportunity came in the spring of 1924 when heavy rains deluged the county. He deliberately drove the car along a cut bank where raging swollen waters were at the very rim. Expecting the eventual collapse, Palmer figured the car would fall in and be destroyed and he would collect on the insurance policy. He was luckier—the car was swept away and never found. The stolen coupe was granted amnesty—not by his aunt, but by Mother Nature. All he had to do was supply the insurance company with an affidavit that proved the car was his, coupled with an estimate of its value, which he did. It was considered bad luck when he was forced to abandon the car that rainy night. The car he stole served him well and paid him back—in spades.

"Well, it was sure bad you had to lose that nice car." Hubbard consoled.

"I got over it," Palmer responded airily.

He did better than that. The insurance paid for a year old 1923 model. Later, as his business became established, he bought a new '26. Now he drove an automobile only movie stars were seen in; a shiny green V8 roadster with leather upholstery, a radio, and side mounts. Royce Palmer was the cock of the walk. He could survive without Jack MacGregor.

Approaching the gray, blue-trimmed two story house, Palmer remarked, "Looks like you'll need some of that money to fix your truck."

Walter merely grunted. He knew Abner was on his last legs before the trip in.

Walter opened the door. Palmer extended his hand. "Maybe I'll be able to get it right someday. Forgive me if you can, Walt."

Hubbard returned the handshake. "You're sure as hell tryin', Royce—I give you that."

****

Clinton Durkee, raised sheep on his buffalo grass ranch twenty miles northeast of Cottonwood. Ranchers from wet climates where grass grows belly deep, would never consider the prospect of maintaining livestock in such a thirsty environment. MacGregor, Durkee and a few others realized the benefits of the tough energy-giving forage. Durkee's sheep were primarily the Columbia and Suffolk varieties grown in Orkney County in his native country of the Scottish Highlands north of Edinburg. His ranch was not as extravagant as the MacGregor's, but his spread of a thousand plus acres was considered large by most. However, when thinking about Durkee's outfit, size was never the consideration; precision was. Durkee ran his business as he ran his life, strict, moral and inflexible. The buildings were painted and the fences were straight. His animals were fat, healthy, wool-bearing and propagating. The Scotsman's word was his bond. His attention to detail was explicit and his decisions were unwavering.

Jack MacGregor and Marshall Reiss' attitudes toward one another were ambivalent, but the same could not be said about the MacGregor-Durkee association. It was hostile. MacGregor's spread ran the length of Reiss' property. Durkee's ranch, much larger than Reiss', shared a three-mile border with MacGregor. Considering MacGregor's philosophy regarding ownership and control, the ingredients for a running battle were set in place. Durkee had no desire to expand, unless a legitimate and remunerative opportunity presented itself. Liam's philosophy was the reverse and he passed the attitude on to his son. The two would grab land in any manner possible. The free open space to which Liam was accustomed was no more, and he never compromised his acceptance to the reality that he couldn't run things as he pleased. The advent of barb wire, according to the cattlemen, was the end of free enterprise. Durkee disliked Liam MacGregor even more than he did the son. The father exacted no discipline or ethical guidelines, and that, Durkee felt, was his duty. The enmity between the two families mirrored the disputes of centuries involving the Scots and Irish.

Durkee never drank or swore. He didn't gamble, speak ill of his neighbors, or fail to pay homage to his maker. With MacGregors, it was the opposite. Durkee's gut roiled because his children were subjected to this infidelity. As much as he was repulsed by the MacGregor habits, he believed that certain annoyances were a part of life. There was, however, one issue he felt compelled to defend himself and that was to dispel a rumor MacGregor and his father spread; that sheep were destroying the grass. The cowmen claimed the dust storms were a result of the animal's presence. They alleged sheep, having upper teeth, tore out the roots which caused soil erosion. Not only did this accusation gall Durkee; it attacked his sensibility toward the land which he felt a genuine stewardship. He rotated his herds regularly to eliminate overuse. The MacGregors were the philistines— the bible told him those people were placed on the earth as a test and such behavior was to be tolerated.

When Durkee learned of the school board's vote, he was furious. The fifty-three-year-old Scotsman and his wife had eight children; two in high school, four in elementary, two at home, and they weren't finished yet. They were obeying the Catholic doctrine. When the scriptures decreed go thou and propagate the earth, they took it as—gospel.

His children were clones of his discipline: studious, honest, stout, hard-working, and most of all respectful. The closing litany of the daily family prayer before meals admonished, may we always be mindful to the needs of others. His devout reverence to his faith approached overzealousness. The father was dedicated his family; he was the trunk and they were his vines.

Irene Pine was universally thought to be the model of perfection. Clinton Durkee never completely accepted the assessment. He appreciated her all right, but he never found any schoolmarm yet who was worthy of his children —until Mildred Hubbard came along. Durkee's younger children would come home leaping with enthusiasm, eager to relate what "Mrs. Millie" imparted to them that day. Unaccountably, they would leave the supper table without having to be nudged to do their homework. Mildred's effusive praise for study took care of that. His children would occasionally complain about the strict discipline; but it satisfied the sheep man. The final stair to sainthood was that Mildred would lead them in prayer before lunch.

Durkee was a powerful block of a man, standing five foot nine and weighing a solid two hundred and twenty. His stride resembled a swagger, but not by design. When he moved, his large driving hamstrings and a burly chest gave the appearance of a pompous rooster.

Durkee made a quick trip to the telephone office where Ethel worked.

"Let me see the minutes of the last school board meeting, Ethel," he ordered.

Ethel's reaction to the unusual request was negative. Those minutes were her domain. "They're not ready yet, Mr. Durkee," she hedged.

"They're ready enough for me. Get them!"

"I have to type them first."

"I don't need them typed. I can read."

"Well, sir. I have never had a request like this before."

"Now you have."

The woman hesitated. "Well, sir, I..."

"Ethel," the stocky Scotsman replied seriously, "Those minutes are public property. Now, I'll get Sheriff Young if I have to, but they'll be available to me one way or another."

Rancher Durkee said the magic words. Ethel immediately rose from her chair in front of the switchboard and stepped into the back room. She returned with a packet of papers. Ethel, by habit, took the minutes in longhand, typing them before the next meeting. Haltingly, she handed the papers to Durkee. He rose immediately, sat down and pored over the minutes.

"Hmmm," he mused. "Palmer and Vogel and MacGregor voted no. That's interesting."

"Thank you Ethel. I may need these again."

He walked out of the phone office and headed for Palmer's office. Royce was in.

"Royce, why did you vote against the re-hiring of Millie Hubbard?" he demanded.

"It sounds as though you've seen the minutes, Clinton."

"I have."

"Well, then, if you've seen the minutes, you should know."

"Royce, the only arguments made were by Felton Caldwell and Jack MacGregor. You didn't say a word. What's your logic?"

Palmer looked Durkee in the eye, surrendering. "It was a mistake, Clinton."

"I know it was a mistake! Why did you make that mistake?"

"You have to know?"

"I didn't come here to visit."

Palmer hung his head. "I let Jack talk me into it."

"Why would he want to do that?"

Palmer rubbed his chin. "If you didn't come to visit, why ask me? — Ask him."

Durkee wasn't totally satisfied. "If you could re-cast your vote, would you change it to retain Mrs. Hubbard?"

"I wouldn't make the mistake twice."

"You may have that opportunity!"

Without another word Durkee spun and stalked out.

Fred Vogel was gazing out his office window when he saw Clinton Durkee's Packard skid to a stop. Quickly, he beat a path into the store room, closing the door and locking it. The store owner guessed what Durkee's visit was about.

Durkee strode in, spotting an employee. "I'm looking for Fred."

"He just went into the store room."

Durkee tapped on the large timbered door. No answer. He tapped again with the same result. He tried the door. It wouldn't budge. This time he pounded with the meat of his fist, shouting, "I know you're in there, Fred. Either you come out or the door comes off!"

Vogel didn't want his door ripped off as he knew Durkee would, so he unlatched it and slid it open, with a frightened look at Durkee.

"Tell me, Fred, why an ex-homesteader like you would vote against re-hiring Millie Hubbard?"

"Well Jack MacGregor..." his voice trailed off.

"Jack MacGregor what?'

"Well, I thought he made sense..."

"About what?" Durkee persisted.

"Well," Vogel stammered, rubbing his forehead with the heel of his hand, "The thing he said about Millie being married."

"And you think that's an argument?"

"Well, yes... I guess it is..."

"That's weak, Fred!" Durkee barked.

"I know it is, but I gotta think about my store."

Durkee glowered at him. Swinging out of the market place, he beat a path to Jim Thurston's station.

"Jim," he asked entering, have you heard about the school board decision?"

"Yeah, wasn't that a hell of a note, Clinton?"

"I don't know if I'd have put it in those words, but you're probably accurate. Do you have any idea why the vote was such as it was?"

Thurston began rubbing his hands with an oily shirt he was using for a grease rag. "Yeah. I got an idea."

"Well, speak up, Jim. What is it?" Durkee pressed impatiently

"I think," Thurston began slowly, "MacGregor may have influenced a couple of members because Walt Hubbard is trying to buy Marsh Reiss' place."

"Ah ha!" Durkee thought aloud, "and he couldn't buy it without Millie's job. Is that what you're thinking?"

"Yup," the station man replied.

"What's your opinion of that?"

Thurston turned, tossing his sartorial wipe onto a work bench. "It's bullshit."

Durkee sighed. "Well, that's an answer, too."

"I'd have voted for her if I'd been on the board," Thurston admitted.

"Jim," Durkee said thinking, "I'd like to organize a community meeting to force the board into another vote. Now I know it could cost you money because MacGregor buys a lot of gas from you."

Thurston pinched his chin in thought. "I don't think it's gonna matter much longer."

"Why is that?"

"There's a new Texaco goin' in, and I don't expect the MacGregor clan to buy from me after that."

"Why wouldn't they?"

"Well," Thurston answered slowly, "They always wanted a kickback and I'd never give 'em one. The word is, this next feller will."

"Would you help me round up some people, Jim?"

"Sure I would."

"You just made a very large sale to the man upstairs," Durkee said extending his hand, adding, "and try and keep this away from the board members."

The sheep farmer spent the rest of the day recruiting people to attend a supplemental meeting.

He made one last stop. Marshal Reiss was in his barn oiling harness for the sale.

"Marsh, I'll need your cooperation."

"You got it. What do you need?"

"I'm arranging a special meeting to see if we can get this Millie Hubbard hiring reversed, and I would ask that you hold off on selling to MacGregor until we see if we can get it done."

"I've already sold it to Walt."

Durkee weaved unsteadily. "I don't understand. I thought you were going to wait until you found out if he could pay for it."

"Well, we've signed a contract."

Durkee eyed Reiss unsurely, "How can he pay for it?"

Reiss shrugged his shoulders, breathing out. "He really can't, Clint. We went ahead with it expecting that Millie would get the job."

"Jim Thurston was right—he was exactly right. Well," Durkee said leaving, "make sure you get to the meeting."

"Wouldn't miss it, when is it?"

"We don't know yet. You'll get it in the mail."

"Does she have a chance?"

Durkee smiled. "We'll determine whether she does or she doesn't, won't we?"

The sheep rancher walked up to the counter tapping on the glass surface. The bank teller recognized him. "Good morning, Mr. Durkee. What can I do for you?"

"Is Felton free?"

"For you, I guarantee he will be," she answered, motioning for him to follow.

Caldwell looked up from his desk, breaking into a smile. Clinton Durkee was his favorite client and he made no pretense of it. He waved the burly sheep man toward a seat.

Durkee flipped his hat in a nearby chair, handing the banker a packet of papers.

Caldwell glanced down at the top sheet which had a typed message which read: "We, the undersigned, as tax paying citizens of the Cottonwood School District #5, request a supplemental meeting to the school board to have it explained to us why Mildred Hubbard was not re-hired to fill the teaching vacancy at Mitchell School."

The message was followed by an irregular stream of signatures—all scratched out in longhand.

Caldwell leafed through five pages, headed with the same information and their particular list of signees. He whistled softly grinning, "How many?"

"Seventy-two," Durkee answered proudly.

Caldwell admitted. "I heard you were putting this together."

"When can we get an assembly?"

"Soon, you can be certain. I may join your church yet—anyone who can perform miracles like this," he mentioned looking down at the packet, "I need to stay close to."

"We've got a spot for you," Durkee quipped, tilting his head. "You've been in the minor leagues all too long."

Jack MacGregor was livid. He stomped around the kitchen holding a cup of coffee, jarring a spill with every forceful gesture. Katherine, who was holding their newest entry to the family, an anemic three-month old girl named Esther, sat and listened submissively.

"I just don't know why Clinton Durkee wanted to open that can of worms! He's got the whole country thinking what we did was criminal!"

Liam was sitting in the corner of the kitchen, who glanced up asking, "You will have to take another vote. That's about it, isn't it?"

His son set the cup down, rubbing his hands nervously, "I wish it was goin' be that simple. I don't have any idea what the hell's goin' to happen."

Old Liam began invectively, "God damn mackerel snappers think they got to save the world! —course he's a democrat on top of all that! People 'ud find out the world 'ud get by a lot simpler if they'd let nature take its course. Let the stronger rule. It's always been that a way— always will be! Look at the animal kingdom. They don't need us to tell them how to run things! The weak have to go and the strong stay. That's what it says in the bible!"

Katherine looked at Liam, then down at her frail baby daughter. She bit her tongue.

****

The emergency meeting was held in the school gymnasium. A recently sanded and varnished maple floor would soon take significant abuse, much to the chagrin of the superintendent who doubled as the basketball coach. The pungent odor of pine sol infiltrated the large room. An odd menagerie filed in taking their seats.

With each screech of a folding chair, the shiny surface took on a new wound. In the rear, a monolithic round stove occupied a significant portion of the corner. The huge heater frequently branded scantily-clad basketball players who slid into it. Upon the stage at the front, the curtains were pulled and five men sat behind two long tables.

The rumblings of conversation were suffocated when Jack MacGregor's mallet struck the table. He wanted to put this exercise behind him as soon as possible. The room quieted.

"The board will come to order," he said curtly, over the dying mumbles of those who either couldn't hear, or weren't finished chatting.

"The purpose of this meeting as you all know," he began, "involves Mildred Hubbard, who served the remainder of the spring term at Mitchell School when Irene Pine died. It was the vote of the board, by ballot, which was three to two against re-hiring Mrs. Hubbard."

Mildred sat in the crowd embarrassed, fidgeting in her chair. She had the sensation of being in a fish bowl with all eyes on her. She would've preferred to be anywhere but there.

"The board, or the majority of the board," MacGregor corrected, "felt that we would have a better chance of having a permanent teacher if we hired a single, that is, unmarried person outside of the district."

Clinton Durkee, sprang to his feet interrupting, "Why would you say that?"

"Why would we say what, Clinton?" MacGregor expected a fight from Durkee; he didn't expect it before the rear door was closed.

"Explain what you mean by, 'having a better chance of having a permanent teacher.' I just don't understand the reference."

"What reference?"

"Permanent."

"Surely I don't need to explain the word, permanent to you, Clinton."

"I well understand the word, Mr. MacGregor. What I don't understand is why you bring it up at all. No teacher being interviewed, to my knowledge, has ever been grilled on how long she intends to teach."

Durkee's intrusion interrupted MacGregor's train of thought. Attempting to cloak his anger, he avoided the debate, "It isn't that we have anything against Mildred Hubbard. It's just that she's a married woman. I think we owe it to the community to provide the district with a permanent, reliable person."

"You make it sound as though finding a good teacher who is willing to live in that environment is a simple matter," Durkee, argued, still standing.

"Well, Clinton," MacGregor said with condescension, "there have been but two teachers out at Mitchell. I don't think that anybody here would criticize the selection of those two ladies."

The audience reacted with a spirited acknowledgement.

"What you say is true, but that has nothing to do with the reason we're here tonight. Mildred Hubbard's employment is the question, and I say we give her the job," Durkee insisted.

"Isn't it the responsibility of the board to decide who is and who is not hired, Clinton?"

"It is, but I think this is an unusual circumstance."

"What makes it unusual?"

The very specter of the stout, well-groomed rancher standing confidently in the center of the group gave him an aura of authority. To MacGregor, he looked like a coyote in the middle of a crop of his calves.

"I've talked to Mildred," Durkee began, "and she informed me that she can be depended on for another five years. Now I think," he continued, turning to the audience behind him, "that I speak for the people at Mitchell when I say that she has done an excellent job..."

As if the Mitchell contingency had expected the accolade to Mildred, they immediately cheered and clapped. MacGregor set his jaw, readjusting his posture.

"...and," Durkee continued, "I think another five years of Mildred Hubbard would be a pretty nice present for our kids out there."

Again, the applause was supportive.

When the reaction abated, MacGregor, visibly upset, snarled, "Shall we repeat the vote? Would that convince you, Mr. Durkee?"

The suggestion caused Royce Palmer to bite his lip. He wanted no repeat ballot. That would cause a problem with MacGregor.

Durkee remained unmoved. "Before you convince me of anything, Mr. MacGregor, I would ask to have something else explained."

MacGregor's stare was invective. "What do you want?"

Durkee asked, feigning innocence, "I don't know what the audience here would do, but I'd like to know what you would do when you hire a teacher and she gets married, do you—*fire* her?"

The audience laughed and MacGregor boiled. "Well..." he attempted to answer, but before he could, Durkee pressed on.

"In the high school here, you have seven teachers. Six of them are married, one is single. So what do we do with these married teachers?"

The audience erupted in laughter again.

Durkee waved his arms for quiet, pausing to address the board president. "Your argument that Mildred should be single to get the job makes no sense." He looked to his friend, Felton Caldwell. "I believe a citizen roll call would constitute a mandate here, and I also believe that I am vested to conduct one, am I not, Mr. Caldwell?"

Caldwell responded with a simple, "You are."

MacGregor was rattled with the unexpected mutiny. He raised his gavel in an attempt to gain control, but Palmer, next to him clutched his wrist, breathing, "Let it go, Jack."

Durkee scanned the assembly. "I move Mildred Hubbard's application be accepted by acclamation. Do I hear a second?"

"Second."

The affirmation was soft and barely audible, but it was there.

"It's been moved and seconded that the contract be ratified. All in favor of hiring Mildred Hubbard respond by saying aye. He raised his arm as if giving a 'go' signal.

A resounding "AYE!" was given.

Again, Durkee raised his arm, nay?"

There was no sound.

"Let the minutes show that Mildred Hubbard is now a member of Cottonwood District #5 faculty," Durkee hastened, as though the whole thing would fall through if he didn't ram it through.

"I now move," he continued, looking at Caldwell, "this meeting be adjourned. Do I hear a second?"

"Second!" came Thurston's strong voice in the crowd.

"Moved and seconded this meeting be adjourned. All in favor signify by saying aye."

"AYE!"

"Opposed, no?"

Again, there was no objection.

"This meeting is adjourned."

The stubborn, insistent Scotsman got his way.

Instantly, there was a rush to the door before MacGregor could gain eye contact with anyone who opposed him.

As the crowd pushed for the door, Millie shouldered toward Clinton Durkee. Reaching him, she stammered, "Mr. Durkee, I, I want to thank you for what you did. It makes a person feel humble."

The proper rancher looked at Millie. His words were gentle, but firm. "You're a good woman, Millie. You're a Christian and a superb teacher. But you'll find I'm a rather selfish man."

"You're not selfish, Mr. Durkee. I won't accept that," she answered.

"We are all selfish if we would choose to admit it. You see, your job was a secondary issue with me."

Mildred tilted her head in puzzlement.

"My children's education," he explained, "is my primary concern."

The next morning Jack MacGregor collared Royce Palmer in his office. "Believe you've got three hundred of my dollars."

"What three hundred dollars?"

"I think you recall an agreement we made about your vote."

"I honored our agreement—your fish got away. Don't expect me to forgive the money. I took the chance. It wasn't the vote I would have made, but I made it anyway. You're a poker player, Jack. Somebody called your bluff and you lost —that's all."

CHAPTER 11

August, 1928

Walter lost his trusted friend, Abner. With a team of horses, the fallen hero was pulled behind a barn on what would be referred as "the Reiss Place." The old truck performed admirably and shared company with the miscellany Marshall left behind. After the seven plus years when Walter drove out of the garage in Denver, Abner was much in demand. In time, he gradually lost his popularity when other cattle trucks came on the scene. The final blow came when Marshall Reiss, the same person who gave him the job of transporting milk, took the job away when he bought his Dodge truck and picked milk up daily. The need and demand was still there, and Marshall showed why he should be running a dairy and not farming. Now, Walter's faithful companion with the leaky radiator, ragged and torn seats, cracked and pitted windshield, and the noisy differential, was played out. Abner didn't die along the side of some road, though; he went down breathing fire.

There would never be another like him, but summer was getting on. In a week, Millie and Andy would be away at school. Walter had to have a vehicle, and asked Felton Caldwell for help.

Walter sat in the president's private office. Caldwell would've liked a bank full of clients like Walter Hubbard. The rangy, uneducated farmer wasn't the bank's largest customer, nor was he the smallest. Hubbard wasn't one to borrow, but when he did, it was for good reason, and the debts he made were, without exception, paid off on time if not before. Walt Hubbard needed help, the bank president saw to it that he got it. Now that Mildred had the teaching job, Walt Hubbard became even more of a valued-customer to the bank. This time, however, Walter didn't come in for a loan; he needed Caldwell's influence with Sam Armling.

One of the qualities that endeared Felton Caldwell to the farmer was Hubbard's simple honesty. When Walter dropped three hundred in cash in his account, Caldwell collared Hubbard in the bank and asked him where the money came from. He knew Hubbard didn't gamble, and nobody paid that much in round dollars for livestock or farm products. The explanation that a bank examiner may want to question such an unrecorded deposit had a modicum of truth to it, but Caldwell was outright prying. When Walter told the bank president the whole story and how he came by it, Caldwell's amused smile was one the farmer wouldn't forget.

Because of the common nature of their professions, Felton Caldwell and Sam Armling were friends. Earlier, Walter mentioned to Caldwell how Armling assisted him in getting a vehicle back in '21. Walter reasoned that since the two executives had telephone chats frequently, would Felton ask Sam if he had another truck Walter could buy. After talking to Armling, Caldwell explained to Walter that although Armling did help him out—it was a one-time deal, and as a rule, such vehicles were put up for public auction. Caldwell went on to inform the farmer that Armling asked about Walter's well-being—that he remembered the raw boned mid-westerner with the money in his boot. Through further conversation, Caldwell informed Armling that Walter named a boy after the Federal Bank president. With that, Armling relented, and told Caldwell to send the farmer to Denver.

Highway 40 was paved from Kansas City to the Colorado capitol. The Greyhound Bus Company began service along the route, and a dollar and a quarter bought a ticket from Cottonwood to Denver. Walter intended to take Mildred with him, but also wanted to bring his favorite son, Sam, along, since the rambunctious tot was the reason for the arrangement in the first place. Mildred agreed to come but refused to bring Sam along.

Armling was pleased to see Walter again and felt a measure of personal satisfaction knowing the farmer was doing well. Armling asked about his namesake, and naturally, Walter informed the director about his unsuccessful attempt to bring the child along. At any rate, he would bring Sam the next time.

Armling inquired, from his conversations with Caldwell, why Mildred shouldn't have a car to drive to school. Walter explained that while have one car was needed, the luxury of having two vehicles was a convenience they hadn't entertained. Besides, Millie would be living on the schoolhouse grounds, so there was no need. Millie, however, was immediately taken by the idea that she would be able drive back and forth, and stay at the teacherage only when she had to. Walter half-heartedly agreed, considering how convenient it would be not to have to pick up and quit what he was doing in order to go get her, then wait until she was ready to go. And he sure wouldn't be cooking his own meals every night. Maybe, he decided, he could go along with it since the money he set aside for the truck never was his to begin with. Surely, two vehicles wouldn't take all of it. The three visited the motor pool.

Armling set aside a 1927 Chevrolet truck for Walter. The vehicle was not yet two years old, but because the 10,000-mile limit had been exceeded, the truck was made available. When Armling showed it to Walter, the farmer wanted the burly one-ton vehicle immediately. It was the Superior model, with a short wheelbase and in prime condition. The truck suited Walter perfectly.

Armling also had a car in mind for Millie. A snappy little Chevy four door was parked in a corner by itself. The body was green, the top and fenders were black. Disc wheels sporting yellow pinstripes rounded out the appearance. In the spring of 1926 the car, new at the time, was issued to a Denver County nurse. Armling swung a loose arm wave toward the car. Millie's squealed covering her mouth.

"How about that one?" he asked.

"I love it! Is it new?" she inquired.

"No," he explained, "In fact, this car is over the two-year cutoff limit, but since it has only eight thousand miles on it, and the nurse objected to letting it go, we kept it around a little longer."

"Could I sit in it?" Millie asked.

"Help yourself."

Millie opened the door. The mohair upholstery smelled fresh. In fact, the car looked new to the Hubbards. While she settled in the driver's seat, Armling gave a running commentary of the vehicle.

"This is the series V model. It has a heater, and electric starter. The metal wheels are first time, and the brakes are a new design." Glancing at Walter, Armling continued, "She'll discover the engine is more than adequate. There are other modifications specific to this car."

"Well, this car is special, it looks to me," Walter observed.

"It is, Walter. The car is the top of the line, and some of the features on it won't appear for a few years on future models as standard equipment."

Millie stepped out caressing the car with the palm of her hand. "What's the S thing behind the back windows? Does the top come down?" she asked.

He chuckled. "No. They're called Landau irons. You see that sort of ornamental stuff on expensive cars. Those things are supposed to doll it up. Personally, I think they do."

"So do I," Millie gushed.

Walter asked haltingly, "What's the price for the two?"

Armling rubbed his chin. "How does two hundred and fifty sound?"

"I think we just bought two vehicles," Walter said to his wife.

Millie thrust her arms in the air, giving Walter a spirited hug. Although the car was Millie's, he was happy to have it in the family. And there would be enough money left over for two payments on the Reiss place.

Walter took the lead. His new truck was shorter, but brawnier than Abner. The engine was more powerful and he could drive at 40 mph, instead of the 30 he was accustomed. This vehicle was equipped with a starter, a vacuum powered windshield wiper and a forced air heater. He knew the truck was perfect for him. Millie stayed close behind. Her smaller vehicle appeared to have no trouble keeping up. The windows were down, it was summer, and the road was smooth. Walter began to daydream.

From the time Mildred took Andy to school with her and left Walter to tend to Sam, the father began to learn certain things about his second son. Early in Andy's maturation, Walter realized there would never be much in common between him and his first born. Andy had no interest whatsoever in what made corn grow or how to milk a cow. Although Sam was barely four years old, he could milk a cow and with the aid of a stool, he could harness a horse. Meanwhile, Andy was getting a jump on learning and enjoying very moment of it. By the end of the school year, Andy began to read and he could write his name legibly.

Unusually large and agile for his age, Sam, unlike his older brother, was a natural in his love for the outdoors, absorbing lessons from his father about the life of farming and tending livestock. Unlike the ranchers who rode the high bred horses to manage their cattle, Walter and his son were forced to employ the services of the work horses. Barney, a young gelding, was Sam's favorite horse, and the boy would spend the time he was allowed on the spirited colt exploring the 1,280 acres of the Hubbard spread. Walter disliked sitting on a horse, but occasionally had to because there was no other way to work his herd. Sam wanted to do the things his dad did, and often Walter forgot that Sam was just a child. In many ways it was good, in other ways it was not. Sam could turn a cream separator, build a branding fire, supply his dad with the irons, and on occasion, brand an animal. Walter was comfortable with him riding a one-horse cultivator pulled by a gentle horse. Sam learned to love the smell of freshly-plowed ground in the spring, and the burnt smell of cow hide when branding and he wasn't five years old. Over Millie's objections, Walter introduced his son to her husband's one bad habit; chewing tobacco. "If he can drive a team of horses," Walter argued, "he can have a chaw now and again." The father and son were becoming inseparable.

Millie was doing her own share of reminiscing while she guided the Chevy down the highway. It had been a while since she last drove a car. Back in Missouri as a young girl, one of her jobs was to escort her cranky father around in his Model T. She didn't like the duty or the car, and grew weary of his constant instructions. After she married, the rare occasion she had to drive, or as the case demanded, steer, was when Walter got stuck in the mud and he drove the horses. The other opportunity was when she guided the old truck on the long pull from Royce Palmer's parking lot to Abner's final resting place behind the Marshall Reiss barn.

But this ride to Cottonwood was different. Her Chevy handled beautifully. She decided it had to be stored inside, no matter how much trouble it would be for Walter to arrange it. Just as Walter named his old truck, she would name her new car. The spiffy little sedan was affectionately christened Olive Oyl. She patted the dashboard when she came to the name. Her car was comfortable and she was enjoying the aroma of the upholstery and the purr of the engine …and she wanted to go faster. The novelty of the sudden and unexpected freedom was exhilarating! Now, she could go to church without having to beg Walter to take her. He wouldn't go to church himself, and he would have to wait somewhere for church services to end. He didn't read, and he couldn't go to Jim Thurston's station, or the feed store, or anyplace, for the matter, because it was Sunday, and everything was closed—everything except the pool hall, and he wouldn't be seen in there. For this reason, it was rare for her to ask him to take her in. She wasn't allowed to drive the truck. From the beginning, Walter would be the only one who drove the truck—not even Marshall Reiss was allowed behind the wheel.

While driving along, she thought about the changes. She would chart a new course of worship and break away from the shackles of the Baptist religion altogether. She'd like to join Felton's Episcopal congregation, but Walter would never stand for that, it was too close to Catholicism. There was a new Presbyterian church being formed in town, she would join that. Her fantasy was interrupted when Walter drove up to the Reiss' home. Eleanor Reiss offered to take care of the boys while Walter and Millie were in Denver, and now it was time for the family to all return home.

****

Liam was talking to two McGregor ranch hands in the privacy of a horse barn. "Just take a pair of nippers and cut the wires," he said in his gravelly voice. "Let them cows stray on that farmer a little, and he'll damn soon see how much fun it is to have a bigger spread."

One cowboy leaning against a horse stall asked, "What if he comes on the place lookin' for 'em?"

"You and Lou beat the hell out of him Marvin," said Liam. "I'd do it myself, but I'm too old."

****

The next morning, the Hubbard's were up early for the busy day that lay ahead. It was Millie's first day of classes at the Mitchell school. She hurried with breakfast amid the boys chirping about the family's recently-acquired rolling stock. Andy rode home with his mother and Sam, with his dad. Both Walter and Millie were proud of their new vehicles, but would let the boys make the noise. Having a car excited Millie, but not as much as the freedom of driving herself to work and to church. Additionally, this time, she would have a family member as on official student. Walter watched as she drove out of the yard with Andy. He walked to the truck with Sam to check the cows. After taking over the Reiss place, Walter kept the cows on property somewhat unfamiliar to him, so he would keep an eye on both until he became accustomed to the new surroundings. After the inspection, he and his son would cultivate beans.

Bouncing down the rutted pathway, Walter thought of Augie Reiss standing on the Abner's floorboard years back when the three were in the truck hauling milk. Sam was standing in the same fashion, excited about the new truck. Walter was happy, but only for a moment. While driving down the road that led into the cow pasture, he immediately knew something was wrong. The fence was down and the cows were gone. Sliding his truck to a stop, he leaped out. Walter inspected the sharp shiny metal ends. The wires had been cut. Before his young son could join him, he was back in the truck racing back to the tack shed.

"Go get Barney and get a bridle for Trixie," Walter told his son. The young boy knew what to do. Snatching two bridles and running to the granary for an ear of corn he hopped back in the truck with his father. Walter was increasingly coming to realize his dependency on his son. His work horses didn't like to be caught; they were conditioned to what happened after they did. It was different with Barney. He didn't have to work, and always got a treat when he saw the young boy, so he would come voluntarily.

Walter saddled the horses, and the two rode out to the break in the fence. The tracks led to the east. MacGregor property. Walter and his son started on the trail of the tracks.

Jack MacGregor was in his father's kitchen. He was furious. His mother stood against a wall as the son was berating his unrepentant father.

"Have you gone plumb loco, Dad?" the son boomed.

"He's just a farmer Jack," the old man returned, "he needs to be taught a lesson."

"What lesson? What did he do wrong?" he asked.

Bonnie stood by in silence. As violent as the dispute might become, she would not be allowed a part in it.

"We're gettin' a real problem with them dirt farmers. I can't have 'em gettin' comfortable—next thing you know, that guy'll be wantin' somebody else's place, then ours," the old man seethed.

"You don't even know the guy, Dad."

"Well, I know he got both them places we were after, didn't he?" the gnarly old rancher grumbled.

"Dad, I don't like havin' him next door, either. We offered too much for Spring Creek, and he turned it down. I stuck my nose in the noose when I tried to keep his wife from getting that teaching job, and that didn't work. The best thing to do now is try to get along!"

"Well, I put Lou and Marv on 'im. Soon's he comes across that fence line, he'll be a wishin' he stayed off that Reiss place."

"What about Marvin and Lou?"

"I told them soon as that farmer comes through the fence lookin' for his cows, to work him over."

"Dad! From what I hear, we don't need any trouble out of that farmer!"

Liam turned leaving the kitchen muttering, "Kinda looks to me like you're gettin' soft, boy."

"I think I see some of our cows, Dad," the youth said peering off into the sun-filled east. Walter stopped to focus, aware of the two riders who approached him from the rear. "You lost, farmer?" one rider sneered. The two were flanking Walter and Sam in clear aggression.

True to his nature, Walter needed no further prompting. Instantly, he was off his horse pulling the insulting cowboy to the ground.

Just as quickly, the other leaped off his horse, slamming into Walter from the rear, knocking him face down to the ground and began pummeling the farmer from the back.

Sam, born with the same impulse as his father, was off his horse jumping into the cowboy's legs, bumping him off balance. Instantly, Sam clutched the cowboy's leg sinking his teeth into the cowboy's calf.

The cowboy yelped in pain, turning to swat Sam away.

Walter was on his feet in an instant, but before he could help his son, the other cowboy began to rise. He was crawling to his feet and up to Walter's waist when the muscular farmer connected with a stunning blow to the jaw that sent the cow hand reeling and unconscious.

The odds just changed.

While the other cowboy flailed at Sam, who had a death grip around the wrangler's leg, and his teeth firmly clamped onto his calf, Walter hit the cowhand with a crushing blow to the rib cage. As the hired hand turned and fell, Walter caught him again full in the face with another right. He too, lay on the ground, unconscious, with Sammy still locked to his leg.

"You can let go now, Sam," Walter said, gathering his breath, looking for his hat.

Sam got up wearing a wide eyed expression. "Are they dead, daddy?" he asked.

Walter took him by the shoulder. "They'll probably wish they was when they come to. Let's go to town and see the sheriff."

Walter walked into the sheriff's office with Sam. The farmer was showing a few marks on him from the fight.

"You look like you've been sortin' bobcats, Walt," Arthur Young, the sheriff offered.

"We got jumped by a couple of Jack MacGregor's hired hands."

"Yeah, and we beat 'em up, Sheriff!" the boy piped in.

Sam Hubbard was getting to be known as a plucky little guy always with his dad and tobacco juice dribbling down the corner of his mouth.

"What's this about?"

"He cut my fence and let my cows out. I went out lookin' for 'em."

"And that'd be lookin' for trouble."

"Those are my cows, Art!"

"How many are gone?"

"Thirty-six."

"So your whole herd?"

"No. Six didn't stray, so I penned 'em up. The rest are out someplace. Sam and I were trackin' 'em when those two birds come up on us."

"You whipped them both?"

"Guess we did," Walter admitted.

"Yeah, and I helped you didn't I Daddy?" Sam bleated.

He patted the boy on the back, "You sure did."

The sheriff smiled, looking at the boy then back to Hubbard. "So where do you figure your cows are by now, Walt?"

"Someplace on MacGregor's I s'pose."

"That's a big spread. You better not go back on the place. I'll go out and see Jack. You sit tight, and I'll get back to you."

"What good would that do, sheriff? He's the one who cut my fence."

"No, I don't think so, Walt. He's a conniver, but he wouldn't do anything like that."

"Then who would?"

"His dad would."

"I don't trust none of 'em, Art," Walter returned.

"Me neither!" Sam parroted.

The sheriff looked down smiling, then back to Hubbard. "Just sit tight, Walt. I'll stop by your place this afternoon."

Walter and Sam stayed in the barn waiting for the sheriff. Walter wanted to search for his cows, but would honor the Sheriff's advice. Finally, late in the afternoon, the sheriff drove in the yard. Walter yelled to him from the bam. The sheriff walked in, leaning against a wall. He was wearing a slight smile.

"Is there somethin' funny, Art?" Walter asked.

"Doc Sutton had to give one of those cowboys you beat up a tetanus shot."

"Who's Doc Sutton?"

"Guess you don't know him. We got a doctor in town a couple of weeks ago."

"Well, that's good."

"Damn right it is. Anyway, your boy," he said, swinging an arm toward Sam, "bit him pretty good, so he had to give him a shot."

"Shot for what?"

"Rabies."

Walter, was confused. "You acusin' my boy of havin' rabies, Art?"

The sheriff put up his palms defensively. "Easy, Walt! Don't matter who bit who. Any time anyone gets bit by a dog or what, you get a shot."

"But by a human?"

"They're worse than dogs."

"Who fed you that?"

The sheriff glanced at the boy with tobacco stains on his cheek, "It's what the doc said, and I can tell you, if Sam got those teeth into me, I'd see a doctor."

The sheriff continued, "I've been to town and back. I had some paperwork to do after all this."

Walter removed his worn felt hat, scratching his head. "Well, I hope you know something about my cows."

The sheriff walked over and sat on a workbench taking a deep breath. "I talked to Jack, Walt. He didn't have anything to do with it. It was Liam. Jack's upset about this thing too."

"So what about my cows?"

"Jack said he'd have them back in and the fence fixed by noon tomorrow."

"I'll believe that when I see it."

"Sounds to me he's trying to get along, Walt. You might think about it yourself."

"Ain't ready to do that just yet."

"That's up to you. But you need to know a couple of other things."

"What's that?"

"One cowboy has a broken nose and two broken ribs."

"He'll get over it," Walter mumbled.

"I know. The other one has a broken jaw. Liam talked the telegraph operator into taking him to Denver to get it wired shut. Doc Sutton said he couldn't do it. He's only a chiropractor, anyway."

"I don't know what that is."

"Means he's not a full-fledged doctor, but he's better than what we had."

"I guess it wasn't that bad of a day, then, Art, so long as I get all my critters back," Walter said.

"The cowboys wanted to sue you," the sheriff continued.

"What for?"

"Assault, or something like that. One of them went over to Palmer and Royce ran him out of his office. I guess it's all over town now that two rough and tough cowboys couldn't lick a man and a boy."

Walter laughed, reaching for a tool.

Walter's cattle were returned and the fence was repaired. He felt vindicated that he'd sent a message to MacGregor and the law had done its job. Sheriff Young's suggestion that Walter set his ill feelings aside and be a good neighbor was one that the farmer would do if and when he was ready. Jack MacGregor and his father were one in the same in Walter's opinion.

CHAPTER 12

Millie was no longer a temporary teacher. Nineteen students showed up for the first day, the largest ever at Mitchell. The one room school accommodated students from the first grade to the eighth. The job facing Millie was a daunting one, she was aware. Her first week, she questioned her ability to get the results expected of her; that is control nineteen students of eight separate ages, mixed genders and varied interests. She would do her best. Unexpected help was coming in the form of Mary Elizabeth Durkee.

The students were settling into the regimen Millie demanded as they became accustomed to her rules and encouragement. The confidence she was lacking returned and she was secure in the belief that her reputation was not just an over-reaction from what she accomplished in the spring.

At Mary Elizabeth's request, Millie gave the girl certain academic challenges to conquer during the summer, and in the three short months, the eighth grader returned accomplishing work that only students years older had learned. In the beginning of the new session, Millie marveled at the Mary Elizabeth's ability to complete her assignments in such short order that she soon became bored. She asked Millie if she could somehow be of assistance. Mary Elizabeth was aware that her teacher was taxed to the limit. Mildred answered that she would very much like to give the girl the opportunity, but first, she had to receive permission from the father.

Mildred sat at her desk across from rancher Clinton Durkee. His comely, tall daughter sat to the side. School had been in session two weeks.

"And if Mary Elizabeth could due further work as you say, what would be your reasoning for holding her back, Millie?"

"I would imagine, Mr. Durkee, Mary Elizabeth could very well be promoted to the tenth grade by the time this school year is out."

"What possibly could be wrong with that?"

"I believe Mary Elizabeth should be allowed to grow up with students her own age when she gets to high school. It's a wonderful thing that she has such an active mind. However, social interaction is as important as intellectual maturity. I think it would be a mistake to promote her."

He turned to his daughter. "And you agree?"

"Yes, father."

Durkee switched his attention back to Mildred. "And what will she be doing for you?"

"She would be teaching the first graders to read, second graders grammar, third graders history, and helping me out with everything else, including grading papers."

"She can do all that and keep with her studies?"

"She's a month ahead as it is, Mr. Durkee. She wants to become a teacher. She can get valuable experience right here."

He turned to his daughter, "And you want to do that?"

"Oh yes, Daddy. I know I can!"

He smiled, reaching for his hat. "It looks like you both get your way." Rising from his chair, he added, "Actually, the idea rather excites me, as well."

****

An unexpected development was the budding friendship between Jack MacGregor's boy, Chattman and Andy Hubbard. Both boys were bright and competed in their studies. The two handsome and talented youngsters were a treasure for the aspiring teacher. Whatever Mary Elizabeth asked them to do, they responded. Mary Elizabeth was finding her niche. Millie watched the exercise, proud of the young girl who wanted to help, feeling satisfaction with the work she was doing, and particularly, for the two eager students she was tutoring. The two mentor's efforts were not going unnoticed by Jack MacGregor.

It was a fit from the start. The two boys responded to the challenge of learning, but more importantly, they were getting to know one another. When they discovered an old Victrola in the teachers' quarters, they

109

discovered they enjoyed singing. At times, finding a private spot behind the teacherage, the boys would spend their spare time lying on their backs gazing up at the clouds dreaming up interpretations as to what the castles in the air really stood for. Andy thought his friend's name, Chattman, was awkward, so he began calling him "Cat". The moniker caught on by all his friends. His father was never comfortable with his son's name that was his wife's family name, so he readily adopted the nickname. From then on, he was Cat McGregor.

Katherine MacGregor had the flu. It was her job to pick up Chattman at the school, but Jack would do it until she was better. The rancher waited outside in his big new Buick. Andy saw him and walked up. The bus took the remaining children home, and the school grounds were empty.

The rancher squinted into the late afternoon sun, his sweat-stained felt hat turned down over his eyes. He saw Andy. "Where's Cat?"

"He's in the toilet, Mr. MacGregor."

"He is, huh?" MacGregor returned. "Well, tell him to hurry it up."

Andy squinted at the rancher. "I'm not going to tell him that, Mr. MacGregor. Sometimes, you can't hurry those things up."

MacGregor smirked at the young man. "You're the little Hubbard kid, aren't you?"

"Yes sir," he answered politely.

"How'd you know who I was?"

"I recognized your new Buick. Cat's mother picks him up in it."

MacGregor eyed the unafraid young boy for a moment. "Your dad and I don't get along."

Andy looked to the ground. "I know that."

"So maybe," MacGregor continued, "you oughtn't to be out here talking to me."

"No, that's okay. My mom knows I'm here."

"But she doesn't like me."

"She says I have to make my own friends and enemies."

"Well, you shouldn't be talking to me. Your dad thinks I'm a bad man."

Andy looked up at the man thoughtfully. "I know that, Mr. MacGregor, but I haven't heard your side."

Chattman came across the school yard. "Come on Cat! Let's go!" MacGregor yelled. He looked down at Andy. "You named him that, didn't you?"

"Yes sir. Was that okay?"

"Sure," the rancher said starting his car. "It fits him. It's what I call him." MacGregor started the car. "It's been good talkin' to you, Andy. We'll catch you the next time."

Mildred witnessed the discourse from the school window, watching the blue car pull out of the schoolyard.

Mildred was sitting at her desk finalizing the day's work, when she noticed a shadow in the doorway. She looked up to see the figure of a large man, his hat in his hand standing against the late sun.

"Could I have a word with you, Mrs. Hubbard?"

Mildred anticipated the confrontation with Jack MacGregor. She was prepared. "Come in please, Mr. MacGregor," she said, looking up from her work.

MacGregor pulled up a nearby chair, sat down, placing his hat, crown first, on the board floor.

"Mrs. Hubbard," he began, whereupon she corrected, "Please call me Millie."

The rancher settled unsurely in the hard chair. His creased, tanned face was a signature of the work he did. Jack MacGregor was a ruggedly handsome man. The gray hair mixed with the dark brown caused him to look older than his thirty-nine years. He rubbed his open palms together, inhaling, "I'll do that if you'll call me Jack."

She returned an easy smile. "I can do that. Now, Jack, What's on your mind?"

Her warm, calm, confident familiarity was a pleasant surprise to him. His expressive pale blue eyes searched the room as though it was his first time inside. Over thirty years earlier in the same room, he was one of Helen Mitchell's students.

"I..." he halted, "want to thank you for what you're doing for Cat."

"Chattman is very bright and a pleasure to have in my school, Jack."

The rancher moved leisurely in his chair. From the beginning, he considered the tall dark haired woman to be awkward and homely. His opinion immediately changed upon visiting with the assured, refined and articulate woman. "He knows a good deal more already than I knew when I was his age."

"As I said, Chattman is very intelligent. He learns quickly, and he enjoys studying."

"You're tellin' me. This school and your kid is all he talks about."

Millie smiled, nodding. "Andy feels the same about Chattman."

"Where are they, anyway?"

"They're in the teacherage."

"Doin' what?"

"They found a cowboy record. They're in there singing along with it."

MacGregor laughed. "Well, I think that's good!"

"You better hear their caterwauling before you come to that conclusion," she sighed.

MacGregor's expression changed. "Millie, I didn't come in here to talk about the boys."

"No," she put in, "I wouldn't think so. What did you come for?"

"I wanted to tell you that I had nothin' to do with cuttin' that fence."

"That word has filtered back to me," she responded.

"Do you believe it?"

She studied the rancher for a moment. "Yes, Jack, I believe it."

He exhaled, massaging his chin. "I'm glad you do. I don't believe your husband feels that way."

"Walter's stubborn streak isn't something I can change. If I could, I would."

"I've canned those two hired hands that nailed your husband."

"I'll tell Walter that."

"I also want to tell you that I'm sorry for the stand I took when it came to gettin' you hired."

Her brow furrowed. "You don't have to apologize for that. You just wanted an unmarried person. I didn't agree with your logic at the time, and I still don't, but I can't hold that against you, Jack. You figured those two teachers before me could be depended on because they didn't have a family to interrupt things. You made your case."

MacGregor scratched his temple. He knew not to take the apology any further, rising from his chair. "I don't expect you to understand all the things we do. I grew up in this country where we do as we damn well please, and I'm havin' some trouble gettin' used to all these changes."

Millie also rose. "I can see why you feel the way you do, and I appreciate your coming in Jack—I sincerely do."

"Well," he said, putting his Stetson on, "I better go get my kid before he loses his voice." MacGregor stepped out the door.

During this period, the town doctor was settling in. Doctor John Sutton could set fractures, prescribe drugs, give shots, and on occasion, pull teeth. He couldn't legally perform surgery, but he could accomplish the most difficult duty required of doctors—he could make decisions, like the severity of the case, whether the patient needed to be hospitalized… and so on. Nobody in that day would report the conscientious man for lancing a boil, or casting a broken arm. The community benefitted from his presence. Cottonwood was growing and indeed, it was becoming self-sufficient. They needed a doctor, no matter how imperfect he was.

Not everything was rosy with Doctor John Sutton. After the difficult delivery of a still birth, the father indicated he might press charges against the doctor. It was an empty threat, but Sutton, the slender bespectacled chiropractor didn't know it, so he paid a visit to Royce Palmer. Palmer recognized the caveat for what it was, but advised the doctor, just to be safe, bring all the necessary papers so the two could prepare a defense. Sutton brought everything he thought was necessary, but failed to include a birth certificate, reasoning the baby was born dead so there was no need for one. Palmer advised the doctor that the baby was, in fact, born, and the event would have to be recorded. As the Doctor was leaving for the certificate, Palmer asked that he bring two copies. Sutton asked why and Palmer replied, with reason, that he should have a copy for his files and, he instructed the doctor, be sure the foot print was on both certificates. When the doctor questioned the need for an additional certificate, suggesting the baby would be buried without a service, Palmer reminded the doctor that one cannot have too much evidence. The doctor agreed.

When preparation for Sutton's defense was completed and the doctor left Palmer's office, the shyster rose, pulled the shades, and locked the door to his office. He was going to do something he had put off much too long.

It was just that the opportunity had never presented itself. Gleefully, he pulled out a map of the United States.

"Let's see," he muttered, running down a list of Virginia towns. His forged law license was from the University of Virginia. He'd better keep things consistent. "Hmmm," he thought, "How about that tiny town up there in the mountains?" Tapp Springs had a population of thirty-seven. "Yeah. That's where it was... that's where I was born! Nobody's going to find any records there. Now what time... how about three a.m.?... on the..." He looked up at his wall clock reading five to seven... "I was born on the seventh of... February..." He took out a pad and pencil and started filling out the certificate. "February the seventh, 1893. Welcome to the legal world, Royce Palmer!" He stopped short, "I don't have a middle name, and I should have one. I won't use Bernard." He sat thinking of the many times when asked his middle name, saying he didn't have one; just an initial. Palmer supported his chin in his palm in thought. Glancing out the window, he watched the large pine bough tossing in the wind. He had four grown evergreens brought in and planted after the office was finished. "Wait!" he chirped. "It's perfect! Now, if I'm pressed, I can reveal my middle name! I'll say that I finally realized there was never any stigma and I should have never been embarrassed by it!" Inserting the certificate in his typewriter, he centered the space and began to type out the words, Royce Branch Palmer... He glanced at the inked footprint on the certificate, uttering a macabre apology, "You never had an identity, little fella... now you do."

Mildred sat at her desk recording grades when Jack MacGregor drove up. Since his apology, he was on a friendly basis with the teacher. Also, MacGregor's wife Kate, had warmed to Mildred, appreciating the teacher's care of her son, and would frequently bring in gifts of food. Mildred avoided telling Walter where the produce came from. Had he known, the food would've be thrown out. Andy didn't have to be told to keep the generosity to himself.

The rancher knocked once and walked into the school room. "Where's Cat, Millie?"

"They're outside someplace," she answered, not looking up.

"What are you doin'?"

"I'm making out grades."

"My god!' he exclaimed, "is it that time already?"

Glancing up smiling, she answered, "I can't quite believe it either."

"Looks like you'll be awhile," he said.

Mildred knew by his tone, he had something in mind. "Quite a while, I'm afraid. I told Walter not to expect me home tonight."

"I've got to go into Cottonwood for supplies. I'll be taking Cat with me. Why don't you let Andy come along?"

She looked up. "Oh, I don't think so Jack. If Walter found out...."

"He won't find out. Besides, Cat needs the company."

"I just don't think so, Jack."

"We'll be back by seven."

"Well, it really doesn't matter how soon you get back" she hedged, pinching her chin. "I guess it'd be okay... just this once."

MacGregor backed his new pickup to the rear of the store.

"We never come in this way," Andy remarked.

MacGregor merely smiled. There was no need to tell anyone he loaded up at owner's cost, paying with nothing but his signature. "You kids go on inside. I'll be in directly."

"Come on, Andy," Chattman boasted, "I want you to see my girlfriend."

The statement was a surprise to Andy. "You have a girlfriend?" he asked in disbelief.

"Sure. Wait'll you see her."

Chattman sauntered up to a thin gentle appearing girl. "Andrea, this is my friend Andy Hubbard."

She turned, looking at the brown-haired boy who was taller than Chattman. Clasping her hands behind her back, she leaned against the wall staring at the boy without speaking. Andy looked into the auburn-haired girl's green eyes. Finally, he smiled. She returned a careful smile. Andy nodded, turned and walked away.

Chattman caught up with Andy. "I don't think she likes you."

"Why not?"

"She wouldn't even say hello to you."

Andy turned to his friend, flashing a casual smile; he knew otherwise.

Halfway back to the school, Jack MacGregor reached in his coat pocket and produced two slender boxes, giving one to each boy.

"What are these Dad?" Chattman asked.

"Take a look," he said.

The two boys opened the boxes. Neither knew what the chrome objects were.

"What are these, Dad?"

MacGregor turned pointing the one side of the object. "Just blow there."

Driving into the schoolyard, MacGregor grumbled, "I don't know why I had to give them those damn harmonicas before we got here."

By the light of the lamp, Millie opened a can of sardines, spooning a parcel on a slice of bread, and repeated the serving for her son. She then poured two glasses of milk to each for dinner. Andy sat at the table waiting for his mother to join him. She sat and smiled warmly at him. "Was your trip to town fun?"

From under the table, he produced the silver harmonica.

"Did Mr. MacGregor buy that?"

"He did, Mother. He bought one for Cat and me."

"Do you think you will learn to play it?" She was accustomed to Andy calling her "Mother."

"Sure. I already have. Would you like to hear it?"

"Go ahead. You don't want bread stuck in it."

He frowned, "I know that, mother!"

She motioned for him to begin, and was astonished that she recognized the song. He finished, wearing a triumphant smile.

"Home on the Range?" she asked.

"It was pretty good, wasn't it Mother?"

"It was wonderful^"

"I told Cat to have a song ready tomorrow. I hope he didn't pick this one."

While they were eating supper, Andy mentioned a problem he was having.

"I met Cat's girlfriend at the store, Mother."

"He has a girl friend?"

"Her name is Andrea."

"The little Vogel girl—Andrea. What about her?"

"When I met her, I couldn't talk," he answered.

"Why not? Cat got your tongue?"

"Yes, but not the Cat I went with, Mother."

The Vogel residence was a large blue and white three-story chalet high on the southeast ridge of town. The stone mansion was considered one of the elegant homes in the area. Fred Vogel's Prussian heritage dictated the house be kept in constant repair, the grounds trim and manicured, and a household regimen to be observed at all times. That included meals served at regular intervals, not to be interrupted.

Maria Vogel knew something was wrong with her older daughter. It was dinner, and she sat, but ate nothing. The father, disapproving, looked on. "If you can't eat, he said, step away from the table."

She rose, walking upstairs to her room. Her mother followed. The girl sat on her bed, with the full early autumn moon boring into the room.

"What is it?" her mother asked.

"I met a boy today."

Her mother moved toward the girl, sitting on the bed. "What boy?" she asked.

"He came in with Cat MacGregor."

"Well, what about this boy? Did he upset you?"

"Oh no!"

"Then what about him?"

She looked away. "I don't know, mother. I just need to think about him."

Her mother patted her shoulder and left the room.

CHAPTER 13

As the decade drew to a close, an interesting social response developed amid the stages of hard times. It was late November 1929. The stock market crashed and the country was reeling from the effects. The rich never felt the privations and discomforts as the poor. For them, the depression never happened. Those of financial means, such as Felton Caldwell, Clinton Durkee, and Fred Vogel, would never flout their ease of living to their less-fortunate neighbors. They kept the good life indoors, but most felt the effects of the depressed economy... particularly in the availability of the dollar. Jack MacGregor was one who feigned hardship, and except for the indulgence of a new car or pickup now and again, he kept his pretensions to a minimum. He could have lost considerable property, or placed himself in a dire situation, had it not been for his ingenuity. Most of the properties he strong armed away from the unfortunate homesteader were still encumbered. There was no reason to pay them off early. He could never replace the low interest rate that accompanied the lands when he snatched them up. It was a different matter after the money crunch. He, as well as everybody else, suffered a reduction of income. Continued payment on those properties would not only drain what savings the family had, it would place them in an untenable financial posture. Over his father's protestations, Jack challenged the U.S. Government. All the encumbered properties were appraised, and he made it known that he would make no further payments on them, but that he had a standing offer to buy them back at the appraisal figure. If the land was worth more, then so be it. The U.S. Government, bankrupt themselves, readily accepted. The re-purchase at a tenth of the prior debt, allowed MacGregor to have his land free and clear. No greater land bargain could have ever been accorded to the rancher through a stable economy.

The Hubbards were struggling, but were grateful for Millie's steady income. The family was better off than most.

Millie completed her first full year of teaching. Predictions for the next year included an increase in student enrollment. She came to depend on Mary Elizabeth and would miss her greatly. Mary Elizabeth, however, had plans of her own, which her father approved. Millie was aghast. The scheme was for Mary Elizabeth to return for another year and have Millie become her high school studies tutor. The girl believed that in two years under Millie's instruction, she could complete the necessary work for a high school diploma. Mary Elizabeth also calculated that she could begin taking prerequisite summer classes at the teacher's college in Greeley, and in four years, she would have her certificate—the same certificate Millie held. Millie agreed the thinking was sound, but Mary Elizabeth should attend high school to experience the lessons of social intercourse. Clinton Durkee, the ultimate pragmatist, placed the importance of learning a profession ahead of self-esteem. Mildred missed out on this part of life herself, so she conceded. Since the girl would be working, Mildred reasoned she should be paid. Approaching Jack MacGregor with the thought, the school board president agreed. In the past two years, MacGregor's opinion of Millie changed. He asked her what percentage of the work the girl performed. Mildred estimated it was twenty percent. The school board approved the compensation, in addition to Millie's, for Mary Elizabeth. The girl was pleased she could earn money doing what she wanted. Her father was jubilant, and Mildred would have the much needed help. That problem was solved, she had another.

The ice on the pond was receding. Harsh winter winds and freezing temperatures were giving way to longer days of sunshine, and according to Doc Sutton, Millie would be giving birth in less than a month. The summer would give her time to recuperate and be ready to teach in the fall. Walter was prepared to take the pauper's oath with a legitimate claim again this time. Together Millie and Mary Elizabeth would care for the infant, Ruth Anne Hubbard, born on June 9, 1930.

Twenty-one students registered for the fall term. The school board determined that a change needed to be made the next year if there was a single addition in the enrollment. The options were enlarging the school or transporting the seventh and eighth grades into Cottonwood.

The day was September 1, 1931. Millie drove out of the yard with Andy, who held his infant sister. Andy would enter fourth grade. In the back seat, an unhappy Sam was starting school. He looked out the rear window of the Chevy at his father standing alone in the yard watching the car drive away.

Walter monitored unnecessary driving with an iron hand. The two indulgences were Millie's weekly trip to church, and the infrequent trips she took into town for food and supplies. Andy, by habit, would accompany his mother. In the few occasions being in the store with his mother, he searched for Andrea, the girl Cat introduced to him three years earlier, but to no success. On one occasion, he asked Andrea's father about her. At the Vogel dinner table Andrea's father mentioned this to his daughter.

"Who was he?" she asked.

"I don't know who he was," her father answered with disinterest.

"What did he look like?"

"Oh," her father answered casually, forking a morsel into his mouth, while chewing, "A tall skinny kid… brown hair and blue eyes…" Andrea immediately knew who he was.

That particular afternoon, the same tall kid was milling around while his mother was shopping. He saw her, as she saw him.

He walked up to her. "I'm Andy Hubbard," he began unsurely.

The high cheek-boned leggy girl smiled. "I know who you are."

"I met you a couple of years ago," he said.

"It was three years ago. You were with Cat McGregor. I've thought about you a lot since then."

"You're his girlfriend, aren't you?"

She smiled, "He thinks I am."

"I won't tell him you said that," Andy said breaking into a smile.

"Do you have a girl?" she asked.

"Yes," he answered.

Her expression fell.

"It's you," he said quickly, at the same time seeing Millie. "Oh, here comes my Mother."

Impulsively, she rose to her tiptoes, kissing him on the cheek. "When will you come back?"

He could sense the flush of exhilaration, feeling himself swallow, "I don't know."

"I would be here for you if I knew."

"I wish I could tell you," he answered. Mildred approached the two. "Mother, this is Andrea."

Andy looked back as he and his mother walked down the steps. The girl stood watching until they passed from view.

In the car, Andy asked, "Did you like Andrea, Mother?"

Millie paused a moment before answering, turning to her son. "Not as much as you, I suspect. She's an unusual looking little girl. I get the impression that she's mature for someone her age."

Andy touched his cheek to feel if the sensation was still there, it was.

Mildred missed her fiddle, and while never playing it at home, she took it to school with her. Sometimes when she was alone, she would practice. One afternoon, when Jack MacGregor came in, he saw the fiddle sitting in the open. It took some prodding, but he persuaded her to play it, and was quite surprised at the hoedown music she got out of it.

Twice a month, the Grange, the beacon of farm enterprise, would meet in a classroom of the Cottonwood high school. The Hubbards never considered joining or attending the meetings.

The trip into town was too long; besides, Walter was offended that somebody who lived in the city could tell him how to farm. Once a month, the association sponsored a square dance that was wildly popular with the old as well as the young. Long time fiddle player Ernie Stone died, so the group lost the heart of its band. Although Jack MacGregor didn't belong to that ponderous order reserved for farmers, he knew about a replacement fiddle player. Immediately, Millie was recruited and was an instant hit, since she was a much better player than Ernie. She was so popular she would perform solos on request. With the five dollars Millie got for each performance, Walter could afford taking the family to the dances. His job was to care for Ruth while Millie played. Her fiddle represented one of the few pleasantries in her simple existence.

The year 1933 came quickly and brought changes along with it. Sam did his schoolwork, but nothing beyond it. He was intelligent enough, but he hated the indoors. Andy had long since worn out his doctor's set, determined someday to be a physician. Chattman's father bought his son and Andy expensive harmonicas. The two were becoming quite good, and couldn't play enough for Jack MacGregor.

Royce Palmer watched as Jack MacGregor bought a new Buick, then a couple of years later, MacGregor replaced his Buick with another new one. But when Clinton Durkee bought a Packard, Palmer would not deny himself any longer. At the nadir of the depression, he bought a new Cadillac Victoria VI6 convertible. The purchase of such a splashy automobile apparently wasn't enough. This car had fat whitewalls, two spot lights, and was iridescent red. A number of people struggling to make a living were offended. Jack MacGregor, Felton Caldwell and Clinton Durkee were amused. Curiously, Walter Hubbard was, too.

While in Denver, Jack MacGregor impulsively bought two Martin guitars, one for Chattman, the other for Andy. Walter was incensed by the expensive gift, and insisted that Andy return it. After a rare angry outburst from Mildred, he never brought it up again. Mildred was not going to admit that she ordered a Mel Bay instruction book. Andy would study and learn proper fingering, she was certain. Each day, the boys spent every spare minute practicing. Later, when they played while standing, it was difficult to hold the instruments, so Jack, the benefactor, bought two braided tasseled ropes, one red; one gold. Andy took the gold.

That summer passed quickly. Sam helped his father farm, and his older brother would ride Barney to the MacGregor fence where the boys practiced their guitars. Jack MacGregor bought the boys a metal apparatus to hold and play their harmonicas at the same time they strummed their guitars. Walter didn't mind what Andy did in his spare time as long as he had Sam to help him. The Mitchell school didn't increase, so there was no need for school enlargement or transporting students. Mildred would have Mary Elizabeth for one more year.

It was a warm November afternoon in 1934 when Mildred drove into Cottonwood for supplies. On the drive in, Andy's mind was on the girl. He hoped he'd catch her in the store. He did. Andy prevailed upon his mother to give him some time with the girl, and she consented, "but just for a few minutes."

"Is there someplace we can be by ourselves?" Andy asked.

"Will it be all right with your mother?"

"She asked that I don't take too long," he answered.

"I'll take you to my favorite place," she said.

The two started across the vacant highway toward a cottonwood grove.

"I'm walking with you, Andrea," Andy began anxiously. "I never expected to ever be with just you."

Impulsively, she took his hand, clutching it firmly. She began halting, "I, I've wanted to be with you from the first time I met you with Cat."

They entered a sandy lane of tall cottonwoods that bracketed the dry creek. The breeze rattled the few dry leaves in the Cottonwood grove. An occasional leaf broke from its root spinning slowly to the sandy earth.

"Cat talks about you a lot, Andrea."

"He talks about you a lot, Andy."

"I won't tell him about us getting together."

The two continued walking; she held his hand firmly, when she offered, "I don't want to hurt Cat's feelings, Andy. He's really my friend, but you're his best friend."

Andy stopped. "I know I'm only twelve years old, but I have a funny feeling about you, Andrea."

Suddenly the willowy girl clutched Andy and kissed him. He embraced her, not letting go, until she gently pushed away. "Don't say anything to anybody about us, please Andy?"

Unsteady, he stammered. "I won't. We'd better be getting back."

The two walked back to the store in silence. Andy's mother was waiting.

He patted her on the shoulder. "'Bye, Andrea."

She smiled,

"Bye, Andy."

In the car, Millie asked her son, "I hope I didn't hurry you. Did you get your visit out?"

"Yes, we did."

"What did you talk about?"

"We talked about Cat."

"What about Chattman?"

"He thinks Andrea is his girlfriend."

"And she's not?"

"No."

"Then who is?"

"I am."

"You'd better not tell him."

"We won't." Millie heard the word we. She smiled figuring the puppy love affair would soon fade.

In the spring of 1938, Andy, recently finishing his sophomore year of high school, was rewarded with an opportunity to pursue his dream. Doc Sutton had as many calls for veterinary work as he did for human complaints.

One of Walt Hubbard's roan bulls broke through the fence on the Hubbard-Durkee boundary, and Walter sent Andy and Sam out on horseback to find and return the animal. The two were having no luck when they rode into Durkee's yard. They found the irate sheep rancher in a shed with Doc Sutton. A Columbian ram was lying on his side.

Seeing Andy, he snapped, "You'll have to wait until the Doctor and I resolve this animal situation."

Andy assumed that Durkee's foul mood was because of the stricken ram.

"How do we fix it?" the rancher asked.

"You don't. It's fatal for the animal," the chiropractor responded.

"Doggone it. That's a fine breeder," Durkee complained, adding, "I'll go get my shotgun and get him out of his misery."

Andy watched the creature writhing in pain on the ground.

"Doctor Sutton," Andy started softly, "Is there a chance it could be something else?"

The doctor looked at him sideways while wiping his forearms with a towel. "Like what?"

"I think he might have another problem."

"I have no idea what you're getting at," the doctor answered.

"I would like to try something," he persisted.

Andy looked at Durkee. The boy's expression begged a response.

The rancher shrugged his shoulders. "Go ahead, son."

Quickly, Andy pulled up his sleeve, lay down beside the animal, and inserted his arm in the sheep's colon. He continued the insertion stopping at a point beyond his elbow. The ram didn't resist as though it somehow understood help was coming.

"Aha!" Andy exclaimed, bringing his arm out with a ball of cud so large that he had difficulty holding it in his hand while stretching the anus to extricate the object. At that moment, the contents of the sheep's bowels emptied in force on the prostate young man covering him with wet warm loose manure. Immediately, the large Ram sprang to his feet and bolted away. Andy looked up with a wide, gratifying smile. Manure covered his entire front and was streaked across the side of his face.

"Yahoo!" Durkee exclaimed, smacking his palms together, watching the animal trot along the fence line. "That was the problem! Just look at my prize ram!"

Andy was now on his feet.

"What gave you the idea he was constipated?" the doctor asked.

"I remember how it was explained in my doctor set when I was a little kid. I just knew I couldn't give that sheep an enema, so I did the next best thing."

Durkee let out a boisterous cackle. "Well, I don't know how to reward you, young man, but I'll figure something out!"

"I'm just glad I could help, Mr. Durkee. My brother and I were looking for a bull of ours, so I'm happy we were here."

"Well," the rancher softened, "I was pretty hot when I saw that renegade cross-breed in with my Angus purebreds, but I just got over it."

"Is he still in with your herd?

"No. We penned him up."

"We looked for a hole in the fence but didn't find any."

"No. I had Cyrus ride the fence," Durkee said, "He fixed it."

Durkee knew Walter's fence fixing didn't measure up to his own, but it was acceptable. He realized that the farmer tried to be a good neighbor, and Durkee held Millie in the highest regard.

He looked at Andy. "I believe you're Andrew, aren't you?"

"Yes sir."

"I understand you to be an excellent student."

Andy smiled, tilting his head apologetically "I guess I am."

"I expect you'll go on to college."

"I intend to, Mr. Durkee."

"What will be your field of study?" The sheep rancher continued the questions, genuinely interested in the youth.

"Medicine, sir."

Sutton cut in, "Would you like to work for me this summer?"

"Wow! This is my lucky day!" Andy cackled.

Durkee was amused by Andy's enthusiasm. "You go on home and get yourself cleaned up, Andrew. I would give you some dry clothes, but none of our things would fit you." He then turned to Sam. "I believe your name is Sam."

"Yes sir," he glowed. "Sam's my name."

"Andrew, you go on home and get yourself cleaned up, and I'll get Aaron to help Sam drive that bull back."

Sam broke in. "We'll get the bull home okay, Mr. Durkee. This ain't the first time Andy's been shit on."

Durkee flashed a pained smile. He knew about Sam's work ethic and admired the rough cut young boy. Turning to Andy, he announced, "I won't forget this, Andrew. I intend to make this right with you."

"It's already made right. Doc Sutton is giving me a job."

The rancher reached out to shake Andy's hand.

Andy drew back. "You don't want to shake that hand, Mr. Durkee. It's got manure all over it."

The rancher grasped Andy's filthy hand. "That doesn't look like manure to me—it looks like dollar bills."

Chattman obtained his driver's license and the use of one of his dad's pickups, so he gave Andy a ride home from basketball practices and games. Both boys were on the high school team. Walter wasn't happy about Cat chauffeuring Andy around, but it was a solution for the time being. Chattman was a decent guard, but not a star. Andy was the star. The team was doing well, and the supporters stacked the auditorium, following its club to away contests. The Hubbards drove to Cottonwood for the home games only. Even Andrea, no sports fan, attended all the games.

Andy, in his third year of high school, was six foot three and still growing. The farm kid, a big coordinated specimen with a fiery desire to succeed that he received from both parents, was the recipe for an athlete. Basketball, the craze of the winter prairie wasteland was all there was to do and watch. Gymnasiums in the small towns were packed on game night. Cottonwood had a prime center in Andy Hubbard. In his last year as a sophomore, he proved he would be a force when he started the last eight games of the season, averaging ten points and ten rebounds.

Cottonwood won its league championship, and the school was introduced to the bright lights of Denver. Cottonwood won its first game and lost the second in the state playoffs. Coach Homer Martin promised bigger and better things for the coming year.

Chattman and Andy regularly entertained a group in sing along sessions afterward congregating in the dance hall in the back of the Derby Hat restaurant. The two boys developed an extensive repertoire of tunes and would sing songs of the day, like "For Me and My Gal," and "Red River Valley" with their school mates. Those were good times for Andy and his friends. Andy and Andrea displayed no obvious affection for one another, and she kept Chattman at arm's length. Chattman assumed Andrea was giving both boys the same treatment. Andy was getting the better treatment and on occasional, he would drive in with Olive Oyl, his Mother's car, and sneak Andrea back to the grove where he first kissed her.

Andy learned much that summer working for the doctor, and was grateful the doctor would come get him and bring him home. Millie could transport him, but because of the doctor's unpredictable schedule, Sutton preferred to have his assistant on call. Much of Sutton's supplies were veterinary paraphernalia stocked at Vogel's store. Andy was able, when picking up such medicines, to visit Andrea. One concern of Andy's was the coolness by which Andrea's father treated him, and Andy didn't know why. The future would give him the answer.

The first confrontation between Andy and Chattman occurred during the same period. The inaugural spring formal was set for the tenth of May. Chattman wasted no time asking Andrea to be his date.

Taken by surprise, she alibied, "Andy already asked me."

127

Chattman recoiled. "He can't take you. He doesn't even have a car!"

"What do you think I should do?" she parried. "Andy had better ask me," she thought, after telling the lie.

"Go with me!" Chattman forced.

"Well," she paused. "Why don't we all go together?"

"I don't want him around!" Chattman hissed.

"I know it could be awkward, but you two are such good friends, and it would make things a lot easier for me."

"I don't want to share you with him."

"Then I'll stay home. I think it's the best way, Chattman."

He eyed her suspiciously. She never addressed him by his given name. "Well, maybe so, for the time being at least," he sulked.

During the noon hour, she caught up with Andy. "I've got a little sticky wicket."

"What is it?"

"Cat asked me to go to the prom with him. I lied and said you already asked me."

"Oh, damn," he responded, "I just assumed we'd go together."

"You shouldn't take me for granted."

"I know it. What did you tell him?"

"I said you already asked me."

Andy laughed. "How did he like that?"

"He didn't. He said you couldn't take me because you don't have a car."

"I have Olive Oyl."

"I wouldn't dare mention Olive Oyl to him."

"So what are we going to do?"

"I suggested that I go with you both. Can you live with that?"

"You know I can."

She stood close to him. "I wish I could kiss you right now."

Andy smirked, "That would really set Cat off."

****

The country was healing from the depression. Earlier in the summer, Walter traded for a '37 Chevrolet pickup. Millie kept her ten-year-old sedan. Pampered Olive Oyl, always garaged when possible, looked good and still ran fine. Sam was in his last year at Mitchell. Ruth was in the third grade. Andy and Chattman's popularity grew as their music improved and were asked to perform at civic and school events. Walter grudgingly admitted that they sounded "pretty good." Andrea walked the tightrope, entertaining her affection for Andy while keeping Chattman happy.

Andrea Vogel rarely walked between classes with anybody other than Andy or Chattman. Often the girl was bracketed by the two sophomores going from one class to another.

Today, Andy had her to himself as the two walked down the long hall. It was one of the two mornings that Andy and Chattman didn't share classes. Chattman was in a two-hour chemistry lab.

"So you've been making out with Cat, I hear," Andy said.

She stopped, staring up at Andy angrily, "Did he tell you that?"

"It's all Cat talked about on the ride in."

Andy was talking about the trip in the Dodge panel the school used to transport the twelve students into Cottonwood.

"He was in the store being a pain, and said he wouldn't leave until I gave him a kiss. I didn't think he'd spread it all over," she said testily.

Andy wished he hadn't brought it up, after seeing her provoked. He turned walking down the hall, "It's okay Andrea. I didn't mean get you riled up. What you do is your business."

"Andy. I would have told you myself, if I thought it mattered."

"It was just a little annoying that he had to brag about it," he said, massaging her shoulder. "I know you're doing your best to get along with everyone, so forget I said anything."

"Are you disappointed in me?"

"No, of course not."

"Are you jealous?"

"Sure."

"Good," she smiled turning away to her classroom. "I would worry if you weren't."

Chattman sulked on the bus ride home. Andy knew the problem, showing no interest until Chattman asked, "Have you noticed anything different about Andrea lately?"

The vehicle was noisy and the bench seats were hard. Andy kept his voice down as much as he could. "What do you mean?"

"She's been treating me like shit the last couple of days."

Andy wriggled his shoulders. "She's a woman. What do you expect?"

"Yeah. Maybe that's it. It's her time of the month, I bet."

"You're probably right. I wouldn't worry myself if I were you."

The next morning when she was away from Chattman, Andy collared her.

"Cat thinks you're mad at him," Andy began.

"He's right. I am."

"Well, don't get sore just because he tooted his horn about you."

She stopped, giving Andy look of disapproval, "Get your mom to pick you up someplace. We need to talk."

"How about Thurston's station?"

"Okay."

Andy was lounging in the living room by himself. Walter left with Sam and Ruthie to visit a neighbor. His mother was in the kitchen finishing supper.

"Andrea wants to talk to me in private, Mother. Could you pick me up at Thurston's?"

"When?"

"After you get out of school tomorrow."

"Okay. What does she want to talk to you about?"

"I don't know—Cat I think."

"I'm sorry. I didn't mean to pry."

"You never pry, Mother."

After entering the station and Andy's request that he and Andrea use his inner office, Thurston rose, turning to the battered white door behind him. "It's a mess. I'll unlock it." His appraisal of Andrea was one of embarrassment to her.

Inside, she mentioned, "He sort of gives me the creeps."

Andy looked at the slim hips and long shapely legs. "He's a man. Don't hold that against him."

"I don't know what you mean."

"You're a beautiful woman, honey. I'm wondering if you know that."

She clutched him, kissing him, not allowing him to break loose.

He pushed away gently, "What was it we came here to talk about?"

She relaxed. "I guess it's about Cat."

"What about him?"

"The problem, I have," she impatiently began to explain, "is Dad wants me to be nice to Cat, who cries to his dad if I mistreat him."

"You must feel a little like a bargaining chip."

She tightened the embrace. "And Jack thinks it's my job to keep his kid happy."

"There has to be a message for me someplace in there," Andy surmised.

"There is. No matter how often we want to see each other, we have to be awfully careful. As much as it pains me sometimes, I have to compromise my feelings toward Cat. It's not that I dislike him, but I'm not going to have the relationship he wants. I had to let you know some of my concerns, so maybe, you'll be a little patient with me."

"I understand completely."

"Can you afford college?" she asked on a different subject.

Andy found the question mildly unsettling. He knew that with or without outside funds, his mother would see to it that he would be taken care of. "Coach Martin said I'll be offered an athletic scholarship, and in all likelihood, an academic one too."

She burst indignantly, "An academic one *too*? He's the superintendent. All these people think about are their cars and basketball! Our own superintendent puts sports ahead of the reason he was hired!"

Andy smiled, impressed with her spunk. "The girls around here," he offered, "think you're a little stuck up for not wanting to be a cheerleader."

"Is there a problem with that?"

"Not with me."

"Those third grade minds think wearing skimpy skirts and showing off their butts is their ticket to success."

"For some of them, it is."

"Well," she surrendered, returning to the subject of Chattman, "It isn't that I dislike him. He's a talented, handsome guy. If it weren't for you, I could possibly bend to Dad's and Jack McGregor's wishes."

"Which are?"

"Marry him and live happily ever after. I might have done that, but you spoiled it for them."

"Did I ruin anything for you?"

"Don't be silly. You know you didn't."

He embraced her. "I wanted you from the first time I saw you—do you believe that?"

"I guess I had a little agenda of my own, too," she returned.

He held her by the shoulders. "Now I know why your dad's always cool to me." He issued a rueful chuckle. "And I understand why the MacGregors drive up to the back of the store to get things."

"At cost!" she replied bitterly. "Jack thinks when he gets things for what Dad pays for them, that's fair. Jack doesn't realize there's an expense to ordering, stocking, selling and the like. Anyway," she concluded, "it sounds like you're going to be fine in school. I don't know if those scholarships give you any spending money though."

"Spending money shouldn't be a problem. I'll work another summer with Doc Sutton. He pays me more than I'm worth, and I'm socking it away."

"You'll study medicine?"

"Yep. What about you?"

"I have no idea, but the time can't pass too quickly. You're lucky. You get out of here in just one more year. I've got two to go."

There was a knock at the door. It opened. "Your mom's here," Thurston announced.

****

The Hubbard family was recovering from the economic calamity of the thirties. Walter was ready for Millie to give up her teaching job, and she agreed that when Andy finished his first year of college, she would become a full-time farm wife again. Andy was in his senior year; Sam was in high school, and Ruth, "Ruthie," to her brothers, entered the fourth grade. Basketball season would soon begin. Andy was six foot four, apparently ending his growth spurt.

Cottonwood didn't win the state championship. The little town came in second, but one of the participants earned a name for himself. Andy's picture appeared in the sports section of the Denver Post.

Andy was riding with Chattman after basketball practice when Chattman opened, "You're a pretty lucky guy, you know, Andy."

"Why's that?"

"You're getting to go to the prom with Andrea and me."

"You asked her?" Andy feigned.

"I did, after you did. She's only letting you come along because you and I are good friends."

"Think I ought to beg off?"

He straightened, glancing wide-eyed across the seat at Andy. "Would you?"

Continuing the charade, Andy said, "I'll ask her to see if it's okay with her."

Chattman slammed his fist on the steering wheel in anger. "Why the hell do you have to ask her?"

"Maybe then, I'll just skip going altogether."

"You can't do that! You gotta be there. They're planning on us to play for them!"

"Then what do you think I ought to do?"

"Oh, hell," he grumbled, "we've gone this far. We just as well get it out of the way."

"I suppose we have to," Andy murmured innocently.

Chattman gritted his teeth gripping the steering wheel focusing inflexibly on the road ahead. He uttered with finality, "But just keep this in mind, Andy. She's really my girl."

"I'll remember you said that."

****

High school was over for Andy and Chattman. The two ended the academic year with Andy achieving top honors, and Chattman second. Much to the delight and satisfaction of the audience, the two boys gave a musical performance with their guitars and harmonicas on Commencement Night, concluding with the audience taking part in "God Bless America."

The postal carrier, Milo Rittenhaus' old Model A, sputtered away from the mailbox. Ruthie cradled the mail in her arms, inspecting each letter. She saw one addressed to her favorite brother.

Running into the kitchen, she chirped, "Andy! There's a fancy letter here for you!"

Andy inspected the official note with its embossed return address, Athletic Department, University of Colorado. Nervously, he took a kitchen fork and tore the envelope open.

"Dear Andrew," it began, "Basketball tryouts will begin August 10 in the University of Colorado field house. If you should wish to compete, bring this letter with you and register at the Athletic Office in the men's gymnasium no later than 10 a.m. on the above date. Should you be selected as a member of the squad, the University will pay your tuition, fees, and books. The Department will also provide you a job occupying a modicum of your time. You will receive five dollars a week spending money. I hope you will consider this opportunity. I look forward to your presence at the above stated place and time. Sincerely yours, Forrest Bruenig, Head Coach, Basketball, University of Colorado."

"Whoopee!" Andy shouted, handing the letter to his mother who read it aloud.

"Okay if I take Olive Oyl to town, Mother?"

"Sure. Where are you going?"

"I'm going to see Coach Martin."

"Take my pickup if you want, Andy," his father offered.

Andy turned, amused. "You sure, Dad?"

"Of course. Why wouldn't I be?"

When Andy pulled out of the yard, Walter remarked, "I guess that takes care of Andy's school costs."

"Not all of them," Millie warned.

"What do you mean?"

"That scholarship just pays for his tuition, fees and books. It doesn't pay for his room and board."

"Damn," Walter grimaced. "Looks like you're gonna have to keep on teachin'."

"I intended to," she returned solemnly.

Andy stopped at the school official's house to be told that the superintendent was in his office at the school. Andy went to the school, and clambered up to the stairs to the superintendent's office. Martin, seated at his desk glanced up. Andy handed Martin the letter.

The stocky middle aged man read the letter. After he finished, he looked up at Andy. "You know, son. I don't know much about managing sports. With kids like you, a man doesn't need to know much. I could just throw you the ball and go back to reading the paper. You'd win without me."

Andy chuckled. "I don't think so, Coach."

Martin appreciated the complement. "But I'll tell you, Andy. There'll be tougher competition where you're going. If you're going to make the squad up there, it'll be through your rebounding. Concentrate on that—don't worry about scoring. Everyone wants to score. Each rebound is worth a point, but they won't tell you that. When you box out properly and that ball comes your way, you treat it's like your best girl's honor, and you rip it away. You're a quick, strong kid. You'll make it if you do what I tell you."

Andy rose to shake the man's hand, when the official turned. "Just a minute, son, something came for you in the school mail." Martin handed an envelope to Andy. It was another University of Colorado letter. Andy stuck in his jacket pocket.

"Aren't you going to look at it, Andy?" he asked.

"Naw, coach. It's just another letter about basketball."

"S'pose it is, Andy," he said extending his hand. "Don't forget your friends, and remember what I said about rebounding."

"I will sir," Andy said, giving a loose wave and walking out.

Andy walked into the farmhouse, tossing the letter to his mother. "That's a nice pickup, Dad."

"Did you see it had a radio?"

"It was the first thing I noticed," he answered, whereupon his mother let out a cheer.

"What is it, Mother?"

"This letter from the University." she began.

"What about it?"

"It's an academic scholarship."

"So? I've already got a scholarship. I don't need two."

"You're so innocent, Andy. This one gives you a choice. Tuition, fees, and books, or room and board."

"Didn't the other one take care of that?"

She shook her head negatively. "Now you have university housing and dorm food. You won't have to eat basketballs."

"I guess we can breathe a little easier, Millie," Walter said. "Maybe you can quit teachin' if you want to."

She nodded. Walter noticed a tear running down her cheek.

The two sat in Olive Oyl in the Cottonwood grove. Fred Vogel, for the first time, allowed his daughter to steal away with Andy Hubbard. The store owner took the chance that the farm boy, leaving for college, would not return.

Andy was fondling her breasts. "I want you now, Andrea," he said.

"You'll have me, Andy. You have to wait. We'll have time for that. When you get to school write me, or phone me if you can. You're leaving tomorrow. Just remember, I love you, and no matter what, I'll be here for you."

"Andrea, we keep coming here, but I never see any other cars here. I don't see anybody walking or anything. Isn't this a part of the town—a park or something like that?"

"No. We're on Herman Schatzaeder's farm."

"Who's he?"

"He owns this land we're sitting on."

Andy straightened, removing his palm from her breast. "We'd better get out of here, before he catches us!"

She giggled, taking his palm. "He knows we're here. I've been taking walks through here before I was in school. You put that hand back where it was."

Andy emptied his savings account. Felton Caldwell congratulated the young man, and walked with him and his father out of the bank. The rawboned farmer, in his blue threadbare overhauls and weathered straw hat, looked the man of the soil that he was. The proud boy, taller than his father, scanned the flat prairie he had so long wanted to escape. Now that he that was leaving, he was feeling pangs of guilt.

At that moment, Royce Palmer drove up in a gleaming blue Cadillac four door. The big car with its twin fender mounts and glistening chrome grille facing them was intimidating. Palmer stepped out, adjusting his Panama hat.

"My goodness, Royce, what is that!" the proper bank president asked.

"My new car, Felton," he said proudly. "It's the top of the line Fleetwood... sixteen cylinders."

"No convertible this time?" Caldwell asked.

"I know. I just couldn't pass this one up."

"I can see why," Walter marveled, turning to his son. "How'd you like to ride to college in somethin' like that?"

Andy merely returned a smile.

"What's that about, Walt?" Palmer asked.

"Oh, I gotta take Andy up to Boulder tomorrow. He's startin' school up there. I'd take my pickup, but Millie wants the whole family along—so I guess we'll take her old Chevy."

"That's quite a jaunt for that old car," Palmer commented.

"Olive Oyl will make it fine, Mr. Palmer," Andy said.

Palmer smiled negatively. "Olive Oyl, eh? Why don't you take my new Caddie, Walt?" he asked waving, toward the car, cigar in hand.

"Oh," Walter stammered, appraising the behemoth, "I couldn't do that."

"Sure you can. You'd be pretty jammed up in that little—Olive Oyl."

"We'll be okay, Dad," Andy protested mildly.

Palmer tossed the keys to Hubbard who reflexively caught them.

"Keys in your pickup, Walt?"

"Yeah, I never take 'em out," Walter answered, heading toward the luxury vehicle, flashing a surprised smile. "I might not bring this thing back, Royce."

"I'll take the chance. Nobody in his right mind would steal a Cadillac." Palmer replied, revealing a devious smirk.

Caldwell witnessed the repartee silently, shaking his head in amusement watching Walter and Andy pull away.

Millie's moments with Andy were special to her, and his entrance to college was her dream. When they left to take Andy to college, Sam and his father rode in the front. Ruthie, sat in the back, nestled between Andy and her mother in the comfort of the smooth, quiet, cushy sedan. Olive Oyl, in all her simple grace, could never match the ambience provided by the extravagant sedan. The ride was symbolic, Andy thought, with the family separated. He and his mother discussed school subjects; whether he'd have an opportunity to stuff in journalism classes with his pre-med. Up front, Walter and Sam talked non-stop about the car and farming. Time passed too soon. Their conversations came to a halt when the sedan pulled up at the red flagstone dormitory structure that was Andy's new home, Baker Hall. A group of boys on the front lawn tossing a football stopped to stare at the Cadillac. Andy stepped out of the car clad in his corduroy trousers and plaid shirt. Shadowed by the moneyed vehicle at the curb, the young farm boy looked out of place in his plain clothes and denim bag slung over his shoulder. Sam followed Andy into the entryway carrying Andy's guitar. The new recruit checked in and with Sam's help was ushered to his room. Back down in the lobby, Walter announced, "I'm buying us all supper if we can find a restaurant."

The university football coach and two of his assistants were sitting in a booth by the restaurant window when the Hubbards drove up.

"Someone's making some dough," one of the coaches remarked eyeing the vehicle.

When Sam stepped out the front of the car, the coach gushed, "Damn, guys, look at that kid! I'm gonna have a talk with him!"

After the Hubbards were seated, the coach stepped up and introduced himself. Directing his attention to Sam, the coach said, "Where do you play football, son?"

The square jawed youngster returned, "I don't play football."

"You don't? Why not?"

"We don't play football where I'm from."

"Where's that?"

"Cottonwood."

"Oh," the coach chuckled rubbing his cheek. "That's right. They don't, but that doesn't matter, son. You come and see me when you're out of school anyway... what do you have, another year?"

"No. "I'm a sophomore."

Andy was embarrassed for his brother, thinking Sam was impolite.

""Only a sophomore! Well, you look me up when you come to college."

"Don't plan to go to college. I intend to farm." Andy was becoming more annoyed.

"Well," the coach said looking toward the parking lot, "I can see why you'd want to do that. Looks like your dad's doing pretty well."

Andy had enough. "He'll hunt you down coach. I'll see to it."

For the first time the coach took note of Andy. "You here for basketball?"

"Yes sir. We start tomorrow."

"Well, bring your brother around when he's out." The coach turned and left.

Andy scowled at his brother. "You should learn some manners, Sam."

"What'd I say?" Sam asked surprised.

Mildred broke in. "It looks to me that fellow could use some manners of his own."

Andy nodded. "I agree, Mother. I hope my coach isn't like that."

The city was dark now, and the family drove away. Watching the night blot the tail lights of the car, he knew he was alone. There were a couple of lessons he would consider from the day's experiences; wealth brings a false respect, and his stock may not be as high as he thought it was. He turned and walked into his new home.

CHAPTER 14

Andy was given his physical exam at the school dispensary and directed to the men's gym. He wasn't told to bring his gym shoes. It was good that he did. Walking into the large granite building, he glanced around for somebody to give him directions. Coming into a hallway, he saw a man carrying a clipboard.

"Could you tell me where I'm supposed to go, sir?" Andy asked.

The kinky haired man in his thirties asked, "What's your name?"

"Andrew Hubbard, sir."

The man looked down at his writing board, taking a pen from behind his ear, making a check by Andy's name "Yeah, you're one of the walk-ons…from Cottonwood…where the hell's Cottonwood? Is that here in Colorado?"

"Sixty miles or so east of Denver, sir."

"Out where the hootie owls fuck the chickens, huh?"

Andy didn't respond.

The man recognizing that this kid didn't fancy to his humor, instructed, "Go down the hall, turn left. You'll see the equipment cage. They'll get you your stuff and assign you a locker. I see you brought your shoes."

"There weren't any instructions whether we should or shouldn't."

"Yeah, I know. That's our fault."

"What do you do if you don't bring shoes?"

"You take what we've got in the pile, but in your case, I doubt if we could fit you. He looked down at Andy's feet. What size do you wear?"

"Thirteen."

The man laughed. "No. You'd be shit out of luck. So go get your stuff."

"Thank you, sir."

"Don't call me sir, call me Duke."

"Okay, Duke," Andy said making his way down the hall wondering if he would have had to play in his bare feet. He was also told he was a walk on. He didn't know what that was. So far, he wasn't impressed with the reception.

The players were seated on the bleachers. A tall heavy graying man was accompanied by a much shorter man with a clipboard. The shorter man was Duke. The tall man was speaking.

"My name is Felix Bruenig. I'm your coach. My assistant here is Duke Turner." Two men, standing in the background were not introduced. They were the trainer and equipment manager.

"I know you all want to make the team," he continued. "Unfortunately, only twelve out of the forty-two here will. We keep that number for our freshman squad. Perhaps we'll make some mistakes judging your ability, but that's how it goes. Today will involve nothing more than sprints, jumps and agility tests. You will be separated according to position. Guards will be with guards, forwards with forwards and centers with centers. You know who you are. I'll take the centers and forwards. Duke will handle the guards."

Of the three centers, Andy was the shortest at six four. The other two at six-foot-seven and six-eight were on scholarship. Andy thought he was on scholarship. He was to find out he had to earn a scholarship. That was why the other two centers wore new shoes.

Later in the afternoon when the squad was dismissed, Bruenig and his assistant met in Bruenig's office to discuss the candidates. Eventually, Hubbard's name came up.

"I think we may as well send this kid home, Duke," the coach said. "I didn't expect that second center to show up."

"You're talking about Proctor?"

"Yeah, Proctor."

"Well, the kid you want to send home can jump, Fritz. In fact, his vertical jump was four inches greater than Burns. I'm not sure Proctor can jump at all. And that country kid's fast. He's faster than your centers and most of the forwards. Hell, Fritz, keep him around as a forward if you have to."

Bruenig hedged. "We've got bushels of forwards. The hell of it is, Duke, these kids from little hick towns never play anybody. They really haven't had the coaching, so they don't know the first thing about basketball, and we don't have the time to back up and teach them—not if we don't have to, that is."

"You must have brought him in for a reason, Fritz."

"I did, but I don't need him now that the other kid's here. I don't need but one center and we've got three. The two other kids are from big schools and are taller than he is."

"They really aren't."

"Aren't what?"

"Taller."

"The hell they aren't. One's six-seven and the other is six-eight. He's only six-four."

"He can out jump them both, so in reality, he's tall or taller than they are."

"Duke, how many kids since you've been here, that came from these little watering holes, ever made the team?"

"None, but this kid has some size, and he can move."

Bruenig exhaled submissively. "Duke. I never expected both of these big kids to show up."

"So you're going to send this kid home without giving him a shot?"

"Oh hell. Let him hang around if it keeps you happy."

That evening after Andy learned his scholarship was provisional, he was upset. Of forty-two men who gathered, four were automatically awarded full scholarships and eight of the thirty-eight remaining would make up the freshman team. At least he was determined to show the coaches what he could do.

The next morning, Bruenig was addressing the team. Four of the beginning group were released a day earlier because they lacked physical ability.

"You men will be scrimmaging against our varsity, so we'll learn in short order how you compare with the veterans," he announced. "There will be four portions of our weeding out process. We will scrimmage for an hour-and-a-half in the mornings and the same in the afternoons. Today is Tuesday. By tomorrow afternoon, you'll know if you made the squad. If we feel you're unable to cut the mustard, you'll be excused at the end of that particular period."

Andy sat on the bench the entire morning while the two centers ahead of him rotated. The same was the case with other position members, but Andy focused on the centers only. The six-eight center's name was Proctor. Andy was embarrassed for the awkward young player. He so wanted to get in to prove he was better than Proctor. It was becoming obvious that Proctor wasn't going to make the cut when he sat the last half of the second session. Andy wondered why the gangly kid was given a scholarship. He concluded it was simply because of his height. The other center, Harold Burns, although an inch shorter than Proctor, was a much better athlete. Andy figured he could compete with Burns.

Bruenig was condescending to Burns, and referred to him as "Hal." Bruenig would say such things as "See if you can post a little faster, or try to keep your arms up; stay away from the dribble." Andy was annoyed by the instructions, knowing the player should already know them; he considered Burns to be an equal to the varsity center.

He sat through the entire afternoon scrimmage, and was becoming increasingly angry. The next morning was a repeat. He noticed Proctor was missing. At the start of the afternoon session, when Andy was on the edge of walking out, the varsity center turned his ankle, and was on the floor writhing in pain.

"He can't play, Coach," the trainer advised helping the injured player off the floor. Bruenig looked around rubbing his chin cursing, "Damn, I wanted to give Burns some more time against the varsity."

Turner stepped up to Bruenig, pointing to Andy sitting on the bench. "Then put Burns with the varsity, and let the farm kid take his place."

Bruenig thought for a moment, exhaling largely. "Yeah, I guess we could do that."

He turned toward the bleachers. "You!" He pointed at Andy. "Get in!" Turning to his center, he said, "Hal. You have to give him your shirt. You'll be playing with the varsity now."

The varsity jerseys were gold; the freshmen, black. Burns pulled off his wet jersey tossing it to Andy, who caught it.

"Mercer!" Bruenig yelled to the manager. "Get this man a varsity jersey!"

Andy slipped on the sweaty jersey, which was cold and uncomfortable. He didn't care. He was on the floor.

Andy's team brought the ball down, passed the ball around amidst shouts of instructions from the coach. Andy set the screen and the guard took the shot. Andy spun for position. Burns boxed for the rebound. The shot caromed off the rim. Andy slipped inside Burns, snatched the ball and in one motion laid the ball in. Burns stared dumfounded.

"Get down the floor, Hal!" The coach yelled. Andy was easily on defense when Burns set up on the post. When the ball came into the large man, Andy had noticed Burns' habit of dribbling once before laying the ball in. Anticipating the bounce, Andy snatched the ball and fired it down the court. Nobody responded to the break, whereupon Bruenig cursed, "You! Get the hell down the floor on a break! You shouldn't have to be told that!"

The opposing team again had the ball. This time, the forward shot from the baseline. It rimmed out, and Andy jumped as high as he possibly could. He and Burns grasped the ball at the same time. Andy remembered Martin's admonition, "Treat it like your best girl's honor! Rip it away!" He did just that and again fired the ball down the floor. This time, the player was there for an easy lay-up.

The next time down the floor the ball was laid in neatly to Burns for an automatic score. He turned for the basket, not dribbling this time, but was shocked when the ball was driven into his face causing his eyes to water and his nose to bleed.

"You've got to learn to put that ball up with the outside hand, Hal," Bruenig yelled fatherly, as the trainer attended to the tall player. Andy saw the coach look at his watch. He knew the practice was coming to an end, and he had made his statement. The next fifteen minutes, Andy moved easily around the slower, larger man. He out rebounded and outscored

Burns for the duration of the test. Near the end of practice, Andy had the ball in the key hole. Burns was between him and the basket. Andy went up faking the shot. Burns went up too, and Andy spun around laying the ball in uncontested. Whether he intended to or not, Bruenig breathed into his whistle. Everyone stopped. The coach smiled. "I guess that's it, fellows. We'll call it a day." He glanced at watch. "Meet back here at nine tomorrow morning, and we'll have the final roster."

Andy showered and walked back to his dorm. He had a peaceful feeling certain he had impressed the coaches.

Andy went to his cubicle the first thing that Friday morning. He lost some change, and thought it could have dropped out in his locker. When he opened his locker door, he saw a new pair of shoes placed on the bottom shelf.

Andy entered the gym and took his seat on a bench of the bleachers with the others. Presently, Bruenig walked in, clipboard in hand. He paused, scanning the group. He took a breath before speaking.

"This is always a chore I'd rather not have to do. Those of you whose names I don't call, don't despair. You can hopefully catch on at another school, junior college or another institution someplace. I want to thank you for showing up. You hung around to the last. At least you weren't the first to be cut. I wish you the best. The rest of you, stay on the bench for the practice to follow."

He glanced down at his sheet and began reading the selections. "Burns, Baker, Persinger, Goodman, St. John, Taylor, Schroeder, Kreuger, Downing, Ramsey, Javernick…" he stopped, smiled looking up, uttering, "Hubbard." You men are our new team. Stick around. The rest of you men, I want to thank you for coming. I wish you good luck."

Those who weren't chosen walked out grumbling and cursing. Out of respect, those who were chosen remained quiet.

Bruenig walked by Andy. "Did I throw you a little scare, Country?"

Andy smiled. "Nope."

The coach looked down at the boy sitting on the bleacher. "You were that sure of yourself?"

"Yup," Andy smiled.

"Now, how could you be sure?"

Andy raised a leg. "New shoes."

Back in the coaches' office, Bruenig heaved a long sigh. "Sheez! I damn near passed on this kid. I would have if it hadn't been for you."

"I was so sure, I bought him new shoes," Turner admitted.

Bruenig chuckled, "Okay. That's how he knew."

The assistant coach turned. "Knew what?"

"Oh, nothing," the coach murmured.

Andy caught the Saturday bus out of Boulder at noon, making connections in Denver to Cottonwood. He was realizing the benefits of success. The athletic department paid for his bus fare home. It would be a weekend trip, because school would begin Monday, but Andy had to get the news to his family, but especially to Andrea.

He hopped off the bus that made its stop in front of Thurston's gas station. Old Jim wanted to chat, but Andy had other pressing matters. He headed for Vogel's store.

The board floor creaked under his shoes as he searched for her. The clock on the wall read 4:00 p.m. Through an office window, he spotted her sitting behind a cluttered desk. Quietly, he opened the door. Seeing him, she turned in surprise; her face was a mixture of exhilaration and frustration, not expecting him. Instantly, she began smoothing her hair.

Recognizing her anxiety, Andy apologized immediately. "I should have called. I'm sorry."

"I—I'm just so surprised to see you," she said, rising from her chair.

He took her in his arms, explaining, "I made the basketball team, and I wanted you to know."

She stood on her tip toes, kissing his cheek. "Was there ever any doubt?"

"I didn't know it, but there was."

"You were given a scholarship, weren't you?"

"It was a provisional thing, but I've got my free ride now. That's all that matters."

She smiled, glancing nervously around the office.

"Is there something the matter?" Andy asked.

"Actually, Andy, there is. Can we meet over at Schatzaeder's later? I'll explain it all then."

"Okay. I'm planning on staying at Reiss' tonight, so I'll walk down there—what say, seven o'clock?"

"No. I'll pick you up at Reiss' place. I know where they live." Andy kissed her, and left the store, heading toward the creamery. She sat back down at her desk, breathing a sigh of relief.

After a short time, Chattman MacGregor, who was back at the dock area loading supplies, walked briskly into the office where Andrea was seated. The MacGregors, by habit, and much to the chagrin of certain employees, treated the Vogel business as their own.

Andrea's expression mirrored that feeling as she glanced up at Chattman.

"That doesn't look happy," he remarked.

"I don't feel good," she replied.

"What's wrong?"

"Something is," she replied.

"Well, you gotta' get better soon, 'cause the show starts at eight."

"I'm not up to going anyplace tonight."

He wheeled. "Aw, c'mon, Andrea! This is the first date you've given me for a long time, and now you're begging off?"

"There'll be other times."

Somewhat placated, he exhaled, "Well dammit, Andrea. That's a good movie."

"There'll be other ones. I'm sorry, Chattman."

He turned, slamming the door in disgust.

The usual banging of milk and cream cans met Andy as he walked into the creamery. Unmistakable smells of dairy products, in various stages of preparation, pervaded the large concrete room. August Reiss, four years Andy's senior, swabbed the inside of a milk tank.

"Hi Augie," Andy said, as he approached him. "Is your dad around?"

Young Reiss turned, "Back so soon from the big city, Andy?"

"Just for the weekend. Is your pop here?"

Reiss swung a free hand to the rear of the building. "He's out back with Fred Sanford, loading a truck."

Andy walked up to the two men who were handling the bulky ten-gallon milk cans into an enclosed truck.

"Hello, Mr. Reiss."

Reiss wiped his forehead. "Why, hello, Andy. Didn't expect to see you."

"I came to ask if I can stay the night at your house. I'll grab a ride out with Milo in the morning."

Reiss placed his handkerchief back in his overhaul pocket. "Jump in and help Fred and me load these cans, and you got a deal."

Sitting at the supper table, Andy noticed something had changed since last eating at the Reiss house. As if on cue, the family bowed.

"Heavenly father, we thank you..." Marshall began.

Andrea approached her mother in the kitchen.

"Mom. Andy's home for the weekend, and I'm meeting him. Please don't let dad know."

"I thought you were going to the show with Cat MacGregor tonight."

"Well, I'm not, and if he calls, please tell him I'm unable to come to the phone."

Her mother shook her head. "I'll tell you, Andrea. I don't like making excuses for you. It'll be a good thing when you graduate and get away from here."

Stepping toward the door, Andrea snapped, "You can say that again! I didn't invent this problem! I can't wait!"

Her mother dabbed her eyes with her apron. "I know, honey."

Andy recognized the sound of the '34 Ford horn. He excused himself from the supper table and walked out to meet Andrea. She was waiting in the sedan her father gave her when he bought a new Lincoln.

Inside the car, Andy asked, "You seemed a little upset when I caught you in your office this afternoon."

Gripping the wheel, she began, "I got pressured into going to the show with Chattman tonight. Sure, you surprised me, but I couldn't have been happier to see you."

"Sorry to upset your plans," he said easily.

"You didn't upset anything. You know that."

"How'd you get out of it?"

"I told him I was sick."

"You lie, little girl."

"I didn't lie! I get sick every time I see him. I swear Andy. You know how Jack MacGregor pampers that kid—and I don't know what makes dad tick—whether he's trying to save the business by trying to get me to go with Chattman, or if he really likes him—I can't believe that he does, but it's tough on me with you gone. Just tonight, Mom was saying what a good thing it'll be for me to graduate and get away from here."

Andrea pulled the car to a stop next a huge cottonwood.

"Come on. I brought a big blanket. Let's lie down under this tree."

The grass was soft beneath them. The sky was clear and the night was warm. The two lay in a quiet embrace on the wool blanket. Finally, Andy spoke.

"I want you to know I understand the bind that you get put in, and if you have to see Cat occasionally, just to keep everyone happy, you have to do it. I don't like it, but you know I trust you."

Andrea explained, "I don't want to hurt his feelings—I really don't. I can't seem to get him to understand that there is nothing, nor will there ever be, anything between us."

"Would it help if I talked to him?"

"I don't believe so Andy. He'll only think that you have your own desires, and will do whatever you have to do to realize them—because that's the way he does things. No, you'd be better staying out of it. He's my problem, I'm sorry to say."

The two lay on the desert floor under the cloudless sky for two hours. She dropped him off at Reiss' house. He would see her once more before going back to Boulder.

Milo Rittenhaus' old Model A rattled up to the Hubbard mailbox. He sorted the mail fingering the Hubbard parcel, moving toward the mailbox, catching himself.

"Hell," the longtime mail carrier barked, "No need to stick these in the box. You take them in."

Andy thanked him for the ride and hopped out.

Millie hadn't expected to see her favorite son, and was not only surprised to see him but happy when he went to church with her. Andy told the family everything he could remember about the two busy weeks he'd had while away. Millie readily offered Olive Oyl for Andy to take in to see Andrea before they dropped him off at the bus station.

Andy met Andrea once more at their adopted place, and she impressed Walter and Millie when she came to bus station with the Hubbard family to see Andy away. Andy and Andrea pledged to write once a week, and telephone frequently.

Andy's life changed dramatically that fall of 1940. He was no longer presumed the brightest among his peers, or the top athlete on his team. Suddenly, he was very average academically and physically. He now had to compete for his accomplishments. Reality struck when he received his first C, and when the coach criticized him for not learning a play. Because of his workmanlike attitudes, such failures were soon turned into successes, and he soon won the admiration of those who studied and worked with him, as well as his mentors.

Andy swept floors at the athletic office for extra money. Most of the money was spent on telephone calls to Andrea. Some of the calls were met with a certain element of difficulty. If Andy was fortunate enough to get Andrea, her mother or sister, he had no difficulty of getting through. If Fred picked up the receiver, Andy was met with the usual excuse that Andrea wasn't available, whether she was or not. This habit frustrated both, but the two resolved to continue calling. Another inconvenience for Andy was there were no phones in the dorm rooms. He would have to rely on the telephone operator to relay the call. Andrea was going to have this problem, too; she just didn't know it yet.

Another influence on Andy was his new roommate. This was a new experience for him. His roommate's name was Bob Snavely.

Snavely came to the University of Colorado on a football scholarship. He came with excellent credentials, except one. The all-state fullback from San Angelo, Texas, was recruited by over twenty Division I schools. He was sought by such schools as Southern Cal, Penn State, and—Texas. This burly six-foot two, two-hundred-twenty pounder was not only fast; he was tough. His unbridled, wild attitude made him a fit for the game he came to play. Snavely's Achilles heel was his scholarship. He was smart enough, all right. But his study habits were not only inadequate, they were absent.

It was only a question of time before athletic ineligibility would catch up with him.

Although Snavely's academic goals in no way replicated Andy's, the country boy was taken by the suave, daring, yet friendly football player's demeanor. Try as he might, Andy had little success in transforming Snavely's study habits. But, Snavely, on the other hand, did exert a certain persuasion on Andy's social habits when he induced Andy to join him in an occasional beer.

In addition to the unfortunate affectation Bob Snavely was having on Andy, other storm clouds on his horizons were gathering—in the person of Chattman MacGregor.

CHAPTER 15

Time was passing quickly for Andy. His studies were going well. Basketball season was half over. He made many friends with his guitar; not only in the dorm, but on the long bus rides on basketball trips. The Christmas holidays were fast approaching. Both he and Andrea felt this particular year would be better if the holidays would pass unnoticed. As Andrea had remarked to Andy during one of their phone conversations, "I can't be seen with either one of you guys." He understood her dilemma.

It was a rare occasion when Andrea would grant Chattman a date. Her standard excuse was that she needed to study, and that she did without compromise. Her class work was superior, and this was partly due to the inactivity she had imposed upon herself. On the occasions she gave in and allowed Chattman time with her, it was normally to a movie where exposure was slight, and she could keep the eager young cowboy at arm's length. To Chattman's frustration, Andrea showed him very little affection.

Chattman was relieved when Andy had gone off to college, figuring competition for Andrea no longer existed. He would have her for himself. Now, full-time on the ranch, Chattman was given total responsibility to do the things he was born to do. It was becoming apparent that Chattman MacGregor was following in his grandfather's footsteps; that of control and greed. He found that acquisitions came natural for him, with one exception—the girl he desired. He concluded that Andrea was just not a warm person. That was okay with him. He would change her. He figured that it would only be a matter of time.

Andrea would indulge Chattman just often enough to keep her father and Jack MacGregor from complaining.

Now home on break, Andrea, with Andy's blessing, agreed to go to a movie with Chattman, and later on, the two boys would accompany her to a dance on a Saturday night. The latter arrangement was not to Chattman's liking, but it kept the peace for the time being.

With the aid of Walter's '37 Chevrolet pickup, Andy stole away to Phillipsburg with Andrea several times when he was home, but spent the bulk of his time around the farm house, much to Millie's enjoyment. While Millie wished this time with Andy could last forever, he was counting the minutes for the holidays to end, so that he could get back to the new life he preferred.

The academic year was coming to a close; Andy made the dean's list, and in a rare accomplishment for freshmen, he was on the basketball traveling squad. But all that would soon be behind him, and he had to figure out what he would do in the summer. Although there were some rewards, he would prefer something other than aiding Doc Sutton.

Ethel Hoagland was the telephone operator in Cottonwood. All incoming and outgoing calls were connected by Ethel, and if she chose, those conversations were listened to by Ethel. She made no pretense of her admiration of Chattman MacGregor. MacGregor, as a youth, had befriended Ethel, when she was being ridiculed in Vogel's store. He shooed the hecklers away, and bought her a handkerchief to cry on.

The MacGregors represented everything she was not. They were handsome, powerful and rich—and they treated her with respect. Not everyone did. She never forgot Chattman's gesture. The homely, gawky, spinstress readily supplied Chattman with bits information that came across the lines in the years to follow. During the past months, her favors to Chattman had been especially valuable, when she would eavesdrop on Andy and Andrea's telephone chats, then relay them to Chattman. Not all of her gossip was appreciated when she described the more intimate, juicy exchanges the two callers had. Often, Chattman's pride was damaged, and once alone, he would express his anger by throwing or breaking things, or cursing. In the infrequent times he was alone with Andrea, he dared not ask about the intimate conversations. That would blow his cover. Ethel informed him that the two were planning on attending the prom. It was never clear to him if he was to be included and neither Chattman nor Andy was willing to share Andrea like they had the previous year. He would sabotage the arrangement. It would require Ethel's help.

Two weeks before the prom, the two had agreed, by letter, to attend the prom together— without Chattman. In the time that remained, the arrangements would be worked out.

For reasons unknown to neither Andy nor Andrea, their communication came to a halt. When Andy called, the line was either busy, or a dead line; the same happened with Andrea. Time was drawing to a close. In frustration, he fired off a letter to her, which was precisely what her response was. She mailed a letter to Andy.

An unfortunate event occurred on the way to this train wreck which seemed destined to happen. Saturday morning was chemistry lab for Andy. His lab partner was Dewey Gentry, a wealthy student from New Hampshire. Gentry offered his LaSalle coupe for Andy to use for the prom. The labs usually lasted upwards of three hours. Bob Snavely was aware of this, so he picked up a girl and sneaked her into his dorm room; an automatic dismissal if caught.

Andrea picked this particular morning to retry an attempt to call the university. For the past week, and reasons she didn't understand, none of her calls were put through; this one was. Andy was still in chemistry lab. Snavely left the room to go the lavatory. The knock on the dorm room alerted the girl. She answered the telephone in the hall. Andrea asked for Andy, and got the shocking response in slurred speech that he wasn't available—from a girl! Shaken, she dropped the phone and began her slow walk down to the cottonwood grove to the Schatzaeder farm.

Later that afternoon, she got one last call from Chattman, again begging her to go to the prom with her. "Sure—what the hell," was her response. He never heard her swear.

It was a cold cloudy Saturday morning. The MacGregors were sitting around the table. "Dad, care if I use the Buick tonight?" Chattman asked.

The gnarled rancher, looked from a plate of eggs, not waiting to swallow, before he spoke, "What's wrong with one of the pickups?"

"Aw. Dad, this is special."

"Then take a special pickup," his dad dead panned, chewing as he talked.

"Are you planning on using the car tonight?" Chattman persisted.

Jack MacGregor chewed and swallowed hard. He had a knife in one hand and a fork in the other. He placed his hands on the table on either side of the plate with his knife and fork held erect. His brawn, coupled with his abundant salt and pepper coiffure gave him the appearance of a ruling king.

"I bought you a goddam car, Cat, and you wrecked it, and I'm not buying you another one. You know I don't let anybody drive my Buick!"

The phone interrupted his tirade.

Kate picked it up. "It's Bob Sherman. He wants to know if you're still going to help him brand this afternoon."

"Sure, I told him I would," MacGregor answered, starting again on his food.

Kate turned again to the phone. "Yes, he is Bob," she relayed. "Oh, I don't know. I'll ask him." She turned to her husband. "He wants to know if we'll stay for supper. Maybe play some pitch afterward?"

"Sure. Tell 'im that's okay by me." A piece of egg was hanging from one corner of his mouth as he talked.

"Sure, Bob, we'd like that," Kate said into the phone. "All right, I'll bring the kids over, but don't plan on Cat. He's going into Cottonwood tonight. All right, goodbye."

Kate hung up on the phone and sat back down at the breakfast table.

Chattman re-opened the case on the car. "I'll wash it, Dad. It's really dirty, you know..."

"Who you takin'?" Jack asked.

"Andrea Vogel," was the triumphant reply.

"Beat your old buddy out, huh?"

"Sure did!"

"Well," his father hesitated. "I knew Fred Vogel when he didn't even have a horse of his own. I've carried his ass longer than a man ought to. His girl can ride in a pickup." The rancher wiped his mouth with his shirt sleeve and rose from the table.

Andy was frantic. His calls to Andrea were being short-circuited, he was certain. He called Augie Reiss at the creamery. That call was delivered.

"Augie," Andy pleaded. "Go over to the store and ask Andrea to get in touch with me, will you. Then call me back?'

Andy's reply came from young Reiss. "Andy, I went over to the store. She left early and nobody knows where she went."

Andy slammed the receiver down. "She can't be with that God Damned MacGregor!" he cursed.

Chattman had an idea. Those pitch games continue well into the night. He would take the sedan, anyway. He wouldn't wash it—his dad would notice that, but he'd make certain the car had a like amount of gas in it when he put it back in the shed.

Ethel Hoagland began to regret what she did. Her mind raced. Neither Andrea Vogel nor Andy Hubbard had ever done her wrong. She agonized that Friday night. "How could I harm to these people?" she asked. Saturday morning came, and Ethel failed to show up at the phone office. She lived alone at the same hotel where Royce Palmer began his business.

It was late Saturday afternoon when Augie Reiss relayed to Andy he heard Andrea was to go to the prom with Chattman. Andrea's stinging betrayal consumed Andy's consciousness. He had to find out why she would betray him, after all they had agreed to do with their lives. Earlier in the month, Dewey offered his car for the prom and while Andy wouldn't be able to use it for the intended purpose, he asked for it now.

As he approached the schoolhouse where the prom was starting, he pleaded with destiny hoping it wasn't true. It was dark and raining now, as he climbed up the familiar concrete steps into the school entrance. He walked into the hallway, hearing the gathering noise of conversation, laughter and clinking of silverware. He slowed his step as he approached the arch opening to the gymnasium. Forcing himself to step into the entryway, he would see what he came to find out. He scanned the tables, the girls elegantly dressed, sitting at the tables with their dates. He heard the piano at the end of the gym where the faculty was seated. Then he saw her. She was dressed in a white formal sitting next to Chattman.

Andy wheeled, bolting toward the exit, unaware that Andrea had caught a glimpse of him. He felt as though a hot knife had been stabbed into his being. His vision blurred as he broke through the heavy outer door.

Andrea sat stunned. She struggled to collect her emotions, wadding her linen napkin and throwing it at her plate of food. The scrape of her chair drew startled glances from her friends, as she thrust herself away from the table. Instantly, she ran in pursuit of the man she loved. Swinging the door open, she saw the lights on Andy's car come on. Racing down the steps, shouting his name, she heard only the tires screeching on the asphalt, and the wild splay of the headlights searching the open highway. Quickly, the car disappeared in the night. Tearfully, she watched the lights fade in the black rainy void.

Andrea stood in the graveled yard, motionless. Glancing up, she saw Chattman standing on the steps under the flood lights.

"Come in, Andrea," he said. "You're going to get wet."

She gazed up at him, not speaking.

"Well, come in!" he pleaded, standing in his shiny black tuxedo, being pelted in the light rain.

She stood in the darkness, silently turning toward her home.

"Andrea! Where are you going?"

Not responding, she started into the night.

He caught up to her, placing his hand on her shoulder.

She shook it off, violently, "Don't you touch me!" Her voice was a mixture of hate and pain.

"Andrea! What's got into you?"

She offered no response.

"The least you can do is let me take you home!"

She didn't answer, quickening her step. He knew better than follow, watching the figure in the white dress disappear into the black rainy night.

During the drive back to Boulder, Andy's emotions ranged from deep self-pity, to a raging cauldron of anger. He thought back over his time with Andrea. Was she really his girl? She always professed to love Andy deeply, and not care for Cat in the same way. But was this really true? Andy remembered the times they spent at the Derby Hat restaurant, Chattman and Andy entertaining the crowd and Andrea displaying no obvious affection for Andy. She said their distance was needed to save Chattman's feelings. But was it really Andy's feelings she was trying to save?

And in high school, Cat talked endlessly in their rides into school about making out with Andrea. She denied it, didn't she deny spending time alone with Andy to Cat? Had Chattman been telling the truth about his relationship with Andrea? Her explanation to Andy had always been that she needed to be nice to Cat for her father's sake, and that it pained her to offer him so much attention. Was this true or did she give the same explanation to Cat about her time with Andy? Maybe Cat didn't even know that Andy and Andrea spent time alone together. Andy had been very careful to hide his affection for Andrea around Cat, and Andy was certain Andrea had done the same.

He knew Chattman and Andrea had gone on dates together. Andrea would tell him so. Was that her way of letting Andy know she was not his girl? Maybe she really was Chattman's girl, something his friend had said so many times over the years. Whether Andrea was Chattman's girl or splitting her time between the two, it was suddenly unclear to Andy. She may not be his.

The possibilities that were now consuming him were more than he could bear, and by the time he reached Boulder, Andy had decided to escape the life and environment he was living in. Although he was enjoying it, he was tired of having to scratch for money. Without realizing it, he was weary of the long hours of study. A significant change had to be made, he decided, and it would be soon.

Snavely was lounging on his bed when Andy walked in the dorm room. He had a beer in one hand, and a smoking cigarette in the other. Both were dorm infractions.

"Jesus, Bob!" Andy burst. "Are you trying to get expelled?"

"Doesn't matter. The dorm mom caught me with a girl in here today, and come Monday, I'll be dismissed."

Andy flashed a tired smile. "What say we go grab a beer?"

Snavely instantly sat up in his bed. "Sounds like you had a rough time of it too."

"That's not the half of it," Andy returned, nodding his head toward the door. "C'mon, Bob. I've got Dewey Gentry's car. Let's hit the Timber Tavern."

Walking to the car, Snavely guessed, "This has to be something serious. I know you borrowed a car to go someplace. Was it Cottonwood? You've been tight as hell all week. What's goin' on?"

"I'll tell you when we get there," Andy murmured.

The two ordered a pitcher of beer and found a quiet corner in the tavern. Andy relayed the night's events to his roommate, and told him, he had decided to join the marines.

Snavely was flabbergasted. "That's exactly what I decided to do!" he admitted "But not you! You've got your school, and you're making A's. That would stupid on your part! I can't believe that girl would do what you said she did, after all you told me about her!"

"Don't try to talk me out of it, Bob." Andy was serious. "Come morning, I'm rousting Gentry out of the sack and I'm heading to Denver and join up. You come along if you like. It's up to you."

Well, Andy," he breathed, "I think it's a big mistake on your part, but crazy as it is, it's just what I planned on doing."

"Good God, boy. You look down in the dumps," Jack MacGregor said to his son at the breakfast table.

Chattman didn't respond.

"What's a matter?" Farnham chided "Wouldn't she let you kiss her?"

Chattman jumped to his feet to hit his younger brother.

"Sit down! Sit down, for God's sake, boy!" Jack commanded. "You hurry up and eat your breakfast. We left a pickup over at Sherman's last night, and I need you to get it back."

Leaving the kitchen, Chattman's mother asked, "Did you have a good time last night?"

"Not really, Mom."

"I could tell by the way you acted when you came into the kitchen this morning. You'd better tell me about it when you and Dad get back."

"Maybe," Chattman uttered and walked out behind his father.

The rain put Jack in a good mood. As the two walked across the yard with mud sticking to their heels. Jack asked, "Did they get much rain in Cottonwood last night?"

"It was raining lightly when I came home. It rained that way all the way home, I guess."

MacGregor scowled at his son. "You guess! Hell, it was rainin' hard by 10 o'clock. What time did you get home?"

"I don't know, Dad. I didn't check the clock," Chattman explained.

That brought another look of askance from his father, who opened the door on the driver's side of his Buick. Chattman entered to the passenger side feeling a reprieve that he did get home before the rain became heavy; otherwise, deep ruts would lead into the garage.

As Jack settled in the car he remarked, "Well, by God, I'm grateful for this rain. This was turnin' into one hell of a dry spring. You can't run a ranch without something for those cows to chew on, and grass can't grow if it doesn't rain."

He continued his commentary, turning on the ignition key and pressing the starter. "What's it been—six weeks since we've had any moist..."

The engine sprang to life and so did the windshield wipers. MacGregor stopped talking and watched the oscillation for a second, before facing his son. "Okay, young feller, you just got caught in a lie," he growled. "How you think you're gonna' get your neck out of this one?"

At the confrontation, Chattman lost his composure totally, and began sobbing uncontrollably. Between breaths, he exposed everything: the arrangement with Ethel, Andrea's disgust for him, the tyranny he brought on his friend. Finally, he gushed, "I'm sorry Dad. I guess I'm just no good."

Jack was moved. He loved his boy. "Okay, okay," he soothed." You just keep your mouth shut. These things have a way of working themselves out." He placed his arm around Chattman. "I'm glad you told me this, Cat. That's what a dad's for."

"Dad, I love you," Chattman murmured.

Jack patted his boy on the thigh as he backed the Buick out of the garage. Chattman detected a tear in his dad's eye as his father glanced back though the rear window.

Andy was eager to get out of the dorm. He loaded Gentry's car with his belongings and was heading out of the building when he stopped by the mail room to see if there was any mail. There were two bulletins which he peremptorily stuffed in his lapel pocket. With Snavely on his heels, he walked out of what had been his home for the past eight months, Baker hall. He failed to notice the letter that was wedged between the two other pieces of mail.

Dewey Gentry rubbed his eyes. He wasn't accustomed to be rousted out of bed early Sunday morning. Worse yet, the information his friend Andy Hubbard just gave him upset him even more.

"You're what?! Join the Marines? I thought you were smart, Andy." He glanced at Snavely whom he met once before. "Did he talk you into this?"

"No, Dewey," Andy answered quietly, "It's my choice."

Gentry crawled out of bed, fumbling for his glasses. "Of all the times to join the military," he groused, "this isn't it. Are you aware that this world is about to be immersed in war?"

"That sounds like an overreaction, Dewey," Andy returned.

"Is it?!" The diminutive wealthy Easterner shouted, placing his glasses on his thin nose. "Hitler's attacking everything in sight, and he won't be satisfied until he's pillaged all of Europe! Japan's expansion is the same threat! They're a heartbeat away from instigating hostilities with us! It might not hurt for you to pick up a newspaper now and then! You'd be a lot better off with a scalpel in your hand than a rifle!"

Andy waved him off. "I've put some things in the trunk of your car. Get them down to my folks if you can. And take us to Denver. Will you do that?"

"This is Sunday, or did you forget?"

"Doesn't matter," Andy replied. "We'll wait until tomorrow if we have to."

On the trip down, Gentry plied his best arguments for Andy to stay in school, but to no effect. Stopping at the induction center, Andy insisted on taking his guitar with him. Goodbyes were given. A cluster of young men standing nearby started giggling. Gentry realized he was still in his pajamas.

An hour-and-a-half later, Andy, along with the group interned in the induction center, took the step forward, repeated the oath and was sent across the street to the Windsor hotel, where the next day they would board a train to San Diego. A strange sensation began to invade Andy's thoughts of anger and betrayal—the idea that he may have acted too hastily.

The house was dark when Andrea stumbled onto the porch. The long walk across the small town without street lights took her more than a half hour. She was cold and wet, but it wasn't the physical discomfort that depressed her; she felt only the shame that engulfed her when she saw Andy enter the gymnasium. She knew a trap had been set, and unwittingly, she had been a part of it.

Her family hadn't gone to bed, and was surprised when the cold dripping girl walked in the door. Andrea didn't intend to review the past hour's occurrences; rather she ran upstairs to change into dry clothes. Shortly, her mother came into her room. Andrea relayed the evening's events. Her mother's compassion was complete. The father would hear the story.

Andrea slept fitfully. The next morning, she intended to resolve her dilemma by driving to Boulder and confronting Andy. She would talk to him face to face.

"I'm not letting you take that old Ford all the way to Boulder," Fred Vogel said to his daughter.

"Dad," she protested, "I have to find out what's going on."

"I know you do," he answered quietly. "I'll drive you."

Andrea was caught in the emotion of the moment. Her father had never expressed compassion for her, until now.

"I'm looking for Baker Hall," Andrea explained to the attendant at the Texaco Gas station. He pointed to the high rise area where the university buildings were located, then the general directions. After a short while, Andrea and her father located the flagstone structure which was Andy's dorm. Her father waited in the car, preferring not to present an uncomfortable atmosphere with a person he'd never accepted. Andrea entered, not anticipating the revelation she received.

The dorm was quiet. Being Sunday mid-morning, students were still sleeping in. Andrea walked into an empty office. The large desk in and chair were unattended.

"Hello?" she called.

Presently, a middle-aged matronly lady appeared. "Yes?" she asked.

"I'm trying to locate Andrew Hubbard. He is a student here. Do I have the right place?"

The woman eyed Andrea with suspicion. "And who are you?" she demanded.

Andrea told the woman who she was and the purpose of the visit, whereupon, the woman asked, "Then you know nothing about why he left?"

This information brought Andrea rigid, "He left?"

"His room is vacant. Neither he nor his roommate is there. It's been cleaned out, and no one seems to know where they went."

"You mean he's gone?"

"Yes."

"Why would he leave?" Andrea asked shakily.

"I don't have any idea why he would leave," the woman answered, referring obviously to Andy. "His roommate was suspended, so I know why he left. But Andy had no reason to leave. He was an excellent student, and we all liked him."

"And you have no idea where they went?" Andrea continued.

"None whatsoever."

"Why was his roommate dismissed?" Andrea continued the questions.

"He brought a girl into his room, which is against the rules."

Andrea stood in a trance. "So that was the girl," she murmured.

"What girl?" the lady asked.

"It doesn't matter," Andrea breathed, then inquired, "Who are you?"

"Miss Curtis. I'm in charge of this residence hall." Her reply was officious. The lady then asked, "Should I get in touch with you if Andy shows up?"

"No, don't bother," Andrea answered, turning toward the exit.

"He was such a good boy." the woman continued.

"I know," Andrea murmured, reaching for the door latch.

CHAPTER 16

The combination of rough tracks and the smell of smoke brought Andy awake as the steam locomotive struggled toward the summit of the continental divide. He hadn't gotten much sleep, considering what happened the past two days. He fell into a deep slumber after boarding the train, as did Snavely. He shook his partner awake. Snavely was wearing a watch.

"What time is it, Bob?" he asked the burly youngster, who awoke, rubbing his eyes.

"Four-thirty," came the yawning reply.

"I'm ready to stretch out a bit," Andy said. "Let's go walk around."

Snavely readily consented.

Approaching the end of the car, Andy asked a grizzled black porter if it was okay to walk from car to car. He was informed that there was no rule against it.

After passing through two passenger cars, the two paused on the short platform between the shaking, clattering vehicles. Andy suggested they pause to get some fresh air and view the pines and snow covered peaks that they were passing through.

"Any idea where we are Andy?"

"I'm guessing we're about out of Colorado," he returned, looking westward where the mountains changed to plateaus.

Discovering the temperature was colder than the two had expected, they decided to return to their seats. Snavely quickly fell asleep. Andy, chilled from the time standing between cars, pulled his jacket down around his waist, which bared the mail he stuffed in his pocket when he left the dormitory. Carelessly, he began to peruse the three pieces, when he discovered the white envelope wedged between the two articles of student mail.

His eyes caught the return address of the letter. A. Vogel, Box 17, Cottonwood, Colorado. He jerked straight in his seat, and quickly with his thumbnail, ripped open the envelope. The letter began:

> Andy,
>
> For whatever reason you have, I haven't heard from you. I have tried several times to call you. Your line has been either busy or no answer. My only assumption is that you don't want to see me again.
>
> Andy's hands began to shake, as he continued reading.
>
> Will you at least acknowledge this letter? I would feel better, knowing what I did, or why you have avoided me this week. I'm shocked and hurt. I haven't seen you for three months, and I so looked forward to going to the prom with you. It was all I could think about this semester. A thousand things ran through my mind this week, and I'm a wreck. I guess you found another girl, and I have given into Chattman to go to the prom with him. You know who I love. Will you write?
>
> I'm alone and confused, Andrea

Andy re-read the letter, realizing that his world just closed around him. He began thinking of his mother, who would be devastated. He wondered how he could have acted so impulsively, without considering anything but his own concerns. His pain was just beginning.

Fred Vogel was putting the car in the garage. Andrea half walked, half stumbled up the porch steps. Her mother was waiting for her. "You don't look happy dear. What did Andy have to say?"

"I never got to see him."

"Why not?"

"He wasn't there."

"Where is he?"

"He's gone."

"Gone where?"

"I don't know, Mother. Nobody seems to know."

"When is he coming back?"

"He's not coming back. He took all his things and left," she said beginning to cry.

Monday, a letter came to Andrea with a Boulder return address. Immediately, she checked the post mark. It was mailed Friday. She hurried up to her room.

It was a short letter.

> Andrea,
> I don't know why I can't get through to you, or why you haven't called me. I've tried so many times to call you, but your line is always busy. I don't know what this means, unless Chattman has finally gotten to you. I guess the prom is off. The least you could do is tell me what's going on. I deserve that. I still love you.
> Andy

She hurried down the stairs and clutched her mother.

"Mother! Andy was trying to get in touch with me! I thought he didn't want to talk to me because I couldn't get through! Neither one of us could get through! It was Ethel Hoagland all the time! Chattman MacGregor put her up to it! I just know he did!" she cried.

Ethel Hoagland's switchboard was positioned so that her back was to the door of the office. She didn't hear Andrea walk in. Andrea leaned against the wall of the room, arms folded, silently staring at Ethel. Ethel, sensing a presence, glanced around. Her eyes met Andrea's, and reflexively, fell shamefully to the floor.

"Why, Ethel?" Andrea asked, her voice demanding, yet compassionate.

"Why, what?" Ethel pretended. The tone of her voice betrayed her true feelings. Andrea eyed Ethel evenly, waiting, hoping the awkward pause would elicit a confession.

"Ethel," Andrea explained quietly, "You've just ruined a young man's career."

The stringy operator swung around in her chair. "What young man are you talking about?"

"Don't play dumb, Ethel! I was in Boulder yesterday, and Andy's gone! He left school, and nobody knows where!"

Ethel pitched forward in her chair, clasping her face in her hands. "It was Chattman!" she sobbed.

"I know it was Chattman," Andrea said. Her voice was even and cold. "What I don't know, is why you did what you did."

"It was something he did for me a long time ago."

"What did he do a long time ago?"

"He did something nice."

"Was it something so nice that you would hurt somebody else for it? Did Andy Hubbard ever mistreat you?"

"No."

"What about me! Have I ever mistreated you?"

"No," she responded meekly.

Andrea slowly turned the door knob, murmuring, as she walked out, "You're sick, Ethel."

The drill instructor (DI), with a hand held loudspeaker barked instructions to the recruits assembled in front of the Item Company receiving yard at the 4th Division San Diego Marine base. The men were assembled, arranged into barracks according to last names, and issued uniforms.

"Hansen, Hinshaw, Hubbard, Jackson, Johnson," the sergeant in charge intoned. Nearby, a corporal assisted in pointing out where the incoming troops could locate their gear.

"Have them stow their personal effects in the aft portion of the barracks, corporal," the DI continued.

Spotting the guitar, the corporal asked Andy, "How well do you play that thing, soldier?"

Andy was standing beside his bunk. "Okay, I think, sir," Andy responded.

"Can you sing?"

"Some songs, yes."

"What kind of songs?"

"Country songs."

"Just wait here," the corporal said, turning toward the barracks door.

The corporal approached the DI. "I may have found a solution for some music for the colonel, Yank."

Yancey Donnelly was the DI, a grizzled first sergeant who was in the corps for his tenth year. The marines had been good for him, and he was good for the corps. Only one thing was missing. He joined the marines to fight and there had been no wars.

This particular night, Donnelly was in charge of a party to be given in honor of the departing battalion commander, Henry Stuart. They were celebrating his promotion to brigadier and move to division headquarters. The small band scheduled to provide music was marooned on San Clemente Island, where they were performing the night before. Their launch developed engine trouble and was detained until the boat could be fixed.

The corporal, whose name was Grounds, was explaining, "He says he can sing and play country, Sarge."

Donnelly shook his head negatively, "Aw hell, I planned on that band. I don't see what one kid with a guitar can do."

"Why don't I go get him and see what he sounds like?"

The burly sergeant moved in his chair. "Okay," he sighed, "after he's suited up and chowed down, bring him here. We gotta' have somethin'."

"You know the colonel—I mean the general   likes country music," the corporal urged.

"I know he does. So do I."

After the men were issued their fatigues, footlockers, and barracks numbers, they were lined up and fed. Part of the standard menu for new recruits was a week's helping of saltpeter. This took the men's mind off their civilian trappings for as long as necessary. Andy identified the taste. He'd been introduced to the element in chemistry classes. He remarked to the recruit sitting next to him, "They're giving us sodium nitrate."

"What's that?"

"It's to keep you from getting a boner."

"I can't taste it," the young soldier replied.

"You can't get a boner, either," Andy chuckled.

The corporal entered the DI's ward room with Andy in tow. The sergeant looked him up and down, gauging the trousers were much too short. "You're gonna' hafta' get this kid over to quartermaster in the morning, Grounds. That kid can walk Mission Bay and never wet his crotch." He then glanced up at Andy. "Okay son. Let's hear what you can do with that thing."

Andy unbuckled the case. Knowing he was going to be asked to play, he quickly tuned his guitar after mess. He removed the guitar and located a pick. "Any requests?" he asked.

"Give it your best shot," the sergeant grunted.

Andy began with his favorite song, "Wildwood Flower," moving into a medley of cowboy songs. Shortly, the doorway was jammed with cadre clapping and stomping their feet. Andy noticed a grin on the DF's face. After he finished the next piece, the sergeant asked him to sing.

Andy sang the old song, "Strawberry Roan."

Donnelly waved him to stop. "That'll do just fine, kid," he said, noticing the twang in Andy's voice. "Where are you from?"

"Colorado, sir."

"Sir! You're learning fast. Colorado—that's out in the country, isn't it?"

"Way out in the country, sir."

"How far out?"

"My basketball coach said it was out where the hootie owls make love to the chickens."

This brought a chuckle from the otherwise grouchy DI. "Okay, Country. Go wait by your bunk. Corporal Grounds here will come and get you when we're ready for you."

Andy stood alone by his bunk. Everyone else was watching a propaganda movie leaving him by himself to think about Andrea, and the mistake he had made.

Discovering Andy was a Godsend for Sergeant Donnelly. Henry Stuart was a crusty old soldier from Kansas, who fought at Verdun in WWI. He was most-pleased with the DFs selection. When the party was adjourned, and Andy was putting his guitar back in its case, the general accompanied by his wife, walked up.

"Private," he began, "My wife was with me when I was stationed in Monterrey. You sing the Mexican songs better than the Mexicans do. There is one song, however, my wife and I particularly liked, and hoped you'd sing. Do you know the song, "Happened in Monterrey?"

"Yes sir, I do."

"Do you mind playing it… and singing it?"

Andy replaced his guitar, strummed the introductory chords, and began in his soft baritone voice, "It happened in Monterrey, in old Mexico. It happened in Monterrey a long time ago…"

As he, his cadre corporal and the DI walked back to the barracks, Donnelly crowed, "You really made it with the general. I think we'll be getting some use out of that guitar while you're around, country."

"I noticed the man sitting next to the general. He didn't seem taken by my music," Andy commented.

Donnelly knew who Andy was referring to. He was Frank Canali, the company commander.

"Yeah," Donnelly grunted, "That's our boss, Captain Canali. He's from New York. They don't have cowboys back there, so you'll have to figure out what he likes."

The following weeks provided the test young men known as "boot" camp. It was reveille at four in the morning to "taps" at eleven at night, with an occasional guard duty sprinkled in somewhere during the night. The days were jammed with drills, marching, combatics, and all forms of harassment invented to dehumanize the human being. Marine boot camp was a test of wills, with the usual number unable to withstand the torment and harassment falling away to be conscripted into a less demanding branch of the services. The new recruits soon discovered that the Marines are proud of their heritage; they were not a haven for the faint of heart. Andy experienced the meaning of total exhaustion. Five days passed before he had the time or energy to write a couple of letters.

****

Dear Andrea,

Your letter was hiding between two other pieces of mail, and I didn't see it; otherwise, I wouldn't be where I am. It's as though it was supposed to be. Now that I know you were trying to call me all this time, I can only suspect we were being manipulated. I know when I called Augie Reiss that Saturday after noon my call got through. And when he went over to the store, you were gone. My only assumption, in my confused mind, was that somehow you changed your mind about Cat. Anyway, I thought I lost you, went off my rocker and joined up. What a mistake!

They're trying to kill us here. Bob Snavely, my old football roommate that I joined up with, says this boot camp is ten times rougher than any football training he ever had. The first week, 15 percent washed out and have been re-assigned. I would probably entertain faking it, except those who don't make it here are doomed to another branch of service. Word is, the first week or so the thing stabilizes. Besides, I'm too proud to think I'm too weak so see it through, so I'll be sticking it out. There has to be a reason for all this happening the way it has. Hopefully, we'll be able to find out and never doubt each other again. They'll be giving us a furlough in a month or so, so I'll bide my time until then.

I love you, Andy

Andrea laid the letter on her dresser. She knew she would re-read it many more times. Gazing across the prairie town from her upstairs window, she also knew her time in an environment she hated was drawing to a close. It couldn't end soon enough.

Emma Birkenmeier was on the phone. If anyone in Cottonwood got news first, it was Emma.

"Yes, I got it from Anna Vogel. Can you believe Andy Hubbard would do something like that? Just leave school without telling anyone? And his grades," she continued, "were good, and I understand..."

As gossip filters through small towns, much of it is carried on the phone lines, and Ethel was hearing it all. Each time an accolade was passed Andy's way, Ethel felt the knife thrust in her side. In her preoccupation, people began to gossip about her. They were saying that one has to repeat instructions to get her attention nowadays.

Sam heard Milo Rittenhouse's Model A pull up to the mailbox, sit idling for a moment, then the sound of the little engine struggling away. He sauntered up, opened the box and casually leafed through the mail when he came to an elongated striped envelope. He broke into a hard run, covering the porch with one step, threw open the kitchen door. Walter was still seated at the round oak table. Mildred was clearing the red and white checkerboard oilcloth that was spotted with spills from breakfast.

"Momma! Momma! Look at this!"

She glanced at the envelope and began wiping her hands on her apron. Taking the folder from her son, she sat at a chair at the table, opened the missive and began reading aloud.

> Dear Mom and Dad,
>   I've gone and done a very unwise thing. I was distraught because I thought Andrea jilted me, and I joined the Marines..."

"Oh no!" Mildred cried.

> I know this was a serious mistake, but I'm determined to see this through, and eventually complete my education. I don't know how this came about, but intend to find out. Andrea wrote me a letter, and I wished I had opened it when I first got it, but I didn't, and there's no use worrying about that now. I know you will take this seriously hard Mom, and I'm sorry. I'll...

"It was one of those goddammed MacGregors, I guarantee you that," Walter seethed. "You know it was, Dad! Sam parroted.

"Now that's not going to help anybody!" Mildred chided through misty eyes.

Mildred fell against the kitchen wall, her apron in her hands, covering her face, sobbing. "Why! Why in the world? Why?"

Walter supported her, gently holding her in his strong arms. "He'll benefit from this Millie. It will toughen him up a bit," he consoled.

Mildred stiffened angrily, "That boy doesn't need toughening up, Walter! He never did and he will never will!" she broke from his arms and started to the bedroom.

"Well, with the situation in Europe and the way things look, he would probably have to go anyhow," Walter rationalized. Millie glowered at him.

"I didn't raise my boys for cannon fodder!" she exclaimed.

"Well..." Walter started.

Millie interjected, "Walter, you never did understand Andy! Oh, I don't know what to do!" she cried as she hid her face in her apron again, bumping into the bedroom, flinging herself on the bed, sobbing.

Walter stood motionless, his hands in his overhaul pockets, staring at the floor. "Naw, I guess I never did," he confessed.

****

"Sergeant Donnelly," the orderly intruded, "Captain Canali will see you now."

The first sergeant walked into the Captain's office, removed his hat and took a seat.

"What's up, Yank?" the dark haired handsome New Yorker asked. Donnelly had been under Canali's command since returning from overseas duty, and greatly admired the young C.O. Canali let the sergeant pretty much run the company as he pleased, seldom getting involved in training practices, since the Captain was pleased with the way things were getting done. When Colonel Stuart was promoted, regimental headquarters assigned an executive officer to assist Canali in his administrative duties, in addition to training. It was common for C.O.s to have an executive, but it wasn't unusual for them not to, either. In Canali's case, he was satisfied, since, during his three-year tenure, Donnelly and his cadre did the job to his satisfaction. Canali's superiors were happy because they, without exception, felt the troops who graduated from Canali's boot camps were well trained and prepared for duty.

"It's this new Exec, Frank." In close company, Donnelly was on a first-name basis with his boss. The subject was a second lieutenant named Perkins assigned to Canali's company.

"What about him?"

"First, he insists that I salute him."

Canali leaned forward in his heavy swivel chair, selecting a wooden box on his desk. He handed the box to Donnelly who took a cigar and handed the box back to the Captain.

"You never smoke these. Why do you have them around?"

"I keep them for you and Henry."

Canali was referring to General Henry Stuart.

Donnelly scratched a kitchen match on the sole of his shoe.

Canali waited for Donnelly to light his cigar, before he spoke, "That's his right, y'know. He is an officer, and those are the rules."

"Well, I ain't salutin' him."

"Suit yourself." Canali said. "What's second?"

"He's a pain in the ass, Frank. I wouldn't mind havin' him around if he knew shit from shinola. He screws up everything I do. He's never done anything firsthand. You know, he doesn't have a damned bit of experience and I wouldn't mind that, except you can't tell him a fuckin' thing. He's learned everything out of a book. He's trade school and you know what that means."

"I guess I don't know. I'm trade school. What does it mean?"

Donnelly choked on his cigar. "You're not a mustang?"

"Nope."

"You gotta' be kiddin' me Frank."

"United States Military Academy, Quantico, class of 1937," Canali announced proudly. "This was my first command."

"Well, damn, Frank," Donnelly stammered. "I've known you over three years. I wouldn't insult you for the world."

Canali rose, took a deep breath, and laid his palm on Donnelly's shoulder. "Yank, you didn't insult me. I didn't ask for this guy, and I'm sure we don't need him. I'm not going to get into any of the details, because both you and I know it would be a waste of our time. Second lieutenants come out knowing everything, and think they have to let the world in on it. Generally, they don't, as you say, know shit from shinola, so try to get along with him and just go about your business—do the things the way you normally would do them..."

"Armour!"
"Here!"
"Armstrong!"
"Here!"
The liturgy continued through mail call with recipients answering the call so the mail deliverer could hand soldiers their letters. Occasionally a recruit would be berated for not answering loudly. "Bruner!"
"Here."
"Goddammit!" He cursed. "Sound off like you got a pair!"
"BRUNER!" the postal clerk repeated.
"HERE!"
"That's better, Bruner. Chapman!"
The exercise continued, "Hubbard!"
"Here!" Andy pushed up to get his mail, pressing by an indolent freckled recruit who never seemed to get any mail. That was Atkins, Andy knew. As he passed by the shorter man, Atkins lipped, "Must be nice, Skinny."

Andy didn't respond, thinking only about the person who called him skinny. He took the letter to his bunk, recognizing his mother's handwriting. The letter was encouraging, as Andy hoped, with his mother looking forward to his furlough. As he read, a passage particularly caught his interest. "People are beginning to talk about Ethel Hoagland. She's acting so strange lately. I was in the phone office the other day to call Aunt Nora, and Ethel actually began crying." Andy's mother didn't know why. Andy did.

****

175

Rusty Atkins' exhibition of physical prowess did little for his popularity among the men in the company. He was treated with deference, mostly out of fear. His dour, unfriendly attitude persisted throughout boot camp. He managed his training without making any friends. He was avoided everywhere, except at mess, where this was impossible. He liked nobody, and nobody liked him, and he was consistently disciplined by being placed on extra duty or detail. Rusty felt a particular dislike and distrust for Andy Hubbard who palled around with Bob Snavely. He expected them both to jump him at any moment. Rusty was openly antagonistic toward Andy and spoiled for a fight. Andy never gave him the opportunity. Cracks appeared in Atkins' armor when, on occasion, Andy was playing and Rusty wasn't on detail. Rusty would crawl up alongside the barracks, in the cover of night to hear Andy play and sing country songs. He barely sneaked away one time when he was seen tapping to the music on the side of the wooden barracks.

CHAPTER 17

Mildred entered the phone office, closed the ill-fitting folding door to the booth and began conversation with her longtime Missouri friend, who recently moved to Denver. Mildred considered her conversation private, forgetting the likelihood Ethel was eavesdropping on her call.

"Yes, Nora. We don't know why Andy did what he did. Actually, I'm heartbroken but I'll get through it..."

Tears began to run down Ethel's cheek, as she reached for her handkerchief.

Stepping out of the booth, Mildred saw Ethel in her grief.

"What's the matter?" Millie asked.

"I could hear your conversation, Mrs. Hubbard." Actually it was a lie, but Millie didn't know it.

Millie placed her hand on Ethel's shoulder. "There, there, Ethel. I appreciate your concern... it's really not your problem."

"It's just...! It's just...!" Ethel sobbed.

"Don't you worry, Ethel. It'll all turn out all right. How much is the call?"

"Nothing, Mrs. Hubbard. I forgot to record it."

That was the truth.

After settling into Walter's pickup, Millie remarked, "Ethel's taking Andy's running away harder than we are."

Walter started the vehicle. "That's strange," he mused over the protesting whine of the gears as the Chevy started up the street.

****

June, 1941:

The Vogels were sitting around the breakfast table.

"Somebody's got to do something about that girl Ethel down at the phone office," Fred Vogel complained. Our girl, Twila, has to tell her three or four times before she gets anything straight. I'm beginning to think we'd be better just drivin' out to wherever we have to go to get an order straight."

"And she looks so distraught, so defensive," Anna Vogel added. "I wonder if she's feeling well. I heard she has diabetes. They might be acting up, and she looks so lean and drawn, lately."

The conversation lasted for a few more minutes, when Fred looked at the clock and remarked, "I gotta get going. Cat MacGregor will be in with a couple of guys to load those camp stoves."

"Mother," Andrea said after her father left, "I think I know what's bothering Ethel."

"What?" Anna asked.

Andrea told her mother the whole story: the prom, why Andy joined the Marines, and her confrontation with Ethel.

"My goodness, my goodness," her mother repeated. "That poor girl."

"Somehow, I don't feel so sympathetic as you, Mother. What about me? What about Andy? I'd say that's poor!"

"I'm not justifying what she did," her mother explained. "I'm just thinking that she must be very mixed up to do such a thing. That poor girl hadn't had the best of things, you know."

"I guess I'm still thinking of me, Mother," Andrea said, "and I'm not just ready to forgive her. You talk about poor Ethel. Well, what about poor Andy. His life is wrecked, just because some poor girl doesn't have a brain in her head! He has no business being in the Marines, no matter what happens with Andy and me."

"You love him, don't you?" her mother asked.

"With all my heart," Andrea gulped.

"I guess I didn't know it was all that serious. You keep so much inside of you, Andrea, but I guess I should have known after all these years."

Andrea excused herself and went up to her room. She wanted to be alone. Anna Vogel sat at the kitchen table staring sadly at nothing, thinking of the things Andrea told her.

****

It happened one hot spring afternoon when the company was on a thirty mile forced march in the southern hill country area. During an exercise designed to test the mettle of a Marine due to the speed and intensity of the operation, an interesting thing happened. This trek went through a particularly grassy area, to simulate a jungle road meandering through the area. This road was used principally as a haul road or an access road for army vehicles. There was only one ten-minute break, and when the reprieve came, men collapsed immediately by the sides of the road. Shortly after the order came to "fall out," the order, "fall in," was issued. An unusually exhausted Rusty Atkins dropped off to sleep along the edge of the road. The evening prior, he was given the usual extra duty; this time for guard detail. He went to bed at 11 p.m., and was ordered to walk guard from 1 to 3 a.m. Reveille came at 4:30 a.m. In his deep slumber, he didn't hear the order to resume the action. Andy was preparing to take his place in the marching column when the sound of a heavy vehicle filtered into his mind. Inexplicably, his mind registered the specter of Atkins who collapsed on the road dangerously close to the curve. Immediately, he turned and sprinted where he remembered the soldier sleeping. In his horror, he saw an armored personnel carrier roaring over the slight rise heading into the curve bearing down on the comatose man. At that precise moment, Andy dove headlong, crashing into the inert form, a split second before the tracks of the machine clattered over the exact spot where Atkins collapsed. The force of the plunge thrust both men barely out of the path of the speeding fifteen ton behemoth. The two lay for a moment in the storm of dust left by the machine. Atkins stared in disbelief at Andy, and then at the vehicle thundering away. Andy rose to his feet clutching the shoulder strap of the shocked Atkins' jacket. "Come on!" he shouted. "They're pulling out!" Without speaking, the two sprinted into the ranks of the company.

That evening in the barracks, Andy was awakened by a jostling of his bunk. Drowsily, he rolled over, rubbing his eyes. He saw a form standing by his bed.

"Did you know that was me?" the soldier asked.

Andy shook his head, clearing his vision, and sat up. He sighed. "Sure—I knew it was you."

"Why'd you do it?"

"You were about to get killed!"

"But I've given you nothin' but shit."

Andy forced a derisive laugh. "You were still about to get your butt mashed. I couldn't just stand by and watch."

"Stand by and watch, your ass! You damn near got yourself killed too!"

"But I didn't."

"You don't even know my name!"

"It's Atkins, isn't it?"

"It is, and call me Rusty, if you don't mind."

"Okay, Rusty," Andy replied easily.

"You're Andy Hubbard, right?"

"Yep."

"Well, is there anything I can do to repay you?"

"As a matter of fact, Rusty, there is."

"Well... you just say the word!"

Andy lay back in his bunk. "Let me go back to sleep."

Atkins watched with an unnatural affection, as the tall man rolled over. Rusty Atkins smiled for the first time since joining the Marines. He had a friend.

"Yank here," Captain Frank Canali began, "tells me you just saved a soldier's life, Private Hubbard."

Andy was standing at attention in the officer's orderly room the next afternoon.

"Yes sir," the tall youngster responded.

"That was a brave thing. I'd like to reward you. Is there anything you'd like?"

Andy brightened. "There is sir."

"Name it."

"Can you get me transferred to Corpsman School, sir?"

"You want to be a medic?"

"I want to be a doctor, but this would be a start."

"I'll see what I can do."

Vera Baker was the bookkeeper at the Ford garage. She was attempting to reach the phone office. Going back to the rear of the garage, she shouted "Ervin!" Ervin Kasstle was the mechanic. The methodical, obedient servant was hired shortly after the garage opened in 1918— just after Vera Baker signed on. Vera was proud of her longevity and clung to her authority as if it were a birthright.

Ethel Hoagland sat in her office chair immersed in self- pity. The pulsating buzz from the switchboard seemed far away. The toy-like incantation, "Central! Central!" issuing through the headphones produced a weak squawk, resembling that of a parrot's. Her demented mind registered another summons from the person trying to get through. She pulled the jack from the board, disconnecting the painful reminder that would never betray her again.

Ervin worked under an old V-8, replacing a pan gasket. He skidded out from beneath the car, struggling to his feet, wiping the grease from his hands.

"What is it, Ms. Baker?" he asked, dutifully eyeing the bulky, officious woman standing above him.

"I can't get through to Central! Go over and see what's going on. I've got to contact the Greyhound bus station in Burlington before the 9:15 gets in!"

Vera Baker never asked. She told.

Ervin continued wiping his hands as he walked the block-and-a-half to the telephone office.

"Bitch!" he chided quietly, "One of these days she's going to shout at me once too often, and I'm going to shove a monkey wrench right up her ass!"

The only person Ervin didn't fear and could threaten and make demands, was Ervin himself. Ms. Baker was in no danger of being abused.

He walked up to the phone office door, threw it open, expecting to see Ethel gabbing with someone, avoiding her duties as telephone operator.

The chair in front of the switchboard was vacant.

"Ethel!" Ethel!" he called out.

There was no answer. He paused, noticing that the door to the rear was ajar.

"Ethel?" he asked gently.

Then he saw her.

"Oh God!" he shouted, leaping backward. He struck a chair nearby, sending it slamming noisily against a wall.

Ethel lay prostrate on the floor. He picked her up in his arms. A .38 caliber revolver tumbled from her dress. He felt a warm sensation on his right forearm as he let the limp figure drop to the floor. Glancing down at this blood-soaked sleeve, he bolted from the phone office, legs pounding the sidewalk as he raced back to the garage, yelling, "Ms. Baker!" "Ms. Baker!"

Ethel Hoagland was dead.

"Now men!" Perkins waxed, "There has been only one group to go over the top of this apparatus since the camp was opened in 1928. I say group, because you will assemble in teams of three men. As you engage this course, you'll need your buddies to assist you. I would like to think that some group will conquer it today."

The obstacle, referred to simply as "The Hill," was made of two mammoth poles jutting skyward with horizontal bars bolted through them. As each participant climbed to the top, he discovered that the higher he climbed, the bar spacing increased, making the ascent not only a physical challenge, but a mental one as well. The structure was conceived with the intention of being a confidence builder. The climb began with an easy ascent, gradually becoming more and more difficult and dangerous, ending with a section that was terribly risky and borderline impossible.

It had been two days earlier when Andy nobly rescued Rusty from the speeding troop carrier. When he heard Donnelly's order to choose partners and get ready for the test, Rusty Atkins approached him.

"Want to buddy up with me?" he asked.

Andy didn't hesitate. "Sure, Rusty."

"We need a third, Hubbard," the gnarly Mississippian offered.

"You can call me Andy."

Atkins smiled wryly. "I didn't want to sound too friendly."

"Let's get Snavely," Andy said. "I'm sure he'll be looking for me."

Sure enough, the muscular athlete strutted up. "Andy," he began, "I don't..." He stopped short when he saw Rusty.

There was a glint in Andy's eye when he announced, "This is Rusty Atkins, Bob. I think you two have met..."

The two eyed one another warily.

Atkins haltingly offered his hand. "Sorry about that, uh, thing, uh, Bob."

Snavely smiled, returning the handshake. "That's okay. I'll get your ass at something else."

Andy broke in. "What do you say we see if we can do what nobody else seems able to do?"

"If we can't," Atkins said, "I don't know who can."

Andy squinted looking up appraising the structure. "There's something unfriendly— nasty— about that thing."

"Like what?" Snavely asked.

"Well, during the movie critique they had on this course, I noticed they showed all the obstacles and the demonstrations on how to complete them—but not on this thing. They only went up a few bars before they came down," Andy explained.

"So what's different?" Rusty asked, "The height?"

"Partly, but that's not all of it," he murmured analytically. "I think it's something they want us to find out."

"Well, it's gotta' be something," Snavely put in, "because how come after all those years, only one bunch finished it...?"

"Well," Andy said. "They're not telling us, and I guarantee that we'd better be prepared for what it is. There's something we're not seeing. Personally, it scares the crap out of me."

The whistle blew assembling the men. "Remember, men, time is important," Perkins began.

Yank Donnelly interrupted him. "Guys," he announced gravely, "There has been only one group to complete this course. Seven have been permanently disabled; three have died. I urge you to be especially careful!"

The order was given and the company broke en-masse toward the obstacle. Andy stopped both of his partners advising, "Time doesn't mean anything. Yank would have agreed with Perkins, if it did. Let's see what those ahead of us do."

The three watched as the men in the company climbed to the fourth or fifth horizontal bar, then drop, bar by bar, back to the ground.

"Well, let's go," Snavely urged.

They muscled into the jam of soldiers clambering up the bars. Andy discovered the challenge immediately, as he began to reach further. At the fifth bar, some forty feet off the ground, Rusty exclaimed, "I can't reach the next bar!"

"Then jump for it!" Snavely yelled.

"There's nothing to hold onto!" Rusty exclaimed.

"Then balance yourself!" Snavely yelled.

Rusty accepted the challenge, springing to the next two bars.

Two bars later, Snavely got his surprise. He discovered the next bar was too far for him. By now nobody was as high as Andy, Rusty and Snavely.

"Shit! I can't reach it!" Snavely exclaimed.

"Then balance yourself!"

Snavely looked up at Rusty standing above him. "I'm not going to do that!"

Rusty noticed Snavely's fists grasping the bar Rusty was standing on.

"I ought to step on those hands, dammit! I did it—you can do it," the redhead swore.

Instantly, Snavely thrust himself up to the above bar, finding his balance, discovering the poles on either side were close enough to support himself.

"Damn! That wasn't so bad," he crowed.

The three were two bars from the top, when Andy discovered what the two earlier were experiencing. "I'm sorry, guys!" shouted, looking down at the soldiers grouped around the stanchion, from this elevation, appeared to be no more than two feet tall. "I can't do it!"

Rusty began softly, his voice strangely friendly, "Andy, it's no different for you than it has been for us. Just spring up the way we did, and trust your balance!"

"I don't think I can do it! I'm afraid I'll fall!"

"So did we!" Snavely cursed. "Just do it! We're depending on you!"

Andy tossed his caution, leaping, unsecured to the next bar, steadying himself against the pillar. He had a triumphal smile on his face. "You're right! It wasn't that bad!" He turned and leaped upward. "See you around!" he chirped, reaching the second to last bar. To his astonishment, he made it, with not a lot to spare. Looking down, he lowered his voice and warned, "Bob. Be damned sure you jump as high as you can, and Rusty. Don't even try it. After Bob's up, you jump, and I'll grab you!"

Rusty knew what Andy said was right, because he was fortunate to catch the bar he was standing on.

Snavely jumped, and his complexion whitened. He caught the bar, but one hand slipped. Andy anticipated the problem, and was bent over. He instantly grabbed Snavely's fatigue jacket, and with Andy's help, Snavely made it up. Balance was no longer the enemy. Space between bars was.

Andy looked down at Rusty who was preparing his jump.

"Snavely," Rusty breathed.

"What?" Andy asked.

Rusty noticed the stout fire plug arms of Snavely's. "I want Snavely to catch me."

Andy repositioned himself on the bar for Snavely to be above Rusty.

"Okay!" Andy barked. "I'm the coxswain!"

Andy noticed a surprised, humorous expression on Rusty's face. "When I say 'Ready,' you both answer 'Yes' when you're ready. When I say 'Go!' Rusty, you know what to do."

Andy yelled and Rusty sprang. Snavely grasped the outstretched arms and easily snapped Rusty up over the bar.

One bar to go. There was not a sound among the troops standing below the hill.

Rusty breathed, "Well, Andy, It's up to you. You've got the worse job."

Andy looked up as he talked, "You're right, Rusty, but it's not the distance. I'm a jumping fool. I can get to that bar easily. It's catching Snavely that's going to be the scary part."

"Well," Snavely answered confidently, "I trust you. Let's get this show on the road."

Andy's leap reached the bar with little frighteningly-little to spare. He readied himself.

"Rusty," Andy ordered, while wiping his palms on his pants. "Dry Snavely's wrists. Use the tail of your jacket. Now Bob," he began seriously, "Make your hands into fists and when I yell "Go!" You jump as high as you can with your fists stabbed into the air. Got that?"

Rusty was wiping Snavely's wrist. "Got it!" Snavely replied.

"Wait," Rusty cautioned. Looking at the muscular athlete, he asked, "How much do you weigh?"

"About two-fifty."

Rusty drew in a deep breath, looking up at Andy.

"I weigh a hundred-thirty. We can't risk you missing Bob. You catch me, Andy, and we'll each go for one of his arms."

"I like that idea better," Snavely offered.

"I do too," Andy agreed. "Okay, Rusty. Let's go."

Andy caught the lighter man who positioned himself across the bar, looking down at Snavely.

Snavely sprang into the sky. When he was at the top of his jump, Rusty grabbed his left arm with both hands; Andy the right. Snavely screamed, anticipating a miss. Steadily, the two raised the strong man up to the bar.

"God! I thought there for a minute you guys missed me!" Snavely cried.

Andy looked at Rusty. "I'm not sure I could have caught him by myself," he admitted. "Me neither," the newly-converted dissident responded. The three stood perched at the pinnacle, reveling in the deafening cheers of the company.

Above the noise, Rusty informed Snavely. "You could probably beat me arm rasslin'."

The three dropped bar by bar the ground. Yank Donnelly stood with an outstretched hand and a wide grin.

Perkins stepped up. "Nice job, fellows. It's a rather tough course."

"Rather tough course your ass!" Donnelly bellowed.

"Oh, come on sergeant, it doesn't look all that difficult," Perkins remarked safely.

"Country," Donnelly said firmly, 'Why don't you and your buddies take the lieutenant over the top?"

"Sure!" Andy responded. His tone exuded confidence.

Perkins whitened. "I don't believe it's necessary to put these soldiers through that again," he seethed, trying to hide a nervous chuckle.

"We don't mind," Snavely grunted.

The lieutenant looked up at the burly athlete.

"Is there something I said that you didn't understand, gyrene?"

"I think you're scared," Rusty intruded.

Perkins wheeled, "What did you say, soldier?"

Rusty smiled, scratching his neck. "I said I don't think you've got the balls to try it— sir."

Perkins glowered at Rusty. "Sergeant! Remand this man to the brig!"

Donnelly smiled. "I don't think that's necessary, Lieutenant."

The enraged lieutenant, unsure of what to do next, turned and stomped away. A disparaging chuckle rustled among the troops who were within earshot. This further angered the lieutenant. He intended to make it rough on the grizzled sergeant.

Andy, standing in the tight circle, asked, "Who was the other group to make it over that thing, Sarge?"

Outside the circle, Corporal Grounds shouted at the top of his lungs, "Earl Harrison— Maxwell Chapman— and— Yancy Donnelly! 1931!"

The company let out another deafening whoop.

Perkins located a megaphone and shouted, "Form up and return to camp!"

He glowered at Donnelly. "I'll take care of you later!"

Donnelly walked away in a mutinous stroll with the three beside him and the company following behind.

"Harrison," Donnelly reflected, "was a Limey... lanky like you, Country. You gotta' have a guy like that to get over those last bars, but then," he chuckled, "It takes a little more than being tall to pull that off. That's where teamwork comes in. It takes strength, agility and length, and you guys did it just like we did. I was afraid you wouldn't buddy up to help this big guy over the last one," he chuckled, eyeing Snavely.

"Who was the brute in your group?" Rusty asked.

"Me," Donnelly repeated, "and I was scared shitless, too."

That comment brought a laugh from anyone close enough to hear.

"Well, that was Rusty's idea," Snavely informed.

"I know. I could hear you, and that was smart," Donnelly responded.

"How high is that thing, Sarge?" Andy asked.

"It's ninety feet, Country. Those top two rungs are bastards. The next to last is nine feet apart and the final one is ten." That means..." He looked down at Rusty. "What's your name?"

"Rusty."

"How tall are you, Rusty?"

"5'8".

"That means that there's no damn way you could have reached the top one – top two, really – on your own, Rusty. I imagine Country here, had to give it all he had to get over the farthest one."

"I did," Andy agreed.

"Isn't that damned thing a little dangerous to have around?" Snavely asked, as the three were becoming familiar with their DI.

Donnelly wrinkled his nose. "I've fought that question ever since I've been here, and I've never been able to come to a conclusion about it. Right now, I'd have to say that I'm for it."

He turned scanning the three. "Y' know, you guys are goin' to get a lot of recognition for what you just did. I can't wait to tell Canali about it. They'll be a three-day pass that goes with it. I tell you," he gushed, "I couldn't be prouder of you guys. To think that happened on my watch!"

As the men broke toward camp, the three, feeling like kings, led the company in. Rusty Atkins now had two friends.

On the walk back, Rusty asked, "When we were on top of that thing, you said that you're a cocksman, Andy. What did you mean by that?"

Snavely broke into a laugh. "He said he was a coxswain, Rusty!"

"I guess I don't know what that is," he admitted.

"We'll get you a dictionary," Andy said, patting him on the back.

"I don't care what it means. I know it took my mind off what was scaring the shit out of me. I thought that's why you said it."

"I didn't think you were ever scared, Rusty," Snavely said. It was an honest comment. "You didn't have me fooled, Rusty," Andy chirped.

Lieutenant Perkins elected not to expose the confrontation he just experienced. Donnelly wasn't concerned whether he did or whether he didn't. The sergeant knew a confrontation was imminent.

Yank Donnelly's dissatisfaction with the exec officer was trying Captain Canali's patience. Although the CO sided with his top kick, he decided to wait for the current training rotation to conclude before he recommended replacing his adjutant. He had no way of knowing at the time that the decision would be accelerated. It happened on a maneuver that was to include a fifty mile forced march. The exercise began from a bivouac area set up on the middle ground on the Camp Pendleton reserve. The site was several miles from the initial training area in the vicinity of Sugarloaf Peak. The mission was to depart the area, and complete the march returning to the starting point. The difficulty was that the trek would commence at sundown in the dense, winding, heavily-wooded terrain. Lieutenant Perkins's assignment was to direct the march, having been given the azimuth settings. He carried the one compass.

Completing the mission was difficult in optimum conditions, but this particular night, a heavy rain that began the night before persisted. In the darkness and inclement weather, visibility was non-existent.

Rusty wandered into the command tent searching for the DI, who put Rusty in charge of a platoon, and the private wanted to review a couple of the instructions. The rain was pelting the large canvas tent as he searched for Donnelly. He found the sergeant along with the CO, Grounds and Lieutenant Perkins standing around a map that was illuminated by a gas lamp. Canali was giving instructions. Unnoticed, Rusty sauntered in and stood next to his first sergeant. He discovered the subject was the upcoming march, and the map was a picture of it. The scrawny private was entranced by the instructions, and how to follow the path. He listened with anticipation.

Canali dismissed the group, and Rusty, to Donnelly's surprise, heard the bulk of the order.

"Understand all that, kid?" Donnelly asked. Donnelly was warming up to Rusty, and selected him to determine if the raw recruit had any leadership qualities. After the exercise at "The Hill," Donnelly thought he identified a certain maturity in the raw youngster.

"Sure, Sarge," Rusty replied, adding, "But I'd be a hell of a lot more comfortable if you were packin' that compass."

Donnelly laughed. "Maybe not. These are unfamiliar surroundings to me. Anyway, the shave tail should be able to follow azimuth settings. Canali gave them all to him."

The weather was miserable, and to compound the difficulty, the company found itself in steep narrow paths interrupted by interstices along the way. Keeping the company in one string was a problem. The trails were steep and rugged, making the project more difficult. The rain was heavy and the night was black. They had been out an hour-and-a-half.

Rusty caught up with Donnelly. Rusty was breathing heavily. "He's got to have missed a compass setting, Sarge," Rusty huffed. He could barely make out the silhouette of Donnelly's big nose.

Donnelly turned. "What makes you think so?"

"I saw the map in the command shack. I made a sort of picture. What do you say when you can see something when you can't see it? You know what I'm sayin'...?"

"Mental picture?" Donnelly prompted.

"Yeah. Mental. And we shoulda' started to head left back there a ways. I saw that topo map, and it didn't go up, and we're goin' up..."

"What do you know about a topographical map?"

"I learned to read 'em when my old man worked in the mines."

Donnelly chuckled. "And you're telling me you can see in this shit?"

"I grew up huntin' varmints in hill country just like this, and I'm used to findin' my way in the dark. And I can tell you, Sarge. We're gettin' fuckin' lost."

"You're certain?"

"Damn straight."

"What do you think we ought to do?" Suddenly Donnelly decided he'd made the right choice with Rusty—he needed him now.

"I ain't the boss," Rusty returned quietly.

"Well, I'm sure as hell not going to approach the asshole. He got us into this mess. He's gonna have to get us out."

Donnelly waited in the downpour considering his options. The sound of rain mixed with the staccato noise of boots striking the wet earth intruded the silence. "Yeah. I do know what to do," he finally admitted. "What chance do we have at getting back on course?"

Rusty's answer was condescending. "You know better'n' that, Sarge."

"Where do you think we are, Rusty?"

"Well," Rusty began slowly. "We're about halfway from where we ought to be, I'd guess."

"That doesn't tell me shit! Where we ought to be is back at camp, god dammit!" Donnelly snapped.

"Then if it was up to me, I'd turn around," Rusty said.

"Think you can you find your way back?" Donnelly asked.

"Cat have an ass?"

Donnelly issued a tired chuckle. "Then I'm gonna' get Grounds to pass the word, and those who want to go back with us, can."

"You can't see my smile, Sarge, but as soon as you're ready, I'm ready."

"You'd better be right, Rusty," Donnelly growled.

"Just get Grounds. I'll wait here."

Donnelly trudged away in the darkness.

Shortly he returned. "Grounds thinks he's got the word spread."

"Okay. Let's go," the private said.

The company, whatever there was of it, followed Rusty and Donnelly back through the serpentine trail through the woods. Not until they reached their destination, would there be any way of determining how many followed. Approaching an hour's time, Rusty stumbled onto a muddy road. He couldn't see it, but he knew where he was. He stopped for Donnelly to join him.

"Yank. We're probably a half-hour from bivouac. I got no idea how we ended up here, but this is in the area where Hubbard saved my life. I can smell it."

The lights from the camp appeared through the rain.

Donnelly caught up with Grounds. The train of troops was dutifully following behind. Entering the marshaling yard, Donnelly ordered his aide, "Assemble the squad leaders and get a count. I'm going to go see the captain. You'd better come with me, Rusty."

"Mind if I chase down Hubbard first?"

Donnelly inhaled deeply, "Come into the command tent after you see him."

Canali was reading under the light of the Coleman lantern when Donnelly burst into the tent. The captain turned, removing his feet from the ammo box he was using for an ottoman.

He checked his watch. "What're you doing here at this time, Yank?"

"We got lost."

"If you got lost, what are you doing here?"

"We turned around and came back."

Canali sprang to his feet. "Wait a minute! Wait a minute! Who came back?"

At that moment, Rusty burst into the tent, followed by Andy.

"What the hell's going on here?" he demanded.

"Captain," Donnelly began to explain, motioning to Rusty. This is Private Atkins, and Private Hubbard who both made it over that obstacle course, a couple of weeks ago..."

Canali softened. "Oh yeah. I meant to have you guys in my office. I'm sorry for that. Time just got away." He squinted at Andy, remembering he forgot about Corpsman's school. But he didn't want to talk about that now. "What's going on?" he asked.

"Captain," Donnelly began, "Rusty—Private Atkins here," motioning to Atkins, "discovered that we were lost."

Canali's brow furrowed. "You what? You didn't have the coordinates!"

"I was in here when you were giving instructions to Lieutenant Perkins," Rusty explained.

Canali was confused and angry. "Now what the hell's going on here? Did the entire company get back?"

Andy interrupted. "No sir. Some are still out there."

The captain turned to Andy. "Out where! What do you mean?"

"Well," Andy started, "I was sort of in the middle of the battalion. We were walking in single file..."

"Single file?" Canali bellowed.

"Well, yes sir."

"240 troops marching single file! Where the hell were you that you had to walk in single file?" the captain asked in disbelief.

"In the mountains, someplace," Andy explained.

"Where were you in all this, Yank?" Canali grilled.

"Bringin' up the rear like I shoulda been," the longtime DI returned.

The captain returned his focus on Andy, attempting to get the picture. "What were you saying, private?"

"We were trying to get through the narrow trail, rocks and all, when someone yelled 'turn around, we're going back!'"

"And you did—just like that?"

"Oh you bet, Sir! We all knew we were lost!"

"And you all turned around—just like that?" Canali's frown was heavy.

"I don't know about how many ahead of us turned around, sir. You couldn't see. I know the ones around me didn't waste any time. We knew we wanted out of there."

Canali removed his garrison cap, scratched his full head of black hair, murmuring, "Jesus Christ!" He turned to Rusty. "So you're the guy who determined that the company was going the wrong direction?"

"Yes, sir."

"And what made you so certain?"

"Like I said," Rusty answered evenly, "I saw the map you were showin' the lieutenant."

"What were you doing in the command tent?"

"I was lookin' for Sergeant Donnelly."

Donnelly came to Rusty's defense. "I know it sounds far-fetched sir, but he had me convinced..."

Canali raised his open palms interrupting his DI. "No explanation needed, Yank. I knew a guy at the Academy who could do that very same thing. He would never get lost—never ever seemed to need a compass."

Glancing at Rusty, he commented, "I tend to think you knew what you were doing." He looked at the two privates, "Go get some sleep."

Rusty and Andy broke for the tent door. Canali turned to Donnelly. "Get me a count, Yank." The captain drew a deep breath. "We'll sort this out in the morning."

Clouds hung heavy, and although the rain had let up, a slight mist persisted, and fog shrouded the wooded hills above the camp. Troops stood in a long serpentine line waiting their turn for breakfast.

"A hundred seventy-one," Canali breathed. He sat at a wooden table in the command tent with Yank Donnelly. "That leaves seventy out there someplace, counting Perkins." Canali took a sip on his coffee tin, while he scanned the map laid out before him. "Wonder where those strays could be," he sighed.

Donnelly standing, also studying the map, breathed, "Maybe we ought to go get the kid." His comment was said in jest, but Canali took him seriously, "Go get him."

Donnelly leaned out the tent, and yelled, "Grounds! Go get Atkins!"

The cadre caught up with Rusty standing in line. "The old man wants you."

Walking away from Andy and Snavely, Andy remarked loudly, "There he goes. We can say we knew him when."

Rusty turned, flashing a smile.

Walking up the line, a large, swarthy marine, seeing Rusty heading toward the front of the line with the corporal, seethed, "Look at the scrawny little runt. He really thinks he's somebody."

"What's his problem?" Grounds asked.

"I don't know," Rusty replied unemotionally, "But if he insults me again, I'm going to knock his ass off."

Grounds looked down at the gaunt recruit, and smiled, "Oh?"

The private stood with Donnelly studying the map. The captain remained seated. Rusty ran his finger along the map, stopping. "We were about here when we turned back."

Canal rubbed his chin. "You were approaching Margarita peak. That's all rough hiking trails."

"Well, that's where we were."

The captain continued massaging his cheek, murmuring to himself, "How the hell could you get way up there?" He glanced at the upstart private. "They couldn't have gone much further in that direction."

"No. I agree," Rusty answered.

"Where could they be?" the CO wondered barely aloud.

"Well," Rusty analyzed, picking up Canali's habit of rubbing his chin, "I'm guessing they turned right."

"Why do you say that?" Canali asked.

Again, Rusty scratched his cheek. "Looking at the topo, that land slips off to the south. We were going right all night long, and that took us up, but, you notice," he drew a path with his finger, "if they continue to the right, it levels out. That lieutenant already has one foot shorter than the other one, and he had to know he was lost, and I'm sure he kept going in a circle. Since he found some terrain that he could handle, I'm thinking he'll pull up and wait for daylight. So," Rusty stopped tracing on the map. "I'm guessing he's right about here." Rusty gave a final tap with his finger.

"Well," the captain surmised, "That puts them in the vicinity of the ammunition depot. Maybe we can raise someone there. I'll give it a try."

The captain rose from the bench. "That'll be all, private."

Donnelly followed Rusty out of the tent. "What was the remark about the lieutenant having one leg shorter than the other?"

"Yeah, that just came out. When I was a kid we used to say it about guys who'd always get lost. Tell the captain I'm sorry about that, will you?"

"No need. If he was pissed, you'd have known it."

"Ammo Depot," the toneless reply came.

"This is Captain Canali, of Item Company of the fourth regiment. We've got some troops missing, and we think they may be in your area."

The clerk's tone changed. "Let me get my section chief, sir."

Canali waited.

"Yes, Captain. This is Major Gregg Babcock."

"Major, this is Frank Canali, CO of Item Company out of the fourth. We've lost about seventy troops, and have reason to believe they are in your vicinity."

"Hang on, Captain."

Canali heard the sound of the receiver dropping on the desk, and sat through an awkward delay before the major returned. "Sorry about the wait. One of my men tells me that a few men belonging to that bunch you're calling about, just wandered in. A mortar outfit is intending to start firing that new four-deuce, and I wanted to call the CO about it, if there are more troops out there."

"I understand."

"Yeah, and we can't have those things flyin' around with your lost troops."

Canali cringed when the officer said, "your."

"We'll round up the rest of them and I'll get the mortar CO to give you a call. I really don't know why they're having exercises in this soup in the first place. Anyway, give me your number, Captain, and we'll be getting back to you one way or another. It's a good thing you called. They were to begin firing at 0800."

Canali checked his watch. Ten minutes away... He looked over at Donnelly, who was seated nearby. "Your private was right on. They found Perkins' men around the armory someplace."

An hour later, Canali got his call.

"This is First Lieutenant Wagner, Captain. I'm in charge of the mortar exercise. We got your troops. A couple of them should to get to the dispensary."

"That comes as no surprise, Lieutenant. How do we go about recovering them?"

"Well, I've been thinking about that. It was probably a good thing you called. With this restricted visibility, we were debating whether or not to go ahead with our training. Now, with the interruption, we've decided to abort. Your troops are pretty wet and cold, and since we've already got trucks and an ambulance, would it help if we ferry them back to the base? We can send out for transportation to bring our own troops in. They're not in any distress and okay to hang out here."

"Would it help? God Lieutenant! I guess it would help! Is there a Lieutenant Perkins with them?"

"Yes. You want him back?"

"Negative, Lieutenant. I prefer he stays with the troops."

"I can't say as I blame you Captain."

Frank Canali Jr., was an officer's officer. Born Antonio Francis in the Bronx, New York, the stocky 5' 11' 180-pound specimen was a superb athlete. His father, Antonio, "Tony" began his career as an iron worker-steeplejack laboring on many of New York's original skyscrapers. It wasn't long before Tony was the owner of a medium-sized steel erecting company, and planned for his son to become president. Upon graduating high school, Frank was offered a wrestling scholarship at Fordham. His father wasn't pleased when his son chose the Marine Academy over the college down the street. But Frank was disciplined mentally as well as physically, and was awarded an engineering scholarship to the Quantico, Virginia institution. In his senior year, Canali was awarded the Helms award in wrestling, and graduated at the top of his class. His father now knew, with his son a military academy graduate and war on the horizon, his dream of his son becoming president may never come to pass.

Canali sat before Colonel Henry Stuart's broad desk at regimental headquarters in San Diego. Outside, in the background, an expansive lawn dotted with palms, extended to the shore of the blue Pacific. In opposite corners of Stuart's office, the Stars and Stripes and the flag of the Corps stood. The banner Semper Fidelis adorned one wall.

The captain came with the expectation he was getting another field assignment which he preferred over his current desk job. With the political scene in the Far East deteriorating, the Marine Corps determined that combat training emulating jungle situations would be in order. For some, boot camp would be cut short. Certain men in Item Company would be affected.

"So, Frank," Stuart explained, "We'll combine a section of armor and artillery with the infantry and get situated down south of here someplace where it's jungle conditions."

"Sounds like about regiment size," Canali put in.

"Yeah. That's about right. So," the colonel continued, "pick out a hundred of your best troops, give them two week's furlough, and we'll get this show on the road. In the meantime, you'll need additional cadre, so get with your DI and select five of your best out of that bunch, give them a stripe before they leave, and explain to them what their duties are going to be when they get back."

"Well," Canali said rising, stating cheerfully, "I'm finally going to get back in the dirt with my troops..."

"'Fraid not," The colonel interrupted, tossing two packets of gold oak leaf insignia on the desk top. "I want you overseeing this operation—not playing in it."

Donnelly and Grounds sat in Canali's office. Canali was wearing his new Major's insignia and the two EM's quickly congratulated him.

Canali outlined the changes which would take place immediately, tossing buck sergeant stripes to Grounds and sergeant major's stripes to Donnelly.

"So Grounds, you're an E-5 and the new DI, and Yank, now that you're an E-8, you'll be my acting exec."

"I'm not going to do that!" Donnelly bristled.

"Why not? Is there something about promotions you don't like, Yank?"

"I'm just not desk material," Donnelly protested.

"Does that mean I have to go out and find another exec? I'm not too good at that you know."

"You don't have to go any further. The man you need is right here in the company."

"What are you getting at?"

"Atkins," the sergeant replied.

Canali's face contorted, "Who?"

"Rusty Atkins—the kid that was in the tent with us—the one that guessed where the troops were."

Canali wheeled in disbelief, "The recruit?"

"That's him," Donnelly replied confidently.

"Why, he's just a kid—he's not even an officer!"

"Brass doesn't mean shit—uh—'scuse me Capt— Major, but you know what I'm sayin'—I don't mean to be insultin' you."

"No, and I'm not taking it that way. You know you're going to have to form a cadre. Since you're so high on this kid, use him there."

"You can be certain I will!" Donnelly cast his eyes to the floor, and spoke softly. "If there's anything I'm good at, Sir, it's pickin' troops who can get the job done, and Atkins is one of 'em. I know he's young and rough, but you'd do yourself proud if you keep him in mind."

"Okay," Canali sighed. "I'll keep him in mind."

Donnelly turned to Grounds. "Sorry to break this to you, Don, but I'm still the DI—okay with you, Major?"

Canali conceded shrugging his shoulders. "We'll find something for you to do, Grounds."

****

June 30, 1941:

Andy, Rusty and Bob Snavely stood at attention in Canali's office. The major entered.

"At ease!"

The three assumed parade rest.

"The reason you're here, gentlemen, is that I've wanted to congratulate you on your conquering that obstacle course, and with all the activity that's going on, I've let it get away from me. As Yank has probably told you, you're the first in eleven years to get through the thing—the second ever. Yank was in the first group. You probably didn't know that..."

"Grounds told us," Rusty interrupted.

Canali responded to the error in protocol with mild askance.

"Yes. Well, it took guts, and I planned on giving you men a three-day pass, but now that's not necessary since you'll going on furlough. Yank informed me the three of you will be promoted to PFC along with the other two who have been selected as cadre, and your courage on the obstacle course will be placed in your records. So, you should feel good about that." Both Snavely and Atkins smiled broadly. Andy's expression remained stoic.

"Also," the major continued, "The time off should do you some good. Dismissed!"

Snavely clapped his hands and skipped out of the room. Canali looked at Andy quizzically. "What is it, Hubbard. You don't act as though any of this agrees with you."

"Did my transfer to Corpsman School come through, Sir?"

"Oh hell, I forgot about that! You'll have to wait until we complete this cycle, and I'll be certain to take care of it then."

Andy saluted and stepped out.

"What about you, Atkins? You don't seem to be too happy either."

"Oh, I'm happy about the promotion..."

"What about going home?"

"I don't have a home."

****

July 12, 1941 Denver:

Andy glanced across the street at the clock on the bus station wall as the cleaner steam pressed his dress blue trousers. The launderer had taken too long pressing his jacket. He would look sharp all right, but time was becoming a problem. He still had to change his clothes in the bus station lavatory in time to make the bus.

The driver stowed Andy's heavy bag in the bus luggage compartment, then reached for Andy's guitar.

"Thanks," Andy offered. "I'll take my guitar with me."

The tall handsome marine entered the bus, taking the front seat opposite the driver. The ride into Cottonwood should take an hour-and-a-half. He should be there by one in the afternoon.

The country was its typical desert yellow, and he mentally made a comparison to the lush green country where he spent the past six weeks. He watched the flat ground flash by, not remembering the endless barren landscape. This wasn't his kind of environment, and he was comfortable knowing he had seen another part of the world. He thought of his new found friends—some interested him greatly—others he tolerated. He liked Bob Snavely, but knew the association was more of acquaintance than close friendship, since there was so little they had in common. Rusty Atkins was another matter. Andy was beginning to admire the recalcitrant waif from Mississippi, seeing a personality and talent he was daily dissecting. He appreciated the dedication, loyalty and drive in the rough cut youngster. Also, Andy could see a latent strain of intelligence few of his peers recognized in Atkins' persona at the time. He knew Yank Donnelly was aware of it.

His thoughts wandered to the kind of life he would lead as a doctor with plenty of money. One thing was for sure; he'd have a telephone. The unavailability made life so awkward, but luckily the Vogels now had a phone. Andrea would meet him at the station.

The bus pulled alongside the chipped stucco wall of Thurston's ancient gas station. Glancing out the side window, he saw her standing under the canopy. She was searching the bus for him, and he knew he could see her and she couldn't see him. He placed his hat on his head, gathered his bag and guitar and stepped down out of the bus. Then she saw him.

The reunion wasn't a reckless impassioned rush to embrace; rather it was a somber recognition. He stepped toward her, removing his hat. She softly fell to his chest while he silently embraced her.

"You look okay," he murmured.

Without moving, she answered, "It seems an eternity since I last held you."

He pressed her away. "Is there someplace where we can be alone?"

"I'm taking you out to the farm. I told Millie you were coming in and she's expecting you. There will be time for us to be alone after that."

Andy felt a special appreciation for Andrea at that moment.

After pulling out of the station and heading east through the buffalo grass and wheat fields, she asked, "What's it like?"

"Some bad, some good. Everything is different."

"What are the people like?"

"Not like they are around here. That part of this escapade has probably been good for me."

"You're there with your college roommate. How's he taking all of this?"

Andy chuckled. "Snavely? Oh, it's probably the perfect fit for him. He's a rough and tumble guy. He's no student, so he should be a Marine."

"When that girl answered your phone, I thought she was yours."

"No. She was Snavely's."

"I didn't know that."

Andy looked over at her behind the steering wheel. The silhouette of her face against the rolling pastures raised Andy's emotions. "You are beautiful, Andrea, in case I forget to tell you."

"Not just okay?"

"Okay, too."

"You're a pretty impressive guy yourself in that uniform," she answered flashing him a gentle smile.

"What's happening with Cat?" he asked, treading into delicate waters.

She turned to him. "You gave him that name, and it was a convenient, affectionate one— as nicknames often are—and maybe it still is for you, but I'll never call him that again."

He returned a warm, indulgent smile, "So how is it with Chattman?"

She inhaled deeply, and began. "You'll never know what it was like that night you came into the gym. I must have been frozen, because I tried so hard to catch you—but I couldn't. Reflexively, she rubbed her eye with the back of her wrist, beginning to cry—but I couldn't!"

He gently touched her cheek.

Quickly, she gained her composure. "I knew immediately that the son of a bitch set us up!"

"He did that for sure," Andy put in.

"Then he has the gall to want to take me home!"

"How did you get home?"

"I walked home in the rain! You think I'm going to get in a car with that asshole again?" She shook her head negatively, turning to Andy. "I'm sorry, darling, to have to use such words, but somehow, they fit precisely."

Upon cue, the two chuckled.

"You see him in the store, don't you?"

Her tone became relaxed. "He comes in, but he skulks around like a whipped pup. I know he looks at me, but he's very careful to avoid eye contact. The whole family has, for whatever reason, changed their attitude toward dad. Jack treats me with respect—he always has, but now he treats dad okay. In fact, dad mentioned to Jack that the ranch ought to have to pay sales tax on what it buys, and Jack didn't object."

"What caused the change of heart?"

"I wish I knew. I know it somehow involves something that Royce Palmer did."

"Royce Palmer? What could he possibly have to do with anything?"

"Again, I wish I knew. I overheard dad telling mom something that Palmer told dad about some lady in Philadelphia, and the store. The part that I heard was that for a period of time, something could somehow go wrong about the store—and not, in any circumstance, to let Jack know that Palmer made the information available to dad."

"What could that be about?" Andy asked, genuinely interested.

"I've told you all I know—I can't get anything out of mom, and she made me promise I wouldn't ask dad anything. She did let it slip that dad had supposedly gotten some letter, and supposedly still has, and it is supposed to have some important information."

"That's a lot of supposing," Andy mused.

"Oh, I know, but somehow or other it's put Jack in some sort of a pickle, and he's cow-towed to dad since then."

"That Palmer," Andy murmured. ""He's a tricky one himself."

"Do you like him?"

Andy considered the question. "I have to admit that I do. I like his brain. How about you?"

"I used to hate him—always making passes at mom."

"Didn't she object?"

"She didn't like it, but she knew how tight he and MacGregor were—and, mom, the subservient German wife always kept it to herself."

"Maybe it paid off."

"I think it must have. I know I don't hate Palmer anymore, now that I know he's not in Jack MacGregor's corner."

"Now if you could eliminate the Chattman thing..."

"It's going to be a thing for only three more weeks."

"What do you mean?"

"I'll be going to college."

"At Denver?"

"Sure. I told you that."

"You said you were planning on going to DU to study journalism. You never wrote me that you already did it."

"I thought I told you. Anyway, in a short time I'll be out of here."

"Congratulations."

"Can you believe it? Free at last!"

Andrea steered her '34 Ford into the Hubbard farm yard. She leaned over kissing Andy. "Here we are, Soldier." She released him with the reminder, "Come see me when you're ready."

The Hubbard family, expecting Andy, respectfully waited for the Ford to exit the yard before they broke from the kitchen screen door. Ruthie was in front, so Andy hoisted her up on his hip, knocking his white hat to the dirt. Mildred immediately picked it up and began frantically dusting it. His brother was next, clasping Andy's free hand.

Glancing at Sam, who had visibly grown during Andy's absence, Andy cautioned, "Careful, there. I'll be needing those fingers."

Now, he hugged his mother while still holding his sister. He looked over at Walter, who simply nodded. Andy nodded in return. Sam picked up Andy's bag and guitar, and the Hubbard family walked toward the farmhouse, Ruthie still on her brother's arm.

Sam wanted to know about the Marines, but Andy centered the talk around the farm, what was happening, how things were growing and the like. Andy asked whether his dad had gotten a tractor. Sam insisted on showing off a Greyhound bus-IHC hybrid affair Walter acquired to haul hay and grain wagons, with the assertion a new tractor would be the next acquisition. Millie was simply happy to have her son home.

The following afternoon, Andy drove into Cottonwood to see Andrea. When entering the store, he was told that Andrea was at home and she would expect to see him there. Andy had never been in the Vogel house, which caused him some uneasiness.

Andrea's mother, Anna, met him at the door, cordially inviting him inside the spacious home. She remarked she was somewhat disappointed he wasn't wearing his uniform. Andrea had given a glowing description of her young Marine. Andrea's younger sister Helga and her mother entertained Andy while Andrea primped in her upstairs bedroom. Finally, she came down the stairs, and the two were on their way.

Inside the old Chevy, Andrea remarked, "Tell Millie I'll trade cars with her."

"Your Ford is worth more than this old crate," Andy said.

"I still would do it—I like this little car."

"I don't think Mom would ever part with Olive Oyl, but I'll mention it to her." Andy took a deep breath. "Where shall we go?"

"Let's go to our spot."

The cottonwoods hung heavy down along the creek bank. They selected a place where the sun was blotted by the heavy foliage. Andy lifted the back seat, and secured the wool blanket, spreading it on the grass under a mammoth branch.

The two began petting when Andrea began unbuttoning Andy's trousers.

"Andrea!" he gushed, "What do you think you're doing?"

"Do I have to explain it to you?" she responded coyly.

"Old Man Schatzaeder will catch us!"

"All Old Man Schatzaeder can do is make us stop," she chirped.

Andy rolled over unbuttoning her dress, and smiled, "I guess that's a risk we'll have to take."

Late in the afternoon, after three opportunities, Herman Schatzaeder missed his chance.

The two planned to go to a diner, then a movie. While dressing, Andy chuckled softly.

"What is that devious laugh about?" she asked.

"I was just thinking," Andy revealed, "That one of the last times I was with Chattman, he reminded me that you were his girl."

"I was never his girl!" She snapped. "It bothers me to think that we went out of our way to be so good to him. Look what it got us. What did you say to him when he said that?"

"It wasn't confrontational. I just said that I'd remember that he said it."

"It should have been confrontational!"

"I wouldn't allow him to crow like that now—-but like you, I was being nice to him."

She embraced him. "I'm your girl and you just remember I said it."

Later in the evening the two entered the theater. After they found their seats, Andrea breathed, "Oh god—look who's across the aisle—I think we should leave."

"I'm not leaving," Andy announced.

When the lights dimmed and the feature began, Andrea nudged Andy. "Guess who just walked out."

"I noticed," Andy chuckled.

"Do you think he saw us?"

Andy smiled, nodding, "Of course Chattman saw us."

Andy spent the remainder of his furlough with the family, and Andrea, seeing neighbors when time permitted. One day, Andrea drove out to the farm. Andy saddled two horses and they rode out to the spring. Andy brought along his guitar and much to Andrea's delight, the two spent the afternoon making love and Andy singing and playing his instrument. It wasn't until the next day, Andy realized he'd left his guitar in a grove of junipers at the spring. He saddled Barney and rode out to get his prized hobby.

Riding down the grove to where he left the instrument, he looked across the fence line and saw Jack MacGregor on his horse. He waved at the rancher, who returned the salute. The two met at the fence. Andy dismounted and hopped the fence. MacGregor slid off his horse.

Andy extended his hand. "Hello, Mister MacGregor."

The handsome-graying land baron smiled and shook Andy's hand. Andy noticed the deep creases in the rancher's tanned cheeks. It suited him, Andy thought, but showed age.

"Andy, call me Jack will you? You're not a kid anymore."

"Okay, Jack. I prefer that. How've you been?"

"Oh," he began slowly. "Not so good, sometimes."

"Why is that?"

"I know what happened and why you left school and joined the service. I'm damned sorry and ashamed about it all."

"You didn't have anything to do with it." Andy said easily.

MacGregor turned and looked into the afternoon sun. The creases grew deeper, and his blue eyes seemed to glaze as he murmured, "Cat's my kid. That apple doesn't fall far from the tree."

"Well Jack," Andy consoled, "I grew up with Cat. I still like him and understand why he did what he did."

The grizzled rancher turned to Andy. "You like him and understand what he did because that's the kind of guy you are. Not many would do that. I just wish my kid could be more like you. Cat's got too much of his granddad in him, and I can't do a damned thing about that."

"No, you can't."

The rancher looked down scratching his thumbnail with his other thumb. "Sometimes, I don't much like who people think I am. Hell, Clinton Durkee thinks I'm in bed with the devil. I admire Clinton and the way he runs his operation. I don't like sheep, but I don't deny him the right to raise 'em. He thinks I do, but it's my dad who started all that. He can raise whatever the hell he wants, but he doesn't know I feel like that. I know what you did for that ram of his was a stroke of genius." He looked up at Andy. "You're going to make a hell of a doctor. And that daughter of Durkee's is one fine girl. She's helping your mother. Hell, Andy, if I'm a little aggressive, I apologize. I like to win—that's how I'm wired. When I didn't want your mom to get that teaching job, it was just greed. I admit that, and it was wrong—and I respect your dad, although I don't ever see us playin' cards together..."

Andy chuckled, "No—there's not much chance of that."

"Well—I'm ramblin'—what kind of a doctor are you going to be, anyhow?"

Andy thought before answering, "Maybe psychiatry."

"What the hell's that?"

"It's a study about why guys go nuts."

MacGregor burst into laughter, slapping Andy on the shoulder. "I liked you when you were just a little buster in grade school—you weren't afraid of me or nobody!"

An awkward pause ensued.

MacGregor studied Andy. The brim of his hat barely allowed eye contact. "Maybe you'll know someday how it is when you got kids of your own and one of 'em screws up. Does that make any sense to you?"

Andy merely nodded.

"Well—I figured you'd understand."

"You said it earlier, Jack. The apple doesn't fall far from the tree."

Andy's leave came to a close. The family, plus Andrea, waited under the canopy for the bus that came too soon. Changes were on the way.

PART II

Millie walked without purpose along the bank, much like the ancient mariner lost at sea, wandering in no direction against a deliberate wind. In the heavens, dark and foreboding skies mirrored her son's misfortune, and she saw him somewhere among the many cattails in the shallow water, bending with the others in the gale, caught, innocent and unable to gain freedom from the sinister force that held them hostage. She was powerless, and could only pledge her faith to the will of God that this tempest would someday abate, and her son, Andy, would again be free.

CHAPTER 18

MIRAMAR TRAINING FACILITY
San Diego, California, July 29, 1941

The '35 Dodge taxi weaved its way through the palms, down a dusty winding road to the Marine station. Andy was mildly annoyed at having to pay cab fare to his barracks, but he didn't want to wait another three hours for the five o'clock shuttle to show up. The cab approached a row of Spanish-style small apartments. Andy figured that the scene didn't resemble a military installation; it was more of a neighborhood, and he mentioned it to the driver.

"This isn't military," the driver replied. "It's Universal Studio's property, and the Marines are leasing it for your training."

"What was Universal using it for?"

"Making cowboy movies."

"I wouldn't think it would be big enough for a training base," Andy commented.

"It's over a thousand acres, and it borders Federal land. It's big enough."

"Well, I guess then it is, but I wonder why there's no activity," Andy mused.

"Be patient."

The cab pulled to a stop alongside a small building.

"Two seventy-five," the cabbie murmured. "Doesn't seem right to have to charge you…"

"I thought that, too," Andy replied, fingering out the change, grabbing his bag and guitar.

Seeing the sign "Orderly Room," Andy opened the screen and walked in.

"Orders?" the clerk sitting at the desk asked.

Andy unfolded his papers, handing them to the aide, who perused them, then instructed "Number four." He arose, pointing, "Halfway down the road on your left. Numbers' on the Building."

"Thanks," Andy replied, heading in the given direction. He located the small structure, and entered without knocking. Inside the simple one room abode, were four bunk-style beds, a writing desk against a wall, a table and chairs in the center. At the base of each bed was a footlocker. He noticed that one of the beds had been occupied. Andy tossed his guitar on one bunk, and began filling his foot locker. He searched the room and was surprised to find a bathroom and shower, plus a small cloak room. A set of corporal's uniforms hung neatly on a rack in the room. He was pleased that his living quarters would be so comfortable and private. It was certainly a departure from barracks where everything was exposed. Meanwhile, he was wondering why there was no activity anywhere. When he had finished arranging his things, he decided to walk around the grounds in an attempt to find the reason for the inactivity. A short walk solved his quandary. A few hundred yards down a gravel road, he found the motor pool where a number of vehicles were being serviced. After a few questions, he learned that Rusty Atkins was close by somewhere—that Rusty didn't go on leave and stayed with Yank Donnelly to help set up camp arrangements. Walking around the corner of a building that had been used as a film studio, he saw Atkins leaning on the hood of a strange looking vehicle, talking with Sergeant Donnelly. Andy strode up. Upon seeing Andy, Rusty broke into a wide smile stepping quickly toward his friend.

"Andy! Am I glad to see you!"

Rusty vigorously shook Andy's hand. Andy nodded to Donnelly.

"How's it goin,' Country?" Donnelly replied to Andy's silent greeting.

"Good, Sarge."

"Yank," Rusty began. "Is it okay for me to take this jeep and show Andy around?"

"Be my guest," the first sergeant replied.

Rusty motioned to the canvas passenger bucket seat of the topless vehicle, and Andy hopped in.

"What is this thing?" Andy asked as the engine came alive.

Rusty let out the clutch and the vehicle eased forward, "It's called a jeep—a utility vehicle. There's a bunch of 'em here."

"It's a cute little thing" Andy commented as they rounded a curve, moving through a row of buildings scattered amongst a heavy stand of palms.

"It is, and it goes anyplace," Rusty replied, pointing to a long building. "There's the mess hall..." then past a cluster of medium-sized buildings, he explained, "The enlisted men's barracks." He pointed to his left, "Across the road's the dispensary..." Continuing along the street, Rusty intoned, "Officer's quarters... the theater... the tank marshaling yard..." He pointed again, "Those are the barracks for the guys in artillery."

"You know your way around, don't you?"

"Yeah."

"Why didn't you go home?"

Rusty mulled the question, "Didn't have anything to go home to. Besides, Yank was grateful for the help."

"What *are* we going to be doing?"

Rusty inhaled deeply, glancing over to Andy. "We'll have our hands full. There's going to be a thousand guys here... infantry, artillery, armor and whatever else."

"And...?"

"And five hundred of that bunch will be infantry. Our job... yours, mine and the other four will be in charge of them... we'll have a hundred each to ride herd on."

"What about the other five hundred?"

"We don't have anything to do with them—just the infantry."

Andy did a quick math. "I don't understand. You said five hundred—a hundred apiece, but there's six of us."

Again, Rusty inhaled deeply. "You'll be in charge of a hundred men, as will the other four guys. I'll be in charge of you five."

Andy chuckled, "So you're going to be my boss?"

Rusty smiled. "Yep."

"What does 'riding herd' involve?"

"Mainly keeping track."

"Keeping track?"

"That's part of it. You'll be present when the platoon leaders take roll call—help in marching, mess, mail call—make sure the soldier has whatever he needs—that includes assisting in anything that the platoon leaders need help, as far as management goes."

"What about discipline?"

"That too."

"We can't be responsible for that!" Andy protested.

Again Rusty took a deep breath. "Do what you have to do, and if you can't, that's what MP's are for."

"So what do I call you?"

"I'm the section leader. You five will be section aides."

"Sounds like we should be getting extra pay."

"There'll be perks that go with it."

"Like what?"

"No KP, no detail, or guard duty, no inspections. We don't stand in line for mess, and we get a lot more freedom about getting off post after hours. You saw our billets."

"Yeah—that's a big time improvement. There will be four of us in that room, I take it."

"That's right."

"Who are they?"

"You, me, Snavely, and some Jap."

"*Jap?*" Andy asked, incredulous, "*What Jap?*"

"All I know about him is his name."

"Which is?"

"Tanaka."

"And what's *his* job?"

"He's supposed to teach us how to kill other Japs."

"God!" Andy responded, "I wonder what else is new."

"Well, the day after tomorrow, Canali will fill us in. That's where you'll find out."

Rusty glanced at Andy's plain shirt. "Where are your stripes?"

"I don't have them on yet."

"You need to get 'em on. We'll get over to the quartermaster and get them sewed on. You'll need all the rank you can get. After we look the place over, we'll go over and get your stuff. Then we can go to the PX where you can buy me a beer."

During four beers, Andy gave Rusty a rundown on his trip home, and Rusty filled Andy in on what he had gained in the interim.

The two sat chatting at the table when Bob Snavely came in, eager to talk. Snavely arranged his possessions in their new environment then headed to the PX, glad that was where is friends were. The talk had centered around each individual's situation when Snavely asked Andy his age.

"I'm twenty, and you?"

"The same," Snavely returned. "How about you, Rusty?" the burly ex-athlete asked.

"I'm twenty-two."

"*Twenty-two*? Where'd you go after high school?"

"I never went to high school," Rusty said quietly.

"Never went to high school?" Snavely grilled. "Hell, I never met anyone who didn't at least go to high school."

Rusty was bent over, casually smoking a cigarette, his elbows on his knees. He glanced up at Snavely. "Now you have."

Andy was registering this conversation with more than a casual interest, since his own roots had spawned similar families. In an attempt to diffuse the impact of Rusty's admission, he put in, "There were several where I grew up who didn't get past the eighth grade."

"So you quit after the eighth grade?" Snavely asked.

"I quit after the *third* grade," Rusty murmured.

"Why?" Snavely asked.

"Had to work."

"Where?"

"Mostly in the saw mills."

"*Saw Mills*! I thought Mississippi was all snakes, niggers and cotton fields."

"You need to get out more often."

Rusty's comment brought a chuckle from Andy.

"You're serious about saw mills?" Snavely prompted.

"Over half the state is timber."

"How come you had to work?"

"It was a big family."

"How big?"

"There was fourteen when I left."

"There *were* fourteen," Snavely corrected.

"That's what I just said."

"No. You said there was fourteen."

Rusty scowled, turning to Andy, pointing with his thumb toward Snavely. "What's with this dude? Does his ears lap over, or did I miss somethin'?"

Both Andy and Snavely chuckled.

Andy exhaled deeply, offering, "Tell you what, Rusty. A few minutes each evening after whatever we do, I'm going to give you a short English lesson."

"Am I that bad?" Rusty's question was laced with innocence.

Andy rubbed the back of his neck. "Rusty, Bob and I both know it. You're no ordinary gyrene. You're going to be speaking in front of troops a lot more than you think, and you'd better learn to improve your grammar."

"Is it that important?"

Andy rose, staring down at the wiry Mississippian. "It's already obvious to me, that you like what you're doing and want to get better at it."

Rusty also rose. "You've been readin' my mind. *Reading*," Rusty quickly corrected himself.

"See?" Andy said. "It won't take long to eliminate a few bad habits that stand out."

At the moment, Yank Donnelly walked through the door, followed by a medium built oriental. Following the oriental was a soldier laden with books and a duffel bag. At Donnelly's nod, the soldier set the books on the table, laid the duffel bag on the floor and stepped out of the room.

"So, Yank," Snavely began, "Got your own Jap valet?" Snavely hadn't been informed of their fourth bunkmate.

Donnelly gave Snavely a sober stare. "Get it all out of your system tonight, Tex. Tomorrow, *we* make the jokes. This is your roommate, Shigimetsu Tanaka."

Donnelly exited the room.

Tanaka immediately sat in the fourth chair at the table, responding in precise English. "I'm *Japanese* – not Jap – get that straight, and I'm here to help you in Jungle training. You should consider me a peer."

"What do we call you?" Andy asked.

He turned to Andy in a show of appreciation. "I prefer Shigi."

Rusty stepped forward extending his hand, which was grasped. "I'm kinda stupid, Shigi. What's a peer?"

The Japanese flashed a warm smile. "According to Sergeant Donnelly, you're anything but stupid. A peer is an equal, which I hope you'll allow me to be."

Atkins completed the shake, smiling, "I'm Rusty, and that works for me."

Both Andy and Bob Armstrong extended their hands, with Snavely apologizing, "Sorry about that, Shigi."

Tanaka avoided responding to the apology. "And I guess, Rusty," he declared, "from what Sergeant Donnelly tells me, I will be spending most of the next few days in your company."

"So I've been told," Rusty replied, looking at the pile of books, "but I hope those aren't for us."

"The books aren't yours, but the information, in them is for you."

"Thank God. I'd never learn to read those signs."

"They aren't signs. They're called characters, and you'll be surprised how quickly you can learn to make certain identifications."

Shigi comfortably began a conversation polling each man as to where they were from, what experiences had they had, what were their likes and dislikes. After a few minutes, the three were engaged in a spirited repartee and had forgotten they had been talking with a stranger from Japan. During the discourse, Andy asked Tanaka where he learned English.

"I learned it in Japan, but I spent two years in San Francisco."

"What were you doing there?"

"Marketing doll heads."

"Doll heads?" Snavely repeated.

"Yes," he explained, "My family paints them."

"Who'd buy them from Japan?" Snavely continued.

"Everybody buys them. I'd venture to guess that if you have sisters, they have a doll painted by Japanese. We paint the faces, then bring them over to sell. Your people then sew them on the bodies and re-sell them. Many, many products, not only in the U.S. but all over the world are Japanese designed."

"Like what?" Rusty asked.

"Dinnerware, plates, cups, saucers, linens, tapestries— all sorts of things."

"It's hard to believe a people who could be so artistic, so expressively delicate, could plan war," Andy mused.

"Believe it," Tanaka said solemnly. "I have just escaped from the Japanese army."

"You don't look old enough," Snavely commented. "How old are you?"

"Here we go again," Andy interjected.

"I'm twenty-six."

"Twenty-six! You don't look old enough to be twenty-six," Snavely exhorted.

"The Asian doesn't show his age as the Caucasian. No insult intended."

"You're no longer the senior member, Rusty," Andy reminded, then asked, "You seem fairly certain that we're about to get involved in a conflict with the Japanese?"

"Not fairly certain, absolutely certain. And it won't be a conflict as you put it. It will be a full-scale war."

"Why?" Andy asked, continuing the interrogation.

Tanaka leaned against the wall. "It's a long story. I suppose It could be traced from the Versailles Treaty."

"That's the WWI Axis powers. It involved the Germans, not the Japanese," Andy argued.

"That's what most of the western world thinks. Actually, Your President Wilson knew what was going on in Asia, but nobody cared to listen to him."

"Like what?"

"While the Allies were exacting reparations from Germany, they granted Japan all sorts of concessions."

"Such as?"

"Control of the Marshalls, the Gilberts, the Carolinas, and the Marianas. They turned their heads as we infiltrated Manchuria and Mongolia. Actually, many people feel that involvement in Manchuria, the

'Mukden Incident,' opened the door to the Japanese designs on acquiring more land, but the nation has been doing this for years. Look at Korea much earlier. And the way we have subjugated China. The Shantung Province was operationally a plum for us. And your 'Open Door' policy. Publically it is touted as a fair way for all countries to trade with China on an equal basis, but it has become an easy way for the Japanese to exploit China without international retribution. President Roosevelt has seen the handwriting on the wall all the time, but nothing has been done."

Tanaka continued, "You people are so trusting. You make such a case against Neville Chamberlain getting manipulated by the Germans, but we did the same thing with your Secretary of state Robert Lansing. Put something before him and he'd sign it. Can you imagine full membership into the League of Nations after all we did to the people in Nanking?"

"Apparently we didn't think any of that was important then," Andy murmured.

"Exactly," Tanaka concurred "Now you're beginning to think it is."

"I still can't see why the Japs want to fight us," Rusty put in.

"You must understand the Japanese," Tanaka said, ignoring Rusty's reference, "We've been taught to fight. It's part of our Shinto religion. A *Bushido*, or warrior, has the same respect as does a farmer, a merchant, or an educator."

"Is Tanaka a common name in Japan?" Andy asked.

Shigi chuckled softly, "Tanaka is a common name in military circles. I'm supposed to be some shirt-tailed relative of General Baron Tanaka, who was the modern warmonger for Japan. My father named me after General Shigemitsu whom you're sure to hear about before this thing is over."

"I thought your main concern was a need for land to put our people on," Andy said.

"That's only part of it. But I'll tell you this. Hitler didn't invent the youth movement. We did. The Samurai discipline was pounded into us when we were just little kids. We'd have big festivals when I was little, and they still do, for acting warlike. They're teaching these kids that dying for the country is inherited, glorious, eternal. I'm sure you'll hear more, a lot more from me in the coming weeks."

Andy was fascinated and pressed, "Why did you defect?"

"Because I know what we're doing is wrong."

"How can their philosophy be changed?" Andy asked

"The Japanese needs to be Occidentalized." Both Rusty and Snavely's brows furrowed.

"Can we win?" Andy asked.

"An interesting question. The Japanese don't think so."

"Why is that?" Andy continued.

"For the same reason the American believes he is invincible. For openers, Japan has never been defeated. Like America, the homeland has never been invaded. It has a natural protective water barrier. And they have been preparing for war for years."

"So you believe we will be defeated?"

Tanaka paused thoughtfully. "No. The Japanese will lose because he's failed to comprehend the inherent instinct in the human race—freedom. And after the war starts they'll find they'll have another problem."

"Which is?" Rusty asked again.

"America's ability to rebound and its capacity to manufacture. Japan can't compete with that."

"I hope you're right," Andy mused.

"Let me give you a for instance. The German, Max Schmelling, just knocked out Joe Louis. The reason Louis was decked, was because he was ill-prepared and overconfident. He wasn't ready. Let's wait to see how the next fight goes."

"But he's a nigger," Snavely remarked.

Tanaka glowered at the larger man. "He's an *American*! And, he is instilled with the same desire for freedom that you are! There's an old Japanese proverb which goes, 'It makes no difference the color of the cat if he kills mice.'" He squared facing the raw Texan, "And you, Mr. Snavely, have much to learn!"

****

The 1057 men of the 4th regiment, 11th Marine Division stood at attention, as did the officer corps and instructor complement on the stage. Six cadre assistants stood rigid in front of the dais as Major Frank Canali rose and approached the microphone.

"Be seated, gentlemen."

The rustle of humanity and creaking of chairs on the wood floor broke the silence.

"You men of the fourth have been selected because you've shown you are a cut above the average Marine. In the next eight weeks here, you will learn the rudiments of jungle training, from where you will be split up and transferred somewhere throughout the world to complete this training as well as to act as cadre for successive jungle training units."

A rumble of response immediately ensued. Andy felt a pang of anxiety. He didn't intend to spend any more time training for combat. He would seek an audience with his commander at the earliest opportunity.

"Seated here on the platform are the officers and instructors of the Fourth. Please take notice of the six corporal non-coms who are standing in front. These men will assist your platoon leaders and will be given the same respect as will permanent cadre."

Upon cue, Andy and his group took their seats. Rusty noticed an angry and swarthy Marine who was glaring at him. Atkins registered the man's features and looked away.

"We are most-privileged to have among us," Canali continued, "the talents of a Japanese officer, who has defected from his country. He has volunteered his services and expertise in an effort to halt and conquer a Nissan invasion which, in this man's opinion, is imminent."

Again there was a spontaneous rumble from the regiment.

"This courageous officer, Shigimetsu Tanaka, a captain by our standards, is here to say a few words. Please welcome Captain Tanaka."

"Jesus—he's an officer!" Rusty murmured.

Tanaka rose, taking note of the smattering of unsure applause.

"Gentlemen, it's an honor to address you." He scanned the sea of men. "It's also a necessity. I've been given divine persuasion in helping, and have come to quell this unfortunate surge of tyranny against our fellow man.

"Your country, as you're aware, is the melting pot of all nationalities. Through its inception it has opened its arms, welcoming anyone who longed to work, to earn, and raise a family. In other words, your country is ready to accept any individual who wants a life of harmony. Give me your tired, your poor... You should know all that."

The company was captured by this hatless Oriental dressed in light khaki clothes.

"But freedom is not free. You must fight to protect it."

At that moment, a meadowlark warbled, in a chimerical expression of agreement.

"In order to fight the Japanese, you must understand the Japanese. Their dedication is something that is difficult to perceive. You think the attitude of the German is maniacal. That type of blind devotion is old hat to the Japanese. They will fight to the death. And they are patient. But you have one large advantage. You are by tradition and habit, an individual. A man who has lived with freedom will, in the disorganized community of combat, become a more effective fighter. He has the natural response to act on his own. You will, in crises, make snap decisions, rational decisions, aside from convention. You will discover," Tanaka said confidently, "that there will be situations where you cannot be led. So you must become your own leader. And you *will*, because it's natural for you to do so."

He halted, scanning the group.

"The Japanese soldier, conversely, *has* to be led. *Obedience* is anathema to him!"

"What the hell's that?" Rusty groused.

"It's his downfall," Andy murmured.

"And," Tanaka continued, "You're resourceful. *But,*" he said in a serious note, "at times, he can be as well. And there is another philosophy that is drummed into him. Surrender is repugnant—surrender is commensurate to death. Don't plan on taking him prisoner. If he's captured, he will accept the worst."

Tanaka's expression grew grave.

"And if *you're* captured, *you* must expect the worst. He has no, absolutely **no** respect for the vanquished, regardless of the fight. So," Tanaka warned, "don't lose."

After the meeting as Andy, Snavely and Rusty were heading for their barracks, Andy saw the large, dour soldier. Andy commented, "There's that Marine who's always giving us the evil eye."

Rusty glanced at the sullen man, commenting unemotionally, "He's got a turd crossways—no doubt about that."

Emil Zamora grew up on the south side of Chicago. Although he bore a Spanish name, he currently knew no Spanish people in his family tree. His father Orlando, when a young man, emigrated from Pensagona, a small fishing village south of Barcelona, settling in Chicago where he found work in the sprawling stockyards. Orlando met and married a Greek girl who came from Athens. The marriage didn't last, and Emil, growing up with only his mother, kept his father's name, Zamora.

Emil was a powerful sharp-featured individual who, from birth, was combative. He liked to brutalize. Throughout his adolescence, this tendency didn't abate. When he was eighteen years old, he impregnated a young woman, and as was a common practice at the time, he joined the military which offered amnesty from his obligation. Zamora was, simply, an angry young man. It was his physical prowess and not his personality that allowed him to be selected for this duty. His combative attitude was a source of uneasiness among soldiers in his ranks.

One night after payday, as tradition dictates, poker games were the order of the evening. Bob Armstrong, a smallish, intellectually-bent marine who was one of the six selected for cadre duty, was satisfying his fetish in a game of seven card stud. Seated around the footlocker, that was the table, were six other troops. One of them was Emil Zamora. The foul-tempered Marine was losing, and Armstrong caught him attempting to exchange a card. The objection found Armstrong on the butt end of Zamora's powerful right fist. Zamora continued to pummel the helpless Armstrong to the point of injury. When Andy Hubbard, not in the game, but a friend of Armstrong's, attempted to help the smaller man, he was restrained by Rusty Atkins. After witnessing his own father squander his earnings through gambling, Atkins abhorred the habit and held no compassion for anyone who would become involved. His philosophy was that those who chose the activity should suffer from its trappings. When Rusty interfered, Zamora unaccountably walked away from the fight, flashing an insulting sneer at Atkins in the process. Both men knew that a confrontation was imminent.

The next morning, Atkins was summoned to Major Canali's office. After putting Atkins at ease, Canali began, "I understand that you broke up a card game last night, Corporal."

"I guess that happened, sir."

Canali flashed a fatherly smile. "Why did you do that?"

Rusty admitted, "I really didn't break anything up. It just happened, but I hate poker, sir. If it was up to me, I'd throw anyone carryin' a deck of cards in the brig."

"Poker games have been a part of the service since time began," the major analyzed mildly.

"They wouldn't be if I was runnin' the show."

The major chuckled. He, as well, disliked the practice. "Well, you may just get your chance to run the show."

"Meaning *what* sir?"

"I'm recommending you for officer status."

"Oh, I don't want to be an officer."

"You *should* be an officer!"

"I want to be like Yank."

"But you're *not* like Yank."

"Well, I don't want to be an officer—not just yet."

Canali was put off by the refusal. "Okay then, Atkins. You're dismissed."

Rusty saluted and walked out. Rusty Atkins was not about to abandon his friend Andy.

****

Things were fast developing that month. The fourth was two weeks into jungle training. Andrea was preparing for college. To Frank Canali's chagrin, Charles Perkins had been assigned as commandant of the armored section, and one evening in San Diego, Andy was given an unexpected opportunity.

The bond between Snavely, Atkins, and Hubbard, particularly the latter, had grown strong, but now there was a fourth—Shigi Tanaka. Tanaka had become quite popular among the men among the company, particularly with his bunk mates. Tanaka's strong, disciplined methods of jungle training, how to contend with the Japanese soldier as well grilling the marines on the Oriental's tendencies was not wasted on deaf ears. This Friday evening the four, enjoying liberal post privileges, took a cab up to San Diego to the Coca Cabana Supper Club. It was purely by chance they picked this night spot. Charlie Spivak had left after having played there for the past two weeks. Tonight, the music would be provided by a little-known up and coming band led by Loren Siffering. Although the management had expected a small turnout, the place was packed, and when the maître d' came to find a place for Andy and his friends, the only empty table was unaccountably in the orchestra pit itself.

The four took their seats next to the vacant band—vacant except for one, the clarinet layer.

"Where's the rest of the troupe?" Andy asked the musician.

"On break," was his answer.

"Why aren't you on break?" Rusty asked.

"I'm staying with the instruments."

"They're not going to walk off, are they?" Andy asked.

"No, but someone invariably will try to play one of them."

"You're kidding!" Andy said.

"It happens all too often. Some joker who's played a tuba in high school thinks he's Tommy Dorsey, and he's got to prove it to everyone."

Rusty noticed the electric guitar. "I can see why. My friend here," he said motioning to Andy, "plays one mean guitar."

The musician looked at Andy. "*You* play the guitar?"

Andy shrugged his shoulders. "I've never played an electric."

"I don't play the guitar," the clarinet player returned, "but from what I understand, they're easier to play than a manual. Are you any good?"

Andy blushed, "I'm okay, I guess."

"*Okay hell!*" Snavely burst. "He's *fabulous!*"

The musician knew that friends always exaggerated, but asked, "You know Satin Doll?"

"Yeah, I do, but where's the guy who plays this?" Andy asked picking up the instrument and inspecting it.

The clarinet player shook his head, grimacing. "Vince Evans. He just cut the hell out of his finger with a steak knife. He's having it sewed up as we speak."

"Andy can play the thing!" Rusty exclaimed.

"Go ahead," the man prompted. "We're on break."

Andy shouldered the instrument. The clarinet player reached over and snapped on the power. "I guess he's got it set where he wants it."

"What key?" Andy asked, advising, "I'll just play the rhythm."

"B flat?" the man said in a half-question.

Andy fingered a smooth introduction then began with a rhythmic beat, to which the clarinet began the melody, quickly nodding his approval of Andy's skill.

After they finished the number, a few of the guests who had witnessed the parlance showed their appreciation with robust applause. The clarinet player extended his hand. "I'm Dean Sears. You *are* a damn good guitarist! How about another?"

"You're right!" Andy asserted. "It is easier to play than a manual!"

"So, how about another?" Sears repeated.

"You know *It Happened in Monterey?*"

"Can you pick it?" the clarinet player asked.

"What key?" Andy asked.

"Suit yourself," Sears answered.

Andy began the melody, to which the clarinet quickly caught up and took the lead.

By the end of the song, the band members were filtering in along with the leader. The clarinet player introduced Andy to Loren Siffering, while bragging on the expertise of the Marine. Siffering considered the moment, asking, "Do you play by ear or by music?"

"Both."

"Let's let him sit in with us, Loren," Sears urged.

"I guess it would be okay," Siffering said, glancing at Andy. "That is if you want to."

"Sure I do!" Andy gushed.

"Okay. We'll see how you fit in with the rhythm section."

The band began with *We 'll Meet Again*, followed by *Body and Soul*—both complemented nicely by the guitar, halting and re-engaging with precision. Andy's ability to follow any song the band played impressed the leader. At one point, he came over to Andy asking his name. The next time Siffering took the mike, he introduced the tall Marine who was filling in. Andy's pals didn't mind waiting through the evening—they were enjoying the music—and getting free drinks.

When the band broke up, Siffering approached Andy. "I suppose you know we've lost our guitar player for a time."

"Yeah. That was bad luck."

"Maybe not for you. We'll be here for a minimum of two weeks. Would you be interested in joining us?"

Andy felt the exhilaration akin to when Doctor Sutton offered him a job. "I'd love it!" He gushed.

"Can you get in to practice with us tomorrow?"

"I can get Sunday off," he parried.

Siffering mulled the answer. "That's the day after tomorrow…" then asked, "You're okay for tomorrow night?"

"You bet!"

"Do you have a suit?"

"I have a jacket and slacks."

"And a tie?"

"I have a tie."

"Wear that. Be here by six. Can you do that?"

"You bet I can! —but," he halted.

"But what?"

"I don't have a guitar."

The bandleader smiled. "Will this one do?" nodding toward the guitar Andy had been playing.

Andy nodded and turned away.

Walking off the dance floor Siffering, with his arm over Sears' shoulder, let fall, "That was a stroke of luck, Dean…hell, he's better than Evans!"

CHAPTER 19

Andy leafed through the pack of correspondence before assembling the troops for mail dispersal. He stopped at a letter from Andrea. Quickly he summoned Bob Armstrong to distribute the letters. Rusty Akins handled mail call one time; considering Rusty's knowledge of pronunciation, once was enough. Andy hurried the short distance to his bungalow and stripped open the letter.

Denver
September 10, 2941

Darling Andy,

Free at last! I'm writing from my dorm room at Denver University. I am enrolled in journalism and have my supplies. It all appears very exciting. I have a roommate. Her name is Johnnie Hickman. She is from Greenwich, Connecticut. Her father was fond of the Song, Frankie and Johnny, so he named her that, with a slight name change. Johnnie suggested she call me Andy. I put a stop to that.

You wrote that your training would be over in three more weeks, and you expect to go to corman's school (sp). Anything new on that?

I'm looking forward to hearing about your playing in the band. You bought…

Andrea's letter lasted another two pages, the entirety which Andy read and re-read. He had to make certain his transfer would come through by the end of this session!

The morning was cloudy and cool, unusual weather for late summer in Southern California. Rusty and Andy had aided the quartermaster in issuing fall field jackets to troops readying for bivouac. Approaching the head of the chow line, which was their privilege, Rusty felt a mild revulsion noticing the open grease trap which was located near a corner of the mess hall. At the back the line, Emil Zamora watched the two walk into the front of the queue.

Frustrated at so frequently being last at everything, since his name began with the last letter, this morning, Zamora, being in a sour mood, had had his fill. He had tolerated waiting for equipment dispersal, records check, mail call and whatever attention that required waiting. This morning, in chow line, he would change some of that.

Approaching the front, he shoved Andy violently causing the tall marine to stumble. Before Andy could respond, Zamora felt a sharp stab under his rib cage. Zamora wheeled toward Rusty.

"'Smatter, Dirty Head? Can't you mind your own business?"

"Line buggers *are* a part of my business, 'Wop'!"

Rusty had learned that the larger man hated the reference, since he wanted it known he was Greek, not Italian that he vastly disliked.

Zamora reflectively threw a heavy right at Atkins which struck nothing but air. That came as a surprise to Zamora, but he was considerably larger than Atkins and very quick, also he felt with his experience in alley fighting, he would finish this little fellow off with dispatch. Suddenly out of nowhere, Zamora felt a vicious slap to the side of his face. By now, a circle of troops had formed a cordon around the battlers. Bob Snavely chirped with delight at the prospect of somebody else experiencing the elusiveness he learned firsthand from Atkins. Although Zamora was quicker than Snavely, he wasn't quick enough.

Bob Armstrong, the incorrigible gambler, realized the fight would offer an opportunity to make a buck. He took out the note card he always carried and began organizing bets. The grunting of the fighters was mixed with Armstrong's verbal auctioning, for which there was a brisk business.

Zamora was quickly the favorite. Men from Rusty's old outfit bet on him, but it was apparent to the majority which man would prevail. Although Armstrong hadn't witnessed the Snavely-Atkins encounter, he'd seen the results. He put twenty of his own dollars on Rusty. The betting abated as the fight heated up. The thick circle around the fighters provided them a ring, a ring large enough for the acrobatics of Atkins which was similar to the Snavely-Atkins fracas, but significantly more vicious. As hard as Zamora tried, he was unable to land a solid blow on the Mississippi water bug. Atkins continued his furious facial assault. Zamora was literally getting the hell slapped out of him, and there was no letup. Atkins was fighting with an open hand only, which was becoming more and more an embarrassment, and a frustration to Zamora, who now sported cuts and rivulets of blood streaming from all parts of his face.

He shouted for Atkins to "Fight like a man!"

A large corpulent cook heard the ruckus and came out of the mess hall with a knife in one hand and his fatigue jacket in his other. He forced his protruding stomach, covered only by a T-shirt, through the ranks of spectators. Zamora saw his opportunity. He snatched the butcher knife from the cook and made a quick circular charge at Atkins. Rusty leaped aside. Zamora's impetus drove him to the ground, the knife slicing through the pant leg and into the flesh of one of the ringsiders. Screaming in pain, the onlooker fought his way out of the inner circle. The front row price for him was too high. It had seemed that all this had happened in a split second since the shocked cook now lost his fatigue jacket. Atkins jerked the loosely-held garment away from him and wrapped it around his own left forearm. Zamora had now gotten to his feet as the crowd began to scatter lest another ringsider get his ticket punched. The next move Atkins put on Zamora would provide conversation in the barracks for days to come. Atkins stood flat-footed with his left forearm at a 90-degree angle providing Zamora a target. Zamora plunged the long knife toward Atkins' midsection. It missed. The next thing Zamora was aware of was a sickening sensation in his groin. Atkins had met the thrust, placing his hand on Zamora's head as a fulcrum, cartwheeling over the lurching half-breed. When Zamora turned around spread eagle, Atkins was waiting for him. The toe of Atkins' boot caught Zamora in the crotch with such force that he was hurled backward, blood emitting from his inseam, and the knife flying backward from his hand into the circle of troops. Screaming in pain and stumbling backward, he fought to regain his balance but fell buttocks first into the grease trap.

An exposed military waste collection tank was enough to turn a man's stomach. All mess halls had a reservoir called the 'grease trap', which gathered waste. When the trap was full, it had to be emptied. The structure was roughly four feet deep and four feet square. This morning the tank was full and because of the cold weather, there had been four to five inches of sediment that crusted to the top of the refuse.

Immediately, two MP's burst onto the scene and fished the floundering Zamora feet first from the gravy-like mess. Grease and slime covered his face, sticking in globs to his heavy eyebrows, as the desperate man struggled for breath. The ringside clamorers were instantly silenced by the figure of Major Canali standing rigid at the side of Rusty. At that moment, an ambulance pulled up and two orderlies, grimacing in the process, wadded Zamora into the vehicle.

"Get back in chow line!" Canali ordered the troops, who sprang like robots into a column. Armstrong would have to settle up later.

Canali motioned silently for Rusty to follow him. Andy and Snavely turned and sauntered into the mess hall, not at all surprised with the outcome.

Rusty, walking alongside the Major, murmured "Guess I'm in a pot of trouble now."

The major casually commented, "That troop could have drowned if the MP's hadn't been called in."

"Hell of it is, I'd probably let him," Rusty retorted grimly.

Inside, Rusty, who by now was well-known by the major, asked cautiously, "Will it be the brig?"

"It will for the guy with the knife," Canali responded easily, as though nothing had happened. He had privately wished to be rid of the recalcitrant marine who had become a constant annoyance, but Zamora had done nothing more than disturb his fellow troops.

"The reason I wanted to see you was to tell you that you'll be going down south for a few days with Tanaka to search for an environment more suitable for our training—somewhere with more swamp land. He doesn't think this place fits and he doesn't feel the troops are learning much."

Rusty's face showed surprise. "He's right. They aren't."

The two stood for an awkward moment. Rusty began unsurely, "Is there something else?"

The Major formed a curious smile. "I was checking your 201 file. I know Rusty isn't your real first name. Where does Rufous come from?"

"My dad named me that."

"I *assumed* that. Was it for somebody in the family?"

"It was for a bird."

"A *what?*"

"It was for the little brown hummingbird. It's not orange or pretty like the rest, and it's smaller, but it chases all the others away from the food."

"It's tougher, huh?"

"It is that."

"Your dad named you right."

Rusty fidgeted. "I don't know about that. My dad said I looked like one when they brought me home."

****

One afternoon after mess, Andy asked Shigi how difficult Japanese was to learn.

"That depends on a lot of things. How well do you want to learn it?"

"Not all that well," Andy returned. "Just a few words."

"Like what?"

"Like, thank you, please, sir, excuse me—words like that"

Shigi's expression was one of confused humor. "Sure, Andy. I'll teach you to say a few things."

CHAPTER 20

Andy filled in with Loren Siffering's orchestra for a week and was feeling part of the band. Siffering paid Andy $35 a sitting. That was more than he could imagine making, so after the fourth day, Andy bought his own guitar. Vince Evans, the regular guitarist, was fortunate that Andy was committed to the marines. Siffering preferred the country boy because, not only was Andy a better guitarist, he could also stand in as a vocalist, which the band discovered by chance. During a rendition of *Marie*, where all members who could carry a tune take part in the rendition, the bandleader heard Andy's soft baritone. On a Sunday night, Andy was first featured in the song *I'll Never Smile Again*. He was an instant hit. One night Snavely was feeling lonely and accompanied Andy, and in the presence of some band members, he inadvertently called him "Country." The moniker stuck with the band members. Andy would sing at least one song a night, and despite his nickname, it was seldom, nowadays that Andy played or sang any of the songs he learned growing up. Andy had sat in for twelve nights consecutively. Because of the fledgling band's popularity, Siffering was offered an extended contract, but first would have to honor a commitment in Minneapolis. In two more nights, Andy would be temporarily out of a job, but he did glean some information that would benefit him in the near future.

To his satisfaction, he was accepted musically as a professional guitarist whose repertoire of chords and knowing when to use them fit in nicely with an orchestra which was rapidly gaining recognition on a par with the established bands. Siffering agreed to hire Andy back when the ensemble returned. When Andy wondered how the travel could be accomplished in such a short time, he was informed that the airplane made it all possible. A seed was planted in his mind.

CHAPTER 21

Rancho San Diego
National Wildlife Refuge,
September 16, 1941

The training unit's move came at an opportune time for Andy. On bivouac, he would be unable to make the commute into San Diego, and that was for two weeks—just the amount of time the band would be out of town.

The maneuver, however would bring problems for Frank Canali.

After learning that his executive officer was the same officer who had given him so many problems in boot camp, Canali complained to the department, Classification & Assignment, who made the replacement with the same officer. C&A responded in that no preferences had been indicated, and Charles Perkins appeared to be the officer who had the desired capabilities and was available. Perkins had performed adequately until this day, when a temporary pontoon bridge was assembled across the Sweetwater River. The process of connecting the components was the first step, followed by the latching. Since the bridge was anchored from both sides, should any readjustment be required, it was done prior to the final latching.

The final section was in place and the engineer gave a flag signal, to finalize the process. Perkins misunderstood the signal and instructed his driver to take him across the river. Standing at the bank, Rusty immediately recognized Perkins' error and shouted to his driver to stop and back the jeep off the bridge. He knew the weight of the vehicle would disengage the unsecured couplings. The driver disregarded Rusty's warning. Couplings came apart when the pressure from the wheels caused the unsecured connections to separate. At the third section, the jeep heeled to the right spilling the lieutenant, then the driver into the swiftly flowing current. Immediately, both ends of the severed bridge began floating downstream. Rusty leaped into the river at the precise moment Frank Canali's jeep came screeching to a halt at the river bank.

The major leaped out. "Who in the hell's in that jeep?" he shouted to Donnelly.

"Our stupid-ass exec!" The burly top kick, spat.

Just then, the driver popped out of the water and began swimming frantically to the shore. A crowd of spectators gathered at the edge. Andy waited for Rusty to surface, since he didn't come up the with jeep driver. In a moment, Rusty burst out, hatless, and gulping for air. Immediately, he disappeared again beneath the surface. After what appeared to be a dangerously long time he came up with a comatose Perkins locked in a forearm. When he reached the shore, Andy grasped the lieutenant, pulling him safely onto firm ground.

"Get down on your stomach, Bob!" Andy yelled to the athlete standing nearby. Snavely quickly complied, as Andy cleared the stricken officer's tongue and placed him face down over Snavely's midsection, starting a rhythmic pumping. Canali stood over Andy as he worked to save Perkins' life.

"You didn't take his pulse. Is he alive?" Canali asked.

Andy looked up flashing the Major a quizzical stare, as he continued the cadence. Both realized that the expression needed no explaining. "We'll find out soon enough," Andy responded.

Andy continued the process, becoming more and more concerned as time slipped away. He had made a mental calculation of the time the jeep went under until the present, noting each millisecond was the difference between life and death. Doggedly, despite his growing pessimism, Andy continued the effort. He was on the edge of compromising his dream of will power and reality, when suddenly there was a cough, a spewing of mucus from Perkins nose, and a cry, as though the sound had come from a baby. Hubbard looked up, euphoric, as a true doctor would, after snatching a life from the throes of extinction. Propriety, rank, protocol, all vanished at this moment as Andy ordered triumphantly, "Get this man an ambulance!"

At that moment, Rusty strode up wearing dry fatigues. Seeing this, the major told Rusty to take a break, grab a jeep, take Andy and Snavely with him and go have a beer at the PX. That's exactly what they did.

On his second beer, Rusty complained mildly, "Sometimes I think I shoulda taken Canali up on that offer."

Andy spun on his stool. "*What offer?*"

"To make me an officer," Rusty returned evenly.

"Well, *why didn't* you?" Andy burst in disbelief.

Rusty turned frowning, "I didn't want to leave you and Bob."

"Why the hell not?" Snavely interrupted, countering, "Andy's been trying to get out of this duty since day one!"

"What's that about?" Rusty asked facing Andy.

Before Andy could explain, Snavely volunteered, "Andy's been campaigning to get into Corpsman School."

"That so, Andy?"

"Sure," Andy responded. "I want to be a doctor."

"I knew that, but I didn't know you're trying to get out."

Andy inhaled deeply, "In this business, we can't tell where we're going to end up, Rusty. Just because I want to go to Corpsman school doesn't mean anybody's abandoning you."

"Hell no!" Snavely cut in.

"It's just... we have to do the best for what's best for us," Andy continued.

Rusty studied his empty bottle, murmuring, "I guess I never thought of it that way. I think I better talk to the Major."

"Be damn sure you do!" Snavely grunted, draining the remainder of his beer, rising. "I'm getting us another round."

The following morning Rusty and Andy stood at attention in Major Canali's office. Snavely was not invited, apparently since lying on one's stomach warranted no special treatment. Sergeant Donnelly was in attendance. Two Distinguished Service Medals with ribbons attached were on the major's desk.

"You men," Canali began, "have been a credit to the Corps since you became Marines. Sergeant Donnelly will attach your awards which you both have earned."

The two stood at attention as Yank did the pinning, peremptorily shaking each soldier's hand.

"Also," the major continued, "A three-day pass is available at your discretion. Dismissed."

The two remained.

"What is it? I said 'Dismissed'. Didn't you hear me?" Canali reminded them.

"I've got a request, Major Canali," Andy began.

"What's your request?"

"Actually two requests. I still want to get into Corpsman School, and what would the penalty be if I overstay my three-day pass?"

"Overstay for *how long*?"

"Hopefully not at all, but I'll be going out of state and I could have problems making connections."

"Regarding the first part, orders will be cut for Corpsman School forthwith, Corporal. Be assured of it." He turned to Atkins. "What's *your* request?"

"I want to be an officer," Rusty stated with conviction.

Canali broke into a broad grin. "I'll have orders cut for Fort Benning. At the moment though, I need you to help me through this rotation. It won't be according to regs, but I'm making you my acting exec for the time being."

CHAPTER 22

Lindberg Field, San Diego
September 25, 1941

The weather was clear and warm that late Friday afternoon. Andy waited in line to board the United Air Lines DC3. He checked his watch; 4:32. He would be in Denver before six. It all seemed impossible.

For the first time in several months, Andy was happy. He had ample reason to be. As he sat in the aircraft that was winging him across the Rockies, he re-read the recently-received orders he held in his hands:

Corporal Andrew W. Hubbard, USMC432, 836: You are hereby ordered to report to   Marine Corpsman School, Buckley Naval Air Station, Aurora, Colorado, no later than 10:30 hours, October 13, 1941…

He smiled, knowing his instruction would be conducted at Fitzsimmons Hospital in Denver, the largest military hospital in the world. He had no idea how long the training would last, and he didn't care—he was comfortable knowing that he was going to be doing something he wanted to do, plus he was going home where he could be with Andrea.

The weather in Denver wasn't accommodating as it was in San Diego. A fine mist was falling. Andrea held her umbrella watching for him to exit the plane. When she saw the tall man in a suit and tie, she dropped her umbrella and ran for him. Andy was wearing the expensive attire he had bought at the request of Loren Siffering. When he stepped away from the bottom tread of the ladder, she clutched him.

"You gotta be the most handsome man on the planet!" she gushed.

Andrea was wearing a flowing dress and high heels. Her long brown hair was damp under his palm, as he felt her soft lips on his. At that moment, a young man retrieved her umbrella, handing it to Andy.

"I was hoping this lady needed some assistance," he said with a chuckle.

"I think she's taken care of," Andy said, taking the umbrella, "but thanks."

Andy hailed a cab, directing the driver to the Windsor Hotel, an elegant century-old inn built in downtown Denver. As the two snuggled in the back seat, Andrea deluged Andy with a train of questions about the band, the airplane ride, the money he was making, his military activities, his new wardrobe, all which he delighted in answering, and told her he had a special surprise, which he would divulge when they were in the hotel. Andrea told Andy they would have to meet her roommate before the two took the planned bus trip to Cottonwood. Andy handed her his order sheet to read while he reserved a room. Her happy squeal caused several heads to turn. The two took the elevator to the eighth floor.

An hour and a half later, the two showered, dressed and headed for the dining room. After they had finished dinner, Andrea reminded Andy to call Augie Reiss to have him while on his milk run, inform the Hubbard family that Andy would be coming in the next day. Andy was well aware the news would come as a big surprise. When he asked the whereabouts of a phone, the waiter informed him there was one down the hall from the bar. Although there was no intent to order alcohol, the two found a bar booth. Andrea would wait there. Andy walked away to make the call.

Andrea was deep in thought when she felt gentle tap on her shoulder.

"May I sit down?" the trim blond man asked.

"I'm sorry. I'm with someone," she answered politely, but succinctly.

"Sorry. I thought you were alone. I didn't mean to intrude."

"He went to make a call," she explained.

"If he went to make a phone call, he may be gone a while. This is a nice hotel, but its old and the phones few and far apart. Sure I can't keep you company 'til he gets back? Any man who is your date, I'd like to compliment him on his tastes." There was a gentle, relaxed manner in his tone.

She flashed an alluring smile. "I'm afraid you can't sit down."

"He'd probably beat me up, huh?"

Her hair swished side to side when she shook her head negatively. "No. He won't beat you up."

"Why not? I probably would if I was that guy."

"Well. He isn't that sort of guy."

At that point, a waiter appeared.

"I'll have a whiskey sour and whatever the lady wants."

The waiter nodded, looking at Andrea.

"Nothing for me," she answered.

"Very good, sir," the waiter acknowledged, turning away.

"You don't mind if I have drink here, while you wait for your man to get back, do you?"

She shrugged her shoulders. "Why are you so persistent?"

"I'm sorry. I'm really becoming an ass. I'll be on my way..." he said, turning to go.

"No," she corrected. "You're really not, but why did you come in the first place?"

He turned, "May I be perfectly candid?"

"I'd rather you would be."

"You're a very unusual looking person. I guess you already know that."

"I'll take that as a compliment," she said, appraising the tall gently-handsome blond man.

The waiter brought his drink, setting it on the table. The man looked at Andrea for her okay while he reached for payment. She nodded a guarded affirmative.

"Sure you won't have something?"

"No, but thank you." He noticed her mood had softened.

"Are you in motion pictures?"

She giggled. "No. I'm not into any of that."

"I've met a couple of actresses, and I'm certain they'd like to look like you."

"Oh, is that so?" she asked. "Who have you met?"

"I've met Theresa Wright and Joan Crawford, for openers."

"I like Theresa Wright," Andrea mused, adding, "What's she like?"

"She's a nice gal—not at all arrogant—just like she comes across on the screen."

"So what do you do?" Andrea asked.

"I sell vacuum sweepers."

She laughed. "I don't think so."

He laughed also. "What do you do?"

"I'm a student at DU."

Again, he laughed. "I don't believe that, either."

"But I am. I'm a student studying journalism."

At that moment, Andy walked up. The man turned and exclaimed, "Wow! Who do you play for?"

Andy paused, extending his hand. "I'm Andy Hubbard. Who are you?"

The man returned the greeting. "Phil Olson. I've been trying with no success to learn this lady's name."

Andy flashed a quizzical look at Andrea, then back to Olson. "This is my girl, Andrea Vogel."

"I knew she was your woman. She made that abundantly clear." He turned, "Hello, Andrea."

Andrea smiled, acknowledging the introduction.

"Well, why don't you sit down?" Andy offered.

Olson sat across from the two.

"Could I buy you a drink?" the man offered.

"You could if I was old enough," Andy replied.

Olson's face was one of surprise. "How old are you?"

"I'm twenty. I won't be twenty-one for another month."

Olson took a deep breath. "Well, you could fool the bartender."

"Am I to believe you're not twenty-one yet, as well?"

"Believe what you like."

"Okay," he surrendered. "Let me buy you a drink anyway."

"I wouldn't know what to order," Andrea said.

He looked at Andy.

"I wouldn't either," Andy followed.

Olson caught the waiter's eye, and motioned to him,

"Bring me another and a couple of margaritas for my friends, Carl."

The waiter left.

"What's that?" Andy asked.

"We'll see if you like it—if not, we'll try something else."

Olson settled in the seat. "So what do you do, Andy?"

"Right now, I'm in the marine corps."

"*What?*" Olson reacted. "What are you doing in the marines?" Olson massaged the back of his neck. "I thought I was a good judge of people, but tonight I'm getting a new education!"

"He was in pre-med and was betrayed by his friend," Andrea explained, beginning the story. In the course of the conversation the first drink was consumed, and they were on their second—Olson on his third.

When Olson described his work, that he was a field writer with the Washington Post Dispatch, Andrea was intrigued, since his work was precisely what she intended to do. Olson told how he grew up in Denver and was in town to witness the reading of his aunt's will. He was her favorite nephew, and amongst her bequeaths, was a new Oldsmobile coupe. She had barely driven it.

"It's a hydramatic," Olson explained.

"I don't know what that is," Andy admitted.

"It shifts itself. You just put it in gear, step on the gas, and away it goes— no clutch or any of that."

"I've never heard of such a thing," Andy commented.

"It's new this year. What little she drove it, my aunt just loved it they said. Anyway, I'm taking it back to DC with me, and I'm not going to be in any hurry."

The three visited about current subjects; that Andy and Andrea would be taking the bus to Cottonwood, what they should be doing in the short time Andy had, and Andy's experiences in the Siffering band, of which the correspondent had heard, and was impressed. Olson explained his work was heating up, considering the state of affairs in the world.

When Olson quizzed Andy about the specifics of his training, the easy conversation changed to serious.

Olson leaned forward on his elbows. "Do you mean to tell me there's a marine regiment, not attached to Pendleton, training specifically for combat with the Japanese?"

"Yeah," Andy responded innocently. "That's just what we're doing."

"Are you under oath not to divulge any of this?"

"What do you mean, under oath? We've taken no oaths."

"Would you be offended if I confirm what you've just told me?"

"Why would I?"

"I'm just asking."

"No. I'd have no reason to be offended—why would I be offended?"

"Because what you just told me is pretty sensitive stuff—I'm surprised it's not classified—that's why I asked you if you were under oath."

"Well, even if it should be classified, as you say, how could that be of any consequence to me?"

"Some people might not approve of what you're doing."

Andrea broke in. "I'm following none of it. You make it sound as though Andy's breaking some law!"

"Andrea," he began in a soft voice, "Relations are very unstable between the Japanese government and ours—*very* unstable. What Andy's unit is doing is not a matter of being right or wrong—it's a matter of being politically correct. There's really no point in going into all of that, except to say that for your benefit, Andy, it might be better if I just forgot I ever heard a word of what you told me."

"Well," Andy responded casually, "I have orders for another assignment, so whatever's going on, politically correct or not, I'll be out of there."

Olson straightened in his chair. "What orders—what are you talking about?"

"I have orders to transfer— I was given them before I boarded the plane today."

"Do you have those orders?"

"Yes."

"Could I see them?"

"They're up in the room."

"When were they cut?"

"I don't know—'couple of days ago, I'd imagine."

"*Where* are you supposed to report?"

"At Buckley—right here in Denver."

"*Here in Denver*? What a stroke of luck that is!"

"You're telling me! I'll be attached to naval air—I couldn't have scripted it any more to my liking."

"So, you'll be training at Fitzsimmons?"

"That's right," Andy returned.

"*When* are you supposed to report?"

"The thirteenth of October," Andrea interjected.

"You've seen the orders?" he asked her.

"Andy showed me the order sheet last night."

"That's a little over two weeks away."

"It can't come soon enough," Andy breathed.

"Phil?" Andrea asked, returning to the prior topic, "Who's to say what Andy's company is doing is as you say, *politically incorrect?*"

"Well, I don't know that it is, Andrea. I'm just saying that I *suspect* that it is, and I don't want to get Andy in a crack by reporting it. I *guarantee* you there are those who would make a big smell with this story if they knew anything about it."

Olson paused sipping his drink, continuing. "I have to confess, though, I would feel a lot better about divulging the information, knowing you have transfer orders, Andy."

"Then I don't see any problem in reporting it," Andy said.

"What about you, Andrea?"

"Well, Phil," she began familiarly, "I'm like Andy. Since he's being transferred anyway, I don't see how it could possibly hurt. Part of my problem is that I like the sort of work you do, so that influences me, although I wouldn't do anything to threaten Andy's future, because it's *my future*, too."

"So what's the verdict?"

"I say go ahead," she answered, "but how do you feel?"

Olson considered her question for a moment, then blew out a volume of air responding, "Hell—it ought to be okay."

An awkward quiet followed, then Olson abruptly rose. "Don't go anyplace. I'm ordering another drink for us. I'll be back quickly as I can." He walked briskly away.

"I wonder what that could be about," Andrea said turning to Andy.

"What do you mean?"

"He was so brusque."

"I thought we discussed it enough."

Suddenly her attitude was unsmiling. "Andy, this is the first time things are beginning to go right for us, and I don't want anything to upset that."

"I'll go catch him and tell him to call it off," Andy said, rising.

She clutched his sleeve. "No—don't. I'm just being a worry wart."

On the sixth floor, Philip Olson was dialing Washington DC from the private phone in his room. The call was made to James Whalen, Editor-in-Chief of the Washington Post Dispatch newspaper.

After several rings, there was a weary, annoyed, "Yes?"

"Jim," Olson began, "This is Phil Olson in Denver."

Philip Olson had been recruited away from the Chicago Tribune to the Dispatch for Olson's seemingly uncanny gift of getting news first. Whalen had given Olson carte blanch on playing by his own rules in uncovering new information. He once said to Olson to call him if there was any blockbuster material—any time, day or night.

After a moment, the grouchy replay came. "Jesus, Olson. It's after one in the morning."

"Jim. I don't have time to explain. I have information that there's a marine detachment south of Pendleton, unaffiliated with the marine base training *specifically* for combat with the Japanese."

"Where'd you come up with *that*?"

Olson hesitated. "I got it from a marine who's in the detachment."

"A marine in the detachment! Are you drinking your own bathwater out there?"

"I have reason to think there's something to it, Jim"

"Phil, if there was anything to that," Whalen's tone rose to a weary whine, "don't you suppose Barnes would have clued me in?"

Whalen was referring to Mark Barnes, Assistant Deputy of Military Affairs in G2 at the Pentagon, and Whalen protected this empirical source of information—but he had also come to trust in the hunches of his lead writer.

"He's probably not onto it," Olson suggested.

"God, Phil—this is pretty off the wall—he's *got* to know."

"I just want it confirmed. You said to call you anytime if it's important. I'll call you back in the morning, eight your time."

Olson returned to the two at the booth, who, not accustomed to alcohol, were in a giddy spirit. Olson's expression was somber.

"Andy," he began, "I have reason to believe what you've told me should have been classified."

"Have you come up with something new?" Andrea asked, leaning toward the journalist.

"Well, as I said earlier, it's a sensitive area. I questioned it immediately. My boss in Washington is looking into it."

"Do you think that Andy's unit will be affected by it?" she asked.

"I'm really unprepared to comment on something like that, but if I had to guess, I'd say it would. This country is isolationist. This country won't react until it's instigated, much to the chagrin of the right wingers. The Japanese know that. They're sneaking up on us the same way Hitler crept up on Europe. America's do nothing attitude is running Roosevelt nuts. The American people need to know the score, so how do we handle Andy's story? Do we just bury our heads in the sand and let the Japs think that none of us cares?"

Andrea studied the writer. "Didn't you just leave us to call your paper?" she asked.

"I did," he replied. "I would have held off out of respect for you guys, but I thought I had your blessing, and I went ahead because, in my opinion, it was the thing to do."

"Then it sounds to me it's too late for you to forget about anything."

Olson flashed a stare of exasperation at Andrea. "You're right it is. Just what sort of message are you sending?"

Andy exhaled deeply. "I have trouble believing the Japanese are as determined as you say they are, although I have a Japanese roommate who agrees with what you say."

"You should listen to your roommate. We already *know* what they're up to."

"Then why doesn't somebody do something about it?"

"I just said it. We will wait for them to make the first move. Roosevelt made that clear. Actually with his Congress along with public opinion, he has no other options."

"Well, I already have orders for another assignment. I can't imagine anything derailing that."

"Andy, I wouldn't have made the call if I didn't believe that."

"I'm not blaming you for anything, Phil," Andrea said. "I know it sounds like I am. There has to be a reason for all this—why we met and why Andy could be in danger, and why he has been given an opportunity to get away from it all— we have to believe that all this will turn out for the best."

"Well," Olson surmised, "That would be nice. In the meantime, let's have breakfast in the dining room here tomorrow morning, and bring those orders with you, Andy."

Denver time was 6:00 AM. Olson was on the phone with Whalen.

"You say Barnes doesn't deny the story?" Olson asked.

"He's just digging into it, Phil. Apparently, it's happening—something's happening, but so far as they can tell, there's been no authorization for it. It's one of those things that could blow out of proportion in a New York minute!"

"Has he talked to Morrison?" Olson asked.

Olson was referring to John Morrison, Marine Corps Chief of Staff in Washington, subservient only to Admiral Ernest King, head of CINCPAC.

"He doesn't want to bother Morrison on the weekend. He did, however, reach Henry Stuart, who didn't deny the allegations."

"Who's Henry Stuart?"

"Apparently, he's head of the 4th Marine Division-- the unit in question is under his command."

"Jim," Olson cautioned, "Wait until we get together before you go any further with this."

"Hell! I can't do anything until it's confirmed—but the monkeys' out of the cage."

"Get your ass back here before this thing gets away from us!"

"You should tell Barnes to protect our interests in case it starts to heat up. Tell him to hold off until I get back."

"I can't ask him to do that!"

"He owes us. We're the ones who raised the red flag. Do it as a favor to me, Jim."

Olson could hear Whalen's heavy breathing, apparently in thought.

"Okay, but get your fanny on the first plane east!" Whalen returned, with a parting shout, "This could really be a hornet's nest."

Olson sat alone at the table in the restaurant dining room. He had searched for a booth, but found none. A cubicle, he considered, would offer better privacy.

The two young lovers approached the newsman. He noticed the smirks on their faces, deciding not to comment about that.

Andy held Andrea's chair, then sat. In one hand, he passed his orders to Olson, and filled Andrea's coffee cup with the other.

"Good morning. I trust you slept well." Olson started.

"As well as could be expected," Andy quipped.

Andrea giggled at the statement.

Olson smiled nodding slightly, acknowledging the message. Silently, he digested the information on the order sheet. After reading it twice, he murmured, "Looks safe enough."

He handed the order sheet back to Andy, and breathed deeply. "Andy. I'm going to give you some advice."

"Shoot."

"You'll notice your orders say, 'On or before October 13…'"

"So?"

"Well, when you get back, tell your CO you like the part where it says 'before'. Ask him to get you on the first plane to Denver."

"He'll do that?" Andrea cut in.

Olson directed his eye contact to her. "If he can, he will. He's finished with Andy. It's a given he's arranged this transfer out of a request as well as respect to Andy."

"You're right about that," Andy put in, "but how would you know about orders?"

"I did my stint in personnel management at Fort Dix. I have some idea about how things function in the military."

"You've been in the Army?" Andrea asked.

"G2— intelligence—two years."

"How old are you?" She asked.

"I'm twenty-eight."

Simultaneously Andy and the girl gasped. "You don't look any twenty-eight!" Andrea exclaimed.

"That's only fair, Andrea. Nobody looks his age. Now," he said in a somber voice, "I'm flying out to DC this morning. Andrea, I'm leaving my car with you. I know you can use it for the time being. I'll try to get back as soon as I can to pick it up. In the meantime, I'll need your address—I can get yours, Andy when you get to Buckley—and your phone number, Andrea…"   "I don't have a phone," she protested.

"You have a dorm number. I want to be able to get in touch with you, and I'll leave my office number with you." He passed a note pad to her.

"Okay," she complied, scribbling the information, handing the pad back.

"I'm not staying for breakfast…"

"Are you in *that* big of a hurry?" Andy asked.

"I am," he replied, tossing the keys and a parking stub on the table. "Cars' in the parking lot next to the hotel here, and the parking is free when you present the hotel stub. Sorry for the rush, but that's sometimes how it is."

He stood, and the couple followed.

"Can we give you a ride to the airport?" Andrea asked.

"I've got a cab waiting" he said, catching the eye contact of both.

Olson turned to leave. "Know the song, *We'll meet again, don't know where, don't know when*? Andy?"

"Sure I know it," Andy replied.

"Believe it, and sing it for Andrea if you ever get back with the band."

He gave Andrea a hug; Andy a handshake and walked to the cab.

As the two watched the cab pull away, Andrea commented, "That was a little unexpected."

"It was," Andy agreed, "At least, we don't have to worry about bus or cab fare."

The two walked back to their table. "Okay. We'll have breakfast and go see Johnnie," Andrea said.

"Then we'll make that trip to Cottonwood we've been looking forward to," Andy said, smiling gravely.

Andrea's sighed. "We can come back early tomorrow, okay?"

"We have to if we intend to spend any time together," Andy agreed.

The two headed to South Denver to the university in a car that was new and didn't need shifting. Andrea's plucky roommate, Johnnie, was duly impressed with Andy and repeated the same several times to Andrea. Now it was time for the trip that neither wanted to take, but both knew had to be done.

The two rode in relative silence commenting on such things as the car, the weather and certain incidentals, when Andrea lamented, "I wish I knew why some things have to happen."

"What are you referring to, specifically?"

"Well," she halted, "I'm thinking that we didn't have to tell Phil—or *allow* Phil to spread that around about your training stuff..."

Andy was driving. He reached over and caressed her cheek. "That's over and done with, Honey. We can't do anything about it now."

"But you *can* get out of your unit right away and that you have to do."

"I'm aware of that."

CHAPTER 23

Entering Cottonwood, Andrea wanted dropped off at the store. Andy walked in with her, immediately met by Jack MacGregor. MacGregor nodded politely to Andrea, who shuffled past him without speaking, and the rancher knew better than to attempt to strike up a conversation with her.

"Cat's down at the Tumbleweed, Andy," MacGregor entreated. "I'd consider it a favor if you'd stop and say hello to him."

"I'll do that Jack," Andy replied, excusing himself after a moment of small talk to find Andrea.

She was standing chatting with her father. Andy had a strange feeling when he approached the two, as though he was no longer the outsider; Fred Vogel was. Vogel practically curtsied for the imposing youth and Andrea smiled noticing this.

Andy acknowledged Vogel, informing Andrea that after his trip to the farm, he'd be around at approximately eleven in the morning to pick her up. When he started to leave the store, she stood on her tiptoes, and kissed his cheek just like she had done many years before.

The old tavern hadn't changed from the time it was nailed together in the '20's. Lonely ranchers, their throats parched and minds dried up, regularly frequented the Tumbleweed for beer or whiskey. There was nothing exotic served at the Tumbleweed; otherwise old Lloyd Barber couldn't be the bartender, since he was the only bartender the Tumbleweed ever had. Some pious citizens wouldn't go in the joint; neither would people who felt it too expensive to imbibe. Still, it was generally considered a place to meet for those coming in from out of town, or for those who had to get in out of the weather, and nobody was blacklisted because of their gambling or drinking habits. There were disagreements and fights over the years, but nobody ever killed anyone.

Andy had been in the tavern once as a child when a spring snow shut down the county, and havens of refuge were scarce. Otherwise, patrons had to be eighteen or older to be allowed.

It was noon Saturday. The business was empty except for Lloyd the bartender and Chattman. Come early afternoon, it would begin to fill, and build to the usual noisy weekend night celebrations.

Chattman looked much older, slumped at the rail, his soiled felt hat drooped down over a tanned forehead, his sole companion being a newly-opened whiskey bottle next to him on the bar. A roll-your-own cigarette dangled from his fingers, and the telltale *Bull Durham* tag hung as a pendulum from the pocket of his faded brown shirt.

Andy walked over and sat, slapping MacGregor on the shoulder.

"Hello, Cat," he said, easily.

Chattman turned, surprised. "Well, hi, Andy. I didn't know you were back in the country. Are you home on furlough?"

"No. I'm here just for a couple of days."

He tipped his hat back; his forehead baring inquisitive wrinkles. "You're still out in California someplace, aren't you?"

"Yeah, I am."

"Well, how can you be here for just a couple of days?"

"I flew out."

Lloyd, the bartender stepped over. "What can I get you, stranger?"

"A beer, I guess, Lloyd."

The bartender brought the beer.

"How much, Lloyd"

"Nothing, for you," he said wearing a grizzled smile. Andy smiled, nodded.

"Goddam! I've never been in an airplane," Chattman trumpeted, slugging a glass of whiskey. "How could you afford that? —isn't it expensive?"

"Not that bad."

"So what brings you out for only two days?" Chattman persisted.

"I had some business in Denver."

"What sort of business?"

"*Personal business.* Let's talk about you. How's the ranch?"

"Couldn't be better. Beef prices are up. Grass's been good. Can't complain." He sucked on the cigarette.

"That's great. Do you still play the guitar?"

He blew a fog of smoke. "Haven't touched it since high school. How 'bout you?"

"I bought an electric. I've been playing in a big band."

"I thought you were in the marines," he said, refilling the glass.

"I am."

"So when do you play in this band—is it a western band?"

"No. It's a dance band."

"That doesn't tell me anything. You dance to a western band."

"Okay," Andy sighed. "It's a brass band."

Chattman chuckled scornfully. "You play a *guitar* in a *brass* band— now how about that? What's the name of it?"

"Loren Siffering."

"Never heard of it."

"I didn't think you would."

"When do you play in it?"

"I play in it after I get off duty."

"When's that?"

"From about seven thirty to midnight—sometimes later, like on weekends and holidays."

"How often?"

"Every night of the week, except when the band's out of town."

"What town's that?"

"Right now they're in Minneapolis."

"That's not in California!"

"I didn't say it was!" Andy protested lightly.

"Well," he said airily, "I don't see how you can be in California and play in Minneapolis."

"I *don't* play in Minneapolis, Cat!" Andy exclaimed in frustration. "I said *the band* was out of town!"

Lloyd stood at the side wearing an amused smirk.

Chattman downed another glass, murmuring. "You ought to get paid if you play that much."

"I do get paid."

"You *do*? —how much?"

"Ten dollars an hour."

"Oh, that's bullshit! Nobody makes that kind of money! That'd be like getting two steers an hour! There's no need to try to impress me, Andy. What do they *really* pay you?"

Andy avoided the question and was about to change the topic when a rangy ranch hand sauntered in.

"Damn, Lloyd, there's a pretty car out front. Whose is it?" he asked.

The dark-haired bartender was polishing a glass. He nodded toward Andy. "Must be his, I'd guess."

"Damn, that's a snazzy wagon, stranger! It says Hydramatic, What kind of car is that?"

"It's an Oldsmobile," Andy replied.

"What's Hydramatic? I never heard of that."

"It's an automatic. You don't have to shift it," Andy explained.

"There's no such thing," Chattman drawled, looking straight ahead.

"Why isn't there?" Andy asked.

Chattman let fall an insulting snicker, "Cause there's no such thing; that's all!"

The cowhand responded derisively, directing his message to Andy. "In case you don't know Cat MacGregor, podner, Cat MacGregor knows what your car is like even though he ain't even saw it yet. Cat MacGregor's a fuckin genius!"

He looked at Barber. "How about a beer, Lloyd?"

Andy noted Chattman's anger at being put down, but considering the specter of the brawny cowhand, he figured Chattman was wise to let it pass.

"I saw your dad in Vogel's," Andy said in an attempt to re-invent a conversation.

"Oh?" he asked, "Is Andrea down?"

"I brought her down."

Chattman downed another glass, beginning to slur his words. "Yeah. You and Andrea. That business sticks in my craw."

Hearing Chattman mention her name, Andy knew he had better get out of there. He finished his beer, rising. "Thanks Lloyd."

"Anytime, Andy."

Out of the corner of his eye, Andy saw the rangy cowhand's wave. Andy returned with a wave of his own.

Chattman scowled. "I thought you came to visit."

"I came to visit an old friend," Andy replied gravely.

"Well, I'm here. What the hell?"

"I don't think you heard me. I said I came to visit a friend. I don't see him in here."

Andy glanced over at Lloyd who was shaking his head sadly. Quietly, Andy slipped out the door.

Fat, brown chickens scurried to escape the path of the shiny maroon coupe. Andy brought the car to a halt and stepped out. A gangly young girl broke from the screened in porch. Andy stepped from the car at the time she leaped into his arms.

"Oh Andy!" She cried. "It's so good to see you!"

"How old are you, Ruthie?"

"Eleven," she said wearing a big wide smile.

Mildred was out of the house by now, who rushed up to Andy and embraced the son who was cradling her daughter.

"What a surprise!" Millie cried. "How did this come about?"

"Let's go inside, and I'll explain it all."

On the way to the farmhouse, Ruthie asked, "Is that Andrea's pretty car?"

"No," Andy answered, "It belongs to a newspaper man."

Out of the corner of his eye, Andy registered a suspicious frown appear on his mother's face. Andy would tell his mother and the rest of the family all about that later.

"Walter and Sam will be in any minute. Ruthie just flagged them."

Millie was referring to the practice of climbing on the windmill and waving a white dish towel, serving as a beacon easily-seen in the table-flat country, which told the field hand it was dinner time. The chore had been Millie's until Ruthie became old and trusted enough to climb the windmill steps.

The family mood became festive when Andy showed his orders. Soon, he would be coming back to Denver and begin pursuing his dream.

In the afternoon, the family went for a drive in the new car, with Sam doing the driving, his father sharing the front seat, and the three in the back. Sam, nearly sixteen, would soon be driving legally. Later in the afternoon, Sam took Andy, in the pickup, on a spirited tour of the farm. The older brother's enthusiasm for agriculture could never be a match for the younger's.

As was the usual custom, Millie was early to bed, and Andy was there to sit at her bedside for the habitual intimate conversation. Earlier, Andy had entertained the family telling stories of his new experiences. Ruthie sat by him hanging on his every word. Among his narrative, he told about meeting Phil Olson.

That evening in the bedroom, Mildred had to know more. "Andy," she started, "It hasn't been easy for me since you joined the marines."

He registered her dark form silhouetted against the barren pasture spreading from her bedroom in the moonlight.

"I know that, Mother. It hasn't been easy for me, either" he consoled, patting her affectionately.

"You say Andrea was hesitant about giving out the information of your transfer?" his mother asked.

Andy looked at his mother, scarcely visible. The breeze blowing through the screen made a lonesome eerie sound. He thought about the outline of her he'd remembered as a child, lined, with the moonlit background of green summer grass, and flat white winter snow outside.

"She's a worry wart, Mother. She admits it," Andy explained.

"You know I am, too, Andy".

"Well, I told you about Phil's suggestion, so I'll get back just as fast as I can."

"Just make sure you do that," she admonished.

Andy's departure wasn't particularly emotional, considering he'd be returning in a couple of weeks or less—except for his mother. He detected a concern and knew that was her nature; that there was nothing he could do about it. He gave everyone a hug and a hand shake and was on his way.

CHAPTER 24

The new Oldsmobile appeared more in harmony with the surroundings parked in front of the Vogel chalet than at the simple farmhouse of Andy's parents. Andrea was eager to be on her way, but Andy insisted on a cursory visit. Privately, he had become the idol of the Vogel women. He did, however, manage to wriggle out of staying around for lunch. Andrea brought a copy of the *Denver Post* with her because the two had planned on seeing a movie in Denver that afternoon. She sidled up next to him as they pulled away from the little western town.

"Mom got a little uptight like you did when I told them about the Phil Olson thing," he began.

She clutched him. "Don't even bring that up. If I thought for one minute that that business could destroy our plans, I would tell you to keep driving."

"Keep driving where?"

"I wouldn't care—Mexico, Guatemala, South America—as far away from it all as we could get… and never come back."

He chuckled. "We'd be going the wrong direction for that."

"Then I'd have you turn around."

Changing the subject, he said, "I visited with Cat yesterday,"

"Why would you do *that*?"

"Jack asked me to."

"I wondered what you two were talking about after I left you in the store."

"Well, I went to see Cat down at the Tumbleweed as a favor to Jack, but I'm sorry I did."

"Why?" she asked absently.

"I think he's brain dead. He drank half a bottle of whiskey in the twenty minutes I was in there, and I don't think he followed much of what we talked about."

"I—I'm not really surprised. I sort of saw some of that when he'd come into the store."

"He's pretty bitter about us."

"Why? What did he say?"

"Something about 'our business sticks in his craw'."

"Well good! At least he finally realizes we *have* a 'business'!"

"So open up that paper—let's figure out what movie we want to see."

Andrea fumbled with the newspaper finding the entertainment section. She began reading: "Here's *Northwest Passage*, at the Orpheum," she said.

"Who's in it?"

"Robert Young."

"Read on."

"*Road to Singapore*, with Bob Hope, Bing Crosby and Dorothy Lamour."

"I don't think so."

"How about *The Barclays of Broadway* with Ginger Rogers and Fred Astaire?"

"Oh hell no! Fred Astaire shows are like going to a circus. I prefer something with a plot!"

Andrea laughed. "I know. Those movies were all we'd seem to get at the Trail Theater."

"Or the ones that are two years old," Andy put in.

"Here's one you might like—*Drums Along the Mohawk* at the Mayan."

"That's a possibility. What else you got?"

Andrea continued scanning, "How about *The Postman Always Rings Twice*?"

"Who's in that?"

"Lana Turner and John Garfield."

"I like that, although I don't know who John Garfield is. Where is it?"

"At the Denham."

"Let's go to that one."

"Okay with me—only one problem," Andrea said.

259

"What's that?"

"It doesn't start until three."

Andy glanced at the clock on the dash. "If that thing's right, we've got two hours to kill."

"That should be no problem—there's plenty of things to do."

"Doing what?" Andy asked.

"Buying something for me," she answered lightly.

Andy didn't comment—he merely smiled.

The Windsor hotel was a block and a half from the theater. Andy pulled into the hotel parking lot realizing a stay at the inn would eliminate parking expense. The country boy was learning the ways of the city.

The two strolled down Broadway, stepping into a jewelry shop. During the browsing, something caught Andrea's eye. It was a silver heart that was in two parts; the heart separated in the middle, but when connected, the line of separation was invisible.

"Oh, this is just what I want, Andy! You keep one half, I'll keep the other, and when we're together for good, we'll keep it forever. Let's buy it! It'll always remind me that half of me is separated when you're away."

"Okay," Andy said, glancing to the clerk, "How much?"

"Thirty-three dollars," he replied.

"Wow!" Andy exclaimed. "That's as much as a ring costs!"

"I'll pay half," Andrea insisted.

"Why would you do that?"

"I'll feel more a part of it," she returned.

Noticing the eyelets on each heart, Andy asked, "Can we get an extra chain?"

"It comes with two chains," the jeweler replied.

CHAPTER 25

Denver, Sunday 27, 1941

The two finished a late breakfast. It had been a long glorious evening. Now it was time for Andy to catch his 11:05 flight out.

Andrea sat at the table, deep in thought. "Andy," she asked, "I read a book the other day, and in the book, two lovers had a code."

"Oh? What kind of code?"

"When they would write or speak in a code, it would be every eighth word."

"So you think we should have a code?"

"Sure," she answered lightly.

"Well, eight is too complicated; how about five?"

"Five, it is," she returned.

The two watched and waited while the silver DC-3 idled its throaty rumble.

"Be sure to call me just as soon as you find out anything," she said.

"I'll try and call you from the airport as soon as I find out."

The serpentine line began to move. He embraced her, kissed her long, turning away.

She stood as the airliner throttled up and began easing away from the tarmac. A strange anticipation gripped her. His return couldn't come quickly enough.

Andy's flight arrived at five past one, Pacific Time. He checked the manifest for return flights to Denver. Western had one leaving at 5 arriving Denver at 8:15 pm. Andy caught a cab to the base and went straight to the bachelor officer's quarters. The locator gave Andy Major Canali's billet number. With the clerks okay, Andy left his bag in the office and found his CO's place. He knocked. He had never seen the major dressed casually.

Canali was smiling. "Didn't you have a nice visit? Hubbard—I see you're back early."

"I had a wonderful time, Major, but I have a question."

"What is it?"

"I ran into a guy who said that since my orders read 'on or before' I could leave before, considering you'd authorize it."

"You can catch the first stage out if you're in that big a toot— but it'll have to be on your own nickel—otherwise you'll have to wait for the army to transfer you."

Andy broke into a wide smile, and saluted, "Thank you sir!"

Gleefully, Andy walked back for his case. "Finally, I'm in luck!"

Andy went to the PX for a pay phone. First, he'd call Loren Siffering, offering his gratitude and a farewell—he figured the band would be back from Minneapolis—then he'd call Andrea.

He caught Siffering in at his hotel.

"Andy," the bandleader was insistent, "You have to sit in with us tonight. Frances Langford is in town and has agreed to appear with the band. We're expecting a sellout. This is a really big opportunity for the band. We will be recording the event, and we've got to have your guitar!"

Andy was torn. He decided to accommodate the bandleader, and take an early morning cab to Lindberg and catch the first plane out.

The night was, indeed, festive. He sang *Swinging on a Star* with Miss Langford, and with a warm tribute from Siffering. He closed with *We'll Meet Again*.

Washington DC, Sunday morning, 8 am
Editors Office, Washington Post Dispatch

Phil Olson met with James Whalen. Olsen filled his boss in on the particulars of his stay in Denver and his concern about exposing the story. Whalen was speaking:

"Well, Barnes at the Pentagon spilled the beans to his boss."

"I thought he would," Olson returned. "How'd you find out?"

"His boss, Paul Schneider called me."

"So what do we do now?"

"Nothing. The balls in our court, but he asked me to table any publicity for the time being."

"For how long?"

"I don't know. He said he'd keep me advised."

"I don't think I like the sounds of that," Olson warned.

CHAPTER 26

4 Marine Corps Headquarters
Quantico, Virginia

Monday, October 28, 1941
08:30 Hours Eastern Standard Time:

John Morrison, Marine Commandant, was summoned away from his morning coffee. Ordinarily he would put the caller on hold; not this time. The caller was Naval Chief of Staff, Admiral Ernie King.

"Ernie! This must really be important!"

"It could be, John. I just got a call from Paul Schneider at the Pentagon. He says that there's an outfit—regimental size—out in Southern California someplace, training for the express purpose of killing Japs."

"Oh? Doesn't sound like a bad idea."

"No, I don't think it does either, but the attitude of this country is so damned tender— everyone's scared shitless of Germany—the Japs are the ones they ought to be worried about. They're really pissed off now that we've shut off their oil—anyway, we can't have anything like this getting into the newspapers. You'd better check into it."

"Sounds like something under Henry Stuart's watch."

"Well, find out."

"And if it's true?"

"Shut it down!"

"When?"

"Forthwith!"

"Anything else, Ernie?"

"No, John. That's it."

The normally-acerbic King promptly hung up.

11th Marine Division Headquarters
San Diego, California

Officer's quarters of Brigadier General H.L. Stuart
05:40 Hours; Pacific Standard Time

Henry Stuart answered his phone on the fourth ring.

"General Stuart," was the crisp reply.

"Henry, this is John Morrison."

"Who?"

"John Morrison, at Quantico."

Stuart gathered his thoughts. "Oh John! What's up this time of day?"

"Henry, do you have a regiment that's training specifically for Japanese confrontation?"

"Yeah. What about it?"

"I just got a call from Ernie King. You've got to close shop."

"Ernie King?"

"That's right."

"When?"

"Just a minute ago!"

"No. I mean when do I have to do this?"

"Immediately!"

"What the hell for?"

"Because he said so!"

"I mean what's the reason?"

"Apparently we can't target the Japs."

"Who started that crap?"

"Now Henry, I don't have time to discuss."

"I ought to be given the courtesy of an explanation..."

Morrison cut him off. "This came down from the Pentagon just this morning! Don't argue with me, dammit! —Just *do* it!"

Morrison slammed the phone down. He didn't like interruptions, either.

CHAPTER 27

Marine Training Facility
Miramar

Frank Canali was just getting into his field jacket when his phone rang. He checked his watch. Ten minutes to six.

"Major Canali here."

"Frank—Henry. I just got a call from John Morrison. You've got to halt maneuvers."

Canali was stunned. "*What?*"

"You heard me. *He* just got a call from Ernie King, who got a call from the Pentagon."

"Why?"

"Apparently somebody got wind that we're doing something with the intent of killing Japs, and that's supposed to be taboo."

"I thought about that, Henry."

"Then why didn't you say something?"

"I dunno." His voice trailed off.

"Well, get to it, Frank. It's a damned shame. We had only two more weeks."

Canali dialed the post MP captain. "Carl, this is Frank. As of this moment, everything is off limits. Place sentries at all roads leading in and out of the facility. Allow *no* traffic, *in or out* until I give the order. Don't ask me what it's about because I don't know myself."

Andy sat in the back seat with his packed duffel bag. He had said his goodbyes and was eager to be on his way. Suddenly, his cab came to a stop.

"What's happening?" Andy asked the cab driver.

"The sentry said the whole post was put on quarantine."

"What for?"

"How would I know? I'm taking you back."

A shocked and dazed young marine carried his bag back to his bungalow. Two of his roommates were there, knowing nothing more than he did. The real cause of the stoppage hadn't come to Andy yet. It would be unthinkable.

Andy sat. "Where's Rusty?"

"He's with the old man," Snavely said.

"Well, he'll know what's going on," Andy said.

"He stopped back by here a few minutes ago," Snavely said. "Canali's in the dark about it, too."

"Where are they now?" Andy asked.

"No clue," Snavely responded.

"Well, I'm going to breakfast. I'll find something from somebody."

The three found Sergeant Donnelly in the mess hall.

"What's going on, Yank?" Andy asked.

"You know as much as I do, Andy," the first sergeant replied.

"Well, I've got to get into town and catch a plane to Denver. I've got orders," Andy protested.

"You can forget about that, Country," the burly mustang replied. "Everything's on hold 'til we get some word."

During the suspension, General Stuart was on the phone to the marine commandant, General John Morrison.

"...And, Henry," Morrison concluded, "the regiment will take the troop train out of San Diego at 17:00 hours arriving Fort Lewis approximately 20:00. The complement will be interned overnight boarding the troop ship *President Madison* for Manila..."

"You say it's about a two week's sail?" Stuart cut in.

"Something like that, and the families of the troops will receive notice of the transfer by Western Union," the four star attested.

"Damn! That's abrupt." Stuart commented.

"Well," Morrison sighed, "Nobody will have any knowledge that this effort ever existed, and that's how it has to be."

Andy agonized the morning away, refusing lunch. Shigi, realizing Andy's predicament, sidled up to him and asked, "Are you getting anything out of that book I gave you?"

"I've been reading it. Memorizing some stuff," Andy said absently.

"Like what?" Shigimetsu asked.

"Oh, I don't know, Shigi. I'm not much in the mood for it right now."

"Try something," the Japanese urged.

Slowly, Andy struggled through a sentence. Shigi was wide-eyed.

"Did you just ask, 'Can you direct me to Kyoto?'"

For the first time that day, Andy smiled. "That's what I *tried* to say."

"Not bad! Not bad! Do you still have that book?"

"Yes, I have it."

"You keep it and continue to study it, Andy!"

At 2:00 0'clock, Major Canali called his staff and cadre together.

"Men," he began. "For reasons unbeknownst to me, and with my sincerest apology, I regret to tell you this regiment will immediately initiate action to ship out—training as of today is concluded—and our destination will be Camp O'Donnell on the island of Luzon in the Philippine Islands…"

Andy heard no more of the remaining message. He was aware only of tears streaming down his cheeks.

The time was 5:00 0'clock in Denver. The weather was refreshingly cool with a few billowy clouds languishing in an otherwise clear blue sky. Andrea was walking back to the dorm from her last class, when at that precise moment, a strange phenomenon occurred. From out of the clouds, a stark bolt of lightning struck, followed immediately by a sharp, angry thunderclap, then nothing—no rain, nor wind ensued—nothing but an eerie void. There was no explaining sudden freakish quirks of nature. But Andrea knew. Unaccountably, she felt a release of the torpor she experienced after the conversation with Phil Olson. Inwardly, she knew her premonition was accurate, and the penalty of disclosure was certain.

The demon was exorcised, and she would no longer live in fear of it. Sadly, she entered her room.

"Andy's gone," she sobbed to Johnnie. "I'm sure of it," she murmured softly.

When Johnnie's efforts to placate her failed, she suggested, "Come on, Andrea. Let's go get an ice cream cone. I'll buy. It'll get your mind off Andy for the time being."

Andrea dutifully complied.

The line at the PX phone was impossibly long. Andy went to the company orderly room. "I need to use the phone," he told the CQ.

"You can't use this phone," the clerk in charge replied. "I have orders to leave it open."

Canali was standing nearby. "Let him use it."

Andy dialed Andrea's dorm at D.U. On the second ring, the operator answered.

"Would you get Andrea Vogel for me?"

A few long moments later the operator came back on. "I'm sorry. She's not in her room."

Andy shook his head, and put the phone back on its cradle.

"I thought you left yesterday, Country," the Major commented.

"I *should have*, sir. That cockeyed guitar of mine caused me to miss the plane."

"Well, be sure to bring it along with you," Canali said.

Andy's response was toneless. "I don't know if there will be room for it."

"Bring it to me. I'll see it's safe."

Andrea and her roommate walked back in the dorm. When she passed the phone room, the girl said, "There was a long distance call for you, Andrea."

"Do you know who from?"

"Somebody named Andy."

"Did he leave a number?"

"No. I asked that, and he said it was from an army post."

The half-eaten ice cream cone fell from her limp hand onto the floor. Mechanically, she wandered into her room.

CHAPTER 28

Washington Post Dispatch, Washington, DC
Editor's Desk, Tuesday, October 29

Jim Whalen punched Phil Olson's intercom: "Come in here, Phil."

Olson tossed his pen on his desk, walked out of his office through the row of staffers into Whalen's office.

"What's up, Jim?"

"Bad news, kid!" the editor growled, "That regiment has shipped out."

"What're you talking about?"

"I just got a call from Mac Barnes in the Pentagon. That regiment you alerted us to has already been disbanded and is aboard ship to the Philippines!"

Olson frowned. "What the *hell* are you talking about?"

"Schneider lied to me. He alerted the marine commandant in Quantico and they put the wheels in motion—pronto. I'll never do a fuckin military jockey a favor again—ever!"

"What's this about them being shipped out? We haven't as yet printed anything about the exercises!"

"That's just it!" Whalen barked angrily. "They didn't *want* it to hit the presses!"

"Hell! If that young marine who broke this story to us is on that ship, I've probably destroyed his future. He was being transferred to medical corps in Denver, where he'd be with the girl he was going to marry. Now, before you know it, he'll be stuck in a God Damned war zone!"

"Well," Whalen stammered, "I don't know what we can do about it now."

Olson turned on his heel muttering, "How in the crap can I ever face Andrea after this?"

The editor remained at his desk, wrestling with the thought of whether he was more upset or disappointed.

CHAPTER 29

Cottonwood, Colorado
Tuesday, October 29,1941

Milo Rittenhaus' Model A came up to the Hubbard yard. This wasn't regular mail; he would deliver it personally. Walter happened to be in the barn. He came out to greet the mail carrier. He clumsily tore the envelope open. Rittenhaus stood watching.

> Dear Mr. & Mrs. Hubbard,
>   As of this date, your son, Andrew W. Hubbard, serial #413,836 has been transferred to Camp O'Donnell, Luzon, Philippine islands….
> General J.A. Morrison
> Commander USMC

Walter wadded the message into his overhaul bib pocket.
"What is it, Walt?"
"Oh, Andy's been transferred overseas."
"I thought he was coming to Denver."
"Yeah. Millie'll be disappointed."

****

Denver October 29
7:20 pm

There was a knock at the dorm room door. Andrea rose from her desk to answer it,

"Long distance call for you, Andrea." the girl said.

Andrea's passions spiraled. "Could it be Andy after all?" she wondered, hurrying to the door.

"From Washington DC," the operator said. "You must be somebody important."

Her heart sank, all expectations abandoning her, as she walked to the booth.

She picked up the phone, "Hello?" Her tone was terse, flat.

"I can tell from the sound of your voice, Andy didn't make it back."

"No," she answered simply.

"I've struggled all day working up the courage to call you. I guess I've caused you and Andy irreparable grief…"

"You have."

"I—I know it doesn't matter a whit to you but I was betrayed, I knew there was always that small chance I took with Andy. But the chance was infinitesimal. I was in control of the situation. I didn't think what happened *could* happen—not in a million years."

"I can't blame you, Phil," she said softly. "I know you didn't expect this."

Olson almost collapsed with relief.

"Oh, Andrea. If only you knew what you just did for me… I…I…"

Andrea was moved. She could tell he was distraught. "Quit beating yourself up, Phil. It took the three of us to cause this. What *did* happen?"

"In a word, the publicity director at the Pentagon lied to us"

"Why?"

"In the vernacular, it's called CYA. It's…"

"I know what it means."

"So he got the head of the Marine Corps to mobilize the regiment… just like that…in one God Damned day! I'm still in shock, and I know that's a dumb comment to make to you."

"Phil," she cut him off mildly, "There's something bothering me and I want to ask you about it."

"What's that?"

"Andy left before noon Sunday and said he'd call as soon as he knew something. He didn't call."

"Obviously, he didn't have anything yet."

"But he had plenty of time. He would have been in California early afternoon."

"Andrea," Olson said fatherly, "You have to understand that when you're in the military it's a whole different world. There's any number of things that could have prevented him from calling. First of all, his CO might not have been available to give him the okay that you were depending on."

"He could have called from the post."

"Calling from a post is no gimmie. Soldiers don't have the freedom with phones that you and I do, and I can tell you this, Andrea, and I know you don't want to hear this, but his window of opportunity was pretty small, knowing what we know now. He *had* to have gotten his ducks in line Sunday, because Monday would have been too late. I'm sure he would have called you as soon as he had some news, or just as soon as he could."

Andrea began to cry. "You're *right* Phil! You're absolutely right! I didn't think of all that you just said…time being so short and all that, and he *did* call!"

"When?"

"Yesterday, but I was out of my room."

"Where did he call from?"

"The post."

"So you couldn't call him back."

"No!" She returned, beginning to lose her composure. "I've got to go, Phil. Please stay in touch!" she cried, hanging up the phone.

****

The *President Madison*
Wednesday Oct 30, 1941

"These things are crowded as hell," Snavely complained to Bob Armstrong as the two climbed the ladder to the ship's galley.

A veteran crew member heard the remark, and growled, "Don't be complaining, Soldier. You've got it pretty nice, This thing's only half full. You'll mind your manners," he admonished, "or we'll be making it plenty tough on you."

The two walked in silence, until they were well out of the shipmate's earshot. They had been ordered to pull KP. The troops had been warned that there would be consistent detail during the voyage, and they had expected it, knowing the military's practice of keeping soldiers busy whether the duty made sense or not.

Rusty and Andy fared better. Canali saw to that. They were spared extra duty, and although they didn't have staterooms, their quarters were eight man bunks; much better accommodations than those in the slings well below deck. The two were upside standing at the prow of the great ship. Under the circumstances, Andy was accepting the new experience with a healing attitude. The two leaned on the rail with a twenty knot sea breeze blowing in their faces. Rusty was enjoying a smoke. Between drags, he held his cigarette away for the wind to make it last. The sun, due west in the clear sky, was starting its dip in the ocean.

"Well," he mused, "That was rotten luck that you weren't able to get on that plane. I suppose that's really got you down in the dumps, and your girlfriend's, too. Hell of it was, you never had a chance." He took a final draw, exhaling and snapping the butt across the bow into the void.

"I just wonder," he uttered above the faint churning of the propellers, "How this fracas all came about." Andy studied the square jaw and the serious scowl of this friend. He had come to admire the man. Rusty *did* convey the image of a leader.

Andy scanned the open water formulating his thoughts. Finally, he spoke. "I'm afraid that's not quite so, Rusty," he began. "I *did* have a chance…*and*…I think I have an idea about how this thing you're calling a fracas all came about."

The sun had made its exodus when he finished his story to Rusty. He told of meeting Olson, the decision to allow the exposure; the suggestion for his early transfer; Canali's acceptance; the decision to play in the bank, knowing the plane and time was available, then chancing the trip until the next morning; eventually the betrayal by Olson, Rusty was spellbound.

"Rusty," Andy demanded, "You can't ever let it be known to Andrea that I could have caught that plane. It would destroy her. Hell, it's destroying me!"

"I won't," Rusty promised.
President Madison

Somewhere at sea
November 1, 1941

Darling Andrea,

Close, but no cigar. I was in the cab, in route to the airport when I was turned back. Olson sure had me fooled. Anything for a buck I guess. But we're not going to let this get us down.

We'll be aboard this tub for the better part of two weeks, but we'll drop anchor at Luzon and I'm looking forward to that. ...

Andy wrote a long encouraging letter, finishing with the instruction that he would have no return address until he was interned at Manila.

He closed the letter to Andrea, and then composed one to his family.

In the next few solitary days with little to do aboard the ship, Andy started to brood about his misfortune. He continued his study of the Japanese language, at least what he could by himself, and he enjoyed playing his guitar for the brass aboard ship, although he preferred playing and singing in the band to large, noisy groups on an immense dance floor. His trouble was he began harboring vicious thoughts about Chattman, then Phil Olson. Chattman ruined his life out of jealousy, and Phil Olson, whom he barely had met, plotted against him for a miserable newspaper story. And he missed Andrea. The few days he had spent with her were the pinnacle of his life. So often, in the past few days, he thought of her words, "We'd go to Guatemala, South America and we'd never come back." He fought the nagging apprehension that he could be thrust in combat; that he may have to kill. Nothing was more repugnant to him. He loved life, and found joy in healing. He recalled the time when he was a young boy, he and his father were sweeping a granary readying for the storage of wheat. A mouse broke from the corner of the granary. Walter yelled for him to kill the mouse. Andy hesitated, whereupon Walter struck Andy, who was holding the weapon, the broom, shouting again. Andy stamped the fleeing mouse with the bristles of the broom. Visions of the dying rodent remained in his being, because he couldn't bear to kill. He never hunted, or owned a rifle, although he scored marksman with the military rifle. His mother conveniently found an excuse for him to be away when it was time to butcher a hog. Life for Andy had reached its lowest point.

CHAPTER 30

Port of Cavite, Luzon
November 10, 1941

Land Ho! Instructions blared from the loudspeaker. Andy joined up with Rusty in the warm moist tropical air, as they made their way down the gangplank. Andy smiled when he saw Zamora.

"There's your buddy, Rusty," Andy jibed.

Rusty turned. "I guess when they said they cleaned the camp out, they meant the brig, too." Andy had heard the unpleasantness in Rusty's growl before.

"I don't expect you'll have any more trouble out of him," Andy mused.

"You can never trust a guy like that, Andy. Never."

Temporary bunks were installed at Nichols Field for two companies of the 4th. After morning mess, the men were split up and transferred to other installations. Rusty and Andy would be separated.

"I'll be in touch with the post locator in a couple of days, Andy, and we can hook up."

"I wonder what's going to happen now?" Andy said.

Rusty extended his hand. "We'll know in a couple of days."

Andy was doing his best to hold his temper as he whacked at weeds with a dull bayonet. "You would think they could find something other than this to keep me out of trouble," he grumbled. Shortly a Filipino drove up in a jeep.

"Corpal Huppard?" he said in broken English.

Andy straightened, wiping his forehead with the back of his wrist. "I guess that's me."

"You go get things—then come with me."

Andy went back into the makeshift barracks coming out with his duffel bag and guitar stepping into the covered jeep. The driver started up a winding dirt road.

"Where're we headed?" Andy asked. His demeanor had changed. He had tossed the bayonet away, and was happy to be relieved of doing nothing.

"Hospital," the diminutive Asian replied.

"Am I supposed to be sick?"

"I take you to hospital—all I know."

Andy decided he'd leave it at that.

The base hospital was some ten miles up the dirt main highway, near Fort Stotsenburg. Andy was in for a dusty ride. Less than two miles away was Clark field. Although Andy wasn't aware at the time, Clark was where Rusty would be stationed.

After a twisting hour's plus ride, the jeep pulled up to the large brown stucco stone fortress and stopped. The driver waved toward the heavy doors at the entrance as a mute suggestion. Andy grabbed his bag and instrument and headed through the threshold. Nobody met him and he had no idea where he was going. He set his things in a corner and scanned the area.

He spotted a buxom American nurse, and asked, "I have no clue where I'm supposed to go. Could you possibly help me?"

"Are you sick?"

"No."

"Who sent for you?"

"I don't have any idea."

She flashed a wry smile. "Well, that's a good place to start. Come with me."

She approached a serious sharp featured man in the usual doctor's white tunic.

"Captain Kohara, have you orders for a corpsman?"

The doctor looked over in mild disgust. "No. I don't know anything about that."

"I'm Corporal Hubbard," Andy put in, saluting. "I've been sent here for some reason."

"Corporal Hubbard," he said holding the salute.

"We never sent for any Corporal Hubbard, and we don't salute in here."

Andy put his hand down, as a tall slim, graying hump-shouldered man wearing thick glasses walked past. He was studying the X-ray sheet he held as he ambled through the lobby. His white coat was sprinkled with blood, and Andy knew he was a doctor.

Andy wasn't to be denied. He pointed to the shuffling man. "Maybe *he* knows."

The captain spoke loudly, as the man walked past. "Art! You know anything about a Hubbard who says he was sent to us?"

The tall man stopped, taking his eyes away from the transparent sheet. His forehead showed heavy well-defined wrinkles. "Who?"

"Andy Hubbard!" Andy blurted.

"Oh?" he said softly. "You the kid that just came in on that troop ship from San Diego?"

Andy's emotions skyrocketed. "Yes, sir!"

"Okay, come in here with me, son."

Andy immediately was taken by the man's soft, deliberate manner.

The tall man pointed to a chair in front of a desk which was loaded with carelessly-piled papers. "Sit down, young fella" The doctor sat, practically falling into the chair as though all his muscles instantly became flaccid. He leaned back, removed his glasses and massaged his eyes with his thumb and forefinger. Andy wondered if he would eventually speak. Finally, he did. Placing his glasses back on and focusing a firm stare on Andy.

"You're the kid who's thick with the high mucky-mucks."

Andy straightened in his chair, "I don't know what you mean, sir."

"You know General Stuart?" the doctor cross-examined.

"I know who he is. I've not met him formally."

The doctor rummaged through some papers on his desk. "You Andrew W. Hubbard?"

"Yes, sir."

"You the fella that saved that lieutenant's neck out in California?"

"I'm one of the ones."

The doctor still held the firm gaze. "The one that almost drowned." It was more of a statement than a question.

"I'm the one who administered artificial resuscitation."

The doctor relaxed back into his chair, absently reaching into a nearby open jar, snatching a gum drop, holding it in his thumb and forefinger for a moment, then waving it as an offering, "Want one?"

"No sir."

"Why not? Think my hands are dirty?"

"On second thought, I *will* have one."

"Are you patronizing me?"

"Yes sir."

The doctor chuckled triumphantly, tossing the candy to Andy who deftly caught it. He then picked out another piece of candy and started talking and chewing at the same time.

"It's unusual," he started, "actually it's a problem for us to have someone come in the circumstance which you've been sent, or which we've accepted—whichever. It's more that you've been ordered to come into this department, and we've been ordered to take you. Although this kind of string pulling infiltrates the corps occasionally, I'm opposed to it—not that things can sometimes turn out for the better. What kind of medical experience have you had?"

"I saved a neighbor's ram, sir."

The doctor displayed amused shock. "Oh? Tell me about that."

After Andy told the doctor the story, he said, "I've always wanted to be a doctor, Sir."

The doctor was genuinely entertained by the story and commented, "Those are the things a good doctor would do. So why didn't you go to college and become a doctor?"

"I did go to college one year, Sir."

"One year? Why only one year? Did you flunk out?"

"No Sir, my grades were all 'A's."

"Then why didn't you stick it out?"

Andy sighed, "The reason I left was unusual."

"You weren't kicked out, were you?"

"No, Sir. I left on my own."

"Were you in some kind of trouble?"

Andy hesitated, "I guess so, Sir..."

"What kind of trouble? Stealing...trouble with the law?"

"Oh no, Sir," Andy said quickly. "Nothing like that."

"Well, what, then?" the doctor asked, becoming impatient.

"Well, Sir," Andy stammered, groping for words. "I thought I was jilted and I was so broken up. So for some silly impetuous reason, I joined the marines. I later found out that I was set up, not jilted at all, and the girl who I was going to marry is broken up about it too. Anyway, if it hadn't been for that, I would be in school right now."

"Do you like the Marines?"

"No," he answered simply.

"Who set you up?"

"The kid I grew up with—my best friend who wanted the girl, too."

"Some friend," the doctor breathed, then added, rising from his chair, "It doesn't sound as though you'll be very happy dumping bed pans, but that's where you'll have to start. Maybe we can work you in. We'll see."

"That's fine with me, Sir. That's a start."

The doctor was impressed with Andy's humility, his attitude and his vocabulary. Obviously, he thought, this was an intelligent, if unfortunate young man.

"Well, son, I'm Colonel Hoffmeister. I have the command of this joint. Uh, you'll be working under Captain Kohara. You might kinda touch base with me from time to time."

The colonel started to leave his office.

"Sir," Andy spoke.

The doctor stopped and looked back. "Yes, what is it?"

"Do you have any materials, books, rudimentary information that I might begin reading?"

A smile crept across the graying doctor's lips. "There's a whole wall of it," he said, waving a casual hand to the lines of medical books shelved on the walls of his office. "Start anywhere you like." Then he left the room.

Andy walked unsurely up to Kohara, who by contrast, was a much neater man than Hoffmeister. Kohara's desk was clean and orderly. His dress, unlike the colonel's wrinkled whites dotted with blood, was crisp and clean. Kohara continued writing a report, aware that the young Marine stood awkwardly by his desk. But Kohara would complete the report before confronting Andy. That was the methodical type of person Kohara was. Finally, he looked up.

"Okay, Corporal, you want something to do, right?"

"Yes, Sir."

"You go down to supply. You'll find a sergeant named Frietas. Tell him to issue your whites and get outfitted. Then report back to me."

"Yes sir," Andy said saluting.

"And remember what I told you about saluting."

"Yes, Sir," Andy said turning away, then he stopped. "Where's supply, Sir?"

The captain waved a casual hand. "Down that way, You'll find it." Then his brow furrowed. "What's that book you've got there?"

"It's one of the colonel's books, Sir."

"Did he authorize you to take it?"

"Yes sir. He gave me access to his library whenever I want."

The captain shrugged his shoulders, tipped his head and pursed his lips in surprise.

The next few days were a boring trial for Andy with a steady diet of mopping halls and cleaning latrines. He was, however, becoming totally immersed in the medical books he read every evening and into the morning; and he enjoyed his quarters in the hospital, which were clean, roomy and private. His bunkmate was a quiet lad named Morgan. By the end of the week Corporal Morgan was needed less to help Andy since he was becoming more knowledgeable in technical practices and procedures. Andy decided he would make a list of technical terms and questions that he would ask Colonel Hoffmeister. He felt ill at ease with Captain Kohara who treated Andy like a serf. He preferred Hoffmeister.

There was a knock on Colonel Hoffmeister's door. Without looking up from the mountain of unruly papers, the doctor said simply, "Yes?"

Andy walked into the office. The colonel glanced up casually continuing his reading.

"How's it going, Cowboy?"

"I think I'm ready to graduate, Sir."

"From what?" Hoffmeister asked, without looking up.

"From the halls and latrines, Sir. I think I'm ready for audience surgery."

Hoffmeister was amused. "You do, Huh? What makes you think that?"

"I've been doing a lot of reading, Sir. I was particularly interested in an article in one of the medical journals, written by you, as a matter of fact, regarding the benefit of witnessing operational procedures from an instructional standpoint."

"Is that so," the colonel said reading, adjusting his glasses as he read.

"Yes. I was particularly intrigued with your technique of reducing and controlling hemorrhaging during operations involving hemostatic crises."

Hoffmeister leaned back, clearing his throat, removing his glasses and rubbing his eyes. "And what is there about it that interests you?"

"The temperature, blood pressure and containing of arterial content was particularly interesting to me, Sir."

The colonel replaced his glasses and stared at Andy for a moment.

"That so? I'm wondering what your expertise in hematology is. I mean, how do you happen to accept my philosophy, or my techniques in preference to, say, the traditional practice of Bartow's?"

"I'm somewhat familiar with Dr. Bartow's techniques, and I'm especially intrigued by Dr. Eisenstaedt's theories at the Mayo Clinic."

Hoffmeister scowled showing genuine attention. "You speak as one who has specific training in procedures involving the blood. This isn't some sort of charade, is it?"

"Oh no, Sir. I have always had an interest in blood. Reading about the blood makes more sense to me than anything because of my knowledge, small as it is, of blood chemistry."

"That's all well and good," the doctor surmised, "But how can you say that you're familiar with Dr. Bartow's practices?"

"Oh," Andy explained, "I'm familiar with his practices from a literal standpoint only. I've read every detailed account of his from both your library, and the hospital's library, but I've only *read* about it. Obviously, I haven't had the opportunity to participate or even witness anything. That's why I suggested that I might be granted the chance to stand in on an operation."

Hoffmeister leaned forward in his chair. "Well, first, I'm not so sure anything is obvious and second, you will be accorded the privilege of witnessing an operation—and soon."

Andy beamed, shifting his weight uneasily, asking, "May I discuss some other things with you—things I have read about, but don't understand?"

"Such as?"

"Immediate and residual etiology, regarding injury, loss of oxygen and blood in cranial area."

"What about it?"

"Because I would consider treatment of injury to the head to be the most delicate, the least forgiving—the least recuperative... and we should be considering group triage—not individual therapy."

Hoffmeister cut him off. "Have you read the studies *Cranial and Spiral Conditions* by Adams?"

"Yes, Sir, but those are specific anomalies. Although it is interesting, I'm more concerned about treatment and containment as a result of injuries en masse rather than specific cases."

"Why do you say that, son?"

"Because, Sir, for the near future at least, I would expect to be involved in treatment due to injury; not condition. We need to adapt procedures to transport the blood. Make it portable, plasma if you will, learn procedures that will serve us under those environments."

Hoffmeister leaned back, looking at the ceiling seemingly supporting his head with two index fingers to his chin. "Seems to me your interests lie more in the political arena rather than the pathological."

"Call it what you will, Sir, but our problems are imminent. We should be focusing our attention out of the garage, and onto the production line."

Hoffmeister leaned forward as though it took a great effort for him to do so. "I'm afraid you're probably right, but aren't you being a bit ambitious?"

"Oh, certainly, Sir. If I could only be of some assistance, that would please me beyond my wildest dreams. And the experience! My gosh! Think how I could contribute when I get back into med school, when this is over!"

Hoffmeister opened a drawer in his desk and produced a thick black pamphlet.

"Here's Raisbeck. Read this. It's the best and latest on blood work. Maybe you can get some ideas from it. And ask Captain Kohara for the uniform for surgery, and whatever you'll need to attend."

"One more thing," Andy said.

The colonel sighed, lifting his glasses. "What's that?"

"I wonder if I might visit the lab?"

"Live in the goddamn place," he said replacing his glasses. "Do whatever you want."

Hoffmeister replaced his glasses and began pursuing his pile of papers. Andy knew it was his cue to leave.

Andy waited for Captain Kohara to come out of surgery. He stood outside the op room for over an hour. Finally, the captain appeared, and looked surprised at the tall young Marine.

Andy began, "Colonel Hoffmeister has given me authorization to witness your next operation. He suggested that you fill me in on the uniform, procedures, and so forth."

Kohara was in a hurry, but stopped. "He what?"

"I'm going to witness your next operation."

"Most of our operations, as you call them, are the stitching of skin, reducing of joints and broken bones which result from drunken brawls." Kohara explained as he started walking back to his office, scanning his clipboard, which he was busily leafing through.

"But you'll take care of it, sir?"

Kohara stopped, began rubbing his chin. "That's a pretty big leap from swabbing out latrines, isn't it?"

"Squeaky wheel gets the grease," Andy said and headed for the lab.

The door to Colonel Hoffmeister's office was ajar. Hoffmeister was bent over his cluttered desktop poring over a report.

"Colonel," Kohara began, "What's this about that corporal getting permission to stand in on an operation?"

"That's right, John. I told him he could."

"Christ, Colonel, I was two years into medical school before I was allowed to witness an operation."

"And our country was at peace, John."

"It still is."

"Not for long, John."

"Well, I think it's rather unusual to have a green kid come into the operating room."

"These are unusual times, Captain."

"It's against policy, you know."

Hoffmeister glanced up. "Are you suggesting that I don't understand the policies of this hospital?"

Kohara was embarrassed and didn't answer.

"Look, John. I've had some lengthy chats with the kid. Don't underestimate him. If there's a chance he may become a good aide, I think we should give him the chance. God knows he wants one."

Hoffmeister settled back in his chair, touched ten fingers together in open hands.

"John, you're the best damned surgeon I've come across in twenty years. There's only one thing about you that has to improve. That's administrative ability, and experience will take care of that. You know the reputation I have for precision. I scare the daylights out of most young doctors, but not you. You're as much a stickler for competent practice as I am—perhaps more so. Now, how many of our operations have come off without one of our damned aids screwing something up?"

"Not many," Kohara agreed.

"Remember that aide's sewing up that patient with the sponge still in him?"

"How can I forget?"

"Well, it sure as shit doesn't take any training to do that," Hoffmeister growled.

"No," Kohara consented, "But the kid has no training at all."

"He will," Hoffmeister said leaning forward beginning to read again, "And much too soon, I fear."

"So the kid has ambition, and that's enough to satisfy you?"

Hoffmeister looked up adjusting his glasses. "Something the matter with that?"

Kohara stammered for a reply but Hoffmeister cut him off. "John, would your career have been advanced by being exposed to operations before two years of medical school?"

"Of course it would."

Hoffmeister bent over and began reading. Without looking up, he murmured barely above a whisper, "You have a nice day," John.

Andy received his chance to attend an operation soon enough. The next afternoon a marine was brought in with a ruptured spleen. He was being wheeled into the operating room as Andy was looking through a microscope studying blood cells. He felt the tap on his shoulder and turned.

"Come with me," the aide said.

Without replacing the slide, Andy followed the aide into the wash room.

"Wash your hands and arms good and put these on," the aid said pointing to a pile of neatly-pressed pale blue clothing that contained a mask, cap and apron.

Andy was in ecstasy. His heart pounded. Nervously, he fumbled through the clothing, shaking as he laced everything in place. He timorously opened the door to the operating room. In time! The surgery had not begun. The moans of the jaundiced patient were interwoven with the noises of preparation, curt orders, the shuffling of people and equipment. Andy shuffled up to the elder surgeon.

"Now pay very close attention, young man," Hoffmeister ordered. "I'll talk it out as I do the operation. The cutting procedures will be standard for most operations. It's only when we're at the spot of trouble that an operation takes on its individual personality. Watch closely and you'll see what we do in pre-op. These procedures are fairly standard."

Andy nodded quietly as Kohara glowered at him from across the operating table.

"This is what we do first, Corporal," Hoffmeister said. "The first thing we do," he repeated, "is to see if the patient is bleeding on the inside."

"How do you tell if he's bleeding on the inside?" Andy asked.

"You do a quick physical exam on the outside. The first thing you do is get him out of his clothes as the nurse is doing now. Then get the I.V. going."

"You take your fingers and evaluate the sound which will tell you what the density of the tissue is underneath. If I thump on a lung that's filled with air, that's quite normal. You get the sound back, that's called resonance

289

which describes what it is. You get an echo. Hear it?" Hoffmeister asked as he thumped the patient's chest.

"Yes," Andy replied.

"If the lung is collapsed or partially collapsed, there's a little more of what you call 'hyper-resonance', what you see in people with emphysema, because it's not quite so dense. If it's completely collapsed and the cavity is filled with air, it rolls kinda, like a timpani drum, and if it's filled with a solid-like blood underneath, it's dull."

"Really, Colonel," Kohara snarled, "This guy's gonna die before you get to the diagnosis It's a spleen! Let's get on with it!"

"Okay, John," Hoffmeister conceded.

"Okay, Andy. See this big bruise?" He said pointing to a spot in the middle by the man's lower chest. "It's discolored. It's called..."

"Ecchymosis," Andy put in.

"Okay—you already know that. Now you notice his blood pressure is falling."

"Yes! His blood pressure is falling!" Kohara barked impatiently.

"That means he is bleeding somewhere inside," Hoffmeister continued. "You palpate all over the abdomen. Listen to the abdomen first. If his bowel is shut down which it more difficult, he'll have peristalsis, or a wave of contraction moving along the bowel every once in a while. Also with peritonitis, it shuts down, so if you've got blood leaking into the cavity, it'll shut down. Which is another thing we look for such as a rupture of any viscera inside."

Kohara's angry sigh was heard around the table.

"The big key to a broken spleen is you'll generally get a fracture of these ribs over the top. He doesn't, but normally he would. Had they been fractured, he would have let me know. Now, you notice that the abdomen is rigid. A lack of peristalsis, or of bowel sounds, the patient feels the greatest pain over the area."

Hoffmeister depressed the spot and the patient grimaced.

"He'll also feel pain referred to the left shoulder because the blood is coming up and hitting the bottom of the diaphragm. Again, here you have a peritonitis."

"You may also be aware, Corporal," Kohara said sarcastically, directed as an insult to Hoffmeister, "that the guy's going anemic, blood pressure's dropping, pulse is getting weak, the heart rate is picking up, and he's going into shock!"

The nurse had cross-matched the patient's blood as Hoffmeister explained the condition.

"Okay, let's get him ready on the table," the Colonel said. "Now," he continued, as the patient was positioned on the operating table, "let's put him out."

The anesthetist quickly administered ether.

"Spleens have to come out..."

"Yes!" Kohara interjected.

"They won't heal themselves. You can't sew them up." Hoffmeister continued. "We're sleeping him with ether. Okay, get him scrubbed and shaved, and we'll get on with it."

"Finally!" Kohara breathed.

"Hair is the primary source of infection..." Hoffmeister said plugging doggedly ahead with his instruction. "Or *one* of the primary sources. So we drape him," the colonel said, as the nurse applied the towels. Hoffmeister made the "T" incision approximately one half inch thick through the subcutaneous fats, talking as he cut. Throughout the operation, Hoffmeister kept a running explanation. Kohara's patience was running thin. He had forgotten, however, during his days as an intern, the old Colonel did the same for him.

Kohara would suture a layer, as would Hoffmeister, until the final layer was closed.

"Okay," Hoffmeister said, straightening. "That's about it. Keep a close observation on him for about twenty-four hours, Corporal Morgan," Hoffmeister said, removing his gloves.

"Thank you for the play by play, Colonel," Kohara said testily. "Fortunately you finished it before the patient expired."

Hoffmeister stopped and looked at the captain for a moment. "John," He began, then turned away. "Forget it" he muttered as he passed through the door.

Kohara stopped by Andy and ordered, "I want you to have this place squeaky wheels clean in an hour." The innuendo didn't go unnoticed.

In the washroom as the two doctors were cleaning up, Hoffmeister mused, "Making the kid clean it up, huh?"

"If you're gonna dance, you have to pay the piper," Kohara replied.

Andy knocked on the Colonel's door after he had cleaned the operating room. "Yes," the colonel acknowledged without looking up.

"Thank you sir, for allowing me into the operating room," the tall corporal said.

The gray haired surgeon looked up. "Learn anything, cowboy?"

"Oh, you bet. I'm wondering if you had any idea on how I can get some practice on suturing?" Andy asked.

"Sure. Go down to the mess hall. They bring freshly-butchered pigs in all the time. Ask for some hide. Make sure it's got fat on it. Practice on that. I'll inspect it."

Andy followed the surgeons' suggestion as the colonel inspected each piece of sutured tissue, then made his criticisms. Andy was allowed to witness any and all operations from that day on. One day there was an operation for a ruptured kidney. Andy was standing beside Hoffmeister. Timing is such an integral part of operation procedure and the colonel expected to have the clamp in his hand at the precise time the arterially-fed organ was to be closed. The aide paused for a split second as blood began to spurt ceiling ward just as Kohara turned away. Andy responsively snatched the clamp and placed the instrument in Hoffmeister's hand, albeit a half-second late.

"Goddammit!" Hoffmeister cursed as he took the clamp. He would counsel the assistant when time permitted. Almost with the same motion, Andy handed a sponge across the table to Dr. Kohara, before the doctor had an opportunity to order it. Quickly, Kohara applied the sponge to the flooded area, enabling Hoffmeister to identify the area to place the clamp. Kohara gave Andy a surprise glance.

"Suture," Hoffmeister ordered. Andy took the needle and the canister of cat, and began to thread the needle.

"How long?"

Hoffmeister was livid, and wheeled to face the aide, shouting, "What the hell you mean, 'how long'?" He had been unaware until that moment that Andy had been assisting him. Andy detected a twinkle in the doctor's eye, although his face was masked.

"Oh," the colonel replied easily, "Bout eight inches, I'd guess."

The contrast from anger to leniency shocked Kohara. Hoffmeister tied off the arterial, knotted the string and neatly nipped off the loose ends. Andy watched, realizing he himself had a long way to go to achieve a similar level of dexterity.

As Kohara was preparing the area for closure, Andy again threaded the needle.

"Suture," was the order. Andy uncharacteristically said in a half plea, "Let me do the last one, Sir."

The elder surgeon stepped aside. "Be my guest."

Kohara's eyes bulged. Andy clumsily completed the suturing, tied the knot and clipped the ends, looking to Hoffmeister for admonishment.

"I can see you were never a boy scout," the colonel joked, causing an uneasy ripple of laughter around the table.

"Wasn't all that bad," Kohara breathed. Kohara's comment drew surprised looks from everyone.

Back in the washroom, Hoffmeister remarked to Kohara, "Boy, you should have seen yourself. I could have knocked your eyes off with a stick when I let the kid do that suturing."

"You amaze me, Art. If you intend to allow this kid to play doctor, don't you think you should have him wear gloves?"

"John, one of these days, you'll have things your way. For now, I'm still the captain of this ship."

"Actually," Kohara conceded, "I was a little impressed with the kid."

"You did give him a bit of a compliment, in a left-handed way," Hoffmeister returned.

"When was that?"

"About the suturing."

"He was pretty timely in anticipating the need for a sponge."

"I didn't know he gave you a sponge."

"He did, and it was at a critical moment. I don't where that aide's head was."

"Maybe we'll give the kid a job after all, John. Us tall guys have to stick together."

"You know, Art. There's something you've got to learn, too."

"What's that?"

"You've got to quit playing favorites."

"Then would *you* be Captain?"

CHAPTER 31

That afternoon, Andy received a letter from Andrea.

Darling Andy,

I was so happy to get your missive and that delighted that you're finally doing what you're cut out to do.

School is okay, although I'm bored stiff. Everything is so easy. I wish I had a second chance to take that new car to Mexico, or someplace with you, which I would do without hesitation. Incidentally, don't be angry with Phil Olson. God knows, he's broken up enough as it is. You must remember that he did warn you that there could be some risk to exposing the story, and he advised you that you could take advantage of your transfer ahead of time. He wouldn't have done those things if he cared more about the story than he did about us. At least he's got me convinced.

Andrea wrote about her roommate, the weather and other items that weren't particularly of interest to Andy. She concluded:

Remember that I love you only, and I'll wait for you as long as it takes.

My Love, Andrea

Andy folded the letter and placed it away. He agreed with Andrea. After having some time to sort things out, he knew he had no reason to harbor any ill feelings toward Phil Olson. It was anathema for him to reconsider it, but the failed getaway wasn't Olson's miscalculation—it was his own—and he would keep that secret away from Andrea as long as he lived. He wondered about Olson's car. He would ask Andrea about that in his next letter.

Hoffmeister was busy at his desk when Andy walked in. Unperturbed by Andy's presence, the colonel glanced up to see Andy reading a reference sheet from the mountain of papers on his desk.

"What are you looking at?" he growled.

"That's a questionnaire from last week's operation."

"*What operation?*" he muttered.

"The one I assisted on—the ruptured kidney."

"What the hell about it?" he griped.

Andy had come to learn the colonel's bark was just a bark.

"Seems to me this sort of thing shouldn't get stale."

"You sound like one of those pencil pushers at the medical center in Bethesda. Maybe I should transfer you there."

"Oh no—it's just that you don't like paper work, do you?"

"Hate it... besides, it's not necessary."

"Why don't you have an aide do it for you?"

"They'd screw it up. Besides, it's my diagnosis anyway—and I have to sign it."

"Doesn't look all that difficult."

Hoffmeister bristled. "Oh, it doesn't, huh? And how did you arrive at that conclusion, my self-made doctor?"

"I read this, and I think I could answer every question. Obviously, I can't sign your name."

"Okay, wise guy. We'll go back and *you* do it."

The two started down the hall; the doctor handed Andy his clipboard containing a sheaf of forms. Upon entering the first room, Hoffmeister pronounced, "Go ahead."

Andy glanced at the patient, scanning the document. "Okay, sir. The time, the condition, the duration of operation is all logged. The recovery, we document—seems simple enough."

"What condition is the man in now?"

"I can't determine that yet."

The colonel turned away from the patient, speaking softly, as he preferred the patient not to hear.

"If you can't determine his condition, how can you calibrate his recovery?"

"I'd have to go back and review his condition prior to procedure."

"Well, let's go back and look up his records."

Andy started to squirm. "He doesn't *have* any records... does he...?"

"Come on Hippocrates," Hoffmeister challenged, "Where do we begin?"

Andy struggled with what order of checkout should be implemented.

"How about starting with the heart?" Hoffmeister suggested, removing his stethoscope handing it to Andy. That was the jump start the youngster needed.

"I guess I forgot my blood pressure gear, too," he pretended, which the colonel smugly handed over.

Andy listened to the systolic-diastolic beats of the heart, making his notation. Then he checked his watch counting the pulse, murmuring "78—that's okay." He then applied the tourniquet and checked the gauge, "140 over 86—a little high," then placed the thermometer under the tongue, as he made notations for temperature and blood pressure. After a moment, he recorded the patient's vitals, and asked, "How are you feeling?"

"A little sore, sir."

"Actually, you're doing quite nicely," the budding doctor said.

Andy then completed his remarks, plus questions regarding follow up, which he'd discuss afterward with the colonel. The colonel, standing the same height as Andy, tipped his head back, visually scanning Andy's diagnosis, nodding, pursing his lips in a display of agreement. Andy turned to the colonel. "Let's catch the next one."

"You go on ahead. You don't need me."

Eleven diagnoses later, Andy entered the colonel's room.

"I have a bunch of questions," he began.

"Not now. I have something else I need you to do."

"What's that?" Andy was getting out of the habit of saying "sir" to anyone. That pleased Hoffmeister, who considered the acknowledgement unnecessary.

"I just talked with your old boss, Henry Stuart. He tells me you play a nasty guitar." The lanky doctor rose from his desk. "You didn't tell me—let's hear it."

Walking down the hall, Andy apologized, "Guess I got a little big for my britches."

Hoffmeister laid his arm over Andy's shoulder. "You just got a little bit ahead of yourself, but that's okay with me."

The door to the room was ajar. Morgan, lounging on his bed, snapped to attention, seeing the colonel.

"You're to see Captain Kohara," Hoffmeister told the corporal, who quickly exited the room.

Andy picked up his electric, and strapped it on. "What do you want to hear?"

"Know *Whispering*?"

"That's one of my favorites, too," Andy said, and began.

A half-hour later, Hoffmeister asked, "Wonder if you might come by and play for me and the missus?"

"I would if you'd let me loose to hunt down one of my buddies."

"I'll do better than that. I'll arrange for a jeep and a driver."

Late that afternoon, Andy located Rusty on a tarmac at Clark Field drilling a company of Filipino soldiers in marching maneuvers. Upon seeing Andy, Rusty dismissed the soldiers, and hopped in the jeep with Andy and the driver.

"How about the PX?" Andy asked, to which Rusty agreed.

The two buddies bought a six-pack of beer and found a vacant table behind the building.

"I couldn't find you," Rusty began. "How'd you find me?"

"I just had the driver hunt around until I found someone who knew you."

The two talked about what they were doing, and what they thought would happen next. Rusty was awaiting orders to be transferred to Quantico, Virginia, for officer training; that he was bored doing what he was doing. Andy told how he was finally doing what he wanted, and was confident, someway, he would soon become a doctor. Both expressed their fear that war was imminent. Neither had seen Bob Snavely, and assumed he was interred at the naval facility at Cavite.

The driver deposited Rusty back to his post. Andy, with his new-found freedom promised to keep in touch.

The clerk touched Andy on the shoulder. "You live with your eye stuck in that thing?"

Andy straightened up from the microscope. He was examining epithelial tissue from an operation the day before. He had taken a specimen to the lab and was engrossed with a magnified sample.

"Old high pockets wants you in his office."

Andy squinted. "Who's 'old high pockets'?"

"The colonel."

"Oh, okay. I should have guessed that."

Andy entered Hoffmeister's office, pleased to see colonel's tidy room. Hoffmeister looked up.

"Hi, Lieutenant," he said cheerily.

"I'm a corporal, not a lieutenant, Colonel. You know that."

"Not now," he said with a satisfied look, tossing two gold bars on the bare desk. "I'm making you a second 'John.' I'm confident that in a short period of time, you'll make a damned good physician. As I said before, I don't want some enlisted man carving up my patients—it doesn't look good."

"I—I don't know what to say."

"Then, don't say it."

"What does Captain Kohara think about that?"

"You worried about him?"

"Sure I am."

"He's okay with it. You're in good favor with him since you're keeping all this paperwork up to snuff. Just quit calling him Sir."

"What about the other doctors?"

"They don't know a thing about you. They've only seen you in your coat or operating costume."

"Well, it just seems kinda' sudden."

"Get off it kid. In my time, I've seen plenty of battlefield commissions. In Verdun back in '17, Pershing made a captain out of a sergeant in one afternoon. Besides," he issued a long sigh, "I've been thinking about what you were saying about getting ready for the crap that I'm sure will be coming our way, and a little practice on some of these drunks we get coming in here can't hurt. Anyway, put those bars on, you won't be a bona fide officer until I get it past the board, but you'll be treated like one."

He directed a pensive gaze out the window into what was a dreary day, "Just think. Maybe one day you'll be a bird colonel like me."

"That's very generous, Sir, but I'll be going back to medical school when this hitch is over. I'm afraid I'm not cut out for the military."

The old veteran continued his gaze out toward the hazy compound. He drew in a volume of air then let it fall, "Yeah. That's what I thought when I was a young ass buck back in '07. I was a medical student at Ohio State, and I was standing in a soup line when I looked across the yard, and saw a bunch of fat Marines marching around. I was hungry, so I went across and joined them."

"Ever had any doubts about that, Colonel?"

"Sure—who doesn't have doubts? If you don't stay in the Marines, you may have doubts too, but..." the colonel continued, "I finished my medical degree at Walter Reed's expense. Whether it's the military or not, this is the kind of thing you're meant to do. I'm sure of that."

Andy radiated. "Boy, Colonel. I've had compliments in my day, but that one tops them all!"

Hoffmeister was in a philosophical mood, and Andy was enjoying being a part of it.

"An operating room," the colonel waxed, "Is never the same twice, and the most important element in that environment is what?" he asked turning to Andy.

"I'd say it would have to be the level of support you have," Andy said without hesitation.

"You nailed that one, Cowboy. Now, I'll ask you the hard one. As a physician, what is the most critical of all any doctor's talents?"

Andy considered for a moment. "Well, I know what I think it should be, and for you, it can't be any such thing as knowledge, experience and precision—nothing like that—those are things any sawbones are supposed to possess, so you're not going to get me to bite on that."

Hoffmeister smiled, "So it appears that perhaps you have thought about it."

"Would you believe me if I told you I've thought about the very same thing since I first got my doctor's set when I was a little boy?"

That brought a surprised chuckle out of the old doctor, "You never told me about your doctor's set. What's that about?"

Andy recounted the experience with Clinton Durkee's ram.

Hoffmeister listened to Andy's story with great amusement, then referring to his original subject, he asked, "Anyway, what's the answer to my question?"

"Well, this probably won't get me a gum drop, but I'd say making a proper diagnosis."

Hoffmeister winged a piece of candy at Andy, which Andy wasn't able to catch.

"Sorry I missed that one, Colonel."

"You didn't miss the answer, Kid! There's not one damn doctor in a hundred that gets that one straight! That's the very reason you shoved your arm up that sheep's ass! Come on Lieutenant. I'm taking you down to the officer's club for a drink!"

The jeep driver dropped Andy off at the entrance to the officer's club with the customary orders to pick them up in an hour and a half. It was a ritual with Hoffmeister to have two double scotches, never more than three, each evening after his daily routine. Upon entering, he was given the normal razzing about his height, or whatever, from the short Filipino locals who ran the club. This night it was compounded being joined with a person as tall as he. He didn't mind the good-natured ribbing from the employers who he liked and they liked him. It was a place where he could unwind and forget about protocol.

Andy had never had scotch, and now it was his turn to be the target. Along in the evening, Hoffmeister, becoming relaxed, began bragging on the successes of his young protégée, leaving no doubt that Andy's abrupt accomplishments were a direct result of the colonel's own tutelage. To this, Andy received an excessive dose of ribbing. Before Andy and the colonel left the club, however, Andy would get the last laugh, plus a renewed admiration from his boss. Hoffmeister became involved in a spirited discussion with some officers from the motor pool about the difficulty of each other's work. After the second round, another colonel and friend of Hoffmeister's named Otto, and Hoffmeister were in a dead end argument wagering a drink, about the difficulties of fixing a person versus fixing an engine. Otto would toss out engine parts and terms that Hoffmeister knew nothing about and Hoffmeister would do the same to Otto. Finally, Otto said to Hoffmeister to get his amazing lieutenant's take on it, to which Andy, feeling his booze as well, responded that the human body was always a tougher fix. Otto, sitting on Hoffmeister's right asked Hoffmeister for the lieutenant's proof. Hoffmeister turned to Andy on his left and urged, "Well? Let them have it, kid!"

Andy, over the din in the club, said to his boss, "Ask him, when he fixes whatever it is, if he gets to turn the motor off?"

Hoffmeister burst in raucous laughter, and relayed the challenge to Otto. The argument ended there, with Otto conceding and acknowledging Andy's brilliance. The two were awarded the fourth scotch.

The next day all those close to the colonel heard the story.

****

Andrea was sitting at her desk. The time was eleven o'clock in the evening. She was reading Andy's letter.

...and he lets me attend and assist in operations. I help him with diagnosis—that's the most difficult part. Anyway, my darling, I finally got the break I've been looking for. I can legitimately call myself a corpsman, and I'm probably more doctor than corpsman—they don't get to operate. Oh, I almost forgot. He's made me a lieutenant. I haven't seen Rusty since this happened. He'll be surprised because he will be commissioned before long, and here I am, an officer before he is. Officially, I have to be passed by some board, but I've got my bars, and I'm called "sir", so I'm getting there. I have a concern that my duty will be in the field and not in a hospital. Either way, I'm better off than if I were carrying a rifle.

I love you and I miss you.

Andy

CHAPTER 32

Fort Stotsenburg, Luzon
Base Hospital
Tuesday, Dec-8-1941

"Sir. You need to get up."

Andy rubbed his eyes. He wasn't accustomed to being aroused so early. "What's up?" he asked.

"There's an emergency meeting in the colonel's quarters—that's all I know," the orderly informed him.

Andy quickly dressed, checked his watch. The hour was just after four in the morning. The hospital itself was still asleep. The only activity was a few others following Andy as he made his way down the long lobby.

He entered the hospital director's sizeable office that was already crowded with staff members. The old doctor's drained appearance mirrored his tired delivery. He was speaking when Andy entered the room.

"General Stuart said the hostilities commenced this morning at approximately eight o'clock— two o'clock, our time, and the destruction at Pearl being massive, with heavy damage at Hickam Field and Schofield Barracks. Casualties are considerable, but estimates as to how severe are not available yet."

He paused, grimacing as he fumbled at his belt line, scanning the group that was still straggling in. Hoffmeister spoke for another several minutes relaying information that was given to him. Summing the announcement, he asked.

"How does this affect you? I can't really be certain, but I would say that anything you have to send—send it; any letters you have to write, write them. Whatever you have to do that's not hospital work, get it done. You don't have much time. We can expect the same treatment here they got in Hawaii, so you need to be ready for the onslaught. When the moment arises, your time will no longer be your own. An invasion may not come today, but General Stuart said to expect it damn sudden, so put your crews on alert, get all your necessities at your fingertips, and be prepared..." He issued a long painful sigh, "as best you can, so, get to work."

Amidst animated rumblings, the staff members slowly filed out. Andy remained.

Hoffmeister had taken a seat behind his desk and was studying a memo, but glanced up seeing Andy. "Well, cowboy? Was there something in there you didn't understand?"

"What's wrong with your stomach, Colonel?"

"Who says anything's wrong?" he growled reexamining the paper he held.

"I'm not blind."

Looking up scowling, he groused, "I got a little bellyache, that's all. We've got bigger fish to fry. You'd better hunt down Kohara and see what he has for you."

Without speaking, Andy turned and left.

Denver, Dec 7, 8:00 AM

The usual tedium of the school cafeteria was not the same this morning. All conversation was on the Pearl Harbor attack. The shock of the disaster created numerous speculations, with a loud continuous commotion from the students. After discussing the news with their friends, Andrea and Johnnie retired to the quiet of their rooms.

"I hear they're going to suspend classes today," Andrea said, adding, "What do you think we should do?"

"I know what I'd like to do," Johnnie answered.

"What's that?"

"I want to go home."

"Connecticut?"

"Yes," she said simply. "I don't want to hang around here after this."

Andrea paused, thinking, but not speaking.

"What about you?" Johnnie grilled.

"I have no idea, except that I don't want to stay here, either. I'm afraid for Andy, and I know I wouldn't be able to concentrate on my studies."

"Then why don't you come with me?" the buxom brunette asked.

Andrea whirled, a mischievous smirk appearing on her lips. "Don't tempt me!"

"That way your newspaper friend won't have worry about coming out here for his car," she said, half seriously.

"You know, "Andrea hedged, "I might just do that. You have plenty of room for me?"

Johnnie flashed a knowing smile. "Oh, I think I can find a corner somewhere we can fit you in."

Andrea stepped over to the closet, and began emptying the racks.

"What are you doing?" Johnnie asked, startled.

Andrea turned facing her roommate. "Well? Are you serious about getting out of here?"

"Sure... but just like that?"

"Why not?"

"You have family, checking out of school, obligations..."

Andrea cut her off. "I can take care of those later."

Johnnie rose from her chair. "Okay. I brought it up. Let's go."

The clock on the dash read 10:00 O'clock. The two had packed up, gassed up, and gathered free maps of Kansas, Missouri, and Illinois, and were heading east of Denver on Colorado Highway 40. Andrea felt the exhilaration of travel, at the same time, dreading the events that were certain to come.

"Turn on the radio," Andrea said. Johnnie complied.

The humming of the radio tubes warming up was audible, then the announcer's voice, "... Hickam Air Field is ablaze... the Pacific Fleet moored in Pearl is a shambles of twisted wreckage; a maelstrom of smoke and burning ships has masked the extent of damage. Across Ford Island,

Schofield Barracks is a mass of flames as the effort to attend to the wounded continues. Stay tuned to this station for more news of this attack."

"Oh God!" Andrea breathed, gripping the wheel. She asked weakly, "How far are the Philippines from Hawaii?"

"I have no idea. They're not far from Japan, I know that much."

"We have another news release," the radio began again, "From Admiral Hart, Asiatic Fleet Commander in Manila who reports the capitol of Baguio, the summer capitol, has been attacked by Japanese bombers. Another new release just in informs that Hong Kong has been bombed."

"Good grief" Johnnie gasped, "They're coming in from all directions!"

An hour later, a sign read, "Junction— Highway 36, Last Chance 46 miles, Chicago 1007; Highway 40, Cottonwood 6 miles, Kansas City 635..."

Andrea slowed to turn left on 36.

"You're not going to stop in your home town?" Johnnie asked.

"It's out of our way," Andrea replied tonelessly.

Luzon, The Philippines, Clark field
Noon, December 8, 1941

Rusty was furious. Major Canali had put him in charge of a battalion of Filipino troops, and upon news of the invasion, many of the troops dispersed. He was complaining.

"Dammit, Major! After they heard about the attack, those Flips are all heading for the hills! They're like rats leaving a sinking ship! I can't organize anything, and Captain Papano overrides everything I try to do!" he complained.

"I'll talk to Papano, but we've got bigger problems."

"Like what?"

"We've got all these damned planes sitting on the ground, and we're unable to get a decision out of MacArthur. We want to get 'em up and bomb Formosa—the least MacArthur could do is let us get them airborne!"

Andy was organizing medications when Hoffmeister came in. "Did you write your folks?" he asked. Andy noticed the Colonel's limp and grimace when he came in.

"I got a short one off to my girlfriend and one to my folks. That's all."

"I suggest," the Colonel added, "You send that electric guitar home. Hang on to the other one."

"What about you?" Andy asked. "You need to see a doctor. You're hurting. I can see it in your face."

"You need to do what I tell you," the Colonel barked, and stumped out.

December 8, 1941

Millions of Americans heard Roosevelt's famous, "Today is a day that will live in infamy..." The Hubbards were huddled around the battery-powered Zenith in the living room when they heard it; Andrea and her friend, heading east outside Chicago listened on the car radio. They kept the radio on as they drove, when at 5PM Central Standard Time, the announcement came... "This is Manila. We have just learned that at 2:00 O'clock, a savage bombing assault has been directed on Clark Field, just outside of Fort Stotsenburg, MacArthur's headquarters. We don't yet know the extent of damage or number of lives lost, other than the airfield is heavily damaged and there are casualties. The airfield is strewn with broken airplanes. The B-17 recently ferried there are reported to be for the most part destroyed, and the landing strip is reported inoperable..."

Andrea was aware of the tears streaming down her face.

"Johnnie," she murmured softly, "That's where Andy is."

"I know," she returned, massaging Andrea's shoulder.

Back on the farm, after hearing the latest news, Mildred Hubbard put on her coat and walked out in the cutting December wind. The chill tore at her face as she walked across the pasture. She was numb to the cold, walking without purpose along the pond bank, much like the ancient mariner lost at sea, wandering in no direction against the deliberate wind. In the heavens, dark and foreboding skies mirrored her son's misfortune, and she saw him somewhere among the many cattails in the shallow water along the pond bank bending with the others in the gale, caught, innocent and unable to gain freedom from the sinister force that now held him hostage. She was powerless, and could only pledge her faith to the will of God that this tempest would someday abate and her son. Andy would again be free.

The situation at Clark was a combination of confusion and disorganization. The combination of explosives dropped from Japanese bombers high above, coupled with fighter planes coming in low strafing personnel, barracks, machine shops, parked airplanes, and whatever was in the way, turning the place into a junkyard of twisted wreckage. A shell fragment crashed into a troop standing near Captain Pompano killing a young soldier instantly. The Filipino Captain lost his composure and began shouting meaningless orders. In an even voice, Rusty instructed twenty or so men to take a position behind a bank on the far side of the landing strip and set up a fifty caliber machine gun, and for the rest to grab bandoleers of ammunition.

"Take cover! Take cover!" Pompano shouted as the small detachment darted across the air strip. "That's an order!"

"Stick the order in your ass!" Rusty snarled back. "We're not here to die! Let's move it!"

The group raced across the strip, bullets from incoming fighters raking the ground behind them. Snavely dutifully carried the heavy weapon across the flat tarmac and set it up. Rusty began firing wildly at the fighters coming in at tree top level. Immediately, he saw smoke belch from the engine of one of the fighters, then yaw out of control to the left and crash into a thicket some five hundred yards away. There was an instant cheer. Rusty stopped for a moment to relish the black pillar winding into the sky.

Over at Stotsenburg, the condition at the hospital was an equal mess. The insufficient three ambulances brought in dead and dying men. Andy learned very quickly the meaning of triage and struggled with making the decisions. The initial fear was gone now, and he was working feverishly in any way that he could. He and Morgan were carrying a wounded man on a stretcher into the main hall of the hospital when his eye caught a prone figure slumped in the corner of a room. It was Colonel Hoffmeister. They gently laid the stretcher down in the receiving room.

"Come on!" Andy yelled to Morgan. "The colonel is in trouble! Get a stretcher!"

The colonel growled, "Let me alone! Get back to work, Hubbard!"

"It's your appendix, isn't it?"

Hoffmeister, in obvious pain, snorted, "What the hell did you think is was, my dick?"

"I knew it a couple of days ago, Colonel."

Morgan arrived with the stretcher. Hoffmeister snarled, "Get that goddam thing out of here! There are men dying out there!"

"You're going to die too is we don't operate. Morgan, go get a doctor," Andy ordered.

"Morgan!" Hoffmeister cursed, "I'll have your ass in Leavenworth if you get a doctor! You will not get a doctor! I forbid it! That's an order!"

Morgan shrank out of the room and returned quickly, reporting there were no available doctors.

Andy moved toward the prostate officer.

"Come on, Morgan. Help me get the colonel on the stretcher."

"You will not put me on a stretcher! That's an order!"

"Morgan," Andy said firmly. "Get his shoulders; I'll get his butt."

"Ouch! Oh God—you're killing me!" the colonel cried.

"Let's take him into that room," Andy said pointing.

Andy looked at Morgan. "Let's get him on this cart and go get soap and a razor."

"Oh Jesus!" Hoffmeister croaked. There was a hint of submission in his voice. Andy began undressing the man as tenderly as he could. He checked the colonel's breathing, his heart, his blood pressure, frowning after each examination.

"Don't worry, Colonel," he said above the frenzied activity coming from other parts of the hospital. "You're a little out of whack right now, but we'll get you fixed up."

"Christ, Hubbard. You've never performed an operation," the colonel said painfully.

"I've assisted on enough of them, sir."

Morgan came in with the soap, iodine solution, sponge and razor. Andy began washing the colonel who began cursing and howling in pain.

"Get the set up," Andy ordered.

"Just us?" Morgan asked incredulously.

"You got it. Now get at it!" Andy's latent temper began to show. Morgan shrank away obediently.

Andy began shaving Hoffmeister who continued howling, cursing and grumbling, Instructing Andy what he was doing was wrong. Andy paid no attention. He was told doctors made lousy patients. Morgan wheeled a metal table containing towels, clamps, sponges, hemostats, ether, and sodium pentothal. Andy inspected the instruments and felt beads of sweat gather on his forehead. By now, he had the colonel's crotch shaved.

"Start the I.V. Morgan."

Morgan flashed a pained frightened expression, "Me?"

At that moment a nurse walked into the room. "We're looking for Colonel Hoff..." She stopped, placing her open palm over her mouth. "My God! What's going on here?"

"Tell me you're an anesthetist," Andy implored.

"I am, but..."

"Thank heavens," Hoffmeister breathed.

"Sleep him, lieutenant," Andy ordered calmly.

"Why, you're not going to operate on this man!"

"You want to cut on him, nurse?" Andy asked derisively.

"Why no, but..." she protested.

"Then shut up and start the I.V." Andy ordered.

"Colonel?" she pleaded.

"Shut up and start the procedure," Hoffmeister ordered. This time, Nurse Wallace obeyed.

"Know where McBurney's point is, Cowboy?" the colonel asked.

"Yes, I'm very aware where it is sir, and your ailing appendix is directly beneath it. Now, don't worry, sir. You'll be all right."

A slight grin of confidence appeared at the corners of Hoffmeister's mouth, and the sodium pentothal began to ease his pain. Nurse Wallace then administered ether and the grouchy colonel was out.

"Thank God you showed up." Andy sighed as he took his scalpel and made the first clean sharp incision.

"Yes," she answered sharply. "Now if we just had a doctor!"

Andy gave her a withering stare; one that she would not chance insulting him again.

The three-inch incision immediately exposed fat and bleeding.

"Scalpel," Andy ordered as he prepared for the secondary deeper cut. The nurse obediently handed him the knife.

"We should have," she said, "toweled and clamped around the area."

"No time," Andy cut her off. "I didn't want to lose you. Somebody is probably wondering where you are right now."

"They are," she answered quietly.

Andy went through each muscle layer. Nurse Wallace sponged and tied off the bleeders neatly. Morgan watched intently, handing instruments as they were called for. Andy cut through the peritoneum exposing the cecum. There was significant inflammation from the appendix indicated by the greater omentum which had become attached to the tissue.

"Not good," Andy murmured as he began peeling the tissue layer. The nurse looked at the young corpsman, thanking the Lord that she didn't have the responsibility of attempting a first-time operation.

"Retractor," Andy ordered to Morgan who passed the tool to the nurse who then opened the area so that Andy could pull the small bowel out of the way exposing the mesentery.

"Hemostat," he ordered then rolled up the cecum and brought the appendix into sight.

"My God!" the nurse exclaimed. "We're lucky this hasn't burst!"

"Don't cough," Andy joked. "It might."

The appendix was elongated, three times its normal width. Andy knew he had to work quickly.

"Clamps," he said to Morgan. Morgan handed him one.

"*Clamps!*" Andy snapped. Morgan handed another clamp. He placed the clamp on the mesoappendix as the nurse continued tying.

"Scalpel," the upstart doctor demanded, cutting between the two clamps. The nurse immediately began the purse string suture; then a secondary layer of sutures on the cecum.

"Better give him a backup," Andy suggested. "He'd never forgive us if the cecum leaked."

"If he lives," the nurse said, as she applied the secondary suturing. Andy knew her comment was not a criticism. The colonel was old and the appendix was in bad shape.

Andy took a clamp which he attached onto the appendix, handed it to Morgan with the instruction, "Save that for the colonel. Put it on ice.

When we're through, I want him to see it." Andy then took the clamp, rolled it inward, inverted it, and tightened the purse string suture.

"Easy." The nurse reminded, as he pulled the suture.

"I know," he replied confidently. Had he pulled too hard, he may have either broken the suture or pulled it away from the tissue, in either case, causing the contents of the bowels to leak into the peritoneum. He removed the clamp, then tightened the second purse string suture, removing the second clamp. He then observed the area for a moment. There was no leakage that he could see.

"I'm closing him unless you see something I've missed, nurse," he said to the lieutenant.

"No" she said scanning the colonel's open wound, raising her eyebrows. "Looks like a good job to me."

Andy began the closure, suturing layer after layer, then finally the skin.

"It always amazes me that you have to close those things a door at a time," she observed.

"Don't be amazed. It can't be any other way. Let's give him a check." Andy said as he laid a bandage over the incision. He looked at the nurse while she checked his blood pressure. The woman was pretty. Her black hair and dark eyes reminded him of his mother.

"What's your name, corpsman?" she asked.

When the attack occurred, Andy snatched the first coat on the rack, one without any ranking or caduceus identification and he wasn't going to go into any further explanation to the nurse at this point. And he wasn't really an officer yet, officially.

"Andy Hubbard. What's yours?"

"Nurse Wallace."

"Nurse *what* Wallace? I can see you're a nurse. I can't imagine you came into this world without a first name. By the way, what's his blood pressure?"

"Rank doesn't seem to matter much to you, does it? He's 141 over 97."

"141 over 97? He's a tough old goat. I'll bet you a beer that it will recover ten points on both ends in an hour—and no, rank doesn't matter much, although I'm a lieutenant, same as you.

She laughed. "You're not old enough to be a doctor, and if you were, you'd be a captain, and I doubt you're an officer. But you know your stuff.

Your dad must be a doctor, and, yeah, I'll take that bet. Ten points is too many."

The activity at the hospital had subsided. The attack happened two hours earlier and the rush seemed to be over.

"Let's check on how things are going in the hospital," she said, "And if we can get away, you can buy me that beer, if you're really a lieutenant and can get into the club."

"Morgan. Stay here with the colonel," Andy ordered.

"Yes sir." The corpsman replied.

"At least he thinks you're an officer," she quipped, as they walked down the hall.

Although the raid on Clark lasted less than a half-hour, over two hundred troops were killed and three times the number injured. The hospital was full of wounded, but the worst had passed. The two approached a haggard major sitting at a table, his whites covered with blood.

He looked up wearily. "You got away, Barb. What happened? Couldn't you find the boss?"

"Well, I found Art all right. This guy," she said turning to Andy, "had him on a gurney ready to take his appendix out."

"He *what*? You're only a corpsman!"

"Whatever he is, he did a good job," she said.

The major looked at Andy warily. "You must be that kid Art's been crowing about."

"We thought we'd get away for a drink if there's any chance," she explained.

"You'd better do it now if you've got someone looking after Art."

"We do," she put in.

"Hell, we may be hit again, and I'm probably the ranking surgeon, now that Art's down. Besides, Art's man, Kohara, was just here, so you'd better get word to him."

Before the two could leave, Andy felt a tap on his shoulder. It was Morgan.

"The colonel has come around."

"Come on Nurse Barbara. Let's have a look."

The colonel was awake, in pain, and crankier than ever. First, he polled Andy about the condition of the wounded at the hospital, to which Andy had no idea, but the nurse informed the frenzy had passed and many of the staff were on break.

"Well, did you get my appendix?" he asked Andy, lying flat staring at the ceiling.

"Yes, we got it, sir," Andy replied.

"Well, tell me about it, but first prop me up a little. I can't see anything like this."

Together, amongst a litany of complaints, Andy and the nurse wadded two fat pillows under his head.

"I'll do better than tell you about it, sir." Morgan had taken his cue and retrieved the swollen body part. Morgan handed the clamp to Andy who displayed the appendix in front of the colonel's nose.

"I'll be damned!" he chirped. "You did get it! I knew it was bad but not like that! Morgan, take that down to the lab. We'll put that on display."

Morgan turned to leave. Andy took his arm, and whispered, "Throw the thing away."

"But he wants it..."

"I said trash it."

"Now tell me, Cowboy," the colonel began, "I'm a little doped up as you know, and I'm in pain, but I want you to describe the operation before I flake out."

Andy described the operation, part by part. Hoffmeister interrupted. Did you get a good hold on the cecum?"

"He did an especially good job, colonel," the nurse offered. "You can be assured of that."

"Okay then... what the hell... I guess I'm going to live, although I want a little more morphine. I got a bit too much pain."

"No luck, colonel. We're boned out. You've gotten all you're going to get until we can figure a way to get some more in," Andy said.

"I could really use another shot," the colonel protested.

"Curl your toes. Clench your teeth, colonel. Take stock in the fact that you'll be all right."

"That's just fine then!" He carped heatedly. "Take your nurse and get the hell out of here!"

The room was a crowded cacophony of medical people, escaping the first-time attack and eager to relate their experiences. Andy found an unoccupied space on a bench at the rear of the club and left to get a drink for himself and the nurse.

Upon returning, she observed, "The staff in here all seem to know you. Tell me how that can be."

"I've been coming in here fairly regularly with the colonel after hours," Andy replied, asking, "I know your name's Barbara. There aren't many female officers here in the hospital. How is it that you're stationed here?"

"It's a convoluted story. It would bore you."

"Then bore me."

She smiled at him with an amused frown. "You're weird." Taking a deep breath, she began. "I was dating this torpedo plane pilot instructor at Van Nuys. I was in nursing school there, and when I graduated, he talked me into marrying him. He also talked me into joining the marines, convincing me his job there was secure, and I could find work at the base. Well, guess what? Two weeks after we got married, he got transferred to the Enterprise and I got this friendly little invite to Fort Stotsenburg."

"Some honeymoon."

"Wasn't it, though?"

"Sorry you got married?"

She sighed. "We should have waited—no doubt about that. Now, tell me about you."

At that moment, Captain Kohara shouldered up to the two. Andy immediately rose.

"Have you seen the colonel?" Kohara asked.

"John," the nurse began. "Andy here just completed an appendectomy on him. I assisted. He's recuperating now."

Kohara jerked, eyeing the nurse, glowering at Andy, spilling a portion of the drink he held in his hand in the process, exclaiming "You what?"

"I was going to get a doctor," Andy explained, "but the colonel wouldn't stand for it and I knew it had to be done immediately."

The nurse added, chuckling, "He and this corpsman were just about to sleep him when I came on the scene. Neither knew anything about anesthesia, but Andy here did a fine job. He tells me he's a lieutenant."

Kohara flashed a derisive glance to Andy. "Yeah. Art's made him one, I guess," adding, "So how's the colonel doing?"

"He's begging for morphine, but we're out," she explained.

"I know we are," he countered. "How could we expect this? I sent a courier down to Cavite for a re-supply over an hour ago. It should get here before long." Kohara slugged his drink. "Come on. Let's go visit the old man."

The three rounded the hall into Hoffmeister's remote cubicle where the colonel lay on the gurney. Morgan stood by. The colonel was still awake. Kohara laid a gentle hand on the senior officer's forehead. "Well, how goes the battle, boss?"

"I'm in pain, John, but I guess I'll survive. I can't get my doctor to give me any more sedative," he said crustily, a faint note of humor in his voice.

"There's more on the way, colonel. It should arrive at any time. Hang tough."

"Thank God!" the doctor breathed.

"Art," Kohara began, "Why in the hell did you let Hubbard cut on you?"

"I told him I'd have him court martialed if he summoned a doctor, and I would have, too, but there wasn't a hell of a lot I could do when he and Morgan began manhandling me onto a stretcher."

"Weren't you scared to death?"

Hoffmeister issued a long thoughtful sigh. "You know I was, John, but when this nurse came along—and what luck, she's a trained anesthetist—I wasn't afraid anymore. I was confident the kid here," he explained, glancing and motioning at Andy, "could do the job okay, but I was afraid of the anesthesia. But," he continued philosophically, "it had to be done. It was as bad as I've ever seen. It was bad, wasn't it, nurse?"

"John, it was the worst I've ever seen. I'm amazed it hadn't burst."

Hoffmeister jabbed Morgan in the ribs. "Go get that appendage, corporal. I want the captain here to see it."

Morgan stood unmoved. "Well, go git my appendix, Morgan!" the colonel cursed. "Are you deaf?"

"I can't sir."

"Why the hell not? I told you to put it in the lab!"

"Hubbard told me to dispose of it, and I did."

`Hoffmeister turned to Andy. "Goddammit it, Cowboy! I gave that corpsman an order! I ought to bust your ass back to a corporal!"

"Easy, colonel," Lieutenant Wallace cautioned. "You wouldn't have ever gotten a chance to see it in the first place if it weren't for this 'cowboy', as you call him."

"Okay," he surrendered, "I guess you're right."

At that moment a supply attendant handed Andy a small sack. He immediately took a syringe and administered to the colonel, who smiled at Andy during the injection.

"You all better go and let me get some rest, now," he suggested. It was more of an order.

As the small group filed out, Hoffmeister caught Andy's eye. "Sorry about that, Andy," he uttered fatherly. Andy merely smiled and nodded.

Soon, the colonel was asleep.

CHAPTER 33

After the jungle training scheme was abandoned, Shigimetsu Tanaka was sequestered at the Marine base in San Diego, but nothing had been arranged for him to do, and he was bored. He longed for the companionship and the responsibility he had been given.

Corporal Grounds, from the old unit, was held back and promoted to D.I. in charge of boot camp, making use of the existing training facilities. After the Pearl Harbor attack, the abrupt distrust of the Japanese plus their relocation made Tanaka a target, although nobody apprised him of this particular liability. He would be under the protectorate of the United States Marine Corps for the time being.

Grounds walked down the old mission hall to Shigi's room. He knocked at the door. There was no response. Gently he swung it open. "Shigi?" he asked. No answer. He walked in and found the room empty. He then returned to the orderly room and asked the company clerk if he knew where Tanaka was.

"He said he was going up town to buy some magazines," the clerk replied.

"I told him not to leave the post without checking with me," Grounds responded angrily. "Where did he go?"

"Shit, I don't know where he buys his magazines," the clerk answered.

"Damn! Call for me a jeep!"

"Is he in some sort of trouble?" the orderly asked.

"Hell, I've got orders to watch out for him. If you don't know that every Jap in this country isn't in trouble, you better wake up and smell the coffee!" Grounds spat. He turned to the window to wait for the transportation.

Shigi Tanaka told the military staff car to wait at the curb outside the drugstore.

"Only be a minute," he said. "Hang on."

The driver of the military olive drab '41 Ford sedan complied. Tanaka walked into the well-lit drugstore and found the magazine racks. The picture of the sports magazine had a picture of Johnny Lujak. He leafed through it seeing articles about Bobby Jones, Joe DiMaggio and Sonja Heine. He closed the magazine and stuck it under his arm. He then picked up another with the picture of Marilyn Maxwell on the front. He began leafing through it.

A counter away, stood a burly simple fellow, his hair combed back in a greasy pompadour. He was with a friend of equal size. Dickie Butler had just lost his brother at Pearl. His brother was on the California, and although Dickie didn't know how his brother was killed, he knew he was dead—and he knew it was the Japs who killed him.

"There's a goddam Jap," he said to his friend. They stood and watched for a moment.

"He's a fuckin' spy, I'll guarantee you that," his friend replied.

"Let's get the sonovabitch," Butler cursed as he fingered the knife in his pocket.

"No," the other said. "Wait till he gets to the door, then we'll nail his ass."

Tanaka picked up two more issues and headed for the pay counter. Butler and his friend waited and watched. After paying for the magazines, he stepped out of the store into the shadows of the street. He felt a presence behind him and should have run to the car, but his instincts told him to find safety in the concealment of darkness.

Butler had his opened knife poised in his eager palm.

The staff car driver watched helplessly.

Had Tanaka dashed into one of the busy streets of any city in Japan, he would have escaped easily. But this was San Diego. Dickie Butler knew the territory; Tanaka didn't. Tanaka turned into the refuge of the blackness of an alley, unaware that the path offered no escape. It was a dead end. Searching for the exit of the street and finding none, he reversed, but was knocked off his feet by Butler's friend. Butler then leaped on Shigi's back, thrusting the knife deep into the Asian's shoulder. Tanaka spun and threw a vicious knee into Butler's face knocking the attacker to the pavement. But now Butler's accomplice had blunted Tanaka's get away, grabbing one leg. Tanaka scrambled to get to his feet, when he felt a sharp searing pain in his left buttock, as the incensed assailant plunged the weapon to its depth.

"Goddam Nip!" Butler screamed, "You killed my brother!"

Tanaka could no longer run as the second stab incapacitated his left leg. But the American sympathizer was not finished. He twisted away from Butler just in time to meet Butler's friend driving on him. The wounded Japanese thrust his thumb into the attacker's eyeball gouging it out of its socket as one would relieve an olive of its seed. Butler's friend was disabled.

Tanaka desperately crawled along to the light of the street dragging his left leg behind, crying out, "I'm an American soldier! You're making a mistake!"

Those were his last words as he felt the knife enter his back again and again; the anguished cries died away in stillness. Butler guided his friend, horrified at experiencing his eye dangling around the base of his nose, and rushed up the street on a run to find anyone who may help. The driver of the military sedan rushed up and discovered the lifeless form of his passenger lying face down in the alley. Shigi, in his fight for life, had almost reached the safety of the illuminated street. But he didn't, and a candle of America's defense had just been snuffed.

CHAPTER 34

In the days following the attack, Andy had free reign to attend to the wounded; a liberty he greatly appreciated. Word was, he saved Hoffmeister's life, and that was enough clout to give him all the liberty and responsibility he wanted. He was absorbing much in short order.

Down at Clark, most of the aircraft were caught on the ground, despite more than ample warning of an impending raid. Rusty, as well as his superiors, was stewing over the fact that so many planes were lost without a fight, and the consensus was that there was a frightening lack of leadership. "Dugout Doug," as MacArthur was referred, was really catching it from the lower echelons. Scuttlebutt had it an invasion from the Japanese was coming at any time, and Rusty's abhorrence for the Japanese tyranny was rivaled only by the Filipino impotence. Then he was informed of Shigimetsu Tanaka's ambush by an American citizen and his anger mushroomed. He was ready to do his part to set things straight in the world. For him, that invasion couldn't come quickly enough. He would get his wish. Four days later the Japanese armada stormed ashore at Lingayen Gulf.

CHAPTER 35

Andrea and her host, Johnnie Hickman, lounged in the glassed-in porch at the family mansion in Greenwich. The father William, senior board member of the Chase Manhattan Bank, sat in his smoking jacket reading the Sunday Times. From a phonograph, strains of a Sigmund Romberg operetta wafted throughout the portico. The family had finished breakfast and was planning their activities for the day. That ritual wasn't interrupted by the minor inconvenience of a war.

The two girls rose and stood at the window that overlooked an extravagant manicured lawn, interrupted only by a solitary gazebo. That drab foggy morning, the lonely structure looked to be the sanctuary for a private visit they were contemplating. Andrea had been a guest of the Hickmans for the past two weeks, and although the escape had been pleasant, she knew it was time to move on; to where and to what, she had been unable to decide. Suddenly, an idea came to her.

"Would it be okay if I made a long distance call on your phone, Johnnie?"

"Be my guest," her tomboyish friend answered. "Would it be nosy if I asked what for?"

"Not if I get through."

Bill Hickman liked privacy, and that extended to the telephone, evidenced by the booth constructed in the hallway of his home.

Andrea entered, closed the door, took a seat and lifted the receiver, dialed "O" and waited. A nasal voice complied, "Operator."

"I would like information in Washington for the *Post Dispatch* newspaper," she replied.

Shortly, the operator came back on, "That's Jefferson 7900."

"I would like to make a person to person call to Phil Olson at that number."

"Olson?"

"Yes. Philip Olson."

"What number are you speaking from?"

Andrea scanned the phone. "It's Belmont, 51216."

As the phone began to ring, Andrea murmured audibly, "Crap, it's Sunday. I didn't think of that."

"Washington Post Dispatch," the interference-laced voice answered.

"Mr. Philip Olson," the nasal operator said.

Andrea could hear the call being transferred. "'He isn't here at the moment." The response this time was clear and articulate.

Andrea felt compromised that Sunday may have been as good a day as any.

"When do you expect him back?" the operator quizzed.

"Sometime this afternoon," she said. "Is there a message?"

"Have him call operator five at this number," the nasal voice instructed.

Later, Andrea and Johnnie bundled up and strolled out to the gazebo. Both expressed opinions about what would happen now that the country was immersed in war. It was chilly in the bower, but it offered seclusion and that was what they wanted. Andrea revealed the purpose of her call and together the two mulled over what to do now that they both had decided to leave school. A young boy, Johnnie's brother, trotted up. "There's a telephone call for you, Andrea."

Andrea was grateful for the isolation the booth provided. This was a conversation that she wanted for only herself and Phil Olson.

"Hello, Phil," she said.

"Who is this?"

"Andrea Vogel."

"Andrea! —God, I didn't recognize your voice! What are you doing in New York?"

"Connecticut," she corrected.

"Okay, Connecticut. I got a New York operator."

"I quit school, Phil."

"I assumed something happened. I called your dorm number the day after the attack, and they said you checked out. So what are you up to?"

"Want your car back?"

"To tell you the truth, I haven't given it much thought. I've been so damned tied up since the attack."

"Well, I'm looking for a job, Phil. Can you help me out?"

The question stunned him. An awkward pause followed.

"I don't mean to embarrass you or put you on the spot," she said.

"Oh no, no, no," he said quickly. "I'm just thinking. Your question sort of caught me by surprise. How soon can you get here?"

"Does that mean you can do something for me?"

"You get that gorgeous frame of yours here and I'll put you to work. With all that's coming down, you bet I can use you. We'll need a couple of days to decide just what, plus we got to get you a place to stay. Call me when you get close."

The next morning, she left the Hickman estate, pledging to stay in touch with Johnnie.

Luzon, January, 1942

Japanese forces, having overrun Port Binanga, pushed southward through the jungle to Mt. Silanganan, a sheer wall, which rendered US military communications all but non-existent. By January 9, the men of the 4th were exhausted from sleep deprivation and starving from living on less than half rations. The American forces could not begin to match the constant flow of fresh troops, ammunition and supplies enjoyed by a prepared enemy. It was soon obvious that the battle was a losing one. The relief promised by Washington was beginning to appear what it initially was intended... a stall. The American forces fought a courageous delaying action, but was gradually caving in. Compounding the already severe predicament was the infiltration of additional Japanese soldiers along the west border into the southern tip of the Bataan Peninsula. The sobering conclusion was that no aid would be coming from the United States. Morale was at its nadir.

Any attempt to evacuate non-combat personnel was rapidly becoming impossible. The Japanese had become aware of this effort, and were sinking the ships and shooting down aircraft used for the planned exodus.

The situation at Fort Stotsenburg was critical. Medical supplies were quickly running out. Andy had functioned for days as a full-fledged doctor but he also was on the verge of total exhaustion. Air raids were commonplace now, and the deteriorating condition of the hospital necessitated a move to the hospital at Mariveles. Colonel Hoffmeister was up and around working as long as his energy would allow. He had sent and received General Stuart's authorization of a battlefield commission for Andy. Kohara no longer referred to Andy as "corpsman". Bataan was rapidly becoming hopeless, and the tortured memories of Andrea and his family made living for Andy even more hellish. It had been a month and a half since any correspondence had been sent or received, and the prospects for getting any mail was all but a dream. Andy thought about Andrea constantly, and more desperately, he wondered if she was thinking of him. Of the six hundred men of the 4th who began the retreat, barely half had survived. Two of the living were Rusty Atkins and Bob Snavely.

Unbeknownst to Andy, he was soon to be separated from a man who had become an inestimable benefactor. MacArthur had been given orders from President Roosevelt to evacuate Luzon. Earlier, he had established his command post on the island fortress of Corregidor. The evacuation would be effected soon and there were a few select men the general would take with on the premise that the chosen provided critical values to the war effort. It was considered that those left behind would most-likely be subjected to periods of discomfort and incarceration, but such were the unavoidable byproducts of war. Among the individuals selected were General Stuart and Colonel Hoffmeister. It was agreed that both Stuart and Hoffmeister could each take an aide. Stuart picked Frank Canali and Hoffmeister would take Andy Hubbard. Initially, both Stuart and Hoffmeister refused to abandon their men, but word was immediately sent down that the invitation was in reality, an order, and being responsible soldiers, both Stuart and Hoffmeister reluctantly complied.

General Stuart walked into Hoffmeister's battered office. It was March 11.

"Go get your kid, Art. Doug says you can take him."

Hoffmeister bolted from behind his desk and asked a corpsman where Andy was.

"He's out on an ambulance run," was the reply.

"How long ago?"

"I'd be guessing,"

In a supreme effort, Hoffmeister jerkily floundered for the exit scanning the area, then hurried back to his office to face Stuart.

"We gotta wait a bit, Henry. My guy's out on an ambulance run and I gotta chase him down."

"I'm sorry, Art. We're leaving now. We're already late. Doug has his schedule and we still have to get the boat over to the rock. I'm sorry, Pal. It's a no go."

Hoffmeister flashed a pained desperate expression. He spied Morgan walking into the hallway. "Go get Nurse Wallace— now!"

Morgan hurried out.

Hoffmeister sadly followed the general to the waiting sedan. "That poor kid's still battin' zero," he mumbled.

"What's that Art?"

"Nothing, Henry—just nothing."

The ambulance pulled into the hospital yard. Andy and a corpsman climbed out and unloaded a wounded man on a stretcher. Morgan met them at the entrance.

"Lieutenant, the colonel was just looking for you."

"Where is he?" Andy asked.

"He just left with General Stuart."

"What'd he want?"

"I dunno—something important, I would think."

Andy found Captain Kohara operating on a comatose soldier. Andy approached the surgeon.

"Colonel Hoffmeister was looking for me, Captain. Do you know what he wanted?"

Kohara turned from the operating table, and even though he was wearing a mask, his sympathetic expression showed through. "He wanted you to go with him to Corregidor."

"Why Corregidor?"

Kohara paused choosing his words. "He is evacuating to Australia with MacArthur. He wanted to take you with him."

"Is there a chance I can still catch him?"

Kohara stopped his work and looked up again. "No, Andy. There isn't. I'm sorry. There's no chance. I really am sorry."

Andy slumped against the wall and uttered a rarely-used word, "shit." Then he asked, "What about you?"

"I've been placed in charge. It wasn't an option."

"What about Barb Wallace?"

"He took her when he couldn't find you."

"Well, thank God for that, at least," he murmured and walked slowly out of the room.

Manila had fallen and the end was in sight for the battle weary, starved, diseased, exhausted and crippled men. The ring was closing and units from every conceivable outfit Including the 4th were being squeezed into the southern tip of Bataan. General Wainwright set up his command on Corregidor and the transference of personnel from Bataan was being conducted en masse. The tragic end came on April 9 when General King, acting in command, surrendered Bataan to the Japanese. On the morning of April 10, thousands of prisoners were herded to Mariveles Airfield on Bataan. When he realized the capture was imminent, Andy gathered his bag and stuffed it with narcotics, antibiotics, sedatives, antiseptics and myriad pain killers, and whatever room was left for bandages. In his other hand, he grabbed his guitar. Merging with personnel of the 4th, he wandered into the company of his old comrades; Rusty, Snavely, Yank Donnelly and Bob Armstrong. Andy was wearing his blood-stained white coat, replete with rank and duty. He saw them before they saw him. They were hollow-eyed and thin.

"You guys look bad," he said, approaching the small circle.

The group, at first, failed to recognize him, then Snavely burst, "My god, Andy! Are you a doctor?"

"I can legitimately say that I am, Bob."

Rusty stuck his thin arm out to shake Andy's. "And you're a lieutenant!"

Andy looked at Rusty's foul ragged fatigue jacket bearing sergeant's rank. "I see you've added a stripe, Rusty."

"Lot of good it's going to do anybody now," he cursed.

"I thought that too, Rusty," Andy agreed.

"Andy," Snavely began, "I really feel responsible."

"For what?"

"Getting you into this mess."

"Oh hell," Andy uncharacteristically snapped, "This is no time for that."

"Well, I do," Snavely persisted.

"Bob," Andy softened, "None of that matters now. Getting out of this mess is all that matters."

Donnelly, tired and emaciated, but suffered no loss of his fire spat, "We'll get these goddamn bastards before this thing's over, I guarantee you that!"

Immediately, an English speaking Japanese officer yelled over a loud speaker to be quiet and prepare for a search. Andy was shocked at the way the men were being searched and brutalized. Personal belongs were taken. Rank chevrons were stripped and thrown to the ground Watches, rings, wallets, everything was taken. Andy clutched his half-heart necklace when he saw this. He knew that he would never again see his guitar. That didn't matter, but the necklace did.

When it came time for Andy's turn to be searched, he was stripped of his watch, wallet and other personal belongings in his pockets. The guard took the guitar, and grabbed the doctor's satchel he had in his hand.

"Take your hands off that! I'm a doctor!" Andy snarled in the makeshift Japanese lingo he had learned. Japanese soldiers nearby scattered, and the searcher cowered as though given an order by an emperor. The guard nodded politely, and started again up the line continuing his vile grabbing and snatching, as though Andy was some kind of saint among thieves.

During the interruption, Rusty spied the empennage of a wrecked B-17 that lay unaccountably at the edge of the line. It might just work, he thought. Touching Snavely's shirt sleeve and getting Andy's attention, he sidled up against it. Rusty crawled into the rudder portion, and Andy concentrated a move toward the vertical stabilizer which would readily admit his height. Bob Snavely quickly moved into the concealment of the wrecked component.

Emil Zamora saw it all. Incensed at being captured, and jealous of not escaping, he motioned to a Japanese guard and pointed toward the wrecked tail section. Andy felt relieved he hadn't jet joined in the attempt. The guard stepped up, spying the two, who immediately stepped out. At this, the guard struck Snavely in the head with his rifle butt. Snavely, severely injured, fell to the ground. As the guard readied to strike Rusty, Yank Donnelly wrestled the rifle from the guard and shot him. Donnelly was immediately engulfed by a hoard of Japanese soldiers, and a guard nodded to another who unsheathed his sword. Donnelly' fate became apparent to anyone who could spell his own name. The English speaking officer ordered that a large contingent form a circle to witness Donnelly's demise. Rusty made certain he was on the outer rank of the ring. The officer gave a short speech informing the upcoming tribunal would be accorded to any subsequent miscreant, while Donnelly was forced to his knees. The multitude of men of all cultures became stilled when the Japanese drew his sword, holding it ceremoniously high in both hands, perpendicular to the earth. Suddenly and swiftly, he brought it in a violent downward motion, striking full on Donnelly's neck. At that precise moment, Rusty broke from the cordon and raced toward the tangle of vegetation. As the gallant sergeant's head fell to the gravel, two guards became aware of Rusty's flight. They began firing wildly in Rusty's direction charging after him in hot pursuit. Witnessing this, Zamora broke in the opposite direction. He felt the sting of bullets driving deep into his back, falling face first on the dry dusty trail.

Emil Zamora had lost his final perfidious gamble. Zamora's war was over.

Significantly into the jungle now, Rusty had things on his terms. He clung catlike to a tree when he heard one of the Japanese thrashing through the dense foliage. As the hunter walked immediately below him, Rusty dropped, clutching the soldier by the throat. He knew that if the soldier could cry out, his position would be identified. There was no sound; only the muffled thrashing in the dense forest. He held his vice grip while he felt the life ebb from the oriental. Quickly, he pulled the bayonet from the soldier's rifle and headed deeper into the jungle.

"That one is for Yank," he murmured.

He now heard added thrashes and yelling. He decided not to run, but wait. He had spent many hours squirrel and coon hunting in his youth growing up in southern Mississippi. The lush vegetation was similar, and Rusty was a master of patience and concealment. He paused until he could identify one soldier who became separated. Stealthily, he crept up behind the soldier, and with one motion, brought the bayonet over the soldier's head perpendicular to the neck, catching the soldier just under the chin. This time it was simple. The force of the blade cut through the jugular before the soldier had any opportunity to utter a sound.

"That's for Hubbard," he said softly.

More activity convinced Rusty not to trust his luck any further. He headed north toward the Mariveles Mountains, a territory more familiar to him. After a hundred yards or so, the shouting from the Japanese faded away. He felt confident that his escape had been successful. Then something caught his attention. He thought he heard a rustle somewhere behind him. They can't still be chasing me in this tangle, he thought to himself. He waited to be certain. Sure enough, one soldier hadn't heard the order to abandon the search and was still out looking for Rusty. He saw a bush move no more than five feet away. This time, Rusty wasn't so lucky. The Japanese soldier saw him first. Had the soldier fired his rifle, Rusty's whereabouts would have surely been detected, but for some reason, the soldier shouted and rushed at Rusty with the extended bayoneted rifle. Rusty leaped aside and thrust his own bayonet into the ribs of the soldier. He knew the soldier was dead as he lay atop him, but now his heart thundered wondering if the shout of the soldier had been heard. He lay still, the inert soldier beneath him, listening for any unwanted sound. There was none. In fact, there wasn't even the sound of the immense column that now began moving up and along the road. Satisfied that he was finally alone, he decided to search the slain soldier.

"That makes it complete," he said to himself thinking of his friend Snavely who he now considered to be dead. He fumbled through the fallen soldier's personal effects when something brought him to a shocked halt. Shigi had printed his name in Japanese. Rusty had memorized it. He read the name over and over as he recalled "Tanaka." He also recalled Shigi's writing the names of his brothers, one named Yoshijiro. He opened a packet containing a picture of four brothers, all in military uniforms. There, indelibly, was the picture of Shigi among the four.

"I'll be a son of a bitch," he murmured in the waning light. "Small world."

Rusty examined the soldier's uniform, recognizing it as being a lieutenant's and wondered why an officer would risk his life, or even be allowed to conduct an independent search such as this. Rusty continued to examine the dead lieutenant's apparel. Attached to his belt was a pistol and around the belt side, a tool resembling a hatchet. Rusty quickly removed the belt clip. He could surely use those two items. Continuing his search, he found a prize—a compass! Although the lettering was nothing he could read, he knew north was north in any language. Thank God, he thought. Turning the dead soldier over, he discovered some rounds for the pistol and a raincoat tightly wrapped in a small backpack. The biggest prize of all was a can of sardines and a packet of matches! In the pocket of the soldier, he found a knife and some Japanese money. He could see no use for the money, but he could certainly use the knife. He took all the contents and pocketed them. He studied the dead soldier again, deciding that the bootlaces may be of value, so he undid them, wadded them up and placed them in a pocket. A strange exhilaration overtook him. Although he was alone in the jungle, he was free. And he was safe—safer than he had been in three months. He looked at the compass and began the long trek northward to the high remote area of Mt. Natib.

****

The mood was somber that morning in Palmer's conference room. The selective service representative from Denver addressed the group seated around the table.

"Because of your standing in your community and/or your service to your country, you've been asked by the Selective Service Board in Washington to serve on this board in order to make decisions as to designating manpower for our armed forces."

Jack MacGregor wriggled importantly, and Adam Fitch glowed. Felton Caldwell and Royce Palmer sat quietly, and Fred Vogel stared at the floor.

"It's a large responsibility, gentlemen," he continued, "And the decisions as to who has to serve and who stays behind will, with rare exception, be entirely yours. As you know, everybody between the ages of eighteen and thirty-three is eligible for the draft. General Hershey's office will undoubtedly make changes, new rules, and new demands. The present attitude of the Washington office is that we shouldn't disturb a civilian situation where there is a legitimate critical need."

MacGregor smiled confidently.

"Obviously, this is a farm land, ranch community, and Lord knows, we'll need all the grain, meat, wool, poultry, hides and so on that we can muster. Basically, what I'm saying is that if there is a need to keep a man here to produce those necessary items, it will be up to your discretion to decide who goes and who stays. It will not be a popular job at best. You've all taken an oath, gentlemen, and I'm confident you'll perform your duties conscientiously, and to the best of your abilities. We will obviously need to elect a board chairman, so you may just as well do that now."

An awkward pause ensued. Jack MacGregor wasn't going to nominate anyone because he wanted the job for himself, as did Palmer, and as did Caldwell. Considering the strained relationship that had festered between Fred Vogel and himself, MacGregor was no longer pleased with his longtime footman, but he knew Vogel would select him after he threatened to divulge the identity of the person who really held the title of the land upon which the store stood. He would do that, if he had to, in order to protect his son, and Vogel knew it. Vogel was in no position to lose a business that MacGregor only used as a convenience. The dependent German had another year and a half before the statute of limitations ran out.

"I nominate Jack MacGregor," Vogel uttered, almost as an apology.

Simple minded Adam Flitch was a WWI veteran, who served as a private and was gassed at Verdun. The inhalant left him palsied. After his discharge, he stumbled into Cottonwood, where for years he toured the county, peddling Raleigh home remedies. He had the disquieting affliction of shaking his head in a negative fashion while he demonstrated his goods giving the illusion he didn't really believe in what he was selling. His old Chrysler coupe was stuffed with bottles, solutions, powders and potions of all sorts as he bounced across the barren landscape. His most reliable client was Kate MacGregor. She always felt sorry for him and he never left her yard with his pockets empty. Today, the MacGregor outfit would be compensated.

"Me too," he blurted.

"You don't need a second on a nomination," the official instructed. "Are there any other nominations?" There were none.

"Okay, then. Can we have a motion?"

Reluctantly, Fred Vogel quietly verbalized, "I move that Jack MacGregor be installed as the board chairman."

"Me too," Fitch repeated.

"Does that mean that you intend to second the motion?" the Denver man asked, showing irritation.

"Okay," Fitch replied.

"Well then, say so!" the official snapped.

"Say what?" the pill peddler asked innocently.

Caldwell and Palmer glanced at each other, smirking.

"Say you second!"

"I second."

"It has been moved, and in a manner of speaking, seconded, that Jack MacGregor be installed as chairman of the board. All in favor signify by saying 'aye'." Felton Caldwell remained silent, a slight that didn't go unnoticed by MacGregor.

"No?" the man asked. Again, Caldwell remained silent.

"Okay, Jack. You're the man. I'll be leaving you all now," he said tossing a pamphlet of regulations before each member. Read and digest the rulings carefully," he concluded, casting a disdainful glance to Fitch. "I wish you all the luck in the world. Good day, gentlemen."

Again, Jack MacGregor had gotten his way.

****

By the time the small patrol had decided to give up the search for Rusty, Bob Snavely had regained consciousness, but he couldn't get to his feet and was disoriented. The rifle butt had struck two inches above the eye, plus the immediate area was crushed. Andy knew if Snavely were to survive, he would, for the rest of his life, bear the depression on the skull.

332

Snavely's injury was serious involving bleeding around the fracture causing intense pain. A subdural hematoma would slowly build up pressure and the bleeding would continue. Andy understood most of this, but waited patiently to see if Snavely was going to be able to get up and walk. Under the circumstances, he knew Snavely would be a dead man otherwise. Bob Armstrong lagged behind with the two when the guard who searched him ordered that they move up to the column. Again, in his broken Japanese, Andy pleaded that he give them just another moment—that his friend would be able to continue. The guard hesitated, then relented.

Seeing the blood coming from Snavely's nose, Armstrong commented, "I didn't think they hit him in the nose."

"They didn't. The blood is coming from the brain." Andy said as he watched blood drip from the left nostril only.

Snavely began to move. "Can you hear me, Bob?" Andy asked.

There was no response.

Armstrong noticed Snavely's left eye was pointing toward his nose. "Look at his eye!" he exclaimed.

Andy flashed an angry stare. "Let's see if we can get him to his feet. If we can't, he's a dead duck."

Together they struggled to get Snavely to his feet as the lone guard was running out of patience.

"Can you hear me, Bob?" Andy repeated.

"I zink so, Angy. It hurts awful. I can't moo my eye."

"Don't worry, Bob. We'll take care of you."

Andy, with Armstrong's help shouldered the limping buddy toward the hoard of miserable prisoners to begin a tormented man-made martyrdom.

Andy was to learn what his comrades already had experienced; yawning hunger and now it was thirst. They were hungry in the morning, hungry at noon and hungry at night. At the first serving of a small ration of rice, Andy began to skim the weevils and larvae off the top, when he noticed that Armstrong was digesting the portion just at is came. He forced it down knowing Armstrong knew something he didn't.

Somehow, someway, the three were allowed to straggle behind, and made the six day, eighty-five mile walk with only an occasional bit of rice and a seldom drink of infected brackish water from nearby ponds.

The scene was one of dead, bayonetted and emaciated casualties scattered randomly along the way. Andy was aware that his energy was quickly fading. His satchel was becoming impossibly heavy, but he divined himself to keep it. He was jealous of his white blood speckled tunic and the medicine kit that made him different from the rest. He hoped he could locate John Kohara who was surely among the captured.

Snavely's pain had subsided and the bleeding had stopped. His strength and sheer desire to survive allowed him to continue. When Armstrong asked Andy why he didn't administer pain killers to Snavely, Andy explained that to anesthetize the brain was to shut the entire system down; that the brain could not be treated like any other facet of the human body. In fact, it was an amazement, even to the Japanese that anyone in an already enervated condition could withstand the rigors of the inhumane march. Andy attempted, on occasion, to converse with the Japanese guard, who admitted he had no respect for the vanquished, but he marveled at the tenacity of the survivors of the march.

The prison camp at O'Donnell was deplorable but by comparison to the march from Mariveles, it could be tolerated. The bunks were wooden. There were no mattresses, no pillows or blankets. Still, the first night sleeping on the hard planking was the most comfort the survivors had in over a week. Andy tried not to think about his plight. Rather, he was constantly haunted by the separation from Andrea and his family. The knowledge of the treatment he received would destroy his mother and the girl he loved, and he was thankful they were spared the particulars. He had lost thirty pounds during the struggle, and he was beginning to recognize the evidence of malnutrition; he only hoped the organic damage would not be permanent. He was exposed to his first dose of hell and feared he was only at the gates.

CHAPTER 36

Milo Rittenhaus drove into the Hubbard farmyard that early Wednesday afternoon in May. He walked up to the house with a Western Union telegram. School was just out. Walter and Sam had not yet gone back to the fields, so everyone was home. Rittenhaus knocked on the screen.

"Got a telegram for you!" he shouted to anyone within earshot.

Millie burst to her feet and rushed to the door, taking the dispatch. Walter was now standing beside her, and she handed the communiqué to him. The telegram bore the letterhead, United States Marine Headquarters, Washington, D.C. It read:

Dear Mr. and Mrs. Hubbard:

We regret to inform you that your son, 2 Lieutenant Andrew W. Hubbard,   USMC 423836, was taken prisoner by the Imperial Forces of Japan. The International Red Cross estimates the seizure took place on the Bataan Peninsula, Luzon, Philippines approximately April 10 of this year. We cannot inform you as to your son's state of health, but will do so when we have further information to report. Respectfully,

Laurence W. Hill, Colonel, USMC, Adjutant General Corps, Washington.

Millie fell into a chair, burying her head in her hands. "My God in Heaven! At least we know he's still alive!"

"They wouldn't send the telegram if he wasn't, Millie," Rittenhouse said.

"Sure, he's right, Millie," Walter countered, "They wouldn't have just sent us that if he's not…" adding, "wonder how he become a lieutenant?"

Millie sprang to her feet, flashed Walter a contemptuous stare, and rushed to the bedroom.

Walter looked at Sam. "Now what did I say to set her off like that?"

His son returned, "Darned if I know, Dad."

Ruthie, now twelve, directed an annoyed look at the two and left for the bedroom to be with her mother.

The word of Andy's capture spread across the prairie like a wildfire. Andy Hubbard was the first grim reminder that war had engulfed the whole world, and that included Cottonwood. The following Saturday in Vogel's store, Jack MacGregor walked up to Walter and opened the first conversation the two had face to face since the many years earlier when MacGregor had ridden into the Hubbard farmyard that frosty morning in an attempt to buy Hubbard out.

"I want to say I'm sorry, Walt," MacGregor began, "To hear about Andy."

Walter spun around, incensed. He grabbed a spade hanging on a rack and hurled it wildly at MacGregor, the blade narrowly missing the rancher's head.

"You son of a bitch!" Walter exploded. "You lyin' connivin' un-American son of a bitch!" he bellowed.

The shocked MacGregor threw up his arms in protection of his head, racing to the door leading out of the store. Walter had now snatched a pitchfork and flung it at the overwhelmed rancher, now outside, beating a path to his pickup. MacGregor scattered gravel across the street as he sped away. Walter stood at the entrance shouting and cursing at the fleeing MacGregor.

Fred Vogel, hearing the activity rushed into the hallway. "We can't have that going on here, Walter," he said in a loud voice.

Walter sneered at the store owner. "And you're no better, you lackey son of a bitch!" Walter spewed. "My kid's dyin' while MacGregor's is out there safe and sound rolling up the money."

Walter wasn't finished. "You'll never see me again in this goddam MacGregor store. And I'll tell ya somethin' else. When you see me comin' down the sidewalk you'd better step off in the gutter, or there's gonna be trouble, 'cause that's where spineless bastards like you belong!"

Walter wrenched loose and stomped out of the store, knocking merchandise off shelves in his path. He then beat it over to the bank and began hammering on a long counter. "I wanna see Felton and I want to see him now!" He cursed loudly enough that the entire bank could hear.

Felton Caldwell came out immediately and ushered Walter into his office, closing the door behind the two.

"What is it, Walt?" Caldwell asked evenly.

"I'll tell ya what it is, Felton!" he replied heatedly. "I just had a run-in with MacGregor!"

"That comes as no surprise. I expected it much sooner," Caldwell replied analytically, pushing some papers aside on his desk.

"Now you're on the draft board and I want to know why MacGregor's kid hasn't been drafted."

Caldwell inhaled deeply. "Walt, simmer down. It's been bothering me too. The federal government says that if a person is important enough to serve in the peace effort, he can be deferred. We've already considered his case, and I don't mind telling you that I brought it up, but you know who's already on the board..." he expelled a long breath, referring to MacGregor. "And having Adam Fitch there doesn't help either. He really has no business being on the committee."

"Yeah," Walter interrupted, "He's just a dumb old pill salesman, and who the hell selects the board? How did that simple old bastard get on?"

"I'm not sure I know all the rules. I was appointed by the Denver office, and I understand Adam served in World War One—that's why he was selected."

"Well," Walter countered, "MacGregor never fought in any damn war!"

"Neither have I. I didn't campaign for the position, but when I was asked, I accepted."

"Well, they ought to get Marshall, and Clint... and me. Guys who really have a stake in this thing."

Caldwell sighed. "I can't disagree with that, Walt."

"So what about that kid of MacGregor's?" Walter pressed.

"The vote to enter Chattman's name into draft eligibility was three to one—MacGregor, of course, Fred Vogel, and Adam Fitch. Royce abstained, and you can guess who voted to make him available. Now, I'll try to see that justice is done here, but it might take time. You aren't alone in this. Clinton Durkee is hot under the collar. They've already taken Paul, and now Cyrus is eligible. Augie Reiss will be going, as will Robert McCullum, and he has a wife. Don't get the notion that because MacGregor has money in this bank, I won't vote my conscience. You may be interested to know that the parameters dictate that a simple majority decision doesn't carry; It takes a two vote margin for action, so that limits Jack's authority, somewhat, I think. In any case, I'll use whatever influence I have to see that just decisions are come to."

Caldwell's words humbled Walter.

"Okay, Felton. You've told me some stuff I didn't know. I'm sorry I busted in here like I did. You've always been fair with me."

Caldwell looked into Walter's eyes. "I always will be fair to you, Walt. By the way, how's your boy doing? Do you know anything? I hear he's a lieutenant, now—he's such a fine young man."

For the first time, Walter relaxed and smiled. "I don't know any more than you. The Red Cross has said they'd let us know when they know. He can't write or get letters, and that's bothering Millie."

Caldwell leaned back in his large leather chair. "Millie's always been so close to him, hasn't she?"

"A hell of a lot closer than me and that makes it rough on her." Walter rose and headed for the door. "So long, Felton, and... thanks."

Caldwell merely nodded. His sentiment at the moment wouldn't allow him to respond.

Fred Vogel sat in his office alone, bent over his desk, his head in his hands. He knew what Walter said was right, and he felt miserable. In a year and a half, he would make amends.

****

Andrea was now, against her parent's objections, living in Washington and working for the Dispatch. Her job was a hot bed of activity and it suited her. Olson made her his personal secretary and was training her to compose and edit articles. She was convinced that her decision to leave college and work in the capital was the right one. Olson made no pretense of his fondness for her. It was on a busy Monday when Andrea picked up her mail. There was a letter from her mother.

"Dear Daughter," the message began. "I don't know whether or not you know. I learned it only today that Andy was captured on Bataan. There weren't any details. Eleanor Reiss got it from Millie Hubbard herself."

Andrea limply tossed the letter on her desk and walked into Olson's office. He knew Andrea had received bad news.

"It's Andy, isn't it?"

"Yes. He was captured on Bataan."

Olson sat quietly for a moment before speaking. "Andrea, if it hadn't been there, it would have been on Corregidor. The whole roof has caved in on that part of the world. I knew six months ago he never had a chance."

"Phil," she said. "I'm taking the day off."

Neither of them could have guessed that Olson had come so close to being wrong.

CHAPTER 37

Griffin and Wayne Yates had come to the Philippines with their father who was an interpreter with the State Department in 1933. They both learned Filipino Spanish as well as the dialect, Tagalog, because their father spoke it also. They learned to operate their father's ham radio and learned Morse code. When Griffin was nineteen, he opened a small radio repair and sales shop, eventually taking the brother in as a partner. When the two weren't selling and servicing electronics, they were refining an amateur radio operation, and complemented by their father's work, they had an extra insight into what was happening around the world. When it became apparent that Luzon would fall to the Japanese, they set up a receiving and transmission operation in a cave well concealed in a lush grotto in the remote Zambales mountain region. Although battles were fought on the island, their outpost throughout the war remained undiscovered. Their fluency in the Filipino vernacular helped provide them with the organizing of an underground gorilla force. A month and a half after the invasion of Luzon, with the supplies continuing to wane, they readily adapted to the ways of surviving in the jungle. It was this general direction that Rusty Atkins headed after his escape.

The Yates outpost was situated some forty miles north of Mariveles in the thickest undergrowth of the island. Rusty thrashed his way toward higher elevation, thankful that he had secured a compass. He was also thankful for the hatchet and knife he used to kill monkeys and sundry small animals. These he cooked at night, being careful that the smoke would not be seen. He had long since devoured the delicacy of the sardines.

It was nearly noon on April 15, when Rusty detected his first sign of human life. He waited cautiously, then followed the man a short way, determined to detect whether or not he was a Japanese soldier. He was a Filipino! — dressed only in a loin cloth. As a cat would stalk a bird, Rusty followed at a safe distance for the better part of a mile. Then he finally saw where the Filipino was headed. He spotted the cave where the Yates brother had set up their watch.

It was cleverly concealed on an escarpment in view of Manila Bay some fifteen miles in the distance below. Rusty waited for a half hour before deciding to creep up the small clearing in front of the cave. He heard English being spoken. When he was confident his entrance would at least provide him with an excellent chance of escape should his surprise visit cause an irrational response, he quickly stepped into the clearing, his pistol drawn and as softly as he could, he said, "Hello."

The three looked up frozen in utter surprise. Then Wayne Yates reached for a weapon.

"Hold on," Rusty said evenly, "I'm one of you."

Wayne Yates halted his reach for the rifle.

"Who are you?" Griffin Yates asked.

"I'm a marine. I escaped the march they started four or five days ago out of Mariveles."

"How did you escape?"

"I broke for the jungle when they beheaded one of my buddies."

"Where did you get that Jap pistol and the hatchet?"

"I took it off a Jap soldier I killed who came looking for me."

"You killed one of them?"

"Actually three," Rusty replied.

"Are you certain you got here undetected?"

Rusty chuckled softly, pointing, "I've been following this guy for over an hour."

Griffin looked at the Filipino and spoke something angrily to him. The Filipino protested. "He said you couldn't have followed him."

"Suppose I show him exactly where I picked him and followed him. Besides, how in the hell would I have found you?"

Yates then spoke to the Filipino who just looked perplexed and shrugged.

"Well, I'll tell you this. If you followed Felemon without his knowing it, you're a hell of a man," Griffin Yates said, extending his hand and introducing himself.

Rusty put his pistol back in its holster and shook Yates' hand.

"Also, this is my brother Wayne."

"Glad to know you," Rusty returned.

"And," Griffin continued, "This is Felemon Abuban."

Yates then said something to the Filipino who bowed.

"Now, I guess it's my turn," Rusty began. "Who are you guys and what are you doing?"

"Well, soldier," Griffin said pointing into the cave, "we might have just the gadget in there that will get you out of here."

The three sat for an hour relating experiences, the Yates brothers not responding to what Rusty told them about the march. They already knew more than he did. Rusty was given a cup of coffee. It was delicious. He took one sip and asked, "Don't suppose you…?" then stopped.

"Don't suppose what?" Griffin asked.

"Don't suppose you have a cigarette?" Rusty asked timidly.

Yates said something to Abuban and motioned. The Filipino went further into the cave and returned with a pack of Camels, tossing them to Rusty. The young gnarled marine opened the pack, popped out a cigarette, lit it with a Japanese match and took an exhilarating drag.

"I never thought a smoke could taste so damned good," he breathed.

"Okay," Griffin Yates began. "You're here. Where do you want to go?"

"I'd like to be reunited with my old unit, if possible."

"Huh! I don't think you would. They're on that god-awful march right now. Who was your C.O.?"

"My regimental commander was Major Canali. Don't suppose you have any knowledge of where he is, do you?" Rusty asked.

Wayne Yates interrupted. "Canali…Canali. Seems like I heard that name, Griff."

"That name kinda sticks in my mind, too. Have you ever heard of a General Stuart?" Griffin asked.

"Sure. He was Canali's boss," Rusty answered quickly.

"Well, Stuart left with MacArthur, I know that. Seems like," Yates said thinking aloud, "that he took this Canali with him."

"Took him where?" Rusty asked.

"Australia. MacArthur took an entourage to Australia."

"How do you know that?" Rusty asked.

"We know just about everything that goes on around here."

"Well, you've got a good spot—no doubt about that," Rusty commented.

Yates scratched his neck. "They know we're around. They just don't know where. You finding us puts a little scare in things."

"Don't worry about it. I'm special."

"How so?"

"No Jap is going to find you. I play hide and seek better than anybody. Just take my word for it. I've done this sort of thing all my life. I sneaked up on Felemon, didn't I?"

"You did, and it was a good thing. He'll be a little more cautious."

Rusty mashed out his cigarette. "Can you get me to Australia?"

"That's a tall order, Rusty. We can try," Griffin Yates said.

The four sat mapping out strategy to evacuate Rusty.

"Felemon," Griffin said to the Filipino. "I want you to go down in the valley this afternoon. See if you can arrange for the Negritos to find a barranca for this man. We'll set up other communications if you're successful. It's two, now. If you're lucky, you should make it back by midnight."

The native started the lengthy assignment, eventually picking his way through the heavily-fortified Japanese installations along the bay. Abuban returned shortly after midnight. He had arranged for the crew and the canoe to meet at a spot along the beach between Limay and Orion. It was chancy, but if they left immediately, they would be able to reach the beach by 4:30. That would allow the Negritos to paddle away in the primitive craft out of sight of the beachhead by daylight. Griffin instructed Abuban to give the instructions as to where Rusty had to be taken. Rusty had the compass, and with luck, the escape could be effected. Abuban was an experienced jungle guide.

The trek westward was strenuous. Rusty wondered how he had been able to keep up with Abuban initially. Although Rusty was unaware, he had crossed the road where the tragic march had begun. The lonely stretch of beach appeared shortly after 4:00 a.m. which was ahead of schedule. Hopefully, the Negritos had done their part.

Rusty's heart sank when he saw no barranca. Dawn was approaching. The lights from the Jap camps could be seen in both directions from the meeting place. Rusty and his guide waited for what seemed to be an eternity, when the gentle slapping of oars interrupted the stillness of the dawn. Felemon and Rusty waded out in the shallow water and met the canoe without incident. Abuban issued instructions to the Negritos. Rusty shook the Filipino's hand, thinking about Pompano and how there could be such a difference between two Filipinos.

Rusty, along with the three natives, set out eastward along the calm waters across Manila Bay, then along the coastline of the southern tip of Luzon on the rendezvous at Leyte. Beginning to relax, Rusty lit a cigarette, immediately discovering that the practice would not be allowed. One of the Negritos cursed, snapping the cigarette away from Rusty and throwing it into the water. He didn't understand the Filipino lingo, but he understood that message. Also he wondered why Negritos didn't paddle to the island shore as had been directed. He could follow none of their chattering, but their conversation had involved a strategy that would be better not to dock, since it was becoming daylight, and their assumptions were correct. They had reasoned it would be safer to stay well away from the coastline, then paddle eastward around the southern tip of the island, staying between Mindoro and the southern tip of Luzon.

In the afternoon, a squadron of Japanese fighters flew over dangerously close, but the small canoe went unnoticed. The planes were obviously not concerned with a tiny canoe. Their target was much larger: Corregidor.

The hot sun beat down on the four in the boat, but Rusty was happy to be getting away, and was confident his liberators knew what they were doing.

They camped at dusk at the shoreline along the southern tip. Apparently there had been some change in plans, because he was awakened around midnight for a continuation of the journey. Again, they stayed close to the bank as the dark hulk of the island remained visible in the night. As dawn approached, the crew pulled the small craft ashore and spent the day hidden in the underbrush. The Negritos had some hard dry meat resembling jerky beef. That was the cuisine for the length of the journey. Again, as darkness fell, they continued their travel. Four days later, a sunbaked Rusty Atkins arrived at an American installation on Leyte. The situation was far from secure. The Japanese had begun air strikes on the island. The Yates brothers had done their job well. The landing party was expected. Rusty offered a half-hearted thanks to the Negritos, who waved awkwardly and began their trip back. Unbeknownst to Rusty, the natives had completed the most dangerous leg of their journey. They had gotten rid of the American.

Rusty boarded the submarine Nautilus with eleven other refugees of varying importance some five hundred yard from the shore that evening for a trip that would take them somewhere in the Celebes Sea. It was a comfort to be among English speaking people, and was announced on the sub that Jimmy Doolittle had led a spectacular and unexpected strike on Tokyo.

It was dawn. The sub surfaced and was sighted by a PBY. The lumbering float plane splashed alongside the submarine. The evacuees climbed into rubber rafts.

The next leg of the journey was far from safe because it required a refueling stop at Darwin, which had sustained a few non-crippling air strikes. Fortunately, the tricky task of landing and takeoff from the shell-pocked airstrip was not a problem for the seaplane. Finally, an hour into the flight south to Melbourne, the pilot's easy, flat southern drawl cracked over the intercom. Rusty smiled. Another Cajun!

"Folks, I think you can breathe a little easier now. We ought to be safely out of the Japanese striking range, so get ready for a long jaunt. These things aren't hot rods. We figure to reach Melbourne around three or four in the morning. I know you're crowded—it's gonna be sorta like sleepin at the foot of the bed, but try to get some rest. If anything comes up, I'll let you know. Oh, and by the way, congratulations—you're a lucky bunch."

At that point, the hatless, exhausted fast-maturing young marine fell into a deep sleep.

The crackling of the intercom woke Rusty. He shook his head, rubbed his eyes and peered out the port bubble, squinting into a bright sun that was just brimming over the horizon.

"Good morning." The voice was strained and tired. "Our flight took us a little longer than we thought it would. It's a little after five right now, so for those of you who have to make connections, we apologize for the inconvenience."

There was a subdued chuckle from the group scattered about.

"We had to throttle back to conserve fuel. Just for your peace of mind, if these motors start quittin' on us, we don't need to look around for a place to set this thing down."

His words brought an enthusiastic response from the passengers.

"Anyway, we ought to be on the water in fifteen minutes or so, and they'll be a launch to pick y'all up. Good luck." The transmitter snapped off.

When the plane splashed down, wild cheers broke out among the passengers. The Navy launch motored up alongside. A crew member stood at the hatch assisting those into the boat. Rusty looked in at the rangy pilot in the cockpit twisted in his seat watching passengers unload.

"Where ya from?" Rusty half-shouted.

"Looziana!" came the hearty reply.

Rusty snapped a salute as he stepped out of the plane, "Thanks for the buggy ride!"

He caught the smiling pilot's return salute as he hopped into the waiting boat.

At six o'clock in the morning, the tired jubilant group docked. They were taken to a receiving station and from there, the contingent was fed a luxurious hot breakfast. A film crew rolled pictures and interviewed the ragged, weary collection. After breakfast and the filming, Rusty asked a lieutenant standing outside, if he knew the whereabouts of a Major Canali.

"You just got off that PBY?"

"Yeah."

The young officer called over to the curb. "Corporal, take my jeep and this Marine to Headquarters Company!"

Rusty hopped in the vehicle, and as the corporal sped away, the lieutenant called, "He's a colonel now!"

The driver pulled up to the white hotel. Two M.P.'s holding rifles flanked the entrance. Rusty thanked the jeep driver and started for the building.

As he passed, one of the guards asked, "Where's your hat, private?"

Rusty didn't respond, walking briskly to the entrance. The other guard shouted, "Halt!"

Rusty stalked into the orderly room with the M.P. beginning the chase.

"I'm looking for Major Canali," Rusty announced.

"You mean Colonel Canali," the clerk responded. "Do you have an appointment?"

Rusty brushed past him, and burst through the door, with the M.P. on his heels. Canali, sitting at his desk, looked up. When he saw Rusty, he was momentarily in shock, then sprang to his feet.

Canali rushed to Rusty, shaking his hand and exhorting, "Rusty! Jesus Christ! Where did you come from?"

Rusty smiled, and responded with a chuckle. "I was gonna say I just came from hell, but it sort of looks like I brought some of it with me."

"How'd you get away? I was sure you were captured and went on that march."

"It's a long story, Maj… Colonel."

"I tell you what, Rusty, let's go over to the club and you can tell me all about it."

"I can't get into the club. I'm not an officer."

Canali didn't comment, but picked up his phone. "Carl. I want you to open the club for me. I've got somebody special I'm bringing over."

Canali made another call. "Get me Captain Brown."

Rusty stood by quietly. "Irv," Canali began, "meet me over at the club. I want you to measure a man for a complete set of uniforms— and Irv, bring along a medium jacket and a cap with first lieutenant's insignia."

Walking to the jeep, Rusty said, "You're making me a first… I don't get to be a 90-day wonder," referring to officers coming straight from three-months of officer candidate school, who were inexperienced and green.

Canali was sober. "That would be an insult."

A balding older man, a captain, met them at the officer's club door.

"Carl, this is Lieutenant Atkins. He'll be visiting you from time to time."

"Oh yeah," the captain said. "You're the guy who was on the 'Death March'."

"*Death March?*" Rusty asked, frowning.

"Yeah. That's what they're calling it," Canali put in.

Rusty looked at Canali. "God—news travels fast."

"Well—what was it like?" the captain grilled.

Rusty visually searched the club manager saying nothing, then issued, "I wasn't on it—I don't know."

"So you don't know anything about it"

The comment angered Rusty, and it showed.

"You'd better let us talk in private, Carl," Canali said to the club manager who then returned to his office.

"I probably know less about that march than any man," Rusty admitted to Canali.

When the colonel asked him to explain, Rusty gave him a rundown on his entire experience including the Yates brothers and their surveillance system.

A man from quartermaster came in and measured Rusty, and followed Canali's suggestion the he leave room for weight gain. After three drinks of Rusty relating his experiences and Canali outlining Rusty's responsibilities, the two left the club.

"And I'll take you to your BOQ and you can get cleaned up and grab a little shuteye. I'll have you a jeep. Your fatigues will be delivered to your quarters. I want you to meet me for lunch, and after that, you're going to G-2. You have information no one else has… Do you have any questions?"

"Yeah. When did they get those helmets?"

"They're new. They're called 'Battle Bowlers'."

"And the rifles? They look different."

"They're semi-automatic. Not bolt action like the Springfields. They're called M I's."

"Do you pick my staff, or do I?"

"I don't know yet. We'll work that out."

"What's a BOQ, Colonel?"

Canali took a deep breath. He'd had enough. "It's your billets – and here we are."

The jeep rolled to a halt. Canali looked at Rusty, "From now on, call me Frank."

As Rusty stepped out, Canali added, "There's something else I want you to indulge yourself in. You look like you did when you first joined up."

"What's that?"

"Food."

CHAPTER 38

11th Marine Corps Training Facility
Wellington, New Zealand, May 9, 1942
Division Headquarters

"I just read the transcript you made at the G-2 board of inquiry Rusty, and I can see that not many of them bought those charges you made against the Japanese about the treatment of our prisoners."

Rusty Atkins, now a basic company commander, sat before Colonel Frank Canali in his office. Atkins sighed. "They can believe whatever the hell they want," the first lieutenant returned. "I can't control what they want to believe."

"Well," Canali mused, "you have to agree that it looks a little suspect to consider that the Japanese would have any reason to exact such brutal, inhumane treatment on anyone who merely surrenders; they are subject to the same international laws—rules of the Geneva Convention like any other country."

"I don't have to agree to any such thing. Someone out of that seventy-five hundred must have gotten away, then whoever gives a shit can get the skinny from that guy first hand."

"Well, I have to say that I have problems with it."

Atkins issued an impatient sigh. "Is this what you called me in here for? You must know I have other things to do."

"Partly that, and I wanted to ask you if you're aware of the results of the battle in the Coral Sea. The significance of it."

"Of course I do, Frank. It means the Japs can't just walk into Australia like they intended. That they got knocked on their butts for the first time."

"Okay, Rusty. The real reason I wanted to talk to you is the number of breakdowns your unit is experiencing. Hell, if all the companies had that many going to the dispensary every week, we'd need to quadruple our ambulances and medical staff."

"So? Have you heard any of them complainin'?"

Canali paused, thinking, "No, but it just seems that there has to be a more reliable way to get this training out of the way. If it isn't your hard-ass discipline, it's broken bones or pulled muscles. If it isn't that, it's fatigue. I'm just saying there has to be a better way."

"If there is, I don't know how to do it."

"It's three and a half weeks into your cycle and you've already lost a quarter of your trainees."

"Only a quarter? I must be getting' soft."

"Goddammit Rusty!" Canali burst, becoming frustrated. "I've got two thousand men here I'm riding herd on, and I expect to complete this rotation with enough men to fight a war."

"Frank," Rusty began in a quiet, controlled delivery, "I've *seen firsthand*, the fruits of piss-poor preparation. I know what a soldier does when he has no idea what to do, and I've seen the look on a man's face when he's surrendered—the embarrassment, the humiliation, the shame. It's not going to happen again—not on my watch. You can relieve me anytime you want, but I would ask you to let me get one scrap under my belt before you do."

"Well, you may get your wish before you want it. Now that we've stood our ground at the Coral sea, we've decided to let the Aussies defend Port Moresby. We've got a bigger 'fish to fry' as you would put it, and that's capturing a certain airstrip on Guadalcanal."

"Sound's good to me," Rusty said, getting to his feet.

As he headed for the door, Canali offered, "I won't relieve you Rusty. I couldn't if I wanted to with General Stuart looking over my shoulder. He heard one of your motivational speeches to your guys out on bivouac the other day."

351

CHAPTER 39

It had been a bitter winter where everything seemed devoid of color. That included the color of money. It had also been an expensive one for the MacGregors.

Although the immediate demand for meat, caused by the war, brought on higher prices, it also created an upward spiral in cattle prices. The vicious winter had more than offset the expected higher profits. Food supplements, necessary because of the lack of grass, not only involved higher expenses, it made for more work.

Liam, though getting on years, prided himself for being able to do his part, and that was driving the wagon for feeding cattle cotton cake each morning. The mineral that came in one-hundred-pound gunny sacks was loaded onto the wagon. Liam drove the horses, while a ranch hand scattered the nutrient to a train of hungry cows.

It was on a feed run this unruly morning in mid-March, when an empty sack blew off the wagon. Years of penny pinching would not allow that sack to go un-retrieved; it was still worth a nickel at the feed store when it came time to restock. Liam feebly climbed down from the wagon, reaching for the sack. Suddenly, a wind gust kicked it up in front of a skittish mare, which bolted, knocking Liam off he feet. The unset brake lever hooked his leg, and he was dragged several yards before the ranch hand, in the back of the wagon, struggled to regain his balance and grab the reins. But it was too late. Liam's eighty-three-year-old body was broken. The land he had so long commanded, now commanded him. With family and the few friends he had, Liam MacGregor was lowered into his grave near the ranch house, in a simple wrought iron fence, that would serve as his permanent marker.

An era had ended. Jack now ran the family business in total, but he was soon to discover something else about death; it was expensive. Though not faced with dissolution as it had been the case during the Depression, the MacGregor ranch felt the financial shock of Liam's passing. The same federal government whose war effort was sending farm and ranch products skyrocketing, demanded compensation for the passing of one of its citizens. Once again, the MacGregor ranch was mortgaged.

A dusty cloud followed the flashy car as it sped into the flat dry MacGregor yard. Jack MacGregor, who was shoeing a horse behind one of the sheds, set the hoof down when he heard the rumble. He walked around the shack in time to witness Chattman breaking a sleek cream yellow convertible to a stop. Jack dropped his hoof clippers and stared. His son stepped out of the car and swaggered toward his father.

"How do you like the looks of that one, Pop?" he asked.

The elder MacGregor simply stared.

"Well, Pop?"

"Whose is it?"

"Mine," the son boasted.

"*Yours?*" he asked incredulously. "Where'd *that* come from?"

"Well," Chattman began. "When I rode into the stockyards with Matt this morning, one of the guys in the scale house was talkin' about a pilot that was stationed at Buckley and got killed in some battle… Midway, or somthin' like that."

"So?"

"So the car was parked at the Navy base. His family was from back East and wanted to get rid of the car."

"Jesus Christ, Cat!"

"I couldn't pass it up, Dad. You know they aren't making new cars anymore."

"Is that Buick *new?*"

"It's not a Buick. It's a LaSalle, and no, it not new; it's a '40, but it's only got thirty-five hundred miles on it," he explained, adding, "and you know it's next to impossible to buy a car nowadays."

"Shit, Cat!" the father cursed, "Do you have any idea what it's taking to keep you out of this war—the crap I'm having to take? And you come home with this?"

"I didn't think you'd mind, Dad."

"Didn't think I'd mind? What'd ya pay for it?"

"Not that much, twenty-four hundred."

"Cat," MacGregor sighed, grinding his molars, "Your granddad just died. It cost four times what that car cost to pay his death taxes, and we're runnin' on empty. You can't be drivin' these fancy cars with their spare tires on the fenders."

"Sidemounts," the son announced proudly.

"I don't care what they are. If Walt Hubbard saw you in this thing, with Andy's bein' in prison, that crazy buzzard might take a pot shot at you. I wouldn't put it past him. You know how he tried to take my head off a couple of weeks ago."

Chattman studied the ground, jingling change in his pockets. "Naw. you're right. He's just crazy enough to somethin' like that."

"Well," Jack softened, "you just park that thing in the shed 'til I say it's okay not to. Understand?"

"Okay, Dad. That's probably the thing to do, but I'm not sorry I bought it."

****

"Phil! Phil!" Andrea squealed as she burst into his office, threw her arms around him and kissed him on the neck. "Look at this! It's a note from Millie Hubbard with a communiqué from the International Red Cross in China." She handed the missive to Olson.

Dear Andrea,

Milo Rittenhaus drove up today (Sunday) with this telegram. Telegrams terrify me! You just know the portentous news they so often bring. Well, not this time. The Red Cross tells us that Andy is alive and being held captive at the Japanese Army base at Clark Field...

"Japanese Base. Clark Field." Olson cursed.

354

.. in Luzon, and that they would advise us later. I'm so happy, I've been crying the past hour.

Hope you feel the same.

Love Millie.

P.S. Liam MacGregor is dead. I'll send details later.

"Thank God he's okay," Olson offered. "Keep your fingers crossed, Andrea. We're rebounding."

"I knew you'd be happy, Phil," Andrea said, plucking the letter from his grasp and turning to leave.

Olson watched the beautiful woman exit, feeling pangs of jealousy in the process. He sat thinking about her, their long hours toiling over script, working overtime to get stories out, and the many nights at the White Horse with Andrea getting delightfully high and parlaying his playful suggestions that she become involved with him. She never considered that Olson's suggestions weren't playful. Olson, despite his better judgment, had become deeply affected and for him, it was becoming more and more difficult to work with her knowing she loved someone else. Lately, he had begun toying with the notion of applying to one of the news services as a war correspondent. It would serve two purposes. One, he wanted to get into the thick of the action, and two, he would get away from that which was beginning to dominate his thoughts.

That day, he considered the option more seriously. Also, he wondered another thing. Who the hell was Liam MacGregor?

Wellington Harbor
August 1, 1942

General Stuart sat on the platform with Colonel Frank Canali anticipating Rusty Atkins' remarks to his troops on their graduating from boot camp. Three hundred plus marines stood at parade rest waiting for their commander's arrival. Also on stage was First Sergeant Grant Wiley who orchestrated the C.O.'s delay. He had a surprise for Rusty.

"Hell of a note when a division commander has to get here before a company jockey," Stuart groused.

"Yeah. He'd better have an excuse for not being here," Canali put in. Canali's attendance was one of duty since he was Rusty's regimental boss. General Stuart had happened onto one of Rusty's fiery motivational talks, so the general was there to be entertained. It could be said he also had a supplemental reason to be in attendance since Rusty's training session had generated so much unfavorable second guessing with the number of men falling out due to the young commander's merciless regimen. The attrition rate from the original complement was over a hundred men, but as Stuart had noted, the dropout rate had fallen precipitously as the men became hardened to Rusty's harsh measures. Being an old Mustang, General Stuart never shared the worry that his subordinate, Canali, did. Stuart had his baptism of fire in battles with the Germans in the forests and trenches of Germany and France in WWI, so a little discomfort was a benefit in matters of preparation, to his way of thinking. Still, Canali would offer his anxieties whenever the general would listen.

The two sat making small talk, when they were interrupted by a thunderous cheer from the troops. When Stuart and Canali glanced up wide-eyed, they saw Rusty making his way up the stairs of the platform.

"That doesn't much sound like an abused bunch," Stuart jibed, as the troops continued their cheering.

"No—it doesn't," the colonel conceded, embarrassed at the show of support.

The cheers were interrupted by boisterous laughter and applause when a group of soldiers unfurled a banner displaying an amazing likeness of Rusty kicking the rear of an exaggerated caricature of a mustachioed Oriental in thick glasses intended to represent the Emperor.

At that moment, the first sergeant took the mike. "Tenshut!" he ordered, and three hundred men snapped ramrod straight. The men holding the banner stood unmoved. "Please recognize the meanest, toughest, and finest commander we could ever have had the privilege of serving under—our C.O., Lieutenant Atkins!" The top kick turned and took a seat. To the sudden quiet of the post, Rusty approached the mike.

"At ease," he said softly, adding, "Go ahead and sit down, guys." The rustling sounds of three hundred men relaxing followed. Rusty surveyed the troops, then seeing the poster, shook his head in feigned disbelief, then with a smile on his face, turned to acknowledge General Stuart and his immediate boss.

"On the stage behind me are our regimental commander, Colonel Frank Canali, and our 11th Division boss, General Henry Stuart," he announced, in an unintended slight to the superior. Rusty cleared his throat. "Sergeant Wiley gave me a nice tribute. You guys have given me a nice tribute, and before I forget, thanks for the nice funny paper you drew down there—I don't know who put that together—I didn't think anyone had time to do it, but whoever it was, he got it right—we're gonna' give that Nip a royal boot in the ass!"

There was an eruption of laughing. Rusty raised his hands. The company became instantly quiet.

"You should be proud. You survived a tough sixteen weeks. You've done what I've asked of you. You did it because I've told you repeatedly that there's no substitute for preparation. I can tell you, in all confidence, that you're prepared. In a few short days, you'll understand what it all means—and you'll be glad you were."

Rusty took a deep breath, and glanced back to his superiors. His troops sat in quiet respectful obedience.

"We have a good team behind us. It's important to have that. General Stuart has been where we're about to go. He's been in battle, and I can tell you we are privileged to have General Stuart behind us." And, he said, turning to Canali, "I've been with Colonel Canali since the beginning, and I'm lucky to be under the command of him. We are fortunate to have both of these men in support of us. You can be certain, we can depend on them."

"Now fellows," he began in a quiet confident voice, surveying the seated group, "starting tomorrow, we're going up north. We've got a little job to do. And we're gonna' by god do it. We're going to teach a few Orientals some manners. We'll be letting them in on a few secrets—some stuff they need to be aware of. We're going to let them in on the fact that we aren't just a bunch of boozers; of lazy lovers. They need to discover that we do other things in our spare time. They're gonna' find out you can't just come into someone's house and trash it without paying a hellova' price. They're going to find out damn sudden that they just *think* they're the world's best fighters—we're gonna' show 'em they aren't even close —and that we're anything but the cowards they've been makin' us out to be. It's going to be a rude awakening for those slanty-eyed bastards. They're about to find what it's like to run into a bunch of pissed off buzz saws out there that have taken just about all the crap they're gonna' take." He paused glowering at his troops. "Men… we're gonna' flat knock their asses off—plumb off. Are you with me?"

Rusty's words were drowned out by instant jeers and cheering, jumping to their feet and stabbing their arms in the air.

Rusty motioned to Wiley, who took the mike and issued, "Dismissed!"

General Stuart walked briskly up to Rusty, extending his hand. "I think you got 'em ready."

Solomon Sea, New Guinea
August 7, 1942 0600 hours

Rusty positioned himself at the bow end of the LCI and kept a running commentary as the battalion plowed toward the landing on Guadalcanal. The mission was to capture the Japanese airfield. So certain of success, they had already named the strip Henderson Field in honor of a Navy pilot who was killed at the battle of Midway. Their overconfidence got Rusty thinking to himself that he might have gone a little overboard in his talk of supremacy, but he wasn't going to let up now.

"Remember, guys," he said loudly, "A bullet's quicker than you. But it's not really that bullet that gets you. It's you waitin' around until it finds you. In other words, it's the exposure to the bullet. What I'm talking about is time management. If you'll notice, we're gettin' some good cover from those destroyers and cruisers out there. Use that bombardment to your advantage. Those Nips are damn well payin' attention to where those rounds are landin', I can you that, so those hits are your signal to move up. When we hit that beach, you run like a striped-assed ape for cover! You'll find it, don't worry about that. It might be a bomb crater, a ditch, a piece of wrecked equipment, or a bank, no matter how shallow. Don't expose yourself to enemy fire any longer than you absolutely have to. What I'm saying, guys, is that the chance of that Jap bastard shooting you is a hell of a lot slimmer when you're on the move—and when you're not on the move, you take cover. Don't be standing around in the open. Movement and concealment, boys! —that's the ticket!"

Whether the troops were digesting Rusty's advice, he was keeping them from worrying about what was taking place on the beach.

The young Marines soon learned the value of Rusty's murderous training. When the troop carrier hit the beach and the gangway was lowered, the hail of small arms fire brought home to each man the reality of war. However, the Japanese defenders were overrun by the determined and expertly-trained invasion force. The Japanese, shocked by the swift advance, were overwhelmed and the partially-completed island airfield was quickly overrun. The Marines positioned their 50 caliber machine guns providing an inescapable crossfire, and the Japanese attempt at a banzai charge ended badly. Hordes of Japanese soldiers were cut down like so many stalks of corn. The battle was a rout, plus, the men of the 11th took every piece of Japanese road building equipment in their path. By afternoon of August 8, the airfield and its approaches were in the hands of the Marines. The entire engagement cost Rusty two wounded leathernecks.

The following morning after mess, Rusty assembled his men. They were exuberant. He was quick to smother the cheer.

"Men," he started. "Congratulations for a fantastic job. It couldn't have gone much better. Japan is a few thousand troops lighter today. Our medics are I.D.'n them immediately before they shove them in the trenches, which is a damn shame, 'cause they're not worth the trouble. Anyway, fellas," he began seriously, "this is what I gotta say."

Rusty had gained back all the weight he had lost during the siege of Luzon, and his bronze, hardened physique presented the look of a serious fighting man. He repositioned his frame, gaining the troops attention.

"I don't know who said it, or just how it was said, but the message is this: If we don't learn anything from what just took place, then we're missing out on the benefit of experience. What I'm getting at is that the reason we beat the crap out of these Japs is because they underestimated us—just like they did at Midway. They themselves have admitted that they've gotten 'Victory Disease,' because they've had it so damned easy for so damned long. They're learning plenty sudden that they better get over it if they intend to win another battle. Now, here's what you have to keep in mind. Don't you get victory disease. We aren't going to have it so easy the next time, because now they got the message, and they'll be taking us serious from now on."

He rose to his feet. "Take the rest of the day off—get your weapons cleaned and do anything else that needs to be done. Don't let any of this go to your heads. The show's just beginnin'."

Later that morning, Canali and General Stuart entered Rusty's tent. He started to rise.

"Keep your seat, Rusty," Canali said.

"You did a good job out there, Lieutenant," Stuart offered.

"Thanks, General."

"Rusty," Canali entered. "We came to ask a favor. We want you to pick out thirty of your guys to serve as platoon leaders. We want to intersperse them throughout the companies."

Rusty flashed a broad smile, "Thirty?"

"Do you have that many you can recommend?"

"Easily."

"Okay. That's all we have," Canali said, starting to walk out of the tent.

"I've got a favor to ask of you," Rusty said quickly.

"What's that?" Canali asked.

"Put my man Wiley in charge of Charlie Company. That fool who's runnin' it damn near got us all killed."

The request caught the two officers by surprise. Canali looked perplexed. "How so?"

"It's not just one thing, Frank. It's a hell of a lot of little things. He's not cut out for the job."

"Your man's only a sergeant," he protested.

"Then promote him."

"What makes you think he'd do any better?"

"You'll have to take my word for it."

Canali looked at the general. "What do you think?"

Stuart mulled the question, then offered, "Why don't we put Atkins here in charge of both companies, and make this fellow his exec?"

Canali looked at Rusty. "How about that?"

"That's fine with me," Rusty agreed.

"Anything else?" Canali asked.

"There is," Rusty offered.

"What's that?" Canali asked.

"I want those thirty I select to be bumped to corporal."

"What for?" Canali asked.

"If they're going to be stuck into companies cold turkey, I want them to have some clout. It just makes organizational sense."

Before Canali could comment, Stuart said, "I'll okay that."

"And one other thing," Rusty said.

Canali's expression was one of annoyance, "And what might *that* be?"

"I want the rest of my kids to get a stripe out of this."

"How could we possibly justify that?" Canali carped.

"We're absorbing another three hundred guys who have damn little discipline. My kids have paid a price to be where they are. To top all that all off, I gotta whip this new bunch into shape in damn short order, and I intend for my guys to help me with it. Don't worry, Frank. It'll pay dividends."

Canali looked at Stuart who merely shrugged his shoulders and nodded in agreement.

The two officers turned to leave the tent, when Canali warned, "Now Rusty, it's going to get rough from here on. While we were kicking ass up here at the air strip, our supply units to the rear took it in the shorts on landing. A squadron of Japs came in off the carriers last night and caught them napping. We lost jeeps, ammunition, food, tentage—every goddam thing."

"Well, what are we doin' settin' here? Let's go after the bastards!" Rusty exploded.

Stuart chuckled. "They *flew* in. There's nothing we can do about it now. They've high tailed it back to the carriers. Those cooks and truck drivers don't make for much of a fighting force and they got shellacked. Without air cover, Turner and Fletcher turned tail and made a dash for open sea. They're on the hunt for the enemy carriers as we speak. You can expect some kind of fracas when they catch up with them."

"Well," Rusty mused, "I told my troops not to let all this success go to their heads. I just hope to hell they heard me."

Stuart merely chuckled. "Get your guys together and send those platoon leaders down to the Headquarters hut. In the meantime, we'll take care of the other business." The two officers stepped out of Rusty's tent.

Again that day, Rusty called his company to assemble. Putting them at ease, he began:

"Gentlemen, you're too damned good. We're going to have to bust you up. General Stuart wants a bunch of guys to be installed as platoon leaders in certain areas, and I need thirty of you to volunteer."

Instantly, a majority of the men raised their hands and yelled.

Rusty laughed, raising his hands for quiet. "Okay! Okay, guys! I half expected that, so Sergeant Wiley, pick out thirty quick as you can. Now, here's the deal. We gotta have thirty of you for platoon leaders, but for the rest of you, I need your help. We're absorbing Charlie Company, and you have to assist me in shaping those guys up. I can't do it without you, and you'll all get a stripe for doing it."

The company let out a cheer. Again, Rusty raised his hands for order. "I guess I've never taken time to say it, but your performance in capturing this airfield goes beyond my wildest expectations. I love all you bastards!"

One private raised his hand.

"What is it, Private?"

"Well Sir," he began timidly, "I think everyone of us bastards loves you too, Sir."

His words were met with respectful applause. Rusty was embarrassed. He turned to his First Sergeant. "Wiley, get those thirty picked out, then come into my tent. There's something I need to visit with you about."

****

The counter assault on Henderson Airfield came as expected. Thousands of Japanese troops flooded in. General Vandergrift had moved the 5th Marines from Tulagi to secure the defenses, but Stuarts's forces were overwhelmed by the forces of Tanaka's Tokyo Express and had to fall back. On September 12th, in a driving rain, Japanese broke en masse out of the jungle and smashed into the ridge positions of Marines defending the precious airstrip. The tired, half-rationed Marines were to prove to the Japanese what Rusty Atkins declared they would. Although the 11th received no reinforcements since their landing in August, they held their position with the aid of a few Army P-40's and Navy SBD's, plus the pitifully insufficient 75 and 105 MM howitzers. Soaked and weary, yet filled with resolve, Rusty Atkins drove his men to methodically pick off enemy soldiers as they struggled up the steep ridges, The Japanese were tasting the sting of American marksmanship, their casualties running ten to one. Tanaka's forces were continually replenished by troops as though there was an unending well of replacements. But by the middle of October, reinforcements of the 164th infantry arrived. That was the transfusion the 11th needed, and by the end of October, the Marines had secured Bloody Ridge and Henderson Airfield once and for all. Rusty Atkins, now a captain, along with the men of the 11th had earned a well-deserved breathing spell.

****

Royce Palmer watched as Jack McGregor closed the door to his office.

"This has to be important if we have to close a door way out here in Cottonwood," Palmer joked.

MacGregor's mood was not pleasant.

"Royce, I'll get to the point. That simpleton Adam Fitch is making noises like he's gonna' vote to take my kid."

"Maybe he's not so simple as we all thought," Palmer chuckled.

"I don't take that as funny!" MacGregor spat. "Now you know it only takes one more for a majority, and I know damned well Caldwell's gonna vote to draft Cat! With that stupid old pill peddler and Felton, I gotta depend on you!"

"It was that stupid old peddler who nominated you for board chairman," Palmer breathed caustically. "There were a couple others of us who wanted that job."

MacGregor bit his lip. "I didn't come in here to debate with you Royce. Now, if it takes a little money on the side, I'm quite willing..."

Palmer grimaced painfully. "You tried that tactic before."

"And you took it before! God Dammit! A leopard doesn't change his spots!"

Palmer stood, preferring to keep his secret to himself. "Jack. You'll have to excuse me. I do have other work."

MacGregor glowered at the lawyer, and stomped out of his office.

The next day Jack MacGregor visited Palmer's office.

"Where's Royce?" he asked Palmer's wife.

"Down in the studio. Shall I get him?"

"Naw," he said brushing past her. "I'll find him."

He found Palmer bent over a photograph of a lone cottonwood framed against a dark, gray sky.

"Didn't mean to interrupt anything," MacGregor said.

"You're not," Palmer uttered, not looking up from the print.

"Say Royce," he began. "I'm sorry about that little spat yesterday."

This time, Palmer did look up. "Don't worry about it—I've forgotten about it."

"How do you take those pictures?" MacGregor asked with disarming innocence.

"There's really nothing to it, Jack. Come in the dark room. I'll take you through the process."

"You can't take a picture in the dark, can you?"

"Sure," he said darkening the room, and taking a flash picture of MacGregor. "Now," he said removing the negative, "we develop, then the stop bath, fix and wash. Usually we let these dry a couple of hours."

"Does it have to dry for two hours?"

"No. We can blot it. Here," Palmer said, showing the picture to MacGregor. "looks just like you."

"I'll be damned," MacGregor said examining the grainy but very distinct print. "Supposing I wanted, say, two pictures of me, instead of one?"

"Nothing to it. Just develop the negative twice, or however many times as you want."

"Be damned." MacGregor said, adding, "Tom Bryant's gonna be up tomorrow. I asked him to stay for poker. That'd be okay, wouldn't it?"

"He's your vet, isn't he?"

"Yeah."

"It'll make seven, but we can handle that."

Tom Bryant, a veterinarian who lived in Phillipsburg, a nearby town, owed his start to the MacGregor family. They'd given him the bulk of his business and normally paid in cash. There was a devious streak in Bryant's personality that Jack MacGregor was well aware, and he would occasionally prevail upon the animal doctor to bend regulations involving certain business ethics of husbandry, such as the transferring and selling cattle that would otherwise be condemned. These unsavory favors would come at a premium. This time, MacGregor prevailed upon his longtime practitioner to perform an unusual act.

"You say it ain't any different than a bull calf?" MacGregor asked.

"Not really," Bryant answered. "You could probably do it yourself."

"You can dope him up, and still get him to do his duty?"

"Sure."

"What with?" the rancher asked.

"It's called 'Spanish Fly'."

"What's that?"

"It's an aphrodisiac."

"And what's the girl gonna cost me?"

"Five hundred, just like me."

"Jesus! Can't you find anybody cheaper n' that?"

"You're welcome to try, Jack."

MacGregor sighed. "Naw, we'll go it at that," and leafed out five hundred for the woman.

The poker circle was composed of six regulars who used the Palmer basement every second Thursday night since the building had been constructed. MacGregor introduced the veterinarian to those who didn't know him and the games began.

As was the custom, the usual amount of alcohol was consumed, and Bryant made certain Palmer's portion contained the drug. Halfway through the session, and unannounced, and intriguing woman in her forties entered the room.

"This is Caroline, fellas," the veterinarian announced. "I'll be giving her a ride home. She can be a waitress, if it's okay with you."

"Oh sure!" Palmer gushed. "I'm ready for another pop, anyway." Two other members voiced their readiness.

After being directed to the bar, she returned with the drinks, having been instructed about Palmer's penchant. She was careful to rub a breast against Palmer when she served him.

After the next round, Palmer massaged the whore's buttock. She merely smiled at the finagler who whispered to her, "Wanna' play? I got a little room just off this bar."

"Your friends will miss you, won't they."

Continuing to fondle her, he replied, "Honey, we've got too many already. Come on."

Palmer's excusing himself came as no surprise to the members, who were well aware of Palmer's affinity to the opposite sex.

After a short while, the group disbanded.

When the group left, MacGregor scurried about arranging the film.

"Okay, Tom," he said at last, "Open the door."

As expected, Palmer was rutting on the hustler.

MacGregor snapped several pictures before the adulterer could react. He then grabbed Palmer from the rear, as Bryant administered the sleeper. The rancher made a quick exit to the dark room, as Palmer sank into unconsciousness.

"Okay, Caroline, here's your two fifty," Bryant said, leafing out the bills. "Now get dressed and get your butt out of here."

"At least we don't have to undress him," Bryant thought to himself, taking out his scalpel.

As MacGregor began to process the film, Tom Bryant took his scalpel to the back of Palmer's scrotum and made a quick incision along the posterior surface, locating the vas deferens, then clamped and tied it off. He clipped it, and removed one teste. Five sutures later, he gave Palmer another sedative. It all had taken less than ten minutes.

MacGregor was still developing pictures when Bryant opened the door. The rancher turned.

"You through already?"

"All done, Jack. How you comin' along?"

"I've got some ready, I think," he said, then interrupted himself, "You sure, Tom, that he can get along with one just as well?"

"One's as good a two."

MacGregor held the negative up to the light.

"Jesus! Tom, look at this!"

The first negative showed Palmer between the woman's thighs, his eyes wide open, as he was being photographed. MacGregor had all the evidence he needed. He paid Bryant the five hundred and the veterinarian left. Then Jack walked upstairs knocking on Margaret Palmer's room. She sleepily came to the door.

"Listen, Margaret. Royce got a little too much to drink, and we put him to bed downstairs," MacGregor explained.

"Should I come get him?" she asked drowsily.

"Naw, you'd never move him. He'll be okay in the mornin'. I already locked up."

"Okay, Jack. Whatever you think," she said, rubbing her eyes, anxious to get back to bed.

Royce Palmer awoke with nausea and a dull ache in his groin. He touched his crotch, and immediately felt pain. He stumbled to the bathroom, and stared in the mirror at his blackened scrotum. Then he noticed the envelope on the vanity, fumbling it open discovering the compromising pictures. Angrily, he threw them back down on the vanity surface. He returned to the bedroom and began dressing carefully. Looking down at a table, he spied a scalpel. Careful to pick it up by the blade, he noticed the blood still on the shaft, but something else; the initials, T.A.B. followed with D.V.M. on the grip. He delicately placed it in an envelope and put it in his lapel pocket. Without awakening his wife, he called Doc Sutton.

The Chiropractor had been asleep, agreeing to meet Palmer at the Doctor's office immediately.

Sutton was aghast, seeing the amateurish incision and suturing. With a significant amount of pain to the entrepreneur, he disinfected the wound.

"This is shocking—this is criminal," he concluded. "We really need to report this to Sheriff Young."

"No, John," Palmer replied confidently. "Let's not mention this to Art. I'm going take this to another level. Remember, I'm in the business of confronting such offenses."

Sutton merely nodded.

"There's something I want you to look at, John," Palmer announced. He then took the scalpel from his jacket pocket. Removing it from the envelope, and holding it only by the blade, he passed the instrument to the doctor. "I think this is surely the knife they used for the dirty work. Take it only by the blade. I want to be certain they can get the fingerprints from the handle. I need you to tell me what you think those initials are all about."

Following Palmer's instructions, Sutton inspected the tool.

"Well," he said, glancing up, "Those initials stand for Tom Bryant, Doctor of Veterinary Medicine. I hope you have something concrete like this on Jack MacGregor."

"I shouldn't have too much of a problem," Palmer answered confidently.

"I wouldn't be so sure of that," Sutton warned.

"Well, in any case, Doc. I may need you as a witness, if you don't mind."

"Of course I don't mind. It wouldn't matter if I did. You'd subpoena me anyway."

Palmer smiled. "I just want your blessing."

"You've got it."

****

The hunger Andy was experiencing was common to all the troops of larger stature, since all received similar portions. To compensate for this, Andy forced himself to consume matter such as grass and leaves which although not digestible, sometimes satisfied the hollow craving to fill his stomach. Bob Armstrong fared much better on similar rations, since he was significantly smaller.

Andy was grudgingly allowed to hang on to his doctor's kit, although the supply of iodine and quinine had long been exhausted on infections and malaria, used both for American and Japanese treatment. One morning a Japanese captain was stricken with what Andy immediately recognized as a tetanic seizure. Without hesitation, and with his thumb and forefinger, Andy secured the stricken officer's tongue stretching it away from his windpipe. He ordered Bob Armstrong, standing nearby to secure the man's hands when Andy was confident the officer wasn't going to swallow his tongue. He quickly filled his syringe with thalidomide and gave the man a healthy injection. Ordinarily, the same needle wouldn't be used over and over, but these were unusual circumstances, and precaution was a luxury. Shortly, the officer was comatose, and Andy motioned for the guards to take him. The guards complied.

Andy's Japanese was slowly improving, and he was occasionally recruited as an interpreter. The right to carry his satchel was no longer contested, and on a long boat ride up to Taiwan, Andy was allowed to travel on the upper deck of the vessel. He had felt this privilege was a result of coming to the captain's aid. After he heard Armstrong's account of the conditions below decks, Andy knew he was fortunate.

A strange situation had developed with Bob Snavely. After the crippling smash to his head, he had endured months of excruciating headaches. They eventually went away, but not without some odd physical and mental changes. His left eye stayed fixed toward his nose, and he experienced a partial loss of motor control with his right foot dragging and right arm dangling limply. His speech had become slurred, and he apparently no longer responded to physical pain. The curious aspect of this decline was that he was gaining weight rather than losing it. The boss of the compound tapped him for his houseboy, so he was being well fed while the other prisoners were starving. When Andy confronted him about the ethics of this duty, he had lost all ability to reason, not being able to understand any of it.

Through the efforts of the International Red Cross, Andy unexpectedly received two letters while on Taiwan; one from his mother, and one from Andrea. Practically nothing was blacked out from his mother's letter. He concluded the Japanese were not concerned about farm news from a family member. His mother's message was cheerful, encouraging and loving, as Andy read and re-read every line. Andrea's letter with a Washington D.C. postmark was another matter. There were but two lines in the two pages that were left undisturbed. Although he treasured the effort from hearing from her, he was unable to glean any pertinent information from her message. He knew she was in D.C., but nothing more; nothing about what she was doing, where she was staying or who she was working with. He assumed, correctly, that she was there because of Phil Olson, and again correctly assumed she was involved in the newspaper business. The most disconcerting aspect of his confinement was that he no longer had the access to information nor the liberties of communicating that had been taken for granted. The struggle of coping with physical deprivation was now confronted with a more heinous dilemma; mental starvation. But the letters were a monumental comfort, and he would re-read Andrea's last uncensored words: "I dearly love you and will wait forever..."

****

Tom Bryant saw the return address on the registered letter: State of Colorado, Department of Veterinary Medicine, Capitol Plaza, Denver:

Dear Dr. Bryant:
You are hereby required to appear before this committee to answer interrogatives resulting from harm done to a Colorado attorney, who chooses to remain nameless, as to why your license to practice should not be revoked. Dr. Ralph Adams, DVM President, Ethics Committee.

Jack MacGregor was branding cattle with Chattman and two hired hands when Tom Bryant slid to a stop, and walked briskly out of his pickup.

"Jack. I got to talk to you," he exclaimed.

MacGregor handed the iron to Chattman, and strode toward the veterinarian. "What's up, Tom?" MacGregor asked.

The vet silently motioned toward his pickup.

After the two were inside, and before MacGregor could ask again, Bryant handed him the open letter.

MacGregor smirked while reading the message and handed the note back, saying nothing.

"What do you think about that?" Bryant asked.

MacGregor hedged. "There's not all that much to think about. Guess you'd better go see what those guys want."

"I know what they want! They want my goddam license!"

MacGregor wore a curious smile, as though he were enjoying the veterinary's dilemma.

"Hell, nobody's making any charges. You don't have anything to worry about."

Bryant snapped the paper with his forefinger. "Bullshit! Somebody's making a charge!"

"Well, what do you want me to do, Tom?"

"I want you to come with me at that inquest."

MacGregor's smile disappeared, and he spoke softly, "You can't expect me to do that, Tom. That letter's not addressed to me."

"You make it sound as though you had nothing to do with this!"

"Hell, the bastard may come after me next. You wanna come hold my hand if he does?"

"I sure as hell would!"

MacGregor drew a deep breath of air. "Well, Tom. I don't know what to tell you. Sometimes things can go sour. You have to expect that when you get those big payoffs for doin' stuff like that. You gonna give me my money back?"

"You can't expect me to do that!"

MacGregor unlatched the pickup door, stepping out. "And you can't expect me to take your blame. You're on your own, Tom." MacGregor gently closed the door and walked away toward the branding fire, wondering what Palmer might have in store for him.

Bryant sat transfixed, not knowing what to do, with MacGregor's words, your blame ringing in his mind. He spun out of the MacGregor pasture, knowing that he was on his own and was without recourse.

Denver: October 10, 1942

Bryant was familiar with the five panel members. Three of the veterinarians were retired. The chairman spoke.

"Doctor Bryant, this committee feels it has no option than to strip you of your license to practice veterinary medicine. Do you have anything to say in your behalf?"

"These charges are false, Doctor Adams."

The balding doctor in his early seventies grimaced, before speaking slowly and deliberately. "The state attorney general has provided us with an account of this brutal act, with evidence that your fingerprints were on your personal scalpel found at the scene, and that the blood on the instrument matches that of the respected attorney's. Now don't insult us by telling us the accusations are false."

Adams paused glowering at the erstwhile veterinarian who wavered unsteadily.

"However," he resumed, "it is not our purpose to indict or prosecute you. We're not in that line of work. We only want your statement. Personally, those of us on this panel can't fathom why no charges are being brought forth, but if I were you, I wouldn't make matters worse. You should be in prison for this, but the martyr, who, for whatever reason, chooses to remain anonymous and not prefer charges. And that's his right. Some people just don't want trouble. We don't even care to hear what your purpose was. We need only your confession to effect the release. Otherwise, we will litigate, if necessary."

The room became still, and the panel waited.

"I did it," Bryant said in a hushed voice.

Adams rose and motioned to the steward who approached Bryant. "Have Mister Bryant sign the affidavit and show him to the exit."

Royce Palmer had cleverly exacted the extent of justice without exposing his own identity.

CHAPTER 40

Sam opened the manila envelope which contained a letter from the selective service department. His official draft status was now I-A. He handed the letter to his father. Walter was furious. He stormed into Cottonwood and into Royce Palmer's office. Palmer barely had time to turn and see the charging farmer. Walter cursed invectively as he dove for the plump man sitting at his desk. Before Palmer could rise, he felt a deafening blow to the side of his head. Suddenly, Walter felt two powerful arms grab him from behind.

"Stop it, Walt! I'll have you in jail so long they'll be piping sunshine to you!" Sheriff Young cursed.

Walter relaxed. "It ain't fair, Art... it just ain't!"

"What're you talkin about?"

"I'm losin' a second son, and that goddam MacGregor kid is still on the loose!"

Palmer, lying on the floor beside his swivel chair managed, "Go over to the bank and talk to Felton."

Walter stared unsurely at Palmer, the side of the proprietor's head turning purple from the blow. Instinctively, Walter broke away. The sheriff moved for the incensed farmer when Palmer demanded, "No, Art. Let him go."

Walter charged into the bank. "I gotta see Felton!" he shouted.

A number of the bank employees were becoming accustomed to this entrée.

Caldwell met him at the door, ushering him into the executive's office.

"Felton!" Walter began, "That goddam Royce…!"

He raised his arms in protest. "Hold on, Walt," he cautioned. "If it's about Sam's draft status, there's more you need to know."

"What more could there be?" Hubbard exploded.

Caldwell was angry, and rightfully so. Walter never saw the simmering emotion from the normally-controlled bank president.

"I'm guessing you're upset about this last draft board decision."

"Why do you keep puttin' my problem off, Felton?" he huffed.

"Because," Caldwell answered evenly, "Neither Royce nor I voted to make Sam I-A. Besides that, both Royce and I voted to make Chattman I-A."

Walter was confused. "How in the hell can that be? My Sam's eligible and that MacGregor kid is not?"

Caldwell explained, "Jack, Fred Vogel and Adam Fitch voted to make Sam I-A. Royce and I voted to defer him—for the time being. Royce, Adam and I voted to classify Chattman I-A."

"Does that mean MacGregor's kid is eligible?"

"I don't why he wouldn't be. It's been voted on."

Walter, who hadn't taken a seat, placed his worn felt hat on his head. "I'm sorry, Felton."

The bank president rose from his desk. "Walter," he began slowly, "Sometimes you need to bite your tongue."

Walter nodded respectfully and walked out of the bank.

Royce Palmer was sitting in another chair when Walter returned. On its side was his prize leather-wooden-inlay chair broken on the floor.

"I'd apologize if I knew what I could say," Walter began.

Palmer massaged the welt on his head. "I don't think it would fix my favorite chair, Walt."

"Well," Walter fumbled, "I'll try to control my temper."

Palmer studied the powerful contrite farmer. "That would be nice."

****

Phil Olson sat at his desk typing.

"The American victory at Guadalcanal plus the seizure of Henderson Airfield was matched by the occupation of Tulagi, and gains in New Guinea. The Australians have wrestled control of the Owen-Stanleys and the Japanese are on the run in that sector of the Solomons. Now that Kiska has been regained, it appears certain that Attu will soon fall. The Aleutians will then, without a doubt, be back under American control, enabling the entire chain to be cleared for the badly needed supply line to Russia."

Olson stopped typing. His mind was not on his work. He was bored writing about a war that was halfway around the world from him. He had considered the life of writing stories first hand and being where the real action was. He had been at the Dispatch nearly three years. His position was secure and he was a well-respected authenticated writer. His position in the paper was one of envy and he could reasonably expect to Replace Jim Whalen as the chief editor one day. The one reason he hadn't asked for an overseas assignment was his personal secretary, Andrea Vogel. He kept thinking about the night before at the White House where they had dinner together. Their conversation kept running through his mind.

While they were having an after dinner drink, he impulsively said, "Andrea. I love you. You know that."

"Yes, Phil. I know that," she answered softly. Andrea had carefully avoided any emotional confrontation with Olson. She slowly spun her drink glass which was her habit when in deep thought.

"I don't suppose that I'll ever have a chance," he said.

"That isn't fair, Phil. The guy is fighting for his life. My God! He's in a miserable hell and you know the lifetime commitment that I've made to him. If you love me, do the decent thing and support me."

Olson exhaled as he patted his desk pensively. Abruptly he rose, took the elevator to Whalen's office.

"You're here to see Mr. Whalen, I assume," the secretary said.

"Yes, Georgia. Is he in?"

She pushed the intercom. "Mr. Olson to see you, sir."

"Send him in," the voice cracked from the box.

Whalen was sitting behind a mountain of papers. "Want to give me a hand with all these trees?"

"Jim. I want an overseas assignment."

Whalen rocked forward in his chair. "You what?"

"I've given it a lot of thought. I want to be where the action is."

"Where do you want us to send you?"

"The Solomons."

"Yeah," Whalen calculated, settling back in his chair. "The South Pacific is your baby. You always do most of your best guessing about that part of the war. Why?"

"I don't know, Jim. Just got headed in that direction, I guess."

Whalen straightened in his chair. "Phil, this sort of puts me on the spot. You're so damned important here, but God, the war could sure use a correspondent of your caliber over there. I'll do whatever you say."

"Okay," Olson said, "Then it's done?"

"Boy. You get right to the point, don't you? I remember the first time you came in here— young penster that you were. But I appreciate that aggressiveness in a guy. Sure, I'll make the necessary arrangements."

Whalen pondered for a moment. "Wonder who I'll get to take your place. Stan Leach, I guess."

"No," Olson objected.

"Then who?" Whalen asked.

"Andrea Vogel."

Whalen scowled. "Aw, she's too young—just a pup—and a female to boot."

"Appoint her. You won't be sorry."

"That's easy for you to say. You don't have to work with the whole crew as I do. Stan Leach has been here a hell of a lot longer than that young siren of a secretary of yours. And, there's a lot of guys along with Stan who ought to be considered."

"That siren as you call her, has written some pretty damned important articles."

"Yes. That she has..."

"And you were plenty surprised at that White House function when she walked up to Cordell Hull and wooed him into a particularly informative interview."

"Well, yeah, I know," Whalen hedged, "But Phil, I know more about this business than you do."

"I know you do, but scoops trump time on the job, Jim."

"Now, don't get uppity, Phil," Whalen bristled.

"Jim," Olson pleaded, "Will you at least give her an interview?"

"Okay," Whalen surrendered, "I'll grant her an interview, but do you know if she even wants your job? Have you asked her?"

"No."

"I didn't think so," Whalen grunted.

"Thanks, Jim," Olson replied, leaving the office.

"Andrea," Olson said as he punched the intercom. "Come into my office."

Andrea tripped lightly into Olson's suite. Her heels made her dress sway back and forth tantalizing when she entered.

"Yezzuh, boss?" she asked impishly.

"Sit down. No time for fun and games," he said seriously. "I'm leaving for the South Pacific, and I've recommended to Whalen that you be interviewed for my job."

Olson's announcement came unexpectedly, and her expression was one of total surprise. She slumped into a chair. "When did this all come about?"

"Just did. I finally came to the conclusion that you're the reason I'm still here, and that isn't right for either of us. Would you consider the job?"

"And become the most unpopular female in this building?"

"Probably for a while, but not for long."

"Phil," she protested, "don't leave just because of what happened last night."

"I'm not. I've been thinking a lot about leaving. I'd love the experience, the excitement, adventure, and, yes, what happened last night. But not 'just' because."

Andrea was confused and undecided for a few moments, then sat bolt upright affirming, "Sure... sure. I'd like the job, Phil."

"That's my girl!" Olson exclaimed, standing, cueing Andrea to leave.

"Oh, don't give me that stand-up routine! You're going to have to buy me a drink."

"I was just standing up to leave with you."

It was Friday morning. Andrea was in a bad mood. She had slept fitfully. Her phone rang immediately as she stepped into her office. "Yes?" she answered crisply.

"This is Mr. Whalen, Miss Vogel. I'd like to see you in my office at your earliest convenience."

"I'll be right up," she said formally.

Andrea was ushered into Whalen's office. She'd been there occasionally, yet this morning, the generous room with the panoramic view of the city and the capital particularly impressed her. Andrea managed a smile as she greeted the editor.

"You didn't sound too chipper this morning, Miss Vogel."

"I don't feel too chipper this morning, Mr. Whalen. And why don't you call me Andrea?"

Whalen was put off balance by the young woman's confident and serious demeanor. On the one hand, he was lightly offended by her take charge attitude, while at the same time favorably affected by very same resolute personality. And she certainly wasn't trying to impress him, which impressed him.

Whalen cleared his throat. "Please sit down, ah, Andrea."

"Thank you, sir."

"Is it that you're not feeling well this morning?" he began.

"I just didn't sleep worth a hoot last night, so I'm not doing cartwheels this morning. I suspect you've had nights like that."

He chuckled, "More than I'd care to recall. In fact, I also had one such night."

An awkward silence followed, and Whalen contributed to the contretemps when he asked, "How old are you, Andrea?"

Whalen's question annoyed her and her expression told him so.

"Twenty-two," she answered shortly.

Whalen immediately concluded that the young lady's chronology need not be an issue in the decision he was obliged to make, so he approached the interview from a different tack. "Andrea, do you think you can handle Phil's job?"

"Certainly, I wouldn't be sitting here if I didn't think I could."

"Would you make any changes?"

"Sure. New leadership always comes with baggage."

He smiled at the simile. "So, for openers, what would you change?"

"For openers?" She curled her tongue around her lips in a coquettish fashion, "I'd roll a couple of heads."

"Oh? Who are they?"

Andrea mentioned the names.

"Seems like Phil said something about them. What's the problem?"

"They're counterproductive. That kind of inactivity undermines morale, and I won't tolerate it."

A slight smile appeared as he continued, "What else would you change?"

"I'd get some people out onto the streets. More face to face contact. We need more interviews—get more opinions—editorialize…"

"Editorialize—that's supposed to a bad word." Whalen interjected.

"Well it's not. We have to sell ourselves—change that perspective of selling the steak—sell the sizzle instead."

"Give me an example of what you're talking about."

"Why Patton is a threat to Eisenhower, or how Montgomery is so annoying to Patton. Is Roosevelt going to fire Morgenthau? Everyone knows they don't get along. Is GM getting too much of the defense pie? There are myriad subjects."

"You're suggesting that we put the news on the back page. That we turn this newspaper into a gossip rag? There is a war going on, you know."

"Of course, I know that!" she responded indignantly, "And I am not suggesting in any manner that we deemphasize what's going on around the world. But this is a politics town and people want to know what other people think. They want their thoughts to be heard."

"Thoughts to be *heard*. That's interesting. Are you implying that Phil had the wrong perspective on how the news needed to be disseminated?"

"No. Phil has done an excellent job. But Phil has his way of doing things; I have mine. And, incidentally, since I'm on this rail, I'd establish a section just for Phil. You give a name to the column, or have him dream up a byline, then commission him to provide us with a periodic play by play on what's happening in those places where bullets are hitting the ground."

Whalen's fist hit the desk. "Bingo! Now that's a hell of an idea! That'll get us firsthand information, and it'll sure please Phil. And before I forget to mention it, I like your ideas of getting out to the people, but you have to be careful. There are such things as libel suits."

"That's true—the bear growls when you get near his cave."

Whalen nodded in agreement, chuckling, "Go clean out your desk. And have an outline of your plans on my desk Monday morning. Oh, and be prepared to be pretty unpopular around here for a while,"

Andrea stopped at the door, turning to her new boss. "Pardon me for saying this sir, but I think I can give you the same advice."

Cape Esperance, Guadalcanal
January 12, 1943

"Colonel Canali wants to see you in his headquarters, sir," the corporal announced to Rusty. Atkins walked into the Quonset hut, and sat down in front of Canali.

"Rusty, you've gained weight," the colonel observed.

"I've gained fifty pounds since Luzon, Frank. I weighed 130 pounds when I got off that PBY in Melbourne."

"Well, it looks good on you," the commander remarked tossing a set of captain's bars to Rusty.

"These will look good on you, too."

Rusty looked down at the emblems. "Y 'know, Frank. You were a captain when I first met you. It seems so long ago."

Canali was somewhat put out at Rusty's matter-of-fact acceptance of the promotion. He chose not to comment about it. "Yeah," he sighed. "A few things have happened since then." He pointed to a pair of eagles on his desk. "I've been kicked up to bird."

Rusty eyed the full colonel's insignia. "Stuart better watch his ass. You're gaining ground on him."

"I don't think so. He just got his second star."

"Well, I can tell you this Frank. All this rank doesn't mean a tinker's shit if you don't have any clout to go with it. Look at Wainwright—a three star—rotting away in a Jap prison camp. Personally, I'd rather be a buck private stuck somewhere in a jungle."

Canali smiled at Rusty's simple philosophy. "I would, too. Anyway, it looks like we're going to be permanent here for a while."

"That so? I thought we'd be moving up the chain."

"No. The big brass are sending fortifications up to the Aleutians—Kiska, Attu, Adak. They don't want that area to be threatened again, now that this section of the Solomons is secure."

"That's okay with me. I don't mind having a roof over my head. Besides, I'm ready to get back to training troops. I like doing that."

"Rusty," Canali began with a tone of advice in his voice, "don't be too demanding on the troops. I know you were terribly rough on the guys in Wellington, and thank God you were. After we got into combat, you lost some guys, sure, but your kill ratio was lowest in the entire 11th. And that's why you're a captain. All I'm saying is that you have to keep in perspective what the guys can take."

Rusty bristled. "Just what the hell do you think our old 4th is going through right now? Half the bastards are dying of starvation! My best buddy is one of them! I'll drive those new men like they've not been driven before! If you think I've been too goddam rough on them, put somebody else in my boots!"

Canali exhaled heavily. "Okay. Just don't come running to me to replace your fallouts, cause I'm not going to do it this time."

"You won't have to. I got some stories what will scare the piss out of them."

"I just don't want those guys dying in your unit."

"Now come off that, Frank. I never killed anyone. I might have busted some of them up a bit."

"If you had to field the complaints I get from medical people… depleting the pool of ambulances."

"Oh, I'm gonna get to sit through that again am I? Well," he said rising, "I'm not listening to any more of this crap." He stomped out of Canali's hut.

Canali placed his head in his hands, grumbling, "Fuckin' bonehead."

Rusty re-entered the hut. Canali looked up.

"I was going to ask you, Frank, if you'd mind if I promote that Cole kid to Lieutenant?"

Canali sighed. "That the kid you were so high on at Bloody Ridge?"

"Yeah. He's superb under fire. He was a real settling force for my guys. I want to make him my exec."

Canali paused. "Okay. Go ahead and promote him." Canali again placed his head in his hands and murmured, "God, help the guys who land in your outfit."

As the new captain walked out, he snipped, "God help the ones that don't!"

****

As a diversion one year at a Western Governor's Conference, someone concocted the idea of conducting a sporting contest. It was called, the One Shot Antelope Hunt, and it became immensely popular. Grant Dunning, the well-received Colorado governor would customarily prevail on Jack MacGregor to host the occasion on his sprawling ranch, where antelope grazed in abundance. MacGregor was very covetous of this association, feeling obliged to nurture this relationship with such influential people. He was careful never to indulge the governor's friendship or ask a favor of him. But now, something changed all this. He would break the commitment, when Chattman came to his father with a letter announcing the pampered prodigal son had been classified I-A.

MacGregor was ushered into the governor's chambers, and after a series of pleasantries, the rancher presented a case in what the governor considered to be a reasonable request; that what MacGregor was asking for was well within the guidelines set down by the Selective Service Department. The governor showed a genuine interest, stating that he would give the matter serious consideration and let MacGregor know his decision. MacGregor, however, spoiled it all by suggesting at the conclusion of his petition, that he was very willing to express a considerable "monetary gratuity" for a favorable decision.

The governor was stunned.

"A what?" the shocked official asked.

MacGregor smiled. "A little tithe," he blithely uttered.

Dunning stood motioning toward the door, speaking in a stern manner. "I will be letting you know, Mr. MacGregor. Please find your way out."

Two weeks later, Jack MacGregor was quite surprised when he received Dunning's personal note.

Dear Mr. MacGregor,

Being one who represents the community of jurisprudence, I feel it my duty to interpret and execute the laws as they pertain to our country in this time of dire need. I am therefore, compelled, despite my misgivings, to endorse what I consider a necessity providing foodstuffs in the defense of our besieged nation. It is for this reason, and this reason alone, that I have acted to defer your son Chattman from military service. It has been a pleasure to have had the opportunity to hunt antelope on your ranch.

Very cordially,

Grant Dunning, Governor

MacGregor knew he had just burned another bridge, but grudgingly concluded that, as clumsily as his quest had been handled, it was worth the price.

Walter Hubbard was in his barn that late January day when Royce Palmer and Felton Caldwell drove into his yard.

"Walter," Caldwell said. "We wanted to tell you personally that Chattman MacGregor has been deferred, but that wasn't our blessing— the decision came from the regional office in Denver."

Walter smiled kindly at the two, which came as a relief to the two bringing the bad news. The normally volatile man began matter-of-factly, "Oh, I expected it. When that kid and Sam got the classifications at the same time and my kid has been gone for the better part of a month, I know politics had been a part of it."

The two board members merely stood quietly.

"It's okay, fellas. You've treated me and Sam fairly, and that's a hell of a comfort, I want you to know that. Personally, we're all better off havin' Sam fightin' for us than that pip squeak of MacGregor's."

The comment brought instant laughter from Palmer and Caldwell. They instinctively extended their hands which Walter shook.

Inside Palmer's Cadillac, Caldwell breathed, "That could have been a lot worse."

Palmer merely smiled and nodded.

****

The Hubbard family, what was left of it, waited at the depot in Cottonwood on a windy March morning, as the train pulled to a stop. A strapping blond buck private carrying his duffel bag and M-1 stepped off the train. Sam was home on his first furlough. Walter was immensely proud as they drove to the farm.

"So how's it goin'?" Walter asked, beside himself with delight to have his favorite son home.

"Oh, I prefer farming, Dad," he replied.

"Aren't you scared, Sam?" Ruthie asked, now a high school sophomore.

"Nope, not at all. Oh, don't get me wrong. I don't especially like the notion of getting shot at."

The words caused his mother to visibly jerk.

"But I'm anxious to get this thing over with and get Andy back home. Listen, we got 'em on the run and I mean dead run."

"Any idea where you'll be sent?" Walter asked.

"None whatsoever. I'll go back for four more weeks then I'll know."

"Any preferences?" Walter asked.

"Sure. I'd like to go to the South Pacific and start shootin' those bastards… those Japs who've got Andy, but Krauts and Japs are both the enemy. Soon as one falls, the other one will be close behind. So how are things on the farm Dad?"

"Well, I'm gonna miss you this summer, son, but there's a tractor comin' at Zumbach's and it's my turn. So at least, I'll be better in that respect."

"Wow! When's it comin' in?"

"Any time now."

"What model's comin' in?"

"An 'H'," his father replied.

"Boy, a new 'H'," Sam chirped. "I can't wait to get on it!"

****

Bob Armstrong sat beside Andy on the doctor's hard bunk.

"Snavely's been shittin' the bed almost every night now, Andy. That head wound couldn't be causing that, could it?"

"No, Bob."

"Then what is it? I wish I had enough food in me to take a healthy shit."

"He can't close his anus."

"Why would that be?"

The subject was one Andy preferred to avoid. He drew in deeply. "He's being sodomized."

"You mean corn holed?"

"To use your vernacular. Yes. And he has no control over his sphincter."

And that'll do that?"

"It's doing it."

"Who by?"

Andy's intonation was one of annoyance. "I would assume the warden of this god awful compound. Snavely' his houseboy."

"Snavely'll never be right again, will he?"

"No, Bob. He never will."

"We shoulda' left him when he caught that rifle butt..."

"I agree," Andy sighed, "We should have."

"The only reason they let us help him is 'cause you're a doctor and can speak a little of their language."

"Don't remind me."

"Scuttlebutt has it we're going to be transferred to Tokyo."

"I've heard that."

"Does it matter to you?"

"No," Andy returned with a disinterested finality.

"I wonder when things will ever get any better," Armstrong lamented.

"You better hope the war will end. Things are not going to get better."

****

Jack MacGregor happened to be in Alton Zumbach's International Harvester dealership. A shiny red Farmall 'H' still sat on the truck.

"God, Al, whose is that?"

"Well," the dealer replied, "Walt Hubbard is line for that one."

"What's the price tag on somethin' like that?"

"A little over fourteen hundred."

"Does Hubbard know that tractor's in?"

The dealer flashed MacGregor a confused stare. "Well, he's expecting it," he replied.

"But he doesn't know it's in?"

"What're you getting at, Jack?"

"Does he know this is his tractor?" MacGregor insisted.

"Ninety-nine percent sure. Now tell me why you're asking all this."

"Well," MacGregor began cagily, "I know a guy who'd pay an extra thousand to take that home."

"Now Jack, I couldn't get by with that."

"Think it over, Al. I'll come by the first thing in the morning to make sure." MacGregor left the shop, saying no more.

Alton Zumbach thought about nothing else that day other than the prospect of getting an unexpected windfall of an extra thousand dollars. The demands of war had placed acute shortages on the products that he had to sell. Before the war, he would sell a tractor a month, and now, he sold two a year, and the price he could charge for them was regulated by a government agency known as the OPA, Office of Price Administration. Black market was illegal, but Zumbach desperately needed the money. He figured and figured how he could manage the sale to MacGregor. It was true that priority lists had to be registered with the state agricultural association. Those lists were the safeguard against black marketing. But Zumbach knew that one could fabricate a list and a story to back it, and any error would be next to impossible to prove. He was aware any objection raised by a farmer could not be substantiated. His thought was to tell Hubbard that the state made a listing error; that it wasn't his foul-up. Besides, no farmer or rancher ever saw the list anyway. They had only to rely in the distributor's integrity to rely on the ordered succession of the priority. He decided to let MacGregor have the tractor, and stored the new machine safely cloistered in behind some outdated machinery. It would be there just overnight.

Predictably, Jack MacGregor came early.

"Well, what did you decide Al?" he asked.

"Come in the back, Jack. I need to talk to you."

After the two were by themselves, Zumbach explained how the priority list worked, and how it would be possible to make the transaction happen.

"But I tell you, Jack," the dealer cautioned. "I have to say that the mistake was the state's; not mine, and that's the story I have to give to Hubbard. Hell! He's a violent man! He could have killed you a few months back!"

"How well I know," MacGregor said, recalling the shovel flying by his ear.

"So," Zumbach continued, "That's the story I'll have to give to him, and if he goes to the state, then we'll have to stick together on this. You'll have to claim you understood you were next in line."

MacGregor began fingering out cash. "That'll work. I don't expect he's smart enough to figure anything like that out."

"Oh, he's smart enough. We better just hope he's gullible enough."

MacGregor slapped Zumbach on the shoulder and motioned for Clete, his longtime ranch hand to come for the tractor.

"I don't expect any trouble," he said easily.

That afternoon, Al Zumbach drove out to Walter Hubbard's farm. He found the farmer out in one of the most unexpected places; fixing fence. Walter tossed his hammer in the seat of his Chevy pickup and waited for the dealer to drive up.

"Don't tell me it's in already, Al!" he said triumphantly.

Zumbach frowned. "Bad news, Walt."

"What do you mean, bad news?"

"The priority list came down from the state. I gotta sell that tractor to Jack MacGregor."

The farmer was crestfallen and his heart sank. "You're shittin' me, Al."

"I wish I was, but there's nothing I can do about it, Walt. You know how the state is."

"Bet he bought some sonovabitch off," Walter cursed, looking at the ground.

"Well," Zumbach sighed, "I'd hate to think that happened, but I wanted to let you know firsthand."

"Is the tractor in?"

"No," Zumbach lied taking a large chance, "But when it does, I wanted you to know what the hell happened."

"Shit! Son of a bitch!" Walter cursed as he kicked the ground. "Now what the hell am I gonna do?"

"Dunno, Walt," Zumbach said wishing for a chance to get away.

"Well, I tell ya what, Al. It takes a hell of a man to come out here and do what you just did. Don't you worry about it. I'll manage somehow."

"Thanks, Walt. We'll get you a tractor somehow."

Walter appreciated what the dealer said, but knew it was a hollow promise.

As Zumbach drove away, he cursed himself. "Rotten, dirty, not good. You've got a debt to that man that you gotta make up somehow, some way."

Stapleton airport, Denver
May 7, 1943

The TWA Constellation taxied up to the gate. Four giant engines whined to a stop. Two attendants rolled the mobile stairs alongside the plane, as the stewardess, topside, swung open the door. A striking woman dressed in high heels and an expensive wine suit stepped out of the first class section and down the ramp. Her family watched as she approached the restricted section. It had been before the war since any member of the family had seen her, and their shock when she walked up was apparent. She had changed. She was a woman now, and she had accomplished much in her tenure as senior editor of the Washington newspaper. Her editorials and opinion columns had been the talk of the city, and her personal interviews included anyone from the Army chief of staff to Churchill to the President himself. Andrea had secured the admiration and trust of those who worked under her as well as influential people around Washington D.C., along with the chief newspaper editor himself, Jim Whalen.

These accomplishments were lost on a family who had no comprehension of what she had learned, or what she was doing.

After hugs all around and walking to the family car, Fred Vogel observed, "You don't look much like my little girl who went away to school."

"Well," she replied, "I'm still your girl. That part hasn't changed, but you're right. I'm not much like the girl who went away to school."

Andrea quickly discovered just how much she had changed. What was going on around her home town was a far cry from the frenzied hot bed of international activity she had just left. So much so, she was absolutely out of her mind with little to impart, and anything that was happening in her hometown was not of the remotest interest to her. She had the haunting suspicion that a similar deliverance had surely developed between her and Andy as an unavoidable product of their disparate environments. But, she knew, given the opportunity, such a schism would soon disappear.

Another day of small talk, and she wandered down along the creek bank to the Schatzaeder farm, stopping and leaning against the tree where she and Andy had made love. Softly, she wept, fingering her heart necklace. She was ready to go back to Washington, although it was only her second day in Cottonwood. She still had to somehow cope with the three remaining days before she would leave. That evening, she and Helga were going to the Cottonwood Theater to see Northwest Passage. Since the weather was warm that time of the year, they would walk the half mile across the simple country town to the theater. She saw the same movie three years earlier in Denver, and wondered what emotions she would encompass.

Chattman walked in as Clete was unsaddling a horse. It was late in the afternoon. "Well," the loyal ranch hand said turning, "guess who's back in town?"

"Dunno. Who?"

"That Vogel girl you was always hot on."

"You sure?"

"Yup. Saw her in the store this mornin'."

Chattman made a fast trip to the ranch house. He knew his father was inside.

"Dad," he began. "'I know you're not going to like me asking this, but can I take my car to Cottonwood?"

Jack stood in the kitchen doorway. "Hell no, Cat. I told you I'd let you know when that car leaves the shed."

"It's been in there over a year, Dad."

"So?"

"Dad—Andrea's in town."

"She is?"

"Yes."

"Who told you that?"

"Clete—said he saw her in the store this morning."

"Then go in and see her."

"But I want to take my car."

"The answer is no, Cat."

"Dad," Chattman persisted. "When you were my age a thousand wild horses couldn't have kept you away from Mom—not for any reason! And you went all the way to New York to marry her. Anything you had to do to get her, you would have done."

He exhaled a long thinking breath of air. "Yeah, I guess I can't deny any of that, can I?" The father thought for a moment, and uttered, "Oh, what the hell, Cat. Go ahead."

Chattman dashed from the house, and into the shed. He turned the key and kicked the starter. Nothing. The battery was dead. He hunted down Clete who came with a pickup, and a bottle of gas to pour down the carburetor. After a short pull, the big V8 sprang to life.

The sun was setting and the top was down on the yellow convertible when Chattman started to pull into the Vogel yard and then he glanced down the gravel road. His timing was perfect. Andrea and her buxom sister were a short distance away, heading into town. He pulled alongside.

"How about a ride, ladies?" he chirped.

Andrea glanced at him, looking away.

"Wow, Cat!" Helga gushed. "Where did you get that fancy car?"

"Got it a while back," he said confidently. "Rides nice. Hop in."

Andrea didn't break stride.

"Oh, come on, Andrea," Helga begged.

"Go ahead. You can get in," Andrea said.

"But I want you to go with me!"

"I don't want in."

"Please Andrea?" Chattman entreated.

She didn't respond.

"Please Andrea?" Helga persisted. "I want to ride in Chattman's snazzy car!"

"Oh, okay! I'll do it just for you. You get in first. And only to the theater."

Helga leaped in next to Chattman, who wore a deflated frown.

"How are things, Andrea?" he asked anxiously, his heart pumping.

Andrea didn't answer.

"I don't think she heard you, Cat," Helga said as the LaSalle accelerated up the road.

"I heard him. Tell him things are okay."

"Well, the ranch is fine," he said loudly, looking over at her.

She turned and their eyes met. He flashed a nervous grin. She stared solemnly at him.

The Hubbards would go a movie maybe twice a year. Mildred was fond of Spencer Tracy and she persuaded Walter to go see the "show." Walter parked his pickup and was walking to the entrance behind Millie and Ruthie when Chattman drove up. Andrea quickly stepped out, and when she did, she turned to see Mildred and her daughter. Andrea's and Mildred's eyes met, and in the split second, Millie covered her face with her hands. Andrea, who hadn't seen the Hubbards since the time she went East, quickly attempted an explanation. "Millie!"

Walter broke for Chattman shouting, "Get out of that car, you coward son of a bitch!"

Helga hopped out as Chattman spun away, catching a last glimpse at Andrea.

At this point, Walter was quite close to Andrea, who began explaining, "Mister Hubbard, I…"

"And you get out of here too, you slattern!" Walter howled.

By now all the females, except Helga, who was dumbfounded, were sobbing.

Andrea was not going to allow Walter to get away without an explanation. "Mister Hubbard, it's not what you think!"

"I know what I saw. You can't deny that!"

"There's a reason."

"A reason, hell! There's gotta be a reason his dad and your dad is keepin' that damn kid out of the draft while they took my last boy and Andy is rottin' away in a Jap prison camp and..."

"Now dammit yourself, Walter!" She was in his face now. "I can curse just as loudly as you!"

Walter was stupefied, and he practically cowered. She was just starting.

"I was in that God damn car only to please my sister! Not because I have any God damned feelings for Chattman MacGregor who I hate with a passion!" She was gasping for breath. "It was a God damned mistake!" She stood nose to nose with him, her arms rigid at her sides, fists clenched, screaming. "It was a God damned mistake, Walter! Have you ever made a mistake?"

Walter stood with his arms hanging limply by his sides, a pitiful specter in his faded blue overhauls.

She began sobbing. "I love Andy. You should know that by now!" She began to collapse to the pavement, but Walter caught her in his powerful arms. It was a strange sight with the beautiful woman clinging to the plain brawny farmer who couldn't have looked more awkward. Millie walked up and embraced the two.

"Walter. We need to go home." Millie said. "I'm not in the mood to see a show."

"No. I'm not either," Andrea said.

"Oh, come on, Andrea," Helga said.

"No, Helga. You go see the show. I'm going home. I'll make sure someone's here to pick you up."

Her sister turned and walked into the theater.

"I'm sorry Millie," Andrea began, rubbing her eyes.

"Andrea, will you be able to see me while you're home?"

"I'll come over to the school when it's out tomorrow, Millie. Will that be all right?"

"I'll wait for you there."

"Uh, Andrea," Walter fumbled, "I uh... I got a temper. Everybody says it. And I'm sorry about what I said about your dad. It doesn't take much of a man to grumble to his children about what their folks..."

She gave Walter an affectionate rub on his shoulder, which visibly embarrassed him.

"You don't have to apologize, Walter. You're a good man. I know that. Everyone knows that. So is my father, although he disappointments me at times." She paused awkwardly. "There are some things you should know about him. I'll tell Millie." She turned to leave. "I'm sorry I spoiled your evening."

On the way back to the farm, Ruthie, sitting in the middle, blurted. "Boy. Andrea can sure cuss!"

A stilted silence followed.

Finally, Walter, focusing straight head uttered, "Andrea's a hell of a fine woman, Ruthie."

Millie patted her daughter on the thigh. "Your father's right about that."

The next day Andrea was at Mitchell School before school let out. When the doors sprang open, Andrea waded through the current of children into the schoolhouse. Mildred was in her customary chair behind the desk in front grading papers and was unaware of Andrea's entrance.

"Millie..."

Mildred looked up in surprise.

"You're all alone here now, aren't you?"

"Yes. Mary Elizabeth has her own school now."

"She was a real help to you, wasn't she?"

"What a wonderful girl—but she's moved on. She's happy, and that makes me happy."

"How many years here, Millie?"

"Sixteen. I began here in 1927, '26 actually, so sixteen and a half."

"I was five years old."

"You've accomplished a lot since then. I understand you met the President."

Andrea smiled. "Actually, I had lunch with his wife only last week; just the two of us."

Millie stiffened. "With Eleanor Roosevelt?"

"Yes. I had met her before, and she's one of my heroines—as you are, Millie."

Millie flushed. "Oh, my, Andrea, I don't know about that... I can't be compared to Eleanor Roosevelt!"

"Oh, sure you can. She's a person just like you. Actually, she's very down to earth."

"Well, you really impressed Walter last night."

"I had no idea he was so gentle, Millie."

"He is, but nobody knows it. He's not polished."

"He's stronger than an ox—I found that out."

"You said last night that you hated Chattman. Was that just in anger?"

Andrea's appearance grew cold. "He's ruined Andy's and my world. How could I not hate him? He's not stupid. He's calculating and vindictive."

"I'm sorry that I have to agree. Chattman and Andy grew up together. Started school right here in this room. Bright, smart and pretty little boys they were—and inseparable. Andy joined and we know the circumstances behind that."

"Andy and I toyed with running away."

"Away from what?"

"Running away. Away from everything into another country, and we could have pulled it off."

"Oh, my," Millie mused. "Wouldn't that have been wonderful?"

"I can't think about it, Millie. I'd go nuts."

"Well, Sam's been drafted."

"I don't know Sam at all."

"He's a carbon copy of his dad."

"Andy was—is—so different," Andrea said.

"Walter saw it when Andy was just a little tyke. Really Andy and his father have so little in common."

Mildred noticed tears running down Andrea's cheeks.

"Anyway, Sam's in harms' way and Chattman is still around driving a new car, healthy and safe. It's not difficult to see why there's some bitterness. I have to admit I have a little of it myself."

"As I do. Don't leave me out. The man who means everything to me is struggling to stay alive."

Millie began to tear.

Andrea began on a serious note. "I wanted to tell you something about my father. Everyone knows Jack MacGregor set him up in business."

"Yes."

"And that wasn't all for Dad's benefit."

"Everyone knows that too," Millie added.

"Around the time Andy had just started college and we were making our plans, Royce Palmer discovered the land Dad's store is on actually belongs to some woman in Pennsylvania. Philadelphia, I think."

"*What*? How could that be? And how could Royce Palmer find that out?"

"Well, you know Royce Palmer..."

"He's a strange one."

"But a good strange, I think."

"I think that, too," Millie agreed.

"Well, Dad's very loyal to his family and wants desperately to provide for us."

"Nothing wrong with that."

"No, there isn't. But Royce and Jack were beginning to have differences, and Royce let Dad in on this information."

"How could Jack have made such a mistake in the first place?"

"It wasn't a mistake!" Andrea snapped invectively. "Jack knew it all along, but he got caught. He thought he could get that ground for nothing. Typical for the way he does things. Anyway, Jack realized he could lose the bonanza he'd been getting for years."

"What kind of bonanza?"

"He gets everything a cost and pays no tax."

"Oh, my," Millie injected.

"Yes. Well, if the word got out, then the lady in Philadelphia, or wherever, would get the whole business. Now there's this thing called 'statute of limitation'..."

"I know what it is. It's generally seven years."

"Not in this case. On land absorption, it's seventeen."

"Seventeen," Mildred mulled the numbers in her mind. "That should be about expired."

"It is. There's only a little over a year left. But here's the rub. Now that the war's on, that store has become second fiddle to Jack. He's most concerned with keeping Chattman out of the draft."

"He doesn't have to worry about the younger son," Millie put in.

"No. Farnham's got some muscle problem, so he'll never have to go."

"Muscular dystrophy. Esther's got it too," Mildred explained.

"Well, I know they had something, and that's unfortunate, but, now Jack told Dad if Dad didn't go along with him with deferring Chattman, he'd let the cat out of the bag. That he doesn't care about the store anymore, and he's got Dad just where he wants him."

Mildred smiled gravely. Andrea noticed and asked what the smile was about.

"Oh, you said, 'let the cat out of the bag,' it was just a weird coincidence."

Andrea forced a smile. "I did say that. Well, somebody should stuff him in a bag, but now you know the story, Millie."

"That helps, Andrea," Mildred said compassionately. "I really appreciate your coming out to see me, and confiding in me." Mildred's expression grew sober. "The big problem still confronts us."

Andrea leaned over, placing her hand on Mildred's.

"I love you Millie. I pray someday you'll be my mother-in-law. I will never marry if Andy doesn't get home."

Mildred started to cry. "Please don't think that way."

Andrea rose as did Mildred. The two embraced and the young woman walked through the weathered doors.

Andrea looked back and saw the pitiful picture of the teacher framed by the doorway watching her drive away.

CHAPTER 41

A light rain was falling that June morning and the Hubbards were in a happy mood not only because it was raining, but because the train approaching the depot in Cottonwood carried Sam Hubbard. He had been assigned as a squad leader and was given a stripe in the process. He was tanned and stronger looking than ever as he stepped down from the train, a PFC chevron on his sleeve, his duffel bag over one shoulder, and his M-l rifle over the other.

Driving out to the farm he mentioned, "I'm guessing the tractor hasn't come in yet."

"Didn't get it," Walter said shortly.

"Why not?"

"Jack MacGregor did."

Sam scowled. "How could he get it? You were next in line!"

"Oh, I think somebody paid somebody off—that's generally how it works. Al Zumbach came out and apologized. There wasn't a damn thing he could have done. Boy, I miss you, buddy, but the horses don't."

Sam didn't hear the rest of his father's words. He was starting a slow burn about his father's not getting the tractor.

****

Sam's furlough came at a time when the moon was full. The next morning, the sun came out bright. Sam had formulated a plan. He would wait until night to carry it out.

When all had gone to bed and everyone was asleep, he took his rifle, slipped out the window, and set out looking for the tractor. His old dog Spook dutifully followed alongside him. He walked in the bright moonlight the two miles to the border of the MacGregor ranch. In the flat, unobstructed prairie with the full moon, the view was as accommodating as it was on a clear day. He walked another two miles to the ranch complex. After two month's training in concealment, he had no fear of being detected. Also, he was accustomed to fifty mile marches, so this trek would be no more than an inconvenience. Cautiously, he peered into every barn and shed searching for the tractor while the MacGregors slept. A dog barked in the giant yard, but that was nothing out of the ordinary, as an enterprising coyote would frequent the surroundings in its quest of an open chicken house door or the corrals for a lone baby calf or lamb. No tractor. He walked down to the original homestead occupied only by Clete in the bunk house and Bonnie in the original residence. Sam searched every barn and shed; still, no sign of the new machine. He headed home.

The next night, he tried again, looking in every conceivable area for the tractor. Again, no luck. There was one more hay bottom he could visit which was on the extreme border of the ranch, some fifteen miles from the Hubbard farmhouse. He would need another night to get to it.

Millie remarked that Sam looked tired, but he dismissed it as being away from the Army regimen.

The next night, Sam doggedly set out to find the elusive tractor. He left at 9:30 this night, because everyone went to bed early. At midnight, he reached the target hay bottom. The moon was high when he spotted something at the far end of the meadow. Fixing his eyes on the object, he walked the half mile across the grassy meadow. The image of a tractor came clearer. It was equipped with a hay loading device, referred to as a "buck stacker". He walked up to the new tractor, climbed onto the seat and started the engine. He savored the even throaty purr for a few moments. He then shut the switch off, patted the gas tank, murmuring, "Sorry buddy—you don't know how much this hurts me to do this."

He walked several yards away from the machine placing one 30 caliber round in the chamber of the M-l. He then placed a glove on his left hand to catch the bullet cartridge, which would eject with force. He was aware, even if he had been close to anyone's ears, it would be impossible to get a vector on a single rifle shot; it would be difficult to triangulate even with two or three reports. He pulled the trigger, and the staccato report pierced the still night.

The steel-jacketed bullet blew through the right side of the cast iron block, gouging a hole the size of a softball as it spit though the brittle metal. The round missed the crankshaft and rods, but tore through the forth cylinder and out the opposite side of the block, leaving a similar size perforation. The bullet, for humanitarian purposes put down by the Geneva Convention, specified that a steel jacket must enclose a lead projectile to prevent mushrooming. That was ideal for Sam's purpose. The projectile would not spread, thus allowing a relative-unimpeded trajectory through the target and an extended distance after impact.

Sam placed the spent cartridge in his fatigue jacket pocket, removed his glove and began the hike back to the house.

Sam had long been given a sad farewell and was on his way to England, when the hay came ready to put into stacks. Clete Fossun had begun working for Liam MacGregor in 1918. In the twenty-seven years of dedicated servitude, he felt a certain ownership to the ranch. He rode the horse at breakneck speed back to the ranch.

That same afternoon, Sheriff Arthur Young was out to the MacGregor ranch to examine the tractor. Al Zumbach, at MacGregor's prodding, accompanied the sheriff.

"Jack," the sheriff said grimly, "I can't imagine what happened to your tractor."

"Well, Sheriff, someone shot through it. That's obvious," MacGregor growled.

"It's not to me. I can't really see what did it. If it was a gun of some kind, you would expect it to spatter. I can't imagine anything that could make it through this block. And it's impossible to tell the direction this came from, because the holes are the same size. That just doesn't happen. Even if it did make it through the block, and it's obvious that it did, nothing that I know could take a cylinder with it. I just don't know what in the world did this."

"Well, it was a gun!" MacGregor snapped

"I know my guns, Jack, and there's nothing I know about that's capable of doing anything like this!" Arthur Young hadn't heard of a steel-jacketed bullet; in fact, Arthur Young hadn't heard of the Geneva Convention.

MacGregor turned to the farm equipment dealer. "Well, Al. What are we going to do now?"

"Do about what?"

"My tractor! What the hell you think I'm talkin' about?"

"What the hell can I do?"

"Well, you gotta do something!"

"Jack, I couldn't get you a new block, and that's what it's gonna take. If I lived in Chicago and was the kissin' cousin of the president of the International Harvester Company himself, I'd have as much luck getting you a tank!"

The comment brought a derisive chuckle out of Young, which obviously angered MacGregor. He failed to see any humor in it.

"You're not gonna get that tractor fixed. It's that simple!" Zumbach asserted.

MacGregor wanted to lay a guilt trip on Zumbach, but didn't dare. Not in front of the sheriff anyway.

"Shit!" he cursed. "I guarantee ya I know who did this!"

"Who?" the sheriff inquired.

"That Sam Hubbard!"

"Now why would you say something like that, Jack? He's in the army! I understand he's in England!"

"I dunno, Art. I just never trusted that kid. You know he was home awhile back."

"So was Geronimo. Why don't you accuse *him*?" Zumbach jibed.

MacGregor turned to the tractor man. "Y'know, Al. You're not makin' me too happy today. Why don't you give it a rest?"

MacGregor turned again to the sheriff. "You can at least check out what that Hubbard kid did when he was home."

"Well, Jack," the sheriff said, "The ice is gonna have to get a hell of a lot thicker than that if you're asking me to skate out on it."

"Boy. You and Al are both full of clever little sayins' today."

"Come on, Alton. I gotta get back to town," the sheriff said.

MacGregor took one more stab. "Al, are you sure you can't find me an engine?"

"Not a chance in hell. I'm sorry. I really am. You better break out that horse buck stacker."

****

The C-47 bounded across the metal runway at Henderson. Phil Olson gathered his papers and stuffed them in his satchel, then picked up his case that held his sturdy Underwood. The plane rolled to a stop and a sergeant swung open the side door. The hot wet south sea island air hit him like a blast furnace. He was used to the cold miserable early spring weather in Washington DC. Walking across the uneven metal strips, he surveyed wreckage that was everywhere. Twisted parts of fighter planes, trucks, cannons and equipment of all sorts lined the boundaries of the air strip. At the end of the runway sat a row of Quonset huts.

He strode into a hastily-assembled orderly room. "I wonder if I could see the officer in charge?" he asked the CQ, a PFC.

He looked at the man dressed in civilian khakis, unfamiliar with the man's rank or purpose. "That would be Colonel Harrington," he said motioning to the rear of the elongated canvass structure.

The correspondent walked in the office. The officer looked up. "Yes?"

"I'm Philip Olson with UPI, and I have been sent here to initiate a new service."

"Who are you attached to?"

"The Washington Dispatch."

"Then you have no specific assignment?"

"No. Can you give me any suggestions?"

It was not uncommon that a new correspondent had difficulty in becoming established, because of the non-combative, or non-affiliated nature of his work, but military brass had sent down a directive that media people would be treated with respect. Plus, this colonel was receptive. He smiled. "Want to cover the 11th?"

"Anything to get started," Olson replied.

"Okay. We'll get you a jeep and a driver."

As Olson departed with the driver, the colonel smiled mischievously. "That ought to break him in right."

The driver drove Olson to the 11th headquarters, and again asked who was in charge.

"What about?" the corporal grilled.

"I'm a war correspondent attached to you."

"Colonel!" the aide yelled through the doorway, "There's a war correspondent here to see you."

"Who is it?" was Canali's response.

"Philip Olson of the Washington Post Dispatch," Olson volunteered.

"Come in to my office!"

Olson introduced himself offering to cover the 11th Division, to which Canali was co- operative, but warned that a certain troop commander may not be receptive to Olson's line of work.

"I'll start anywhere if you can tell my driver where to find this outfit."

Canali handed Olson a map, and pointed outside. "Take that jeep out front. Send that driver back. You won't need him. You'll be on your own. Before you leave, check in at the BOQ and they'll find you a place to sleep." Canali stood and offered his hand. "Good luck. You might need it."

Olson followed the map, not knowing what to expect when he neared the area. Coming into a clearing, he spotted a complement of men seated on the ground. There was a medium sized officer attired in dirty fatigues, walking and talking as he moved amongst them. Rusty Atkins had completed the training for the day and was addressing his troops. Olson couldn't have come at a better moment. After parking the jeep, he strolled to within hearing distance, took out his pencil and pad and leaned against a tree.

"And I'll tell you this," the muscular reddish-brown haired captain harangued, "Despite what you've always heard, experience is not the best teacher. Experience is the worst teacher! When some Jap sniper hollers out, 'Corporal Davis!' and some dumb shit looks out of his foxhole just in time to catch bullet in his face, you don't need to rise up when he hollers twice. Just because somebody makes a mistake, don't you make the same mistake. You don't have to feel a bullet to know it's real! You gotta think! You can't be influenced by tricks! And you gotta be patient! What I'm sayin' to you is you learn from Corporal Davis' experience. That's the only way experience can be valuable. It's a sad fact that you have to profit from someone else's mistakes."

He strode around in a commanding manner, making certain he had full attention.

"Now crazy things happen in the jungle. Your mind plays tricks on you. I can tell you that a foxhole after three days is a damned uncomfortable place, but it beats the shit out of a permanent home in this hell hole. A land crab, for example, can sound like a Jap crawling on you. In those situations, you're on your own. Many, many men were killed on Guadalcanal for shooting at some damned animal, then giving away his position, eventually getting himself, and worse yet, his buddies killed. I'll say it again. You've gotta be patient!

"In regards to night fighting," he continued, "The Japs are better at it than we are. That's only natural, I suppose, since they're sneaky bastards by nature. Now they got a 25 caliber rifle that doesn't have the punch like the one we have, but the thing doesn't smoke and it doesn't give off a flash. That's an advantage they have at night, because it makes it hard sometimes to see where in hell the round is comin' in from—so pay special attention to that. And you've got to distinguish the light given off by a rotting log from an enemy signal, and I'll show all that as time goes on. You're luckier than hell you have the benefit of this island to prepare you for the next. Those before you didn't have that luxury. Learn to keep to keep your cool. Don't over react and end up shooting each other! Another thing about seeing at night. Don't look directly at anything. You can see farther and better out the sides of your eyes."

Rusty was closing his daily message. He was oft criticized that the pattern of his advice seldom followed in any order, and that was okay, he would argue, since "nothing in combat did either."

"Remember boys, if it can be of any comfort to you, I'll be right alongside you and so will my staff. And if I find anyone in this outfit without a steel pot and an ammoed-up M 1 within arm's length, and that includes cooks and anybody, I'll personally shoot him in the butt!"

The five hundred sitting on the ground clapped and cheered.

Rusty walked over and picked his helmet off the ground, but before he put it on, he stared at the gathering.

"Men. We aren't gonna lose this war no way, no how. Know what makes me sure? Just look up when you see that lead duck get shot. The rest of them don't know what the fuck to do. That's how the Japs are. Not us.

We aren't like that. If I get it in the nuts, Corporal Green over there," he said motioning to a troop, "jumps in and takes my spot. Every one of you men is a leader, and boy, if you don't think that's power, then you don't know what power is!"

Phil Olson, witnessing the moment, could actually feel a surge of pride in the air.

Rusty placed his helmet on his head. "Okay, boys. If you got anything to ask, this is the time, then we'll get the hell out of Dodge."

There were several questions asked; good questions. Olson was impressed not only by the quality of what was asked, but the manner in which they were directed.

When the question and answer session had ended, the DI gave instructions to fall in and begin the five-mile trek back to the regimental headquarters. Olson walked up to Rusty.

"Excuse me, Sir. I wonder if I may ask you a couple of questions?"

Rusty scowled. "Who the hell are you?"

Olson explained his purpose.

"If you really want to be of some use, throw that pencil and paper away and grab a rifle."

"You have something against reporters, Captain?"

"You guys write. We shoot. You're here to make a name for yourself; we're here to end the goddam war."

"Reporting is important," Olson said, standing his ground.

The troops were several yards down the road, and the captain was becoming irritated.

"I gotta go. I walk with my troops."

"Just one question, Sir."

"What is it?" he asked impatiently.

"Have these troops been in battle?"

"Nope."

"Then it seems to me that you're trying to have them make logical decisions to what in reality are emotional conclusions."

"Well," Rusty said slowly, "I suppose that's true."

"How can you expect them to respond when they don't actually know what they're up against?"

"We try to make things are real as possible. Hey! I'm getting out of sight of my troops!"

"Would you consider riding back in the Jeep?" Olson asked.

"Oh shit! I just as well now."

Over the hum of the engine, Olson returned to the topic. "We were talking about the troops reacting as though a training exercise was an actual situation."

"That's right," Rusty said removing his helmet and scratching his bristly copper hair. "I'll answer it this way. When I was in basic training in San Diego, it was playtime. Nobody was shooting at us and nobody was going to be shooting at us. Maybe we should have done what the Germans did."

"What was that?"

"They had one live round randomly placed in their clip on training exercises."

"You'd get a guy killed that way, wouldn't you?"

Rusty looked over in surprise. "Sometimes they did, but they had a pretty damned good discipline system."

"I would think so."

"Anyway, when you get one of these trainees crawlin' through the jungle and he comes on what's left of somebody' s arm, that's when he learns it's not playtime anymore."

He saw Olson grimace.

"I can tell you haven't seen much war."

"No, but I expect to."

"I'll believe that when I see one of you guys near the front line. Hell," Rusty chuckled, "you could get it right now by some Jap straggler who is still out here somewhere. It happens."

"I thought you got them all," Olson jibed.

"No. They'll be hid out here for years to come. Does that scare you?"

"No. Should it?"

"A little bit, I think."

"Did you have a correspondent assigned to you before I showed up?"

"Yeah. We had one."

"Where is he now?"

"Probably back in the states."

"Couldn't he take it?"

"Didn't have a hell a lot of choice. He's dead."

"Thought you said my kind stayed way back."

"Oh, he was. Got hit by an errant round from one of the ships out in Savo Bay."

"Japanese or American ship?"

"Who knows?" It could have been from either one. Things get a little disorganized in those slugfests."

"So the guy got killed behind the lines."

"Him and a bunch more. Cooks, doctors, nurses. It was a bad deal."

The troops arrived at the compound.

"Can I buy you a drink, Captain?"

"I suppose so," Rusty said, pointing to the officer's makeshift club. They entered. The smell of canvas and cosmoline hung heavy inside the Jamesway hut.

Rusty had a gin waiting for him when he sat down. Olson pulled up a chair.

"What'll be?" the sergeant asked Olson.

The waiter recognized Olson's insignia which was neither military nor civilian; but correspondents enjoyed the same privileges as officers.

"Whisky sour."

"Sorry about the sour, but we got whiskey."

"Got bourbon?"

"We got bourbon."

"Then make it a bourbon and water, please."

"I can't take mixed drinks," Rusty said wrinkling his nose.

"Just drink gin, huh?"

"Gin and beer, I guess" Rusty took out a cigarette, offered one to Olson, which the correspondent took.

Earlier, when Olson was in the Quonset waiting for registering to be completed, he overheard some conversation in the background about being attached to 'that bad-ass captain' who was on Bataan.

While sipping his drink, Olson decided to make a gambit. He thought he had the right person. "Understand you were on the Bataan March."

Rusty flipped the correspondent a surprised and amused look. "Yeah."

"Want to talk about it?"

"Not much to talk about. Got away too quick."

"I knew a Marine who got caught on that."

"That right?" Rusty asked, dragging on the cigarette.

"Yes. It was a sad deal."

"They all were," Rusty interjected.

"This one was particularly sad. This guy had no business being in the Marines."

"Oh?"

"Yeah," Olson continued. "This tall kid from Colorado wanted to be a doctor."

Rusty could feel the hair stand up on his neck, as he looked straight ahead. "If you tell me his name was Andy Hubbard, a monkey's going to fly out of my ass!"

"You just gave birth to a monkey because that's who it was."

"Son of a bitch," Rusty murmured softly, "I thought when I killed a Jap out in the jungle who was the brother of a friend of mine, that could never happen—now this!"

"You ought to tell me about it sometime."

"I will tell you, sometime. Shigi deserves it."

"Shigi huh?"

"Shigimetsu Tanaka. What he taught me about Japs saved my ass many a time, but getting back to Andy, how do you happen to know him?"

"I met him and his girlfriend in Denver."

"Andrea?"

"Do you know her?"

"Just saw pictures of her. Do you know her?"

"I wanted to get to know her better, but she would have none of it, Captain."

"Call me Rusty."

"I'm not sure I want to do that."

"Do it. It's an order," he said with a smile. "What was her last name?"

"Andrea Vogel."

"Yeah. Vogel's her name. So where's she now?"

"She has my old job right now. But let's talk about Andy. How well do you know him?"

Rusty looked up at the waiter. "Bring us another, Larry!" then back to Olson.

"He saved my life."

Olson drew a deep breath. "God, Rusty... I was worried about whether I could find anything to write about, but in one short afternoon, I've got enough to keep me busy for a couple of days! Do you think Andy's still alive?"

"He was before I busted away from that miserable surrender."

"How'd you get away?"

"Well," Rusty sighed. "that's another story."

"You'll fill me in on that, won't you?"

"Sure, when we get time, but Andy's the one you should be writin' about. He's the real hero."

"Sounds like you know him pretty well."

"Better 'n any man alive."

"God! I'm glad I left Washington!"

"You may change your mind about that when the bullets start flyin'."

Olson was in high spirits when he headed for his hut. He and Rusty had swapped stories for two hours. With some difficulty, he located his billets. He started a wire to Andrea. "Hello Dear," he began. "The story I'm sending along is bizarre, yet extremely interesting, I assure you. I trust you'll make certain it reaches my column in the Dispatch. Normally, my accounts would go directly to the printing department, but this narrative involves you. Also, I would suggest that you see if you can get it printed in Andy's hometown paper."

Andrea was mildly annoyed that Olson failed to mention that it was her hometown paper, too.

"I'll write you a personal note later. It's been a hectic day. Love you. Phil."

The correspondent unstrapped his typewriter, took out a paper and a carbon. He began:

"Strange things happen in wartime, but in my first day as a correspondent attached to the 11th Marine Division here on Guadalcanal, I discovered, quite by chance, the most-unusual coincidence in my life.

Frustrated initially, I drove my jeep out into the jungle where a battle-tested leathery captain was lecturing his troops that afternoon. Captain Rusty Atkins, an escapee from the surrender on Bataan was the CO. He was addressing some five hundred spellbound troops on the do's and don'ts of jungle combat…"

Olson rhetorically parlayed the story of Rusty's speech to his troops, then he eagerly bit into the heart of the story; how two people, a correspondent and a Marine captain could meet on a remote island in the South Pacific and discover that their paths had somehow crossed through a mutual friend. Olson related how he had met a tall Marine, then related the story of how this same Marine had saved the captain's life. He wrote how this unfortunate Marine, through his heroic act, had given the captain, then a corporal, the encouragement which led to the captain's successes. The final segment of the story related to Andrea; how she was the Marine corporal's desire and a former employee of the correspondent himself.

Phil Olson's future as a war correspondent began with a bang, similar to his start with the Washington Dispatch, and Andy had played an integral part in both stirring accounts.

Andrea read the story in disbelief sending a copy of the story to Millie requesting that it be referred to the newspaper in Cottonwood. Unfortunately, the same story couldn't be printed in Rusty's hometown paper. Rusty had no hometown. But then, he was more fortunate than Andy Hubbard.

CHAPTER 42

Alton Schritter was the first implement dealer to get a Waterloo Boy power plant in Platte Center, an agricultural town on the northeast corner of Colorado, six miles from the Nebraska state line. That was in 1918. The dependable and solidly built machine was not mobile. It could, however, drive stationary balers, milking machines, silage blowers, hammer mills, wheat threshers, and anything around the farm that could get along without horses. The little single cylinder workhorse eliminated a significant amount of manual labor and was a boon to the farming industry. In 1921 the firm that produced the machine was purchased by a company located in the same town as the power plant manufacturer: Waterloo, Iowa. That company was John Deere.

The parent company, intent on growing their business potential, added another cylinder and four wheels. From the Waterloo Boy, the highly-successful John Deer tractor line was born.

Early John Deere tractors were not glamorous, partly because of the cacophonous staccato sound that only two cylinder engines could produce. Plus, they were hindered by their prosaic design. Other tractors with four or more cylinders had a pleasant purr and a certain amount of styling. By 1939, John Deere decided their machines should be pleasing to the eye. Though after making them pretty, they still discharged the same racket. Still, to the faithful, the timbre created by the "Johnny Popper" was a symphony. The window dressing championed by other companies, mattered to some, but not to the farmer who wanted a reliable uncomplicated machine that could be depended on day in and day out. An unwavering respect was harbored by many, many aficionados of John

Deere. Walter Hubbard was one of them. He would have preferred a Deere to any tractor manufactured, and that should be expected from a man who, too, was reliable and uncomplicated.

Zumbach's phone rang that morning in early July. He was sitting in his office with not much to do. International Harvester's contribution to the war effort was responsible for that.

It was Aunt Bertha in Platte Center.

"Alton, your uncle died. We need you to be a pallbearer."

He wasn't a foreigner to blunt demands. Genteel mannerisms were not the personality of Germans at the time.

Alton Zumbach, the namesake and nephew of the John Deere dealer, Alton Schritter, worked in his uncle's shop until 1935, when he was given the opportunity to open an International Harvester dealership in Cottonwood. He felt somewhat of a traitor leaving John Deere, preferring to stay where he was, but his uncle convinced him the opportunity was too good to pass up. Zumbach was young, energetic, and he knew the business. He also knew his uncle was dying.

"I expected it. I'll be there, Aunt Bertie."

"And we…"

The transmission wasn't good, and he urged, "You'll have to talk louder, Aunt Bertie."

"We want you to be a pall…" she forced.

"I got that part. When is it?"

"Tuesday—two in the afternoon at Shaw's."

"I'll be at your house at noon."

"That'll be good. And Alton, before you hang up, I need to talk to you."

"What about?"

"There's a tractor out in the shed. What'll I do with it?"

"I dunno. What is it?"

"It's an 'A' I think. It came in from Waterloo a couple of weeks ago."

Zumbach paused. "That's the factory! It must be new."

"Yes, it's new."

Zumbach's heart raced. "How the hell did this happen, Aunt Bertie?"

He could hear her breathing. "I don't know, Alton. I've been so caught up with Al's being down and all. They brought it up the alley, and I didn't know what do to with it. People are all showing up to buy the place, the business and all."

"Why didn't they take the tractor to the center?"

"I don't know why they didn't do that."

"Has anyone seen it yet?"

"Not that I know of. What should I do with it. Do you want it?"

Zumbach, startled by the question, fumbled, "Sure, sure, Aunt Bertie, but it's not mine."

He waited. The phone was silent. Finally, she said, "I don't know who it's supposed to go to. Somebody, I'm sure of that, but I don't know who. Al paid for it. You have to do that these days before they'll deliver anything. Why don't you just come and get it out of here, so I don't have another problem?"

"You sure, Aunt Bertie?"

"Sure. You're like a son. I named you, you know."

Zumbach was on the road at five the next morning for the one hundred ten-mile drive to Platte Center. At three o'clock that same afternoon, he drove into the Hubbard yard.

He hopped up onto the weathered board porch and banged on the screen.

Millie opened the door, shielding her eyes from the afternoon sun.

"Where's Walt, Millie?"

She stepped out on the porch. "He's out cultivating corn, Alton," she said, wiping her hands on her apron. Seeing the shiny new tractor on the truck, she asked, "Is that Walter's?"

"It is if he wants it."

"Oh. He'll want it all right. I just hope he can afford it."

"He can afford it. See if you can raise him while I get it off the truck."

By now, Ruthie was out of the house.

"Ruthie. Get a tea towel and go wave to Dad!"

She grabbed the towel and scrambled up the windmill tower, which had been the standard practice of alerting Walter out in the field.

Zumbach had the tractor in the yard by the time Ruthie was off the windmill.

"Want to come along, Ruthie?" he asked.

"Can I ride on the draw bar?" she asked.

"No. Get on one of the fenders."

"It's got fenders?" Millie asked.

"Yup. One for you and one for Ruthie."

Across the flat plain, Walter saw the signal from the windmill and headed to the end of the field. Shortly, he spotted the bright green and yellow machine speeding down the corn row. He stopped the horses, and removed his soiled hat. His heart leaped as the sound of the engine pierced the quiet summer afternoon. Shortly, Zumbach drove alongside as Walter wiped his forehead with his red handkerchief. The implement dealer shut the engine off. The horses fidgeted.

Ruthie and Mildred climbed down.

Walter, confused, stared speechless.

"Like John Deere's, Walt?" the dealer asked.

"You know I do, Al!" Walter flushed. "Where did you get that?"

"Doesn't matter where I got it. You got a thousand dollars?"

"Hell yes! But it's worth more than that, Al."

"I know it is, Walt, but I haven't felt right since you lost out on that 'H'."

Walter wrapped the reins over the cultivator lever, stepped off the implement and began inspecting the tractor.

"This thing's new—it's still got the tits on the tires."

Millie winced, wishing at that moment that men could have a more delicate way to describe machinery.

"It's brand new, Walt."

Zumbach climbed down, and focused on the young girl.

"Can you keep a secret, Ruthie?"

She looked at the dealer, perplexed.

"She can keep a secret," the father prompted.

"Ruthie, You're not to tell anybody where your daddy got this tractor, understand?"

Innocent and pigeon-toed, the gangly girl growing fast, and a little long for her dress, asked, "Is it stolen?"

"Oh, no! It came from my uncle's shop in Platte Center, but there are many jealous people around this country," he said winking at Walter.

"I won't tell anybody, Mr. Zumbach," she replied dutifully. "I heard about Mr. MacGregor's tractor. He'd be pretty mad if he found out that Dad got this beautiful tractor."

Walter continued appraising the new machine. He climbed on the seat.

"God damn, Al. This thing has a cushion with arm rests and headlights. Hell, it's got gauges like a car, six gears… and fenders!"

"Start her up."

"It's got a starter?"

"Yup. Give 'er a little gas."

Walter adjusted the throttle lever, weaving back and forth searching through knobs and levers. "Where is it?"

"Down there by the belt pulley."

Walter kicked the starter lever and the engine sprang to life.

"Take her home, Walt, and we'll get you signed up," Zumbach yelled over the pop of the engine. "If Millie'll hold the horses, I'll unhitch and drive them back."

"You sure?"

"For sure."

"Can I go with you, Daddy?" Ruthie asked.

"Hop on, honey. You okay with that, Millie?" Walter asked his wife.

She nodded. "You two go on. I'll keep Alton company." Her smile was a mixture of joy and pathos.

****

Late in May, 1943, the 11th was gearing up to begin the 'ladder' up the Solomons. Rusty's unit was tabbed to ship out and begin an offensive at New Georgia the second week in June. Sam was training in England preparing for something, he didn't know what. He was given enough clues to think it was something big; he just didn't know what or how big. Previously apprehensive from being without Sam, Walter was learning the advantages of having something that doesn't need rounding up in the morning, fed, harnessed or having to be rested periodically. After re-tooling and converting his horse-drawn equipment to function behind his new John Deere, he had caught up fast; and his farming practices were much improved. Millie would return to teaching, and though pleased to be a part of Walter's enthusiasm, she was tormented by the circumstances of her sons; mostly Andy.

In the meantime, Andrea was delighting the newspaper board of directors with the activity that her style of reporting had generated. Her last splash was an interview with Clark Gable who was on special leave from the Army Air Force and in town to sell war bonds. She looked forward, in years to come, when she could brag to Andy that she dodged an entrée from the famous movie star.

For Andy, it was another stop. The shocking losses in troops, shipping and materiel in the South Pacific had necessitated a decision by the Japanese High Command to employ prisoners of war to work in the shipyards, at the same time siphoning the *issen gorin*, "penny men" the price of a post card-poor Japanese, off the streets and into uniform.

Curiously, Bob Snavely didn't travel on the packed troop trucks to the wharf in Taiwan; nor was he seen in the rotten dank hold of the Jap cargo ship that transported the unfortunate captives to the Fujiyama Ship Works in Tokyo. He did, however, show up in the dismal barracks provided to house the prisoners there. Nothing was done to improve the living conditions in Tokyo. The food was no worse, but was it no better, either. Although he was continually exhausted by the lack of decent food and the shabby living conditions, Andy's health became stabilized by the fact that he had something to do. The eternal boredom on Taiwan, sitting for endless hours with nothing to do had an enervating effect not only on his physical stability, but his mental outlook as well.

He was not searched when he entered the prison in Tokyo, so he was able to hold on to his precious silver half heart and the oft read faded yellow letters he had gotten from his mother and Andrea. Andy was put to work building radios. It was a good job in clean surroundings and the conscripts, because of their need for various components, were given a fairly general access to the inventory. After prisoners started working in the shipyards, they were searched when they returned. If a Marine was found with any item taken from where he worked, he was beaten.

After the first few days of work, Andy met his first compassionate Japanese soldier, Hideki Ikeya, a guard, who spoke a modicum of English. With the little knowledge Andy knew of Ikeya's language, they would have friendly talks whenever possible.

Ikeya was a gentle lad from the farming country near Mitsumo. He never liked the childhood hate games that were popular, nor did he partake in the Bushido gatherings or competitions that were so linked to violence. He preferred pitchforks to swords. Unlike his compatriots, he didn't believe the Americans were the barbarians who started the war. His classification as a prison guard was much to his distaste, but he knew there was worse duty. He, like Andy, was new to the camp, recently transferred from Tarlac on Luzon, and happy to be on the mainland. He could see the direction the war was taking, and wanted to get back home. Ikeya realized when the firing stopped, the Japanese would have to vacate the lands they pilfered and competition for jobs and property in their native country would be frenetic.

Andy had long been separated from his doctor's kit. His medicines, short lived, received no replacements. Still, what he knew about doctoring made him desired by those who continually experienced aches and pains and whatever else goes wrong. One night, that included the enemy.

One of the guards, Matsuo, a burly foul mood sort, developed a tooth ache and his temperament had become yet worse. Ikeya prevailed upon Andy to give the guard who had an impacted wisdom a look. Neither was particularly receptive to the examination. Matsuo was contemptuous to the captured, obeying to the Bushido philosophy that to surrender was to die. So in his opinion, Andy didn't represent a living person. Andy was a horyo; a prisoner. Ikeya, knowing that Matsuo wasn't going to be able to see a Japanese doctor, convinced him that the *horyo* was his best bet if he wanted to get rid of his pain.

Andy succeeded in getting the recalcitrant guard to open his mouth and let him make an inspection. The wary guard's dialect was one that Andy had little success understanding, and he relied on Ikeya to be the go between.

"He wants to if you're a tooth doctor."

"Tell him I am. Ask him why he doesn't get one of his own doctors to pull it."

"I can answer that myself. We don't have any doctors. Our doctors are all at war. We don't have much more than you do, and that includes our food. We don't even have sake. That's only for the soldiers at the front."

When Andy touched the man's jaw, he let out a yelp.

Andy smiled. "Tell your friend that we speak that language in my country."

"He's not my friend, but I'll tell him."

The burly guard growled when Ikeya passed along Andy's message.

"He doesn't think you're funny," Ikeya related.

"You tell him that tooth has to come out. Tell him I need some tools and antiseptic."

Ikeya relayed the message whereupon the guard bellowed, "No! I'll be killed immediately! NOOO! No *mondai desu!*"

Andy rubbed his chin, thinking. "You tell him since he's the one who searches me, to let me bring a pair of pliers, a small knife in along with antiseptic when I come back from work tomorrow."

The guard looked at Andy menacingly. Finally, he spoke to Ikeya who spoke to Andy.

"He says he won't do that."

"Okay," Andy said, walking away. "It's *his* mouth."

The next morning the guard stood with Ikeya at Andy's bunk. They began the awkward question and answer session complicated even more with the delays involved in the interpretation.

"He says to get the pliers and knife," Ikeya said. "And he wants to know what antiseptic is."

"Tell him its pain killer."

"He says he doesn't need pain killer."

Andy smirked. He knew otherwise. He would steal the alcohol stored in a propellant station, a compartment near the transmitter section. The fluid was also available for compass gyros, but he could get a larger amount from ordnance. He wouldn't have to go through the straining process to get what sailors knew as "torpedo juice". Andy also requested that Ikeya be at his side when he performed the extraction. He didn't want the volatile guard doing something unexpected.

After passing inspection, Ikeya had located a tall three-legged stool he had placed in a remote area of the compound. Matsuo squealed "O itai!" when Andy touched the infected molar with his finger.

Andy looked at Ikeya. "That word doesn't have to have a dialect."

Ikeya smiled and nodded.

Andy reached for his canteen, pointing with his finger. "Antiseptic." He explained to Ikeya that his friend must drink a portion. Andy would tell him how much, then come back fifteen minutes later.

After a verbal exercise, the guard, through interpretation, agreed to do what he was told. When the two returned, Andy now inspected the guard's tooth. Although Matsuo's demeanor had softened considerably, Andy still didn't think he could withstand the pain of the extraction, so he gave Matsuo another dose, with the same instructions. This time, Ikeya assisted his counterpart to the stool, who sat, wobbly. Ikeya held him by the shoulders.

"Open up."

The guard, no longer angry, understood and complied.

Andy knew the circumstances were terrible; the light was dim, but he took up the carbon knife he had carefully selected which was razor sharp. Luckily, and at the last moment, he had grabbed a fistful of packing cotton and shoved it into his baggy pocket.

Ikeya had passed the word that Matsuo had to keep his mouth as wide as open as possible. Andy squinted. He knew he would have to lance the bulging infected gum. He may miss; the Jap guard may erupt—he didn't care. Puss squirted, and when it did, the guard uttered a sigh of relief.

Andy nodded to Ikeya. "Hold him as tight as you can."

Andy struggled to clasp the sharp-nosed pliers around the barely-visible molar. Weakened as he was, but with all his strength, and using the jaw as a fulcrum, he pried against the guard's jaw. After two forcible pries, he wrenched the tooth from its mandible.

The guard's head snapped sharply when the tooth came free, as Andy tossed the tooth away. He then put his canteen to the guard's his lips.

"Tell him not to swallow!" Andy ordered Ikeya. "Tell him not to swallow!" Andy repeated. "Just keep it in his mouth! After that, I'll tell him what to do."

Both guards knew the importance of Andy's commands, and Andy, himself, thought of the times when a wild, "range" cow, having difficulty giving birth, would lie on her side, readily accepting assistance. This ill-tempered guard was doing the same.

"Now, tell him to spit it out."

Ikeya repeated the instructions, to which the guard shook his head no.

Andy, smiling, held up the canteen, pointing and smiled, "There's more," whereupon, the guard, expectorated, and drank from Andy's canteen.

The three, unusual as they were, started their separate ways.

"Tell whoever is in charge…"

"He is in charge," Ikeya interrupted.

"That's lucky, because he can't work tomorrow, and," Andy said, handing Ikeya his canteen and another wad of cotton, "Tell him, in an hour or so, take a cotton portion out and mash this in that hole." Andy glanced down at his flask, "Tell him not to drink that all at once. And I want my canteen back."

"He's too drunk to care," Ikeya replied.

Andy merely chuckled.

The next day, Andy had secured a gyro canister which he filled with the grain alcohol. Ikeya was the receiving guard. Ikeya warned him that Matsuo was in a foul mood. He was right. The ill-tempered guard berated Andy, angry that his jaw ached. Andy handed him the flask, advising him, through Ikeya's interpretation that after he had consumed another dose of alcohol, the pain would subside.

Apparently, Andy was correct. The next morning, Matsuo was at this normal station, looking the worse for wear, but able to tolerate the pain. Ikeya had taught him an English word. As Andy stood before him for the usual inspection, he handed Andy the canister and mouthed a word Andy could understand, "More."

CHAPTER 43

RICE INLET, NEW GEORGIA
July, 5, 1943

So far, landings on neighboring islands had been met with little resistance. New Georgia posed a different problem for the Allied invaders. The largest island in this chain was especially important, with its vital air strip that would provide a base for the invasion of Bougainville, but there was a problem of accessibility. Narrow coral reefs cordoned the inlet and beaching was possible only through constricted channels. It was easy for the Japanese small arms fire to pick off the invaders approaching where the Japanese knew the Americans would have to land. Rusty Atkins led a regiment ashore on the first wave. His tactics were to take cover and attack from concealed positions, but a ship-to-shore flare exposed a bare, flat shoreline revealing little opportunity for coverture.

Seeing this, Rusty grabbed the phone and instructed his platoon leaders in the LCI's as bullets began to hit the metal boats, "Tell the LCI captains to drop the ramps right now and get out of these coffins! Spread out and run in all directions."

Two machine gun nests raked the landing area. "Thank God it's night!" Rusty muttered to his first sergeant.

General Stuart wanted to land the next morning, but Rusty convinced Canali that a night landing would be preferable. Another regiment, the 43rd was facing combat for the first time, and although they weren't under Rusty's command, he felt certain their casualty rate would be greatly less if they attacked under the cover of darkness since the enemy knew the precise landing location.

"Get into the trees," he continued to shout as the hoard of his troops pounded across the barren sand.

Once into the jungle, he continued with litany of commands. "Take cover! Secure radio contact! Get me a casualty count! Get down and stay down!"

On the water's edge, the 43rd was pinned down and taking heavy casualties. Aa corporal crawled up to Rusty with a walkie-talkie. "It's the colonel, Captain."

Canali was on the bridge of the cruiser Hampton four miles off shore. "What's your status?" he asked.

"We're in… We're okay," Rusty shouted.

"How bad did you get hurt?"

"Not bad at all. We bailed off the LCI's before they got to the shore. We had to wade through a couple feet of water, but it looks like it was the thing to do."

"Where the hell's the 43rd? I can't raise anybody over there."

"They're pinned down. They're in a bad spot."

"We gotta get them loose. Do you have any ideas?"

"We have to take those machine guns out, but I had planned on making an end run. If we have to spring the 43rd, we gotta go across the damn beach where we don't have any cover!"

"Well do what you can. Keep me informed."

Rusty turned to his exec, and said, "Cover me, Dan. I'm gonna see if I can drop a couple of grenades in one of those nests."

"I'll go, Captain."

"No. You get that BAR set up and give me some cover."

The first sergeant, Maynard Skinner, now beside the two said, "I'll get the other nest!"

"No. There's no need of both of us to take the risk," Rusty said.

"I'm from Kaycee Wyoming where there's no trees. I'm better than you are when it comes to fighting with nothing to hide behind."

"All right. Suit yourself. When I break for one nest, you take the other!"

Rusty and the sergeant streaked across the bullet pelted sand. The signalman crawled up to the exec. "It's the colonel again, Sir!"

"Yes sir?" Cole shouted into the phone.

"Rusty" came the reply.

"This is Lieutenant Cole."

"Okay, Cole. Tell the captain not to try any heroics. We'll figure out something!"

"Too late, Colonel. He took off with sergeant Skinner!"

There was a pause. "Jesus Christ! Did he make it?"

"I don't know, Sir. If I looked up right now, I'd probably get my head blown off!"

"As soon as you know anything, get back to me!" Before Cole could respond, the colonel hung up the phone.

"Okay," Rusty said, lying on his stomach next to his first sergeant, in the cover of darkness and the edge of the jungle. "I'll get the nest that's the closest. You get the far one. Try to get two grenades in there." He slapped the sergeant on the behind and raced away into the black night, illuminated only by the muzzle flashes of the machine guns. He crawled in amongst Japanese riflemen who mistook Rusty for one of their own. Rusty pulled the clip with his teeth, waited three counts and lobbed the grenade into the machine gun pit, and waited for the blast. It came suddenly, chopping the crew and ammo bearers into bits. Rusty wheeled in a 360 firing his carbine into the startled troops around him. The grenade explosion was just what Skinner needed. It distracted the far gun crew for a split second. Skinner lobbed his grenade into the pit, then sprayed the area ahead of him with his carbine. He then let out a Wyoming coyote howl. Rusty felt a grin of exhilaration, beating a path to his first sergeant.

The troops of the 43rd instantly got up and rushed into the safety of the jungle.

"Looks like that's what they needed, Skinner," Rusty said gleefully.

"Sure did, Captain. How about a smoke?"

Normally, lighting a match was an error one wouldn't commit, but the Japanese retreated en masse, and Rusty knew his men were hot on their heels.

"Damn! I'm proud of those bastards; they knew just what to do, didn't they?"

"They sure did, Captain."

The light of the match illuminated the close area, and Rusty noticed a red blotch on Skinner's right leg, and yelled, "MEDIC!"

"Who's hit?"

"You are. Look at your leg!"

"Be damned!" the sergeant exclaimed, "I think it went right through my calf!"

The medic raced up. "Where are you hit, Sergeant?"

Skinner pointed to red splotch, "In my leg."

"Well, let's get at it," the medic said.

"Let me finish my cigarette first."

Rusty laughed. "Damn, Skinner. Would you like to be an officer?"

"Sure. Who wouldn't?"

"Consider it done," Rusty said when his exec walked up.

"You'd better call the colonel, Dan."

"No need. The 43rd CO already has."

Rusty had his command tent erected. Quickly, it filled.

"You're a very brave man, Captain," a familiar voice in the dim light uttered.

Rusty looked around. "Olson! What the hell you doin' here? You had orders to stay aboard ship!"

"My old boss told me something Andrea Vogel told him. She said something to the order of 'If you want to hear the bear growl, you have to visit his cave.' Besides, Captain, what are you going to do, demote me? I have a story to write."

Later, when the area was stable, Rusty was sitting in his tent. He had one leg propped up on an ammo box, his helmet propped loosely on his head as he smoked. Phil Olson was against a tent wall at his typewriter. Rusty folded a copy of Yank he had been reading and placed it his case.

"You know, Phil, You're important to this outfit," he said. "Those damned kids just love to hear about what they've been doing. You're really giving them a pat on the back."

The compliment stirred Olson. "Thanks, Captain. It's always nice to think that you're appreciated."

"Six months ago," Rusty mused, "nobody could have told me that a correspondent could be a part of a fighting unit, a member of the team—but you are."

An awkward silence followed. Olson murmured, "Rusty, at this moment I realize for certain, that my leaving Washington was the right choice."

By the first of September, the island was secured. Rusty's unit was credited with eleven hundred enemy killed. He had lost seventy-six of the five hundred men he had brought. Militarily, this was a sparkling achievement; but not to Rusty. Those seventy-six weighed heavily on his mind. By his standards, his kill ratio could be no more than one of his Marines to twenty of the enemy; an ambitious goal to be certain, although his successes, to date, challenged the figure. The losses on New Georgia fell considerably short of his objective. He had personally written a letter to each dead Marine's parents.

This erstwhile unenlightened distrustful waif had, in three short years, become a rugged, mature, compassionate, battle-hardened Marine officer.

****

Johnnie Hickman flew in from Greenwich for the weekend. As she slept on the couch in Andrea's apartment, she dreamed she heard somebody screaming. Half awake, suspended in the twilight of deep sleep and consciousness, fighting for awareness, she became aware that her hallucinations were real. It was Andrea. Johnnie leaped off the couch and fumbled for the light switch. The light blinded her as she felt for the doorway. The screams grew louder as she approached the door. She entered and shook the distressed Andrea who was thrashing in her sleep.

"Wake up! Wake up!" she shouted.

Andrea convulsed serpentine-like in her bed, then came awake. She rubbed her eyes in the dim light of her bedroom.

"What is it, Andrea?" Johnnie demanded.

Andrea sat up and began to cry. "I saw him, Johnnie! I saw him!"

"You saw who?"

"Andy," she sobbed. "I saw him."

Johnnie took her by the shoulders, shaking her. "You're still asleep, Andrea. Come to your senses!"

Andrea blinked her eyes, and began speaking softly, "No, Johnnie, I saw him."

"You saw him where?"

"He was in a wooden bunk. It was dark. There were wood floors and walls. He was so skinny. His knees and ankles stood out so ugly. He was staring up and he was thinking about me." She began to whimper, "Oh, Johnnie, I could hardly tell it was him!"

"It was a nightmare, Andrea," Johnnie consoled.

"No, Johnnie," she said, controlling her emotions, "it was real. I know it was real and I don't know why I was given the vision. I saw him as vividly as I'm seeing you now. And I could feel his thoughts as clearly as I can feel my own. He's in terrible condition and I know he'll never return, Johnnie!"

"Andrea, we have no information yet to how prisoners are treated. Why, you haven't even heard from him since he was captured. You can't be sure of anything. You don't even know whether or not he's alive."

"He's alive," Andrea whimpered. "I just saw him."

"You're sure."

"I'm sure."

Johnnie patted the back of Andrea's folded hands. "Can you go back to sleep now?"

"Yes. I'm all right, Johnnie. Thank you for waking me."

****

Major General Henry Stuart led the 11th ashore on Bougainville. The date was November 1, 1943. The 3rd landed simultaneously on the nearby islands of Treasury and Choiseul in an attempt to divert the Japanese attention away from the more massive landing of the large force invading Bougainville. The diversion strategy was working. Coupled with General Hyakutake's speculation that the low wet terrain around the north shore of Empress Augusta Bay would be unsuitable for any enemy landing and the attention directed toward the ghost invasion off the other two islands, the landing was met with little resistance. Within hours, Stuart's men had secured the area. By November 8, there were more than 43,000 Americans entrenched at Empress Augusta Bay. Now the island was occupied by two large military forces; the Americans on the southern border and the Japanese occupying the eastern tip and the northern border of the island. The Americans were content to hold this beachhead and made no attempt to enlarge it. Stuart's men, however, were not to enjoy the respite in the fighting for the island of Bougainville. Encouraged by the successful landing at Empress Augusta Bay, Nimitz transferred the 11th to Tarawa in the Gilberts where their ill-fated landing was made November 26. The battle was one of the bloodiest of the Pacific Campaign. Nimitz's conservative shore bombardment placed a burden on the invading 11th, but the main culprit was that the inlets of the island were linked by a ring of coral reefs. The landing at Tarawa was met by withering fire, as the Japanese had a commanding advantage. Landing crafts ran aground on the reefs while the Japanese directed murderous fire on the hapless trapped Marines. Rusty Atkins was furious. The only choice his men had was to bail out of the stranded landing crafts and clamber in waist to shoulder deep water to the sandy shore. He watched helplessly as his men were hacked to pieces. Smoke billowed up from the disabled LCI's and LCP's unable to move. Confusion reigned. Lead spit from the heavily-fortified concrete and iron pill boxes as Rusty, Dan Cole, and a piteously small number from the landing party lay pinned down in a shallow bomb crater near the water's edge.

Finally, Rusty had all seen the carnage to his men offshore that he could take.

"Pass that flame thrower, Dan!" he yelled to his exec. "I'm gonna French-fry those bastards or die tryin!"

"And you'll die trying, Captain!" Cole yelled back. "You've got to attack that pill box from the front. They're Japs all over the place behind it. You won't have a chance!"

"Start shootin!" Rusty shouted as he strapped the incendiary weapon to his back. Impulsively, he jerked his body out of the shallow cover and ran a zigzag pattern into the teeth of the guns from the pill box. Cole watched as Atkins ran the irregular pattern toward the front of the bunker. Bullets hit around Rusty as he ran. Cole watched, shaking his head in amazement.

"That lucky sonovabitch could walk straight toward it and they'd still miss him. God! He's got an angel riding on his shoulder!"

Rusty was diving straight at the pill box on the dead run, his weapon spewing a ten-foot spray of fire ahead. Quickly the screams of the gun crew became silent and the acetylene-fueled weapon literally barbequed those inside. Witnessing the distraction, Cole snatched another flame thrower and raced toward the adjoining pill box. Troops in the rear rushed up behind him. Quickly, he disabled the second pill box, as the troops attacked the enemy assembled behind the pill boxes.

"Call the old man!" Rusty ordered the radioman, "Tell him we're finally ashore."

After four days of hell, Marines secured the beachhead, but at a price of eleven hundred lives for the 11th alone. Lieutenant Dan Cole had escaped injury, but half of Atkins' regiment was dead. One of those casualties was a man who just received a battlefield commission, Maynard Skinner. Rusty would have many letters to write.

Seated in his command tent, Rusty was approached by a young corporal.

"Sir," the corporal began, "Mr. Olson has been hit. I didn't know if you knew."

Rusty jumped to his feet. "When?"

"Yesterday."

"How bad?"

"Pretty bad, I think, Sir."

Rusty put on his helmet. "Let's get going. Do you have a jeep?"

"Yes, Sir."

The jeep bounced along the sandy road to the hastily-erected field hospital.

"Any idea how it happened, Corporal?"

"Yes, Sir. A Jap grenade fell by a private. The grenade hadn't exploded and the private froze. Mr. Olson was lying nearby and when he saw the private freeze, he jumped up and knocked the private off his feet. The explosion completely missed the private, but tore into Mr. Olson's side."

"Were you there, Corporal?"

"No, but several guys told the same story. I guess we've gotten pretty fond of Mr. Olson."

"Brave bastard," Rusty mumbled above his breath. Rusty walked through the large tent where wounded lined both sides of the canvas enclosure. Alcohol, disinfectant and fresh canvas provided a pungent aroma.

"I'm looking for Philip Olson. He's a war correspondent," Rusty said to a doctor operating on a wounded soldier. The masked surgeon looked up, mutely waved a hemostat in Olson's direction. Rusty saw his friend. With the corporal tagging behind him, Rusty walked up to the prone man and placed his hand on Olson's hot swollen forehead.

"How's it goin', old warrior?"

Olson only looked weakly at Rusty, too enervated to speak.

"You hang in there. Be strong. You'll make it. I want to tell you how proud the men and I are of you. That was a courageous thing you did. That was, to coin an old phrase, 'above and beyond the call of duty.' And let me tell you this; what you did will have an amazing effect on the troops. We're all praying for you, I can assure you that."

"He's right, Mr. Olson," the corporal put in. "Everybody's asking about you."

"Oh, and by the way, Phil," Rusty continued warmly, "the private wasn't even hit. You saved his life."

A trace of a smile came across the weak man's face. Rusty knew he must leave. The emotion of the situation was too much for him.

"I'll keep a check on you. You'll have to fight for it, and I'm sure you will."

Rusty gave Olson an affectionate gentle pat on the forehead, turned and walked out of the tent.

"You're to go over to the commander's headquarters, Sir," the clerk announced.

"Okay," Rusty said. He laid his pen on the table, picked up his helmet and started over.

Rusty had been in a foul mood since the Tarawa battle. He opened the door to the colonel's temporary headquarters. Canali looked with a serious smile. "Here," he said passing an order sheet across the desk, "You've made major."

"Shit," Rusty chuckled derisively as he glanced at the sheet. "I lose three hundred and seventy-nine guys and they promote my ass. Christ!"

"Those losses were not your fault, Rusty."

"You're goddamn right they weren't my fault, Frank!" Rusty snarled, "And we can't let that sort of thing happen again!"

"How are you going to stop it?" Canali looked up.

"Look, Frank, you've got some clout. By the way," Rusty interrupted himself, "did you get a star out of this?"

"I think so. My name had been placed in nomination."

"Hell, that's great! You belong in general's clothes. Anyway, as I was saying, you and the old man get along great. I got an idea that might turn this bullshit massacre around."

"There was no other way to invade that beach."

"Colonel, when I was a kid, my old man used to round up stray cats for the different farmers he worked for, put them in cream cans and drown 'em. Oh, he didn't much like it, but that was one way he could squirrel money away for booze. I got a whippin' one time when I yanked the lid off that can letting those poor bastards escape."

"What are you getting at?" Canali asked.

"I'm saying that those guys in those barges had about the same chance as those goddam cats!"

"You're probably right," Canali admitted, "But there isn't much you can do about coral reefs."

"That's a defeatist attitude if I ever heard one!"

Canali sprang to his feet bristling, "And that's a hell of an accusation, Rusty!"

"I'm sorry, Frank. That just came out," Rusty surrendered. "Look," he began quietly, "I got an idea. First we pummel the shit out of those beachheads with our big guns and air support. Then we send in some swimmers to search those approaches, make charts..."

"What a hair-brained idea!" Canali interjected.

"It's not a hair-brained idea. Let's go to the old man and have him..."

Canali cut him off. "General Stuart has other problems. He doesn't have time to think about something like this."

"Like a cat in a can, huh?"

"Just don't rock the boat. Let it drop. That's an order."

Rusty stood and sneered. "Just don't rock the boat! That's a good one, Frank. Don't rock the boat!" he repeated. "Well, my guys couldn't rock those fuckin' boats, and that's why they won't be goin' home!" Rusty stomped out.

Canali sat considering Rusty's response. "I can't argue with that," he mused.

Three weeks had passed after the fateful, yet successful, landing on Tarawa. The young exhausted major had completed his three hundred and twenty seventh letter, writing them in alphabetical order. He looked at his watch. 0300 hours. "Dear Mr. and Mrs. Skinner" …Skinner! Rusty gritted his teeth, flinging his pen across the tent.

"That gallant bastard," Rusty cursed quietly. "He never had a chance."

Rusty left the letter unfinished and went to bed. He lay awake engulfed in angry frustration as he had so many nights since the battle. He made a decision.

Rusty visited Phil Olson regularly. Olson had lost a kidney, but he was improving, able to do spot work. This morning he was propped up on pillows with his pad in his lap.

"God! You're beginning to look worse than me. What's eating you?" Olson asked as Rusty approached.

"Phil," Rusty said solemnly, "I want you to make me a story."

After Rusty explained, Olson refused. "That sort of a report will ruin you, Rusty. Give it some thought," he advised.

"Phil," Rusty sighed, "I have given it all the thought I intend to. You always tell me how the pen is mightier than the sword. Now you have my story. It's your responsibility to print it."

Rusty turned and left Olson's ward.

"It's Admiral King," General Morrison's secretary, Madeline, said stepping into his office.

"Yeah, shit, Madeline," the three star said. "I knew it was coming."

"George," the CINPAC commander's voice came sharply over the phone. "I assume you've read this article in the Stars and Stripes!"

"Yes, Sir," Morrison answered. "I've read it."

"Do you realize the impact that article will have on the troops in the entire Pacific Theater?"

Morrison breathed heavily, "Well, what the hell do you want me to do, Ernie?"

"I want you to get in touch with Henry Stuart," the clipped, acerbic voice answered. "I've already talked to Chester about it. He's gravely concerned. We have a serious situation on our hands here, George. These are no small potatoes. That was no private writing that article. He is a heavily-decorated major!"

"Okay, Admiral," Morrison said. "I'll get in touch with the general. The senate is due to vote on his third star. That article may cost him that!"

"I know, George. Let me know what you get from Stuart and get back to me!"

"Yes, Sir," Morrison said and hung up the phone. He looked up at Madeline. "You still haven't been able to get General Stuart, Madeline?"

"Not yet," she answered.

"Well, keep trying," he said and looked back down to re-read the article.

It began, "As I lie in my hospital bed, I consider the pros and cons of relaying the conversation I had with a battle weary compassionate Major Rufous 'Rusty' Atkins. I finally decided that it's my duty to report our conversation, and I take full responsibility for the repercussions that it may have on this man's future in the Marines as well as reprisals to those who may also be affected. I will give the testimony as I best recall it.

"'It was an insult,' the major said, 'to the fighting Marine who will never see another Christmas, or never know the joy of love of a family and a home. All he needed was a chance which he never had, and had he been given that chance to live to fight for his country, he may be alive today. But he was a dead man when the davit lowered his waiting LCP from the cruiser. It was an inexcusable error to assume that he could have ever made it ashore as his craft ran aground to be skewered without any means to defend himself, or even escape the impossible situation he was in. The complete lack of coordination between the Navy support and the soldier wading into hell was an intolerable situation...'"

Morrison threw down the paper in disgust as Madeline interrupted him. "I finally got him," she announced.

"Same son of a bitch that blabbed about that Jap training camp in '40," Morrison cursed, picking up the phone. "Henry," he said, "what the hell are we going to do? Ernie King just chewed my ass!"

Stuart was equally hot. "And Admiral Nimitz just chewed mine. We'll give the kid a special. I'm even thinking about a summary."

"That'll cost him a rank, Henry," Morrison warned.

"It'll cost me a star, I goddamn guarantee you that! And I've got an excellent bird colonel who will probably be passed over," Stuart seethed.

Morrison breathed deeply, "Well, get back to me, Henry, as soon as you have something."

Stuart didn't answer, but slammed down the field phone in his command hut halfway around the world.

"Let's go see the general, Rusty," Canali said as he came into Rusty's tent.

While driving to the division commander's headquarters, Canali broke the silence. "You really stuck your foot in it this time, pal."

"I know, Frank," Rusty admitted. "I just hope I didn't screw you up."

"Well, it's your fat that's in the fire, buddy. I sure as hell don't envy you."

Rusty stood at parade rest waiting for the general.

"Tenshun!" Canali announced, when the general entered. Rusty snapped to.

Stuart glowered at him. "So you're the guy who is running the show these days. What do you have to say for yourself?"

"Nothing, Sir," the ramrod straight junior officer said, looking straight ahead.

"That article, Major, 'was a bizarre, an intolerable lack of coordination,' to use your own words, and an insult to your superiors. A total slap in our faces. Did you realize that?"

"Not at the time, Sir," Rusty answered unemotionally.

"Well, you can expect a court martial. You expected that, I hope, and you're going aboard with us to present your case to the old man himself. Do you have anything to say on your behalf? Hell, we just made you a major!"

"My rank is of very little importance to me when it comes to the lives of my men, Sir."

"Go out and wait in the jeep," the general said angrily.

Rusty saluted which went unanswered, and stepped out of the senior officer's quarters.

"Court martial, General?" Canali asked.

"Oh yeah. Hell, yeah, Frank. And it's a damned shame. He'll be lucky if he's only busted to a captain. I only wish he had come to us. Maybe we could have done something."

Turning to go, Stuart said sadly, "Hell of it all is, the kid's right."

The signalman flashed the blinker to the carrier moored three miles offshore. Permission to come aboard was flashed back. The PT sped across the choppy waters until it approached the gray monolith lying at anchor. As the boat came alongside the huge carrier, the accommodation ladder was lowered. Three men started up the steps.

The small party coming aboard was met by a commander who ushered them onto the bridge. It was a somber group who was seated in the conference room. Nobody spoke. The commander issued one order when all in attendance, including General Stuart, snapped to attention. Then a craggy-faced, white-haired admiral entered the room.

"Be seated," he said matter-of-factly, then the heavily-decorated four striper sat down behind his gray desk and laid his arms on the flat surface. His steely-blue eyes searched Rusty questioningly.

"I decided to bring the major in question aboard, Sir," Stuart volunteered.

"All right, Henry," the admiral resigned. "Since he's the star of the show, I think that's just as well."

The fleet admiral then glanced toward his aide who handed him a sheaf of papers. The admiral leafed through them, page by page, saying nothing. Finally, he looked up and stared at Rusty. Softly, he began.

"How can it happen that an individual with such an impeccable record, a young man who has done so much for The Corps do something like this?"

Admiral Nimitz then again glanced down at the papers, mouthing, "Bravery unequalled through basic training up until now. Just look at these accomplishments—the Distinguished Service Medal, the Navy and Marine Corps Medal, the Bronze star, two purple hearts, an outstanding combat percentage. It's saddening." He then looked up, fatherly, expecting an answer. "How does it happen?"

Rusty fidgeted in his chair. "Sir, I owe everything to the Corps. I respect and feel responsible to my superiors. The thought that the article would affect those above me concerns me greatly. I didn't intend that. My main concern, Sir, was that l had let my own troops down."

"How?" the admiral asked, his elbows resting on his desk, hands clasped.

"Sir, those men believed in me. I did everything within my power to make them battle- worthy. So often I was advised to let up on my troops; that my training practices were too harsh. But I intended, Sir, that should one of my men get killed, it would not be that he was not properly prepared. They sacrificed, Sir. They paid a heavy price before they ever made that landing on Tarawa."

Rusty's tired, blood-shot eyes began to mist. "They believed in me. They knew how my men before them performed on Guadalcanal, on the landing on Bougainville. As bad as that was, I lost seventy-nine men, Sir. I write letters personally to all my troops' parents, and every time I'd seal an envelope, the senseless manner in which they died stuck in my craw a little deeper."

"Was it senseless, Major?" The admiral asked, adding quietly, "The battle was won."

Rusty faced Nimitz resolutely. "Admiral, I've met banzai charges and thought to myself, what a medieval way to fight a war. But it didn't bother me because they were Japs and that's the way they do things. But us! We have a higher regard for human life. We win battles by outsmarting our enemies, not by throwing hordes and hordes of our excellent men at them. I understand that we are not fighting the war because we like it and we intend to conquer the world. It is my understanding that our boys are in this thing to get it over with so they can go on living the decent lives we Americans do. The Japs' most precious ingredients are their materiel. Ours are our men. The perspective of this battle was planned and fought in direct opposition to our philosophy of life."

Stuart cleared his throat and wriggled uneasily in his seat. The admiral looked at Rusty, pondering the young officer's words, before responding.

"The invasion was not planned in disregard to human life. That's a pretty serious charge. However, I can see that it might have appeared that way to you. You may be surprised to know that we have no charts of the land areas surrounding these islands. It's a hit and miss proposition for us. We can only estimate from our geological surveys and hope for the best. Obviously, Tarawa was a miss. Now, since you seem to know so much about military strategy, how would you have my Navy provide better support?"

Stuart sat in the room in disbelief. He had taken a serious chance bringing the major along in the first place. Now to have a fleet admiral in a discourse with a condemned man shocked him.

"I know you don't have charts, Sir. But you do have the availability of bombardment. Those shorelines have to be softened up. Just a little more shelling of those beaches would have helped us immensely."

"We've concluded that, Major," Nimitz said almost apologetically, "But what about those coral reefs? How do we contend with them?"

Rusty was growing easy, putting protocol aside. "I've considered that too, Sir. You must have any number of seamen who can swim five miles."

"Can you?"

"Yes. I can if it means protecting the lives of my men." Rusty said quickly.

"Okay, Major. Go on."

"Bring subs in," Rusty continued speaking comfortably. "Eject those guys from the subs, at night, preferably, and have them inspect the shore areas, make charts and plan the avenues of approach from their observations. Prepare avenues by means of depth charges, Bangalores, if necessary."

The admiral paused, commenting, "That sounds a bit far-fetched."

"It'll work," Rusty broke in. "I've already thought it all out."

Nimitz rubbed chin, then slowly rose from behind his desk.

"Okay, Major. We'll take that under advisement. For now, that will be all. The commander will see you outside. I expect that after this you will consider there are channels to work through before you go popping off again."

Rusty snapped to his feet. "It'll never happen again, Sir, but I do have a couple of other ideas."

The admiral looked Rusty in the eye sternly although there was a glint of surprise and humor in his eyes. "And I'm sure the Colonel here will be happy to hear them. Now, Commander, if you'll see Major Atkins out."

The aide left with Rusty, closing the door behind him and leaving the three men in the room. Thoughtfully, the admiral looked at Stuart, then at Canali before speaking. "Henry," he said gently as he settled into his chair. "There'll be no court martial. My God, how in good conscience can we try that young man?"

Simultaneously, Stuart and Canali issued a sigh of relief.

"Now," he continued, "I think he may have stumbled onto something. As it turns out, the whole island of Tarawa is cordoned by a coral reef. There *was* no avenue of approach, so it wouldn't have mattered where we tried to land. We realize now that we must shell the hell out of the next atoll. Still, it would be well to consider that there are avenues of approach, and we must assume that Tarawa is unique; that the Marshalls will allow us a way in, one way or another. In the meantime, I want you to relieve Major Atkins of his command. It will serve two purposes. One, I want him to feel that he is being disciplined, so a little whack on the wrists will be good for him. Secondly, I want him to present his ideas on paper as to this reconnoitering the shoreline; then get it to me within the next couple of days. Confidentially, and this is classified, we're going right into the Nips' living room. We're going to bomb the daylights out of them. I don't care if it takes a month. Then we're going into Kwajalein."

Both Stuart and Canali gasped.

"That's right. We're skipping the other islands. You see, another upstart young officer, one of Spruance's men, came up with an idea that's so offensively obvious that you're ashamed you didn't think of it, and that's the question of, 'why try to knock the Japs off island by island?' Get to their main island, disable it, and without supplies, it'll die on the vine. Let starvation, malaria pneumonia and the like kill them. Why risk our own men? You have to realize, gentlemen, that some of these young bucks have just as good a grip, maybe better in some cases, as us old salts. Kwajalein's smack dab in the middle of things, so Ray Spruance's kid's idea couldn't come at a better time."

"By the way," the impressive fleet commander said, rising from his chair, "I don't want you gentlemen to be concerned about any delay in your promotions. I'll have a cable to Frank Knox and Ernie King this afternoon."

"Ernie King! Thank God!" Stuart thought to himself. He wasn't looking forward to a confrontation with George Morrison.

"And," Nimitz concluded, "I'm glad, Henry, that you brought the young man aboard."

On the ride back to the Tarawa shore, Rusty was in much better standing with his superiors. Each time the speeding boat slapped the water, a fine spray anointed the three officers leaning against the forward rail. Canali was the first to speak.

"Y 'know, Rusty," he said turning toward the heartened young officer, "perhaps one of these days I'll have the patience to listen to some of your concoctions. Maybe that surveillance idea wasn't such a nutty thing."

"Don't worry about it, Frank. The one who can do something about it heard it. That's what matters. I get the opinion Nimitz is a reasonable enough guy."

Canali gazed at the upstart major in amazement.

General Stuart heard the comment, but since he knew nothing of Canali's apology, he expressed no response. He was impressed, however, that Rusty showed the courage to present his case to a man of Nimitz' power and influence. Stuart was career. He himself was a Mustang and held a special fondness for Rusty. Stuart felt that anyone who stood up for a cause, at all costs, belonged in the Corps, confident Rusty would make the Marines his career.

In January, 1944, Nimitz' Navy unleashed an unprecedented assault on the island of Kwajalein. The sixteen inch guns of the Iowa and Wisconsin bombarded the shore while SBD's and F4-U's pummeled installations further off shore. F6-F fighter planes even bombed with their belly tanks, setting pill boxes afire.

Rusty Atkins didn't go ashore. Instead, he remained aboard the Yorktown, prowling the bridge, being recognized as a VIP, and a landing route advisor. Nimitz' intended slap on the wrist missed its target. Rusty calculated that his being placed aboard ship was a reward for his meeting with the admiral. To him, his opinion was confirmed when an ensign walked up to him and handed him a note from Admiral Nimitz:

Major Atkins:

My naval planning committee has elected to adopt your design regarding submersed blockade investigation, and will be so registered in your 201 file. The name Sharkmen has been selected for group identification. We trust this nomenclature meets with your approval. The Navy applauds you for your thoughtful and timely contribution to the war effort.

Cordially,
Chester A Nimitz, Admiral
Chief Operating Officer
Pacific Fleet, USN

The ensign stood close by as Rusty perused the memo.

"You know Admiral Nimitz?" he asked, awestruck.

"We've met," Rusty answered unemotionally, re-reading the note as he walked away.

****

As was her custom, Ruthie wrote Andy a letter once a week since his capture. Her mother would do the same. In her room, she had a large box full of censured and returned mail. The Japanese would ink out words, phrases and sometimes entire sentences. But Ruth loved her brother and felt, if she persisted, at least a part of the censored correspondence would make it past some sympathetic Japanese. She knew from simple counting, that her mother and Andrea didn't get a letter back.

May, 27, 1943

Dear Andy,

The weather has been warm and pleasant. My studies are coming along well. I plan to go to college as you did. Maybe, we could be in college together.

Ruth repeated some previous messages many times because there were things she wanted Andy to know, and partly because she would run out of anything to say.

Sam is home. He looks good.

Ruth knew if she mentioned anything about war or the Army, the letter would surely be returned. She continued:

Andrea was home last week. We went to the show, and while we were waiting, Chattman drove up in a new convertible with Andrea in the car. Mom and Dad were so hurt. But it was all a mistake and everything is straightened out. Both Mom and Dad are so fond of her. She loves only you and will wait for you. I love you too. Ruthie.

CHAPTER 44

Millie read the letter aloud.

"Dear Folks," the message began, "I don't know how long I'll be here at Plymouth. It's been almost a year now, but it seems forever. I hate this damp cold rainy weather, but Dad, we sure could use some of this water on the farm."

Sam rambled on about army life adding, "Great news about getting a tractor! On the subject of tractors, I got a letter from Josh Durkee and he said Sheriff Young told his Dad that Jack MacGregor thinks I ruined his tractor. Can you believe that?"

"Jack is such a suspicious person," Millie uttered. "How could Sam have had anything to do with that?"

Walter smiled privately. The tractor incident would be a well-kept secret between him and his son.

Sam concluded by saying, "Something big is happening, but nobody's saying anything about it. There's a lot of activity and I'm guessing I'll finally get my chance at killing krauts."

Millie winced at the words

"And it can't come soon enough for me. Write when you get time, Love Sam."

"Well, it couldn't last forever, Millie," Walter said caressing her shoulder.

She laid the letter on the table, not responding.

****

May, 1944

News from the Pacific was that New Guinea had been neutralized while MacArthur was gearing up for his celebrated return to the Philippines. The Solomons and Gilberts were back in Allied hands, and from all appearances, the Marshalls soon would be.

On the European front, Germany's eastern borders were being overrun by the Russians, while the Americans and British were closing the ring. Only France, it appeared, was the Fuhrer's lone remaining bastion. In England, Operation Overlord was in its final phases of implementation.

Back in the states, it was a star, or stars, displayed in the front window of a home of a son or sons serving overseas. If it was a silver star, the son was still alive. A gold star meant he was killed. To aid in the war effort, mountains of scrap iron and aluminum were piled in all corners of rural and urban America. Rations stamps controlled how much one could buy and thirty-five miles an hour was the highway speed limit. *Marzy Doats, Don't Fence Me In*, and *As Time Goes By* were hit songs of the day. *Thirty seconds Over Tokyo, The Postman Always Rings Twice* and *Going My Way* were earning academy awards. Fibber McGee, Henry Aldridge, Amos n' Andy and Kay Kaiser filled the airwaves for adult listening. For the kids, it was Captain Midnight shooting down the enemy and Hop Harrigan disrupting the evil forces with his underground intrigues. Isiah was Clinton Durkee's second son in the war. Jim Thurston was heard to mutter, "A hell of a lot of good it does you to go to church." Jack MacGregor paid the estate costs from Liam's death and the war was making him a very wealthy man. Andrea Vogel had been promoted to associate editor of the Dispatch.

****

Sam Hubbard got his chance to go to war, in spades. Suddenly he was a pawn in the largest, most-complicated military exercise attempted by man.

The LCI pitched violently in the heavy seas on its path to the Normandy coast. This was Omaha beach. By far the most-difficult and grisly objective of the five beaches in the assault. Tetrahedrals, water obstacles, systematically positioned further out in the water, made it difficult for the landing crafts to get in close to shore. The shallow-draft boats dropping simultaneously from their mother ships, instantly took on water and at the same time received heavy fire from gun emplacements strategically positioned across the assault lanes.

Sam knew he was fortunate to be in a secondary echelon as he witnessed the activity in the boats up ahead. In an attempt to keep their vehicles from being swamped, troops were frantically bailing water with their helmets. When the ramps were dropped, those exiting were systematically mowed down by murderous machine gun crossfire. Many drowned, unable to negotiate the rough seas, under the sheer weight of back packs, rifles and ammunition. On the shore, American casualties were piling up. Sam Hubbard determined he would not be a part of this. He knew all the preparatory paraphernalia he was saddled with would be nothing but a detriment. Anything he had to have, he could take it off a dead soldier when— if he made it ashore.

Sam stood at the rear of his boat as it surged ahead approaching the moment to lower the ramp. He dropped his rifle and released his back pack, allowing them fall onto the pitching, sodden floor of the boat. He would leave the four grenades clipped to his jacket. Flinging his helmet away, he cartwheeled over the back of the boat and into the water.

He surfaced for air, utilizing the boat for protection, peeking around to get a view of what was taking place while formulating his thoughts, registering the disorganized racket of war, the chatter of machine guns, cries from the wounded, the constant pinging of rounds striking vehicle hulls, water, rocks and worst of all, flesh.

Sam reasoned that if he had any chance of reaching the beach alive, he would have to stay submerged, so with all his energy, he began paddling furiously, bobbing up only for a precious breath of air. Nearing the shore, he was becoming aware of the awful carnage floating in the crimson water. Fighting the specter of panic and futility, he spied a disabled LCI that had made it within a short distance from the water's edge. Dead bodies lay disarranged around the vehicle. There was no movement aboard the landing craft, and he concluded that all had been slaughtered on approach. Still, he must swim toward it, since it offered some measure of protection. He surfaced behind the metal chassis of the craft, gasping and concentrating on what to do next.

Glancing around the left corner of the frame, he had an unobstructed view of the premonitory where a small group of those lucky enough to make it ashore huddled helplessly against the precipitous cliff. He decided not to make an attempt to join them. Swimming to the left side of the craft, he noticed the terrain sloped gradually away from the steep cliff, leading up a long incline. It was well-defended by two machine gun nests, and slightly upward and to the left, a concrete pill box was anchored in the cut bank All three bristled with automatic weapons spitting a flow of fire evidenced by the stream of tracers.

Since Sam left his helmet, his complete pack, plus his rifle, back where he had bailed out of the LCI, the only fighting gear he possessed was the four grenades, and two ammo packs of 30 caliber rounds which were of no use to him without a firearm. He decided it would be too risky locating a rifle which would certainly be under water, plus, the benefits of having a helmet would not justify the exposure of searching for one. Hastily, he studied the terrain leading up to the first machine gun nest, spying a gnarled bush ten yards off shore. Closer to the gun emplacement, positioned to the left, in the uneven surface, was a boulder, small, but large enough to serve as a shield.

Without further thought, Sam again ducked underwater half swimming, half crawling to the shore. When the water no longer presented any concealment, he scrambled toward the bush. Exhilaration tugged at his lungs at the good fortune of sliding head long next to it and not receiving so much as a scratch. Above, myriad projectiles snapped the air all around him. Now, he had to take his chances of making it to the protection of the small rock. Impulsively, he crawled as fast as he could on his belly, as would some terrified creature, not chancing to present any more target than was absolutely necessary.

He was not so lucky this time, as he was spotted. The ground around him became a fog of dust from the incoming 50 caliber machine gun rounds tearing at the earth, He grabbed a grenade from his ammo strap. Holding the ring pin in his teeth, mentally counting the seconds before detonation, intending to make certain there would be no interval for the gun crew to return the incoming grenade. Lying on his side, he lobbed the grenade where he best calculated the nest to be located, praying for a kill.

At the explosion, he glanced around the rock to see the results. It was a direct hit. Anticipating the crew to be dead, he charged to the gun pit for the safety it offered. Luck was again with him. He now crouched amongst the bodies of dead German soldiers.

Sam wrestled a corpse away from the gun mount and trained it toward the other unsuspecting gun nest, and was shocked when a stout American officer piled in beside him. Downhill and to the left, Sam could see a stream of American soldiers breaking from the cliff wall, now free from the immediate machine gun fire.

"Get 'em, kid!" the officer shouted, readying the band of cartridges. "I'll man the belt!"

Sam sprayed the startled crew killing them all.

The excited officer slapped Sam vigorously on the shoulder. "Damn son! That was a bit of good work! What's your name?"

Sam responded, "Hubbard, Sir," glancing across to the pill box enfilade to the upper final machine gun that was parallel to the two disabled gun pits. It offered no threat to Sam nor the officer, but a fortified bunker prohibited the advance of American soldiers massing below. The unprotected pill box was too large a plum for him to pass so he yelled to the officer, "Cover me. I'm going to give those Krauts in that pill box a treat!"

Sam started to leap out of the gun pit, and only then felt a sharp pain in his right leg. He felt his thigh, soaked with blood. Undaunted, he hobbled across the ground then over and around to the rear of the structure, clambering onto its short roof, dropping two grenades down into the gun deck. The successive explosions silenced the twin 57 caliber automatic cannons that had been raking the beach below since the beginning of the invasion. Instantly, troops down below began streaming up the hill.

Sam wriggled off the roof to see the officer standing before him. It was at that moment the young ex-farmer saw the star on the officer's helmet.

"Good God!" Sam exclaimed. "You're a general!"

General Theodore Roosevelt smiled, having noticed Sam's private-first-class chevrons, "That's right, son. Let's find you a helmet and get you to the first aid station!"

Sam beamed, nodding, "I'll go for that, Sir!"

The Rangers, with the aid of ropes and grapples, neutralized the enemy on the cliffs, while troops of Sam's contingent stormed the plateau to the north. The enemy fled westward only to be confronted by the 82nd and 101st Airborne. The German army caught in the pincer, began surrendering by the hordes. At ten o'clock the next morning, Valognes, Sainte Mere Eglise, and Bayeux had been neutralized. French inhabitants poured onto the streets, wildly throwing flowers and embracing their liberators.

Sam missed out on the welcoming. He was in a field hospital. His thigh wound was serious, but he would survive. That day, he was visited by a one-star general, accompanied by an aide. In the aide's possession were two medals: A purple heart and a distinguished service ribbon. And a gold set of 2nd lieutenant's bars.

****

Milo Rittenhaus' Model A sputtered into the Hubbard farmyard. It was four thirty, Friday afternoon, June 8, 1944. Walter was home. He had finished cultivating beans earlier than expected.

"O my God, Walter!" Millie exclaimed. "It's Milo!"

Walter bolted from the kitchen table where he was seated, flinging open the door. Milo was grim-faced stepping onto the porch. Walter motioned him inside.

"It's Sam, isn't it, Milo?" Walter asked, anxiety lacing his voice.

Rittenhaus took a deep breath, handing the Western Union telegram to the farmer.

"It's Army. That's all I know, Walt. So far it hasn't been good news for you."

Rittenhaus had delivered three telegrams announcing sons that had been killed, and he despised the chore.

Walter gritted his teeth, snatching the missive from the mail carrier. He fumbled in his pocket for his knife, trembling as he ripped open the message.

"If they killed my Sammy," he seethed invectively, "I'll murder that draft dodgin'..."

Millie grasped Walter's wrist allowing her a view of the paper. Impulsively, she began to read.

"Dear Mr. and Mrs. Hubbard. It gives me great pleasure to inform you that your son, 2nd Lieutenant Samuel L. Hubbard, has been awarded a purple heart and a Distinguished Service Award for unequaled bravery on the Normandy Invasion."

"He's been hurt!" Millie cried.

"He's a lieutenant!" Walter cut in, snatching the paper, continuing to read aloud.

"…as he disabled two machine gun nests and one pill box in an Alvin York-style humili…"

"What's that word, Millie?" Walter asked placing his forefinger on the place.

She took the telegram from him and started again, "… humiliating single handed rout of an established enemy. Because of your son's heroic action, the beach was cleared of gunfire allowing the troops to advance. Lieutenant Hubbard's injury, while serious, is not life- threatening and he should be leaving the field hospital in due time. Again, my congratulations, Omar S. Bradley, Lieutenant General, commanding."

One would expect Hubbard to embrace his wife, but instead he and the mail carrier jumped around the kitchen shaking hands.

"How'd he get to be a lieutenant, Walt?" Rittenhaus asked.

"Damned if I know, Milo, but I'm pretty proud of that boy right now," he exclaimed.

Walter turned to see the telegram lying on the kitchen table. Millie was unaccountably gone.

"I gotta go find Millie, Milo," Walter said. "Thanks for bringin' that good news."

Rittenhaus smiled walking out, commenting, "Wish they all could be that good."

Walter found Millie in the bedroom softly crying. "What's wrong Millie? You oughta' be happy," he began.

She turned, embracing him. "I'm pleased, but I'm not happy."

"Then what's the matter?"

She issued a long sigh. "I'm worried about Andy."

Walter attempted to express the compassion he knew Millie would like for him to, and put on his best face nodding, but he couldn't cloak his elation. He released her and returned to the kitchen, and picked up the telegram.

"My God, I'm proud of that boy!" he glowed, re-reading the dispatch.

****

Ikeya stood next to Andy who sat on his hard wooden bunk. The two had become friends as seemingly impossible as it might have been. Ikeya was in charge of the ward room that Andy inhabited. Had the Japanese guard been caught fraternizing with an American POW he would have most-surely been executed. But now that all Nippon was losing the war and all elements necessary to conduct an offensive were being exhausted, discipline was waning. Surveillance was practically non-existent since nobody on either side had any energy. Hunger was a concern with the guards as well as the captives. The only times Ikeya was summoned was to help carry a dead prisoner outside to the grotesque pile of emaciated humanity. When the stack of dead bodies became large, it was doused with gasoline and set afire, the sickening odor filtering into chambers throughout the bunk chambers.

Andy and the Japanese guard shared many similar philosophies. Both were gentle people, each in love with a woman who was waiting. Each had come from a farm.

Ikeya had been some help to Andy when he would occasionally sneak a morsel of food, a potato or a fragment of bread, to the starving prisoner. Andy's size was a disadvantage since all inmates received a like serving. Large men needed more nutrition than their smaller counterparts to sustain them, so they were likely the first to go. Andy was slowly and surly starving to death. His main concern was food as his stomach tugged at him to fill the ever-present need to provide life.

Silver bombers were filling the skies over Tokyo now. Ikeya and Andy knew that they were American. Ikeya also informed Andy that Snavely was being sodomized. Andy didn't need such bits of information. He knew, these things, and with a certain measure of guilt, he was taking advantage of his confidant. Each night, the tall marine would smuggle a radio component into the barracks. With Armstrong's help, he would position and connect the part, apply the liquid solder, then replace the board in the wall concealing his work for another day.

CHAPTER 45

Kwajalein Island, The Marshalls
May, 1944

Siffering's letter to Andrea began,

"I've finally gotten my wish. I'll be accompanying the
Marilyn Maxwell entourage to Kwajalein, presenting my
Sounds of the Pacific to the boys in uniform."

She answered his note.

"Congratulations, Loren. I'm delighted for you. Do me a favor when
you're there and look up an old friend of mine. He's a correspondent
recuperating on that same island. Seems he got a little too close to the war.
I'm certain if you contact UPI or the field hospital there someone can put
you in touch with him. His name is Philip Olson."

The courier stepped into the Adjutant General hut where Olson set
up his work table and handed him a large red white and blue bordered
envelope. The scribe glanced at the USO special services logo. He reached
across his desk for a letter opener.

"Dear Mr. Olson," the message began. "Our mutual friend, Andrea
Vogel, informs me that there's an opportunity to make your acquaintance
while our troupe is performing on the island the 18th, 19th and 20th of this
month. I'm enclosing two on-stage passes for the 18th. Hopefully, you'll be

able to attend, and enjoy the performance. I'd be most-appreciative if you will look me up after the show. Cordially, Loren Siffering."

Rusty Atkins had been retained as a regimental commander in charge of training. New replacements plus some elements from the old 11th had moved on to invading the Caroline island chain. If he was bored by the non-combatant duty, he wasn't complaining.

Olson called Rusty's number and was informed the major was in his office.

"Keep him there. I'll be right over," Olson said, cradling the phone.

Rusty glanced up as Olson limped into his quarters, asking, "When're you goin' to throw that cane away?"

"I'm not sure I ever will. My hip was broken and knocked out of kilter by that damned grenade. Doc said not to put too much pressure on it, so I'm not. Anyway, I didn't come here to talk about my hip."

"What did you come to talk about?"

Olson pitched the envelope to Rusty who appraised the ornate printing. He cursorily opened and read it. Rusty stuck the message back in its sheath, drew a deep breath and grunted "Okay. She knows this band leader. What's this got to do with me?"

"I just want you come along to the show. That's all. I think you'd have a good time."

"Oh hell, I wouldn't know what for."

"Just come and enjoy it. It wouldn't hurt you to meet this guy."

"When is it?"

"Tomorrow afternoon. Four o'clock. Come around at 3:30 with your Jeep and pick me up."

"I guess I can do that."

The immense crunch of GIs sat on the gentle hill that sloped down to the scene of action. Siffering's band was playing songs of the day and the atmosphere was at a carnival peak. The correspondent and combat officer were making their way around the side to the stairs, when Rusty was spied by a large contingent of troops from his regiment. They had found their places early at the front of the stage area, and at this moment, they began chanting his name.

"You go on ahead, Phil," Rusty said. "Looks like I'm gonna have to stay here with my kids."

"Aw naw, Rusty," Olson protested. "You have to sit up on the stage."

Rusty knew the boisterous collection of his men would never allow him to be anywhere but with them so he waved Olson on ahead knowing it would be of no use to try to get away. Plus, he didn't want to be anyplace else.

The show was an extravaganza, and was the perfect tonic for the soldiers' morale. Rusty was yelling and cheering along with his men forgetting for the moment that he wasn't one of them. Then something happened: During a break from the comedy act, Siffering approached the microphone accompanied by a petite brunette songstress wearing a skimpy dress.

"This is Sally Boggs," he began, "and we're going to play Swingin' on a Star, but, can you believe it? Sally wants to dance and she can't find anyone who'll dance with her. Is there anyone who'd volunteer to help this sweet little lady out?"

Instantly, two sergeants grabbed Rusty and literally pitched him up on the wooden stage deck. Before he could get to his feet, the band struck up with the song while the dark-haired girl skipped over to Rusty. She stopped, stood, legs apart, arms akimbo looking down at him with a naughty smile. As Rusty, embarrassed, rose to his feet, the audience roared.

She embraced him and began the dance. Rusty's face showed red beyond his normal complexion, but he gamely attempted to make it a reasonable showing. He couldn't dance, and everyone knew it, which made the exercise all the more of a spectacle. Still he persisted good-naturedly until the song ended. At this point, the girl planted a kiss on his lips then waved to the crowd while she pointed to him. The awkward charade was, for the troops who knew the hardened, no nonsense major, the highlight of the afternoon.

As requested, Olson waited outside the stage door for the band leader to show. Presently, the slim blond maestro stepped out.

Olson extended his hand. "I know who you are. I'm Phil Olson, and this is my friend, Major Rusty Atkins."

Siffering returned the greeting, offering, "Can you give me just a few minutes? I have a couple of things to work out with Miss Maxwell and the program director. Then maybe we can go someplace to get acquainted."

The three rode to the officer's club in Rusty's jeep. Rusty chose a quiet spot in the corner of the dirt-floored lounge. Shortly, the orders were taken.

"That must be some sort of thrill playing for those troops," Olson began.

Siffering paused, exhaling. "You have no idea. I've played in the White House to all sorts of dignitaries, but nothing I have ever done is as rewarding as this."

The three continued small talk for a few moments, when Siffering offered, "I understand that's *your* old job Andrea has, Phil."

"She does, but I don't quite understand how you got acquainted with her."

"She covered the going's on from the little dance venues the First Lady would arrange," Siffering began to explain. "Mrs. Roosevelt took a liking to Andrea, and I just happened to be one of the groups selected to play for one of these things. After that, I became a regular."

"Did she ever mention her boyfriend who was in the Marines? His name is Andy," Olson asked.

"Yes, she did," Siffering answered, "Quite often, as a matter of fact. Why do you ask?"

At this point, Rusty's brow began to furrow.

"Rusty, here," Olson started to explain, is a good friend of that soldier's. In fact, they were in basic together."

"Then after basic in San Diego," Rusty put in. "You're not the man he played the guitar for are you?"

"Sure am."

Rusty rubbed his chin. "Dammit. I knew your name when I first heard it. I just didn't make the connection. There's been so damned much that's happened these past couple 'a years."

"I know," Siffering agreed.

"He was a good guitar player," Rusty mused.

"Still is, I hope. He's as good as there is," Siffering put in.

Rusty's nod was one of silent apology.

""Now this is something," Olson said. "You two are sitting here talking about someone that we all know."

"Well, I don't know Andrea," Rusty explained, rubbing his eye brow, inhaling deeply. "But Andy Hubbard's my best friend. I just hope we can liberate him before he starves to death."

"That's war," Siffering countered. Quickly changing the topic, he added, "Sally took quite a liking to you, Rusty."

Rusty blushed. "That the little gal I danced with?"

"If that's what you did."

"I know. Hell, I've never danced in my life."

"She wants to meet you."

"She said that?"

"She did."

"You tell her I'm game—any place, any time."

"Come around back stage after the show tomorrow."

"Count on it," Rusty responded.

The officer, in his sun-tans, waited in the large room for the members of the production to filter in. Presently, the place came awash with a cacophony of animated conversation as the rush of performers and musicians, free from the scrutiny of the audience, crowded into the chamber. Rusty searched for the girl. Presently he saw her and elbowed his way over. She flashed a warm smile. He did his best to act normal, but his heart betrayed him and he felt his face reddening.

Impulsively, he reached for her hand. "Do you need to change?" he opened.

"Not necessarily. It's pretty warm here, and I'm comfortable," she responded.

This was the first time he had heard her speak and he liked the sound of her voice.

"I'm Rusty Atkins," he began.

"I know your name," she said.

"Well, I know you're Sally Boggs," he put in. "Is there any chance we can get away from here?"

"What did you have in mind?"

"I have a jeep. I thought you might like to see around the island."

She brightened. "Sure. I'd be for that. Is your jeep near here?"

He took her arm. "Right this way."

As they drove along the sandy beach away from the congestion, he jibed, "You're pretty trusting, getting into a car with a stranger."

"I don't think so. This drive is just perfect for me. I need to get away for a bit. Besides, you're a famous major. I don't think I'm in any danger."

He chuckled nervously. "I'm not famous."

"Sure you are. I read that newspaper article you wrote. That was pretty courageous."

He blushed. "Think so?"

"Absolutely. I have two brothers in the service and it'd be nice if their commanding officers think as much about them as you do about your guys. It's pretty obvious how they feel toward you. That display from them yesterday…"

"I thought it showed a lot of disrespect."

She chuckled knowingly. "No, you don't."

"Naw. I guess I don't."

"Well, I thought about you when I first read that article. That's when I was back in the states. When I found out you were stationed here, I told Loren I'd like to have the opportunity to meet you. I just didn't expect it to come about in the manner that it did."

"Yeah. It must have meant to happen."

"Providence, I think," she put in.

"Whatever that means," he uttered.

She merely smiled. The article which contained his controversial article also shared some background of his simple Louisiana upbringing.

The two bumped along the shoreline in silence, when she sighed, "This is lovely, Rusty. I'm really enjoying this. I hadn't realized how confining the work I'm doing is."

"Is it too hard on you?"

"Oh, no! I love it. It's just that it's nice to get away."

"Well, why don't we go back to the mess hall and I'll talk one of the cooks out of a couple of steaks, and we'll have a barbeque?"

"That'd be great! I'll tell Loren and grab a couple of bits of clothes."

Rusty picked up the steaks. He also gathered two blankets and a jug of gin from the officer's club.

The sun had long set, and the moon, above the horizon now, cast a shimmering beam on the gentle water. Sally, pleasantly drunk, not accustomed to the trappings of gin, lay in Rusty's arms, gazing at the last embers of the fire. Demands of the moment, that neither wanted, had come, and the two knew it was time to pack up and make the short trip back to civilization. The evening had been lovely, and, as has happened so many times in periods of conflict, two passionate people accidentally, inexorably, fell in love. They planned to meet again in Australia in another month when the troupe was scheduled to perform in Melbourne. By then, Rusty figured, the Marianas would be in the hands of the allies, and he would be able to meet her "Down Under." Obviously his calculations were more than a little optimistic.

****

Ruthie dashed to the house. She sprang into the kitchen calling to her mother. Once again, her father was in from the field. They tore open the letter from Sam, registering the heading,

PARIS FRANCE
Aug 6, 1944

Dear Folks,

Here I am in the city of sin and bright lights. The only difficulty is, practically everything is off limits, and added to that, they've made me exec officer of this company and am supposed to set an example. ME! Can you believe that? I won't be 21 until June!

My thigh has pretty well mended but I've been kept back because it's a little stiff, and that's fine with me. I may be here for a while. It'd be okay if they left me here, but I don't expect that to happen. I'll just have to play it by ear.

Mother, I remember you playing songs on your fiddle and one of them was, How We Gonna Keep 'Em Down on the Farm, and I want to get back down on the farm. That brings me to my next subject. Dad, I've been doing a lot of planning, plotting and conniving—call it whatever you want. The Hun's on the run, and after Normandy, we've been "going through them like a dose of salts through a widow woman" as you used to say. So I'll get to my point. Wilbur McCullum must be about ready to sell his farm. That's a section close to us. He doesn't have any kids to pass it on to. What I'm thinking is this. We're going to be rewarded for fighting over here. I can get a G.I. loan to buy it as soon as I'm discharged. I'm young and I can pay it off. Would you mind going over and talking to him?

""Gosh, no!" Walter burst. "Wonder why I didn't think of it myself? Imagine! Sam owning his own farm!"

That's about it. Ruthie, I miss you. Bet you can have the pick of the boys when this thing's over. I pray for Andy all the time. I love you all, Sam

Walter's Chevy pickup rolled into the McCullum yard. It was Saturday morning. Walter was anxious as he sprinted up the porch steps of the farm house. McCullum's wife came to the door.

"Wilbur around, Grace?" Walter asked

"He's out separating, Walter," she answered.

Walter tipped his hat, stepped off the porch and walked briskly to McCullum's milk house.

The whine of the cream separator bowl was winding down. This was a good omen, Walter thought to himself; Wilbur was finishing the chore. The bright sun cast a shadow behind the burly farmer as he stepped through the doorway.

The old farmer turned, seeing Walter. McCullum and Hubbard had never been particularly close friends, probably do their age difference, but they were both good honest farmers, respectful of one another.

"Mornin' Walt. How's it goin'?"

"No complaints, Wilbur. And you?"

"Wouldn't do any good if I had any," he responded.

"Listen, Wilbur. I'll make this quick. I just got a letter from Sam…"

"Oh yeah! How's Sammy?"

"He's fine."

"A officer now, they tell me."

"He is, Wilbur, and …"

"God. You must be proud of him."

455

"I am proud of him, Wilbur," Walter said, "But there's something I want to ask you."

"What is it?"

"Any chance you might have given any thought to selling this place?"

"Sure is," the farmer replied.

Walter's heart leaped. "Well that's great! That was what Sam was writin' about. See, he wants to buy your farm, and I understand the Army's goin' to give those vets some financing."

"Too late, Walt," McCullum interrupted.

"Too late what?" Walter asked, stiffening.

"I made a deal with Cat MacGregor."

"When?"

"Just last week."

Walter flung his hat out the milk house door in disgust. "Shit, Wilbur! My boys are fightin' and dyin' for this goddam country and you sell your place to that chicken shit coward bastard!"

"Walt! Walt!" The old farmer broke in. "I had no idea you or Sammy wanted this farm!" He paused eying the wet concrete floor. "I would rather have sold it to you, or Sammy. We don't need the money—Hell, Walt… I just didn't think."

Walter would hear no more. He stomped out of the milk house, picked up his hat that had sailed a good distance, marched over to his pickup and spun out of the yard.

Grace met Wilbur halfway between the yard and milk house. "What was that about, Wilbur?" she asked.

The old man rubbed his forehead with the back of his sleeve. "Guess I just made a mistake, Grace. He come to see if we'd sell the farm to his boy, Sammy. He's pretty upset."

"Why, Wilbur. I never even thought about Sammy Hubbard. We sure should have thought about Walt. He saved our necks more than once with that truck of his, back when he moved on the Harper place."

"That's sure right. I never gave it a second thought."

"I wonder if you can talk Cat out of it?"

"I don't know, Grace. It's worth a try I guess."

McCullum returned later that morning announcing to his wife. "That kid's got a mean streak, Grace."

"Why?"

"He said some pretty unlikely things to me."

"He wouldn't let you talk him out of sellin'?"

"I don't have the heart to tell you what he said."

The two gentle people stood in the yard lamenting the circumstance. Finally, Grace suggested, "You ought to go in to town and see Royce Palmer. Maybe he can think of something."

Wilbur's expression softened, "I'll do that Grace. That's a good idea."

Palmer was in his darkroom when McCullum drove up. His wife Margaret dutifully went to get him.

Palmer came up and as was his wont, he greeted the simple farmer warmly.

Without delay, McCullum reviewed the problem, specifically his concern.

"Well, Wilbur, you were not about to talk the MacGregor kid out of anything. That served no purpose, plus, you just got him suspicious. Particularly after you already signed the realtor' s contract."

Palmer sat, deep in thought.

Finally, he exhaled. "The only thing we can do at this point is file a lis pendens."

"I don't know what that is."

"I know you don't. It puts a hold on any further negotiating on your property."

"You can do that?!" McCullum guffawed.

"I can if you're willing to sign the edict."

McCullum looked stunned. "Sure," he uttered. "show me where to sign."

"You don't do it here. We go down to Phillipsburg. That's the county seat. And you're the one who has to do the signing."

McCullum smiled. "Do I get to ride in a Cadillac?"

"You get to ride in a Cadillac."

On the ride to Phillipsburg, while answering the many questions the lawyer put to McCullum, one involved the amount of the earnest money. McCullum recited the figure, admitting he thinks he forgot to endorse the check when he mailed it to the bank.

"Are you certain you didn't sign it?" Palmer grilled.

"No. Why? Will that help?"

"It won't hurt," Palmer mumbled.

"Ruthie, go out and see what that racket in the barn is. Sounds like a horse or a cow is hung up," Mildred said to her daughter.

Ruth came back on the dead run. "It's daddy!" she shouted. "He's yelling and cussing and hitting the manger with a big board!"

Millie wiped her hands and bolted for the barn. Walter was whaling away at the insides of the barn with a board.

"Damn sonovabitch! Damn sonovabitch!" he ranted.

"Walter! Walter!" she shouted.

Walter hurled the board out of the front of the barn, barely missing Ruth who was coming in.

"Wilbur McCullum sold his farm to Cat MacGregor, Millie!"

"Oh no!" she said painfully, "When?"

"Just did! We barely missed it!" Walter collapsed to one knee and began to sob. That was a first for her. She had never seen him break down.

Walter remained in the kneeling position, his head in his hands. "How in God's name," he began unevenly, "am I gonna tell my son that some goddam draft dodger bought the land he's fightin' for?" He looked up. "It ain't right, Millie!"

"No, Walter," she consoled, softly massaging his back, "it's not fair." She stood by, pursing her lips to keep from crying. He looked up. "Get a letter off to him today, Millie. We can't have him wishin'. He's gotta know."

The mood was somber the next morning. The sky was a leaden gray, and a light mist was falling. Walter happened to glance out the kitchen window, when he saw Royce Palmer's yellow '42 Cadillac pull into the yard. He rose to his feet.

"I think Royce Palmer's out there," he said to Millie, who was finishing up the dishes. "Go let him in."

She wiped her hands on her apron, walked to the kitchen door and turned the knob, just as the corpulent attorney approached.

"Good Morning, Royce," she said cheerily, putting on a happy face.

"C'mon, Millie. You can't be all that happy," He sneered, sardonically, issuing a crooked grin. "I just talked with Wilbur McCullum."

Walter, standing by the table now, asked, "You talked to Wilbur McCullum?"

Palmer avoided the question, turning to Millie. "Got any of that coffee left, Millie? Your husband and I need to talk."

Walter was confused, and patronizingly affixed a chair for Palmer to sit. Millie set a cup on the table and filled it. The lawyer slid into the chair, laying his elbows on the table surface, focusing on Walter, who took his own chair.

Palmer took a sip of coffee, and began. "Wilbur McCullum and I went down to Phillipsburg yesterday…"

Millie slid into a chair focusing on the lawyer.

"…and signed a lis pendens."

"I don't what that is."

"He didn't either, Walt. It puts the kybosh on any further negotiating involving his property."

Walter yelped in delight. "You can do that?"

"We can, and we did."

Walter's immense grin was dowsed, when he saw Palmer's expression change.

"Don't get excited Walt. It doesn't mean much at this point, but the sale of that property of Wilbur's is no done deal now."

"God, Royce!" Walter gushed, "I don't know what to say. I mean, I was so goddam mad when I found out what Wilbur did. I wanted in the worst way to see if I couldn't get that farm for Sam."

"Don't give up on that idea, Walt. There's a chance we can still make it happen."

Walter, animated, open hands, asked, "How, Royce? I'm completely in the dark."

"Well," Palmer began calmly. "Wilbur made a mistake. He knows it. Now the thing we have to do is see if we can't get the courts to decide his way."

"How can we do this, Royce? I don't have any money for this!"

"I'll do it pro bono."

Out of the corner of his eye, Walter saw Millie's smile.

"What's it mean, Royce?"

"Means, I'll do it for nothing."

"You can't do that, Royce."

"Well, I can, but it could get a little ouchy down the road."

"I don't understand."

Palmer gained both Millie's and Walter's eye contact. "This objection will initially be filed in the court down at Phillipsburg, and they'll refuse it, prima facie."

"Meaning what?" Walter asked.

"No chance."

"Why not?"

"I don't have time to explain it."

"All right. Then what?"

"We'll take it to an appellate court in Denver. But before we do, there's a chance there'll be enough public sentiment, since Sam's fighting for his country that MacGregor will cave in."

"I wouldn't hang my hat on that," Walter put in.

"I'm not, but if he doesn't, we start to play hard ball."

"I like the sounds of that," Walter put in.

"I sort of do too, but it could get a little nasty. MacGregor might wish he never heard of Wilbur McCullum."

"Why do you say that?"

Palmer smiled.

He looked the farmer in the eye. "The answer, Walt, is when you take your argument to places where they never shut the lights down, court costs can get plenty steep for the side that loses, but we'll take that chance. I know something MacGregor doesn't."

"What's that?"

"Pardon my choice of words, Millie, but I have to answer Walt's question." He flashed a mischievous grin to the brawny farmer. "It's not smart to get in a pissin' contest with a skunk."

Walter erupted in laughter. Palmer rose from his chair, heading for the door. He looked at Walter. "Just sit tight and don't do anything unless I tell you to. Kapish?"

Walter nodded submissively. Palmer gave him a half-hearted wave and walked out the door.

After he had left, Walter asked Millie. "I wonder why he's doing this."

"I thought about it too, and I have no idea. He's helped us before," she said as an afterthought.

Walter murmured as he stood with his wife, "I wish I knew what makes him tick."

****

Phil Olson stood before Rusty, seated at his large desk. Spread across the major's table, were connecting maps of the Caroline and Mariana island chains.

"Know what the word 'ambivalent' means, Rusty?" the correspondent opened.

Without looking up, Rusty responded, "So far, I've managed to survive without ever hearing it." He looked up at the tall writer. "Why do you ask?"

Olson leaned against a post in the hut. "A while back, I put in for a transfer to cover MacArthur's 'return' to the Philippines. Well, his big splash is approaching, and guess what? I got the job, or, I should say, I'll be one of several who'll be reporting it."

Rusty pushed away from his desk, rising to his feet. "When's all this coming about?"

"The manifest just came in. I'm leaving this afternoon. I'll be on a C-54 that'll take me to Rabaul, then I'll board a destroyer that's supposed to support MacArthur on the Leyte landing. I understand the big event is due to take place sometime this next week."

"If you'll be with MacArthur, you should be safe," Rusty grunted.

"You don't think too much of the general, do you?"

Rusty's tone would give the impression that he preferred not to be asked the question.

"No," he uttered shortly, adding. "I'm gonna miss you, Phil. You've gotten to be a part of the furniture around here."

461

Olson knew the simile was intended to be one of warmth. He extended his hand. "Whether you realize it or not, you gave me my start in this racket, and I'll be forever grateful to you for that. Although I'm ready to go, it's going to be tough to leave."

"So, that's what that word means, huh?"

"That's what it means."

Rusty felt his voice cracking. "You taught me more than a few things about life, buddy. Be sure we get back in touch when this crap shoot's over."

Olson wiped his eye, nodded, and without a response, stepped out of the hut.

Rusty sat in Frank Canali's office.

"Any notion on how long we're going to be stationed here?" the major asked.

The one-star replied, "Stuart thinks it depends on who gets his way— Nimitz or MacArthur."

"Explain that one to me."

"Nimitz wants to starve them out; MacArthur wants to invade."

"Whose side are you on?"

"Nimitz's. Look at Rabaul. It worked there, didn't it? Makes sense to me. Why do you ask?"

"Well, I just got a letter from Sally Boggs and her band is down in Australia for a couple of weeks. I want to get down to see her."

"Go ahead. I think we're going to mobilize, but not any time soon. You should be able to catch a hop heading that way. Take a couple of weeks off I'm sure we can get along without you."

The C-47 hit the runway, bounced hard, with black smoke billowing out behind. It bounced again before settling on the runway, with the clattering roar of the engines reversing. Riding the bench seat had been uncomfortable enough, so the rough landing seemed only fitting. The army workhorse taxied to the end of the tarmac and circled to a stop. Metal stairs were rolled up to the waist door. A tanned Marine in his dress blues was the first out. Sally squealed and ran to him. He picked her up and swung her around. She clutched his waist with one hand and grabbed his white garrison hat with her other to keep it from flying away. They kissed carelessly and passionately.

"Normally we have to pay to see a show like that," the tall blond in a white suit said. Rusty wheeled, breaking into a wide grin upon recognizing Siffering.

"Sally, did you mention to the major that we have a little welcoming for him?"

"I haven't yet…"

"Then I will," Siffering said, motioning to the waiting staff car.

Siffering walked briskly alongside a thick hedgerow. At the end, pink chairs and round tables were arranged on an expansive lawn. Rusty noticed white-clad cooks standing next to a pig on a rotating spit. Off to the side was the band stand, with its microphones scattered throughout the seating area.

An instant cheer rose when Sally walked in with Rusty. The band members had welcomed their prize dancer with humor and compassion. Instantly, a scantily-clad waitress stepped up to Rusty with a gin in her hand, offering, "I believe this is what you drink."

He responded with a chuckle, "I believe you're absolutely right!"

After a half-hour's imbibing and getting acquainted, Siffering stepped to the mike and announced, "Since we want the major to feel at home, it's time to eat, so let's all get in the chow line. Major, you and Sally first!"

After dinner, Siffering rose, stepped up on the dais and took the mike. Chattering around the tables subsided.

"People who know the major," he began, "call him Rusty."

"Rusty," he repeated, feigning astonishment. "I wonder why… why would anyone ever call him that?" He glanced over and smiled at the bronze-complexioned officer.

Ripples of polite laughing and applause followed.

"Rusty asked me if I'd planned anything special tonight. I told him that I had. What I didn't tell him was I had planned on his generosity of saying few words to us. That would be special, wouldn't you think?"

Band members applauded enthusiastically, and started to chant, "Rusty! Rusty! Rusty!"

Rising to his feet, he confessed to Sally, "I didn't count on this."

"Too late. You're stuck." she giggled.

He knew he was stuck, and that was okay. He had expected it. In the four short years since he had been a skinny, wandering waif from Louisiana, the fiery cauldron of hell had forged him into a man of inspiration and determination. No longer was he a creature of uncertain resolve. He was a man confident of whom he had become and what he intended to do with his life. His voice had grown deep and resonant now, leaving no doubt to anyone who heard him that he said what he meant and meant what he said.

Rusty walked up and clasped the microphone. Instantly the crowd cheered and began applauding. He had learned the practice of standing erect, and gaining the audience's attention before speaking. He smiled and began, "It's a privilege to stand before you. It's special to me, and I'll tell you why I say that in a bit." He glanced to the bandleader. "So, thanks for the opportunity, Loren." He scanned the crowd.

"This is not my first trip to Australia. I've been to Melbourne, before. It was in the spring of the year—May 1941, to be exact. I had escaped the Bataan capture. I didn't know they called it the Death March until I got off that PBY and made it in. But that's just what it was. It was a march to kill." Rusty paused to wipe his eye. "I wasn't the same man then that I am now. I knew nothing about war. But for some reason, I was spared the return to battle so I could try to avenge the wrongs forced upon my comrade and my countrymen. For me to be told what one man is capable of doing to another, I would have not believed. I would not have believed the celestial kindness of the good, nor would I, nor can I, comprehend the decaying depths of the wicked."

He strode in a small arc on the stage, and started again. "There's a fellow...my best friend, by the way, who played the guitar in your band. His name is Andy Hubbard... Anyone remember him?"

"Yeah! Sure!" were a couple of shouts.

Rusty exhaled. "He saved my life. On that particular occasion, he risked his life to save mine, and I couldn't understand why one would do that for another. It was a grand gesture, and I couldn't appreciate it then. I can now. He was on the Bataan... death march with me. I escaped. He didn't. I couldn't help him. Today, he's in a Jap prison in Tokyo. Andy's a great man. He'll someday be a doctor... and... what's most important, he's still alive. I can't stop believing that I can be there to save him. So help me with my thoughts of Andy. Hopefully, there's a way... and God willing, there's still time.

"I mentioned that it's special for me to be able to talk to you, and I said I'd tell you why. When you were in Kwajalein, Loren told me that playing for troops was more fulfilling than anything as he had ever done before." Rusty's words were drowned out by instant cheering and applause. He waited until it abated. "And you visiting us dog-faces out there in the war zone was a kiss from Heaven. We knew, and so did you, that bullets were still flying around. And you think that's not special? We love you for risking your lives to give us a piece of home!"

Again, Rusty was greeted with applause.

Rusty rubbed his chin waiting for quiet.

"I'm coming to the end of my little talk, but I have to tell you why I came back to Australia this time. I came down here to ask Sally a question." He paused, looking across the grounds, with a mischievous smile. "...And it's not, will she teach me to dance."

A rustling spread through the group.

"There's another request I have. Can any of you help me out?"

Instantly, the band members began chanting, "YES! YES! YES!"

Sally rushed to the stage and embraced Rusty.

Rusty held his wife in his arms. In the background, the C-47 sat at an idle.

"And you don't know just where you'll be going?" she asked tearfully.

"In the direction of Japan, you can be certain of that. The war is the same as over in Europe, but the Japs haven't learned their lesson yet, so there's plenty of fightin' to be done. But don't worry about me, Sally. We've got the upper hand. We'll take it one step at a time and trust in the Lord."

Rusty kissed her again and headed for the open waist door of the cargo plane.

****

Patches of snow dotted the prairie landscape that cold November morning. Milo Rittenhaus drove into the Hubbard yard. An icy wind blew unchecked across the flat farmland. Walter had finished morning chores and was removing his gloves, when he saw the mail carrier.

Rittenhaus drove alongside Walter, stopped and rolled down the window of his Model A. Not that it was comfortable inside his simple car, but it was warmer than it was outside, and he wanted to keep the conversation as short as he could.

"I'm not gettin' out, Walt. I just stopped by to tell you that Royce Palmer wants you to stop by his office when you git time."

"Did he say what for?"

"No. He didn't tell me nothin'."

"Wonder if he wants Millie to come in too." Walter mentally thought how he could arrange it so she could be away from her teaching duties, if Palmer needed her, too.

Rittenhaus wiped his dripping nose with his forefinger. "I wouldn't know any of that. Oh! He said to tell you to bring in an egg, too."

"He what?"

"He said to be sure to tell you to bring in an egg."

"One egg?"

"He said an egg."

"That can't be right."

"I know. I asked about him that too, and he said, 'just tell him.' You know that Royce. He's a weird one."

Walter walked in Palmer's office at ten o'clock. The barrister was at his desk, and waved the farmer over. Walter glanced at the fancy French leather-inlay chair he had broken. It looked okay. He hadn't realized this was the first time he been in Royce's office since that temper tantrum.

"Mornin', Royce."

"Good morning, Walter." Palmer waved to a chair. "Please have a seat."

Hubbard sat, and removed a fresh white egg from a frayed side pocket of his mackinaw.

"Oh yes. You remembered that."

The lines on Hubbard's face deepened. "Was Milo right? You want just one egg?"

"Yes. That's right. Now…"

"Mind telling me why?"

Palmer raised his hands in mild protest. "Just lay it on my desk, Walter. We've other things to discuss, and I'm short on time this morning."

Hubbard did as he was told and sat as would a docile child.

Palmer pulled out an official-looking document. At the top of the sheet was a bold imprint stating, Circuit Court of Appeals Denver Colorado.

"That thing looks important, Royce."

"It is," he said crisply. "You need to sign at the bottom next to Wilbur's. Don't ask me a bunch of questions, but," he pulled out two long sheets filled with signatures, "then look these over and see if there's anyone you can think we should add to them."

Walter dutifully signed the edict, took the list from Palmer and started scanning the signatures... Marshal Reiss, John Sutton, Jim Thurston, Felton Caldwell. "What's this, Royce?"

"It's a petition. These are character witnesses—people who believe your son should be awarded the judgment. People sympathetic to your cause, as it were."

"What's it for?"

Palmer, controlling his patience, turned facing the farmer. "We have to ask for a hearing in an appellate court, Walter. We have to prove to the court that such a legal action should be warranted, then hope they grant us a court date. There's nothing automatic about it. That's why we assemble things like this list to establish opinion. There are many things I have to do in preparation, like registering our complaints, appealing to the triumvirate, filing…"

"I didn't know any of this."

"I'm aware of that. Just read the list."

Walter began scanning again, but stopped when he came to the name, Sam Armling.

"Jesus Christ, Royce!" He chirped. "You know Sam Armling?"

"Of course I know Sam Armling. Why wouldn't I know Sam Armling?"

"I named my kid Sam after him!"

"I know that," Palmer answered brusquely.

Walter flashed a surprised stare at the attorney, and resumed scanning the list of signatures: Carl Reichert, Clinton Durkee, Herman Schatzaeder, Fred Vogel. He jerked visibly when he came across the name, Fred Vogel.

He turned apologetically to Palmer, staffing softly, "Royce, did Vogel sign this?"

"That's his signature."

"Why that sonovabitch!"

"Better not be calling him that any more, Walter."

"How the hell did you get him to sign that?"

"You don't need to ask."

"Goddam, Royce! You could talk a sailor into buyin' a bottle of salt water!"

Palmer issued a slight smile. "I take that as a compliment."

Walter stood. "Well, I sure don't need to see any more of that that list you put together. I could never add anything to it!"

"Ok, then," Palmer said rising, "If you're satisfied, that takes care of our pressing matters for the time being."

"Oh," Walter asked as he was leaving, "Royce. Do you mind tellin' me what it is with that egg?"

Palmer looked around and delicately picked it up off his desk, holding it between his thumb and third finger. "I have to take care of this egg," he said, flashing a furtive glance at the farmer. "You see this is a pivotal element of commerce."

"How come?"

"Well," he began, "Jack MacGregor's kid has retained Al Zarlingo for his counsel, and in case you don't know who he is, and I wouldn't expect you would, Zarlingo is the mouthpiece for the Smaldones family. If you don't know who they are..."

"I know who they are."

"Good. Well," Palmer said grandiosely, "word has it that it young MacGregor is spreading the word to anyone who'll listen that I'm doing all this for nothing."

Walter stood speechless, unable to comment.

Palmer shook the egg. "They're wrong. Now, I'm not!"

****

LIPPSADT, GERMANY
March 24, 1945

Dear Folks,

I suppose you noticed that I'm a 1ˢᵗ lieutenant. Big deal. I have to tell you I was pretty down in the dumps when I received your letter. It sort of makes me wonder why I'm over here fighting those people who have been trying to take what we have, while the same type of thing is happening back home. Is that my purpose here? To keep the Germans from stealing our land so that Chattman McGregor can acquire it? I'm here risking my neck and I can't do a thing about it. I think they should at least make the draft dodgers wait until we all get home before they let them buy more property. It seems fair that I should have a shot at competing for a piece of America.

This country is all a mess of broken concrete. Scuttlebutt has that we'll be furloughed shortly, so I'll keep you informed.

****

MANILA, LUZON
March 2, 1945

Dear Andrea,

It's been a while since I've taken the time to write you. A lot has taken place since we touched base back on Kwajalein. Meeting Loren Siffering and the troupe was a real highlight of my stay there. Loren was taken by Rusty Atkins, Andy's buddy. I wasn't aware if you knew, but the major married a young girl who sings in Siffering's band. I've lost track of Atkins since then though I'm assuming he is somehow involved in what's going on in the Marianas, because that's where his old outfit went, and knowing him, he has to be in the thick of it. I covered the MacArthur landing on Leyte (You knew that) and off the record, it was a lot of BS—but we played his narcissistic game. What a show off! I'm cooling my heels in a pleasant little cove here called Cavite, looking for something to write about. Rumor has it that there's a colorful old marine surgeon who is in charge of the base hospital at Fort Stotsenberg, not far from here. I'm in the process of tracking him down, so wish me luck.

I trust your work is going okay. I share your gnawing concern about Andy, and say a daily prayer for him.

Write if you get time. I read your columns religiously, but a personal note would be nice.

Much Love, Phil

****

April 1, 1945

Dear Folks,

Just a quick note. I got the strangest memo yesterday. It was a copy of a signature request to General Roosevelt from, guess who? Royce Palmer! If anybody has an inkling as to what that's all about, would you let me know?

Walter smirked. "Royce said he was going to play hard ball."

****

Civic Center, Denver

10th CIRCUIT COURT OF APPEALS

April 7, 1945

Wilbur McCullum, Mildred and Walter Hubbard sat to the left of their lawyer, Royce Palmer in the cavernous marble edifice. To the farmers, the aura was cold, foreign and forbidding. Walter looked ill at ease and out of place dressed in his blue pin striped suit jacket and denim overhauls. On Walter's right Mildred sat, and on her right, appearing discomfited was Wilbur McCullum. McCullum didn't understand what his purpose at the trial was, but Palmer ordered he appear and he didn't argue. On Walter's left, the heavy-set lawyer, dressed in a handsome tan suit, appeared comfortable and confident. Across the courtroom, Chattman MacGregor sat next to a balding dark-featured man dressed in a black silk suit. On Chattman's right, was his father, hands folded on the oak table. Both camps made it a point not to recognize the other, with one exception. Mildred caught Chattman's eye, whereupon he immediately looked away.

A most unusual poster was erected next to the plaintiffs table. It was a life-size cardboard facsimile of Sam Hubbard in full officer's dress. Homer Martin had a Denver photographer create it.

Presently the bailiff walked in and sat. Momentarily he glanced up.

"Are the plaintiffs present?"

Palmer half stood and replied, "We are."

"And the respondent?"

"Present," MacGregor's attorney replied.

Momentarily, three justices, replete in their flowing robes entered.

The bailiff rapped the table. "All rise! Justices Byrnes, Wallace and Coughlin presiding. Case 1041, MacGregor versus McCullum/Hubbard filed in the tenth circuit court of appeals for the City and County of Denver this 12th day of May 1945."

The arbitrators took their stations behind the wide bench. The bailiff called, "Be seated."

Shuffling of seats raked the marble floor and the courtroom came to order.

"Is the defendant prepared to make a statement?" the bailiff asked.

MacGregor's lawyer stood, stalked around the room as though he was offended at having to appear.

"We would like, on the outset, that that thing…" He pointed to the poster, "be removed from the courtroom. It's a distraction and such theatrics have nothing to do with this hearing."

Palmer rose, "If Mr. Zarlingo thinks that it has no bearing on the case, then what's his complaint?"

"Sit down, Mr. Palmer."

Judge Byrnes turned to the litigant. "Well, Mr. Zarlingo. What is your specific objection?"

"It could unfavorably prejudice the court."

"How so?"

"The spectacle of a serviceman may possibly arouse unwarranted sympathies."

The judge cut him off, and asked Palmer, "What's the purpose of this?"

Palmer stood. "Your honor, my co-client can't appear in person. It seems reasonable that the court should have some idea about who he is and what he looks like. I cannot find any rule that disallows this sort of exposition, and besides, he is a hero of the D-Day invasion. If the visual image of an American officer offends anyone, then it seems to me our priorities are a little out of whack."

The justice turned to confer with the other two justices. Presently, he announced, "We'll allow it. Proceed with your opening statement, Mr. Zarlingo."

Zarlingo was visibly upset.

"We feel we are unnecessarily conscripted having to argue a case that has absolutely no legitimacy. We have therefore, filed a petition to end this charade and rule in our favor."

"Duly noted. We have denied the appeal on the basis of the plaintiff's challenge that there may indeed, be extenuating circumstances, Mr. Zarlingo. Proceed with your case."

Zarlingo's eyes burned. "The law is the law, your honor. Mr. MacGregor made an offer in good faith and Mr. McCullum accepted it. He not only accepted it, but he signed a binding agreement, and received a check of two hundred dollars' earnest money. This is an open and shut case, and the letter of the law needs to be upheld."

Zarlingo waved his arms in animated frustration.

"I've been practicing law a long time, and I'm at a loss for a justification in this case. There isn't an argument—none whatsoever! I consider this exercise a gross waste of my time, my client's time and the court's time. The defense asks that you do the obvious and terminate this proceeding at once."

Zarlingo returned to his chair.

Palmer smirked inwardly. He was aware of Zarlingo's reputation and political clout with the Denver Mafia, but this small town lawyer realized it was chancy to insult a district judge, under any circumstance. Al Zarlingo had just offended three at one sitting.

"Your request is denied, Mr. Zarlingo. Mr. Palmer, are you ready to present your case?"

Palmer rose, ran his thumbs around the inside belt of his ample waist. He relaxed, even smiled. He sucked in a voluminous breath and exhaled.

"I've practiced law for some time myself; perhaps not as long as my esteemed opponent, but I can tell you this for certain. I know when I've got a problem... and I've got one. It's these times I'm glad I'm not a judge."

He glanced up at the judges, formidable in their robes and imposing presence.

"My opponent is absolutely right! It is, as we say in the business, a prima facie case."

He glanced over at Zarlingo who was wearing an expression on contented shock. Zarlingo delighted at this unexpected path Palmer was taking. Surely, there should be no need to object.

"It's an open and shut case on the surface. Wilbur McCullum did sign a binding agreement. And Wilbur McCullum did accept a check. He never cashed it, he never even endorsed it, but, all the same, he accepted it. And though Wilbur McCullum wished he hadn't, he did all these things. After thinking about it, he wished he could take it all back, that he could have given Sam Hubbard the opportunity to buy his farm instead. Wilbur McCullum is a nice old guy. He's a great old guy. He doesn't have an enemy in the country, but just like all of us, he makes a mistake now and again. And you really can't blame Wilbur, because Sam Hubbard was away in a strange land risking his life protecting things that most folks around here consider valuable."

Once again, Palmer paused, strolled around the room, hooking his thumbs in his belt line. "Now, I ask you this. Does Wilbur McCullum get just one strike? One strike and you're out? Should the MacGregor family be given more land? They already have over thirty thousand acres. These robber barons have no more conscience than a cormorant in their ravenous quest to satisfy their gluttony!"

Palmer's statement was ill advised and unfortunate. He regretted it instantly.

Zarlingo rose. "Objection! This verbal attack is vengeful and undeserved! The existence of the MacGregor ranch has no relevance in any manner to this contest! The counselor should be censored!"

"Sustained. Be careful with what you say, Mr. Palmer."

"My error, your honor. I do apologize for that. However, let's look at the situation as it exists. My opponent wants you to think this transaction is a done deal. Well, it's not. Nothing has changed hands. As a general rule, a deal is made when 'constructive receipt' has taken place. That, in layman's language, is, if you want something of mine, you pay me for it and I release it to you. Now, it's yours, because I have your money and you have your whatever was mine. That's 'constructive receipt,' and it's that simple. Well, that hasn't happened here. Nothing has been released and nothing has been received."

Zarlingo sprang to his feet. "Objection! Quite to the contrary! A contract has been given and money has been accepted. I demand that statement be stricken from the plea!"

"Overruled. We'll allow it for the moment. Proceed with your contention, Mr. Palmer."

Palmer began again. "We concede that an initial transaction was arranged. But is a verbal ascension and a written response binding under these circumstances? I say no, since Wilbur McCullum clearly wanted to abrogate this transaction before anything was consummated. He asked to get out of the contract and was refused. Remember, the all-important 'constructive receipt' test had not been satisfied. Wilbur had not cashed the check and MacGregor had not invaded the property."

Palmer turned to the judges, pleading.

"We have to have the latitude of changing our minds from time to time. Good God! Just imagine what life would be like if we had to adhere to every piddling decision we made? We make a zillion choices every day! That's what separates primates from the rest of the animal kingdom!"

He turned facing the courtroom, adding, "Whether some of us primates practice this empowerment is another matter."

Chuckles rumbled throughout the courtroom.

Palmer walked over to his table and took a drink of water.

"There are, indeed, extenuating circumstances at work here. In my way of thinking, Sam Hubbard should be given a chance to buy that land. He's surely earned it. As a matter of fact, at this time, our government is underwriting that opportunity as reward for his heroic efforts. And Wilbur McCullum should be given a chance to change his mind. In support of this contention, I'd like to read something to you."

Palmer strode over to his table, removed a letter from his file, and unfolded it. He scanned the courtroom, then the judges. "This is a letter from Lieutenant Hubbard to his parents. I'll read it verbatim." Out of the corner of his eye, Palmer saw Zarlingo begin to squirm. Palmer began reading. "Lippstadt, Germany. March 24, 1945. Dear Folks, I have to tell you that I was pretty down in the dumps when I received your letter. It sort of makes me wonder why I'm over here fighting these people who have been trying to take what we have, while the same kind of thing is taking place back home. Is that my purpose here? To keep the Germans from stealing our land so that Chattman MacGregor can take it? I'm here risking my neck and can't do a thing about it. It only seems fair that I should have a shot to compete for a piece of America..."

Palmer stopped reading and looked up

"I think you get the lieutenant's point, and who can disagree with him?" He focused on the audience.

"How in good conscience can we deny Sam Hubbard the opportunity to buy this farm? Mr. Zarlingo talks about an open and shut case. Well, I got myself in trouble a few moments ago when I questioned his ethics, so I don't think I'd better."

"Objection!" Zarlingo exploded, charging the bench. "Apparently this John Doe intends to engage in character assassination, so why doesn't he just come out and tell us what's on his mind?"

The presiding justice was flabbergasted.

"This is highly unusual. Does counsel for the plaintiff care to respond?"

Palmer turned, facing the court and announced, "If this *'John Doe'* fails to be intimidated by an adversary who is an express coward, and by his counsel who makes a living defending a family organization that operates outside the law, you'll have to forgive me."

Immediately, the courtroom erupted in an uncontrollable hostility. The emotion of the crowd reached a crescendo in support of Palmer's little speech, and the bailiffs repeated hammering on the bench did nothing to restore order.

The justices convened. Shortly, they waved the two attorneys to the bench.

After a brief discussion, the two attorneys went their separate ways. Zarlingo wore a vicious scowl while Palmer appeared relieved. Subdued quiet followed as the bailiff approached his bench. He rapped heavily on the surface.

"The judges have determined a mistrial," he announced. "These proceedings are closed. You can all go home."

Cheers rang throughout the courtroom.

Palmer returned to his table, mumbling, "It's not what I anticipated, but I'll take it."

"What happened there?" Walter asked.

"It's a mistrial. Didn't you hear the bailiff?"

"Yeah, I heard him, but what's it mean?"

Palmer collected his satchel and briefcase and headed for the exit. "A mistrial cancels all litigation."

Walter was frustrated. "Goddammit, Royce! Talk so I can understand you! What does that mean for Sam?"

"Means he gets his farm," Palmer returned.

The next morning in Reiss's creamery Walter and Marshall were discussing the trial.

"Well, I can tell you this, Walt. You've got a real ally in Royce Palmer. It takes balls to do what he did."

"There's absolutely no doubtin' that, Marsh."

****

CLARK FIELD THE PHILIPPINES
May 3, 1945

One of the hangers on Clark had been renovated into a large administration building. Phil Olson had set up his operation in one section, and after a short time he had gotten the information on the legendary doctor he intended to interview. His name was Harold Hoffmeister, one of seven Marine surgeons to have attained the rank of brigadier general. Hoffmeister had run the hospital at Fort Stotsenburg early in the war, before escaping to Australia with MacArthur when the Japanese overran the island in April, 1942. Now, with the re-capture of Luzon, Hoffmeister was back at his old station, busy renovating the place to accommodate the American wounded.

Dusk had settled on the island, and Olson entered the yawning lobby of the stone edifice. Approaching a young doctor, he asked where he could find Hoffmeister's office. He was told, but was advised that the old officer was crusty, busy, and not particularly receptive to correspondents. Olson had tolerated that stigma throughout the war, so it presented nothing more than a simple annoyance.

"Does he have a preference for drink?" Olson asked.

"Schnapps," was the curt reply.

Olson made the quick detour to the officer's club and purchased, what he was assured by the bartender, the surgeon's libation.

Olson stood at the open door, eyeing a graying figure behind his desk. The lamp, inadequate for the large room, gave little detail of Olson's subject. A cursory appraisal indicated to Olson that the individual was quite tall and appeared to be too old for military service. Upon closer inspection, Olson could see that the man's uniform indicated no rank or insignia. He saw the man's crew cut, and his thick glasses reflecting from the white light of the fluorescent table lamp. His mouth made the posture of a whistle, except that his mouth was too open to whistle.

Olson held up the bottle, breaking the silence, "Schnapps?"

At first, the man seemed not to hear, as he continued studying his paper, but slowly glanced up.

"Who the hell are you?" His tone was not angry, just tired.

"Phil Olson. I'm a correspondent."

"Did you have an appointment?"

"Correspondents are sort of like insurance salesmen. We're better off not to announce our arrival. We stand a better chance sneaking up on you."

Hoffmeister chuckled. "Well, that's a new one. You must have heard about my love for reporters."

"I did, but we get this sort of thing all the time. If we had to give shots too, we'd really be popular."

Hoffmeister laughed aloud. "Okay. I'll have a drink with you. What's your name?"

"Phil Olson. Where are your glasses?"

Hoffmeister motioned to the window. "Over there on the window sill."

Olson glanced at the ledge, and frowned. "Those are specimen bottles."

"They are? Well, I'll be damned! How careless of me!"

"You use those?"

"Did you come in here to question my sanitation practices, or did you come in here to have a drink?"

Olson stumped over to the window and gathered two urine specimen containers. He set them on the surgeon's desk, and filled them.

"This'll probably come as a shock to you, Olson, but the inside of that glass is a hell of a lot cleaner than what's inside your mouth."

"Sorry, Sir."

"And don't call me sir. We're like you guys. We don't need that."

Olson reached over, touched Hoffmeister's small container and downed the contents. Hoffmeister did the same.

477

"See that wasn't so bad," the general said, whereupon, Olson did a refill.

"Where'd you get the gimp?" Hoffmeister asked.

"I'm supposed to be here to interview you."

Hoffmeister was taking a liking to the reporter, answering, "You'll have your chance. Now what happened?"

"I got hurt."

"I can see that! Where?"

Olson hesitated. "It was on Tarawa."

"How'd that happen?"

"I was covering a landing, and got a little close to a grenade."

Hoffmeister rocked back pausing. "You're not that reporter that saved that young marine by knocking him away from a grenade?"

Olson exhaled, "That's what they tell me."

"You lost a kidney in the process, if I recall, right?"

"I did."

Hoffmeister softened. "I'll let you in on something, kid. I'm a Marine first, and a doctor second. I read about that incident and I'm damn-well impressed. Come 'ere. Let's let me examine that hip."

Olson stumbled over and the doctor took him by the waist. He began manipulating the hip while holding his ear to the joint.

"Ah, crepitation in the acetabulum. And you've got a real messed up joint here. We better get that fixed."

"I was told I was going to have a bad hip for the rest my life."

"Ah, naw. That area's bad, but we can make it right. I'm surprised you can get around at all."

"What can you do?"

"It'll take a bone graft."

"Bone graft? I've heard of a skin graft, but…"

"We're doin' bone grafts nowadays."

"Where do you get the bone?"

"Probably off your shin. Without getting too technical," the old doctor drawled, "the hole in your hip where your leg goes into is chipped all to hell, and we have to patch it up. Smooth it out. Sorta like puttying up a hub so the axle can move freely."

"Jesus, when did they start that?"

"Not everything's bad about war. Are you up to an operation?"

"Hell, yes." Olson responded, adding, "but can I do what I came here to do?"

"Hell, yes, yourself," Hoffmeister answered. "But pour me another drink first."

Olson refilled the glasses, picking up his tablet and pen. "Okay, Doc. Start at the beginning."

Hoffmeister described his early career, leading up to his experience in Luzon.

"We were setting up this very same hospital. I was in charge, and things were changing by the day. The Japs were making a lot of noise, and we knew they were coming. About then, we had a slug of Marines dumped on us. We didn't expect them, and had little room for them. One kid, and I'll never forget him, a persistent young Marine corpsman, came in and went to work for me. He hung around with me in the operating rooms, and before long, I let him, much to the chagrin of my colleagues, cut on a few people. It turned out to be a lucky thing. He learned fast and became a damned good surgeon in short order. A day after the Japs bombed Pearl Harbor, they came over here and bombed us. We found ourselves in the middle of a first-class war. Conditions in the hospital were in chaos. All of a damn sudden, I collapsed from an appendicitis attack. I knew I had a problem, but with everything happening, I just lost control of it. I was crumpled up in a corner, and while all that crap was goin' on, that same corpsman that I had taken under my wing—smarter 'n hell and as tall as me..."

Hoffmeister paused taking another swig of his Schnapps and Olson felt his skin start to crawl.

"...grabbed another corpsman, laid me on a gurney and took out my appendix! Otherwise, I would have died then and there. I will never forget that young man. God! What a talented kid! —played a hell of a guitar."

"I was told he made a lieutenant," Olson breathed.

"*WHAT?*"

"It's Andy Hubbard."

"You knew him?"

"I *know* him."

"Jesus Christ! How?"

"His ghost has been following me all across the Pacific."

"He's still alive?"

"Yes. He's a POW in Tokyo."

"He got nailed on Bataan. I knew he had no chance. But how did you meet him?"

"Actually, I met his girlfriend, first."

"Oh yes. A pretty thing as I recall. He showed me pictures of her."

"Pretty! That's an understatement! She turned down a date with Clark Gable when we were in D.C."

Hoffmeister lay back in his chair, sighing, "You'll have to tell me about that one sometime. God! What the hell's the reason for all of this? You come in here bothering me, and in the process, tell me about a young lad I've never been able to get out of my mind."

"Since you're going to saw on me, Doc, I can tell you a few more things about him and this war—like why you got that batch of Marines you didn't expect, and why he got there in the first place."

"Really?"

"Yes, really."

"Okay, Olson," the doctor muttered while refilling his glass. "Start talking."

FIFTH MARINE AMPHIBIOUS CORPS
GUAM
March 20, 1945

The venue was the airdrome of the former Sumay Naval Airbase that had belonged to the Japanese before it was captured by 2nd Marine Division in late July, 1944. Since that time, the island, because of its location and size, had become a valuable center for military training and airborne operations.

Colonel Rusty Atkins was addressing 1200 troops of the 77th Marine Division, a green regiment scheduled to go ashore on the island of Okinawa, Easter Sunday, 1945.

He approached the podium, amid a thunderous ovation. The popular young colonel waited for the applause to abate and began.

"I was just thinking how time flies in this business." As was his habit, Atkins would begin, and then pause, as though he forgot what he had to say. He scanned the large group and a slight smile came to his lips.

"In Melbourne back in the summer of '42, we had a situation very similar to the one we have here. It seems like yesterday. I was addressing a garrison of young soldiers, and like you, they had not yet felt the sting of battle. I, as a young company commander, was expounding my philosophies about what to do when we would soon find ourselves in a desperate situation. I imparted all the secrets I had been taught or been told. How to conduct ourselves when we we're being shot at. I told them how to protect themselves. How and when to advance. I told them all kinds of little hints and secrets, real or imagined, that would give them an edge. I even characterized the enemy as evil and sub human, and if their leader was killed he had no direction and would become completely disorganized. I explained to them that we were destined to win because we were smarter and better fighters and we would not accept defeat. I filled them full of all the *bullshit* I could dream up, because I wanted them to fight hard. Guess what? I found out afterwards I only had to do half that. They needed to learn the techniques, but Marines sure as hell don't need any prodding! They don't need to be told that they have to fight!"

A deafening ovation drowned out Rusty's last words.

"We were on our way to Guadalcanal, and if you remember, we kicked the Jap's asses."

More applause.

"I wasn't much older than my guys then, but they didn't know it, because I had brass on my shoulders."

Atkins walked over to a table, took a drink of water, and returned to the microphone.

"After that, it was Tarawa, Kwajalein, and Iwo. Now, we've got one more, and hopefully, that oughta' do it. I can't image they're stupid enough to let us invade their home islands; a lot of guys do. I don't. But," he added philosophically, "if we have to we will."

The comment brought a rumble through the ranks.

"Things are changing now and I want to discuss them with you. The first thing is the enemy. In our first encounters, they were arrogant and condescending. They thought all we ever did was lie around drinking and fucking. They believed they were incapable of losing. Well we broke them of all that."

Laughter interrupted the speaker.

"...and you'd think it would make things easier, but that's not necessarily the case. The majority of the old guard is dead now and the younger bunch doesn't have much confidence. In fact, they're scared shitless of us. And why shouldn't they be? They haven't won a significant battle since the first few months of the war. Now they know their homeland is in jeopardy. They've been told that we're going to kill them all, so they'll most likely fight to the last man because there's no reason for them not to.

"Next, let's talk about our leadership. There are about thirty guys in this regiment acting in cadre capacities who served in those battles I mentioned earlier. That's a real benefit to you, so pay attention to them when the bullets start flying. What they know will save your necks."

Once again, Rusty went to the water glass.

"Lastly, all the elements for success favor us. Our ordnance, in all phases, has become vastly superior. Our strength in numbers is undeniable. Indications are that this war should be over soon. The only real enemy we have is ourselves. Two things affect that. They are overconfidence and under commitment. We know our chances of survival are much greater now than they were when we left Melbourne for Guadalcanal. That, in itself, can be detrimental to your surviving though, because you can get a little too careful. Be assured our chances are in your favor when you're on the move. Be aggressive. I know you will. In the words of General George Patton, 'nobody ever became a hero dying for his country. He became a hero for making that other dumb bastard...' Well, you know the rest. Go get 'em and remember and honor the credo that binds us all as brothers, SEMPER FI!"

The audience responded with a thunderous, "SEMPER FI!"

Aboard the battleship CALIFORNIA
March 29, 1945

The oiler Wassau, tethered to the giant resurrected warship, bobbed in the heavy waters, while supplying fuel, groceries, medical supplies and other items. On a return boat line, a canvas mail basket contained the final opportunity for invasion-bound soldiers to communicate with the outside world. One such piece of correspondence was a letter from Rusty Atkins to his wife Sally, addressed to the United Service Organization, Mindenhall, England.

Dear Sally,

Enjoyed your note, and am happy to hear the Limeys like your singing as much as we do. Guess you see they kicked me up a grade. Apparently the best way to get promoted is to stay as far back from the action as you can. That's not entirely true, and I've realized the value of having an overall view of hostilities in order to direct traffic. Still, there's that pang of guilt not being up there with your guys. We expect this battle to be a last-ditch effort on the Jap's part. Keep up the good work. It's as important as carrying a gun. I can tell you that first hand.

Will get back to you as soon as conditions allow.

Love, Rusty

Sally smiled knowing her husband intended that the statement be taken as a compliment.

CHAPTER 46

AOMORI BASE POW CAMP
TOKYO, JAPAN
APRIL 10, 1945

It was midnight and quiet in the barracks. Andy turned on the knob and watched as the amber glow of the vacuum cathode tube, faint at first, grew bright. Abruptly, faint static broke the stillness of the stark quarters. Andy anticipated this and set a low volume control. He experimented with the frequency dial until he found a clear channel. Carefully, he advanced the amplifier. Bob Armstrong crouched silently behind him. Andy took the mike, one originally designed for the AM-6 Zero fighter, and began speaking softly and succinctly.

"This is Lieutenant Andrew W. Hubbard in Tokyo. I say hello to my mother Mildred, father Walter, brother Sam, sister Ruth, and to Andrea. I sit here in my spacious room and I love it here. I live for the wonderful time when you and the Japanese people will learn harmony. It has never made sense why we die foolishly and unnecessarily. Our food here is not a problem. There is no thought of starvation. We can find food everywhere. My friend in camp, Bob Armstrong, and I appreciate the fair way we are treated. Bob Snavely is here but not with us always. The good people here are people I appreciate. It is a wonder to me often just how we are treated so well. Rusty Atkins would really have it made if he could be out here with us. Our friends here are so far above what the world considers. Regular and often we are going to church. We pray that for always and forever that those of us can become friends. The need for peace is the food of all mankind. I still wish I could possibly have the unreachable yet so precious ability to weld the silver and gold Japanese-American memento together so that no goodbye would ever be a need. This is the very sustenance of a world that's starving for peace. Please work to the very end, even death, to bring tranquility as soon as possible. Andrew Hubbard signing off."

Andy shut the switch off.

"Think anybody heard it, Andy?" Armstrong asked.

"Oh, sure, Bob. It was heard all right. Now we'll just have to wait and see what happens."

The two emaciated men lay down on their bunks, hoping some good may come from the broadcast.

Andy's transmission hit the United States as a shock wave. On April 11, five o'clock in the afternoon the next day, Los Angeles radio KICX picked up the message, and made the first recording. In reality, the broadcast had been received immediately.

Andrea's phone rang in her apartment at 8:15 PM. It was her boss.

"Jim Whalen, Andrea. Glad I caught you. You need to get down here to the office right now."

"What is it, Chief?" she asked. Andrea had the phone cradled in a towel. Whalen's call came just as she was heading for the shower.

"Your man, Andy Hubbard just made a transcontinental broadcast."

She felt the room spin.

"What?" she asked, standing naked, struggling to maintain her balance.

"KICX in Los Angeles just picked it up. I'm going to record it and should have it by the time you get here."

Andrea hurriedly dressed and ran to her Olds coupe parked behind her apartment. Her mind became a maelstrom of reflections as she sped to her office.

The dimly-lit garage was empty except for a vehicle scattered here and there belonging to someone working late, or extending the working day in some nearby tavern.

She rushed through the empty lobby grabbing the nearest elevator. The travel to the twenty-first floor was taking an unusually long time. She would look for her boss in the transcribing section; not in his office.

485

Andrea rushed in and quickly located Whalen who was standing with his back to her, bent over the short-wave recorder. She was startled when she identified the voice she hadn't heard for what seemed to her a lifetime. Rushing forward, she laid her arm on his shoulder, exclaiming, "It's him! It's *him!*"

She felt tears streaming down her cheeks while straining to grasp his words to the end.

Then, she broke into a convulsive sob.

Whalen supported her, offering no interruption until she composed herself.

"That's your man?" he asked tenderly.

"Yes," she answered. "When did he make this broadcast, Jim?"

He searched her anxious expression. "Why... why he just made it."

"You mean just now?"

Whalen was confused. He looked at his watch.

"He made it in the last hour."

"So he still alive?"

"Well, of course he is."

"Oh Jim! Can we play it back?"

After two playbacks, agonizing for Andrea, Whalen grumbled, "It's a hell of a note to use a prisoner of war like that, Andrea."

Andrea tilted her head, remarking absently, "There's something strange about that, Jim."

"There's nothing new about using a prisoner of war as a propaganda pawn."

"Get me a copy of that tape, Jim."

"I intended to. I'll also get you a print-out and have a record made."

"He made that broadcast on his own."

"What makes you think that?"

"I don't know. There's a message in there, somewhere..."

"You just listened to the message—twice!"

"I'm aware of that. But I know him, Jim. You don't. Let me study the tape."

Suddenly, Andrea began crying again and laid her head on Whalen's chest.

"I love him so much, Jim! To think that message was made less than an hour ago. Andy made it! I can feel him! I can almost touch him!"

"Take it easy, Andrea," he consoled. "Let's go get something to eat. You haven't eaten, have you?"

"No. That's very thoughtful. I'd like that."

That night, Andrea sat at her desk in her apartment, continuing to study the transcript. It was 2 AM It was no use. She would go to bed. What Andy was saying, she couldn't decipher, but was convinced that there was another message someplace. In her semi-conscious state, the riddle was becoming clear. Suddenly it came to her! She recalled the ride on the Greyhound bus when they went to Denver to see a movie. The conversation started rolling over and over in Andrea's mind as she pictured herself cradled in Andy's arms, her head resting on his chest.

"You did hear I Love a Mystery last night?"
"Yes, darling," she answered as she nuzzled Andy's ear.
"That was pretty slick about that message... every eighth word."
"Maybe you and I should have our own secret code, honey."
"Okay, Andrea. Our code will be every fifth word."

Andrea sprang out of bed, fumbling for the wall switch. She then rushed back to her study and snapped on the florescent table lamp. She hastily took the transcript from her drawer, and reached for a pencil.

"Okay. Every fifth word," she said quietly to herself.

"This is Lieutenant Andrew W. Hubbard in Tokyo. I say hello to mother Mildred, father Walter, brother Sam, Sister Ruth, and to Andrea." Andrea underlined Hubbard, hello, Sam.

"No, that's not it. It should say 'Hubbard, hello, Andrea.'"

"I'm just starting in the wrong place. I'll start at the message," she said audibly.

"<u>Andrea</u> I sit here in <u>my</u> spacious room and I <u>love</u> it here. I live <u>for</u> the wonderful time when <u>you</u> and the Japanese people <u>will</u> learn harmony. It has <u>never</u> made sense why we <u>die</u> foolishly and unnecessarily."

Andrea re-read the underlined words: "Andrea my love for you will never die."

"Oh, my darling," she sobbed as she read on.

"Our <u>food</u> here is not a <u>problem</u>. There's no thought of <u>starvation</u>. We can find food <u>everywhere</u>."

"Oh, you poor, poor man," she cried aloud.

"My friend in camp, <u>Bob Armstrong</u> and I appreciate the <u>fair</u> way we are treated. <u>Bob Snavely</u> is here but is <u>not</u> with us always. The <u>good</u> people are people <u>I</u> appreciate. It is a <u>wonder</u> to me often just <u>how</u> we are treated so well. <u>Rusty Atkins</u> would really have <u>made</u> it if he could be <u>out</u> here with us."

"I know he made it fine, darling," Andrea sobbed. "I only wish you could have been as lucky."

"Our <u>friends</u> here are so <u>above</u> what the world considers. <u>Regularly</u> and often we are <u>now</u> going to church."

"Friends above regularly now... friends above regularly now... I don't get it... aha! Bombers over Tokyo!" Andrea blurted

"We <u>pray</u> that for always and <u>for</u> forever that those of <u>us</u> can become friends."

"Pray for us," Andrea read.

"The <u>need</u> for peace is the <u>food</u> for all mankind."

"You poor baby. If only you could have all the food in this house right now," Andrea murmured.

"I <u>still</u> wish I could possibly <u>have</u> the unreachable, yet so <u>precious</u> ability to weld the <u>silver</u> and gold Japanese-American <u>memento</u> together so..."

Andrea completely lost her composure at the last clue. She fingered her heart necklace as she sobbed, before gathering her emotions.

"...that no <u>goodbye</u> would ever be a <u>need</u>. This is the very <u>sustenance</u> of a world that's <u>starving</u> for peace. Please work <u>to</u> the very end, even <u>death</u> to bring tranquility as <u>soon</u> as possible."

"Oh my God!" Andrea gasped and began crying out of control. She wanted to run, but to where? She was alone. Nothing could change that. Morning couldn't come soon enough. There were many people she needed to talk to.

By the next morning, the impact of Andy's radio broadcast had begun its tsunami effect. News of the transmission spread like brush fires from islands in the Pacific to groups and individuals across the United States; military and civilian alike.

Andrea's paper broke the story about the broadcast, but she purposefully withheld the secret in the surreptitious message for fear of reprisal from Andy's captors. She desperately wanted to tell certain people about the event, but there were complications. First, Phil Olson needed to be told, but she didn't yet know how to reach him. She knew he had covered the MacArthur landing, but he'd moved on after that, and she didn't know to where. She needed to reach Rusty Atkins. One of her latent intentions had been to get in touch with him, since both Andy and Phil were such close friends. Plus, Andy had mentioned Atkins in his message. She felt, in a way, she knew him. But she couldn't reach Olson and didn't know how to contact Atkins. Finally, she wanted to visit with Millie Hubbard. The problem was that Millie didn't have a telephone. Andrea had tolerated that for years. She'd write occasionally, but when something important like this came up, she had no way to get a message to Millie in a hurry.

As it turned out, Andrea's concerns were unwarranted. Harold Hoffmeister, in Luzon heard the transmission on Armed Forces Radio. He immediately recognized the young man he had so agonized over, and since his hip surgery patient also knew Andy Hubbard, Philip Olson was also informed. Frank Canali aboard the California, received the teletype coverage from Associated Press, and remembering Hubbard from basic training, radioed Rusty on shore. Across the US, hundreds of people owning short wave radios picked up the broadcast and sent so many letters, Milo Rittenhaus had to carry them to the Hubbard farm in a peach basket. One enterprising ham radio owner made a record of Andy's talk and mailed the disc. The Hubbards were unable to play it back because they didn't own a record player. Royce Palmer offered to make his Victrola available.

AOMORI PRISON CAMP
APRIL 12, 1945

Ikeya was waiting at the gate for Andy when he came home from work. The young Japanese guard was sullen. "Perhaps I search you after this."

"Hope I didn't get you in trouble."

489

"Oh, I in trouble all right, but maybe not too bad. But you disgrace me. You fool me. Anyhow, you get to meet the commandant." Ikeya gave Andy a shove. "Follow me."

Andy was led into a small office. Glancing around, he noticed discarded sake bottles and among two chairs, there was a yellow canvas covered rattan couch—the same-type canvas Snavely always wore as puttees when Andy saw him. He was met at the door by a pasty-faced diminutive officer.

"You're an extremely clever man, Hubbard," he said in perfect English.

Andy didn't respond.

"You made my guard here look rather stupid. Why did you make that broadcast?"

"Because I want our peoples to end this conflict and cohabitate this earth peacefully. We've had enough war."

The officer looked suspiciously at Andy for a few seconds. "I quite agree, but things must run their course. I don't like the war any better than you."

"I hope my broadcast has not caused you undue concern, Sir," Andy paraded.

"Quite to the contrary, Hubbard. You have done me a service. Your broadcast reached your homeland."

It did! Andy thought.

"And I'm not upset with your message. As a matter fact, I think it was an honorable thing to do, even though your means of transmission were dishonorable. We're thinking, however, of having you make regular transmissions for us."

"I'd be honored doing that, but you'd be better off passing it around."

The commander scowled. "Why do you say that?"

"A message like mine has less authenticity if the same American gives it repeatedly."

"I see, Hubbard. That's a very intuitive statement and you're quite unselfish."

Andy knew the chance of discovering the code in his initial message was slim but would increase significantly should he give any more broadcasts. Besides, his conscience wouldn't allow him to give a broadcast for the purposes they wanted.

The commandant spoke harshly in Japanese to Ikeya and waved the two out of his room. Since he hadn't angered the commandant, he'd give it a try "Is there any possibility I could get something to eat?"

"I'm sorry Hubbard. I genuinely am. We have a certain amount of food that is distributed to us and that is all we get."

"Wish I could just a little bit of what Snavely's getting," Andy thought.

The radio had been ripped out. Andy and Armstrong sat on the bunk. After Andy had answered Armstrong's questions about the visit to the commandant, Andy considered, "Bob. I've been thinking about it. We handled that radio thing all wrong."

"Why do you think that?"

"We'd been better off keeping it here and listening to what was going on outside."

"It's too late now, but it'd be nice to hear what's going on out there."

"I know. Those big silver airplanes aren't theirs."

"I agree, Andy."

"I just hope I can hold out. I'm getting awfully weak."

Armstrong patted him on the shoulder. "Don't even think like that, Andy."

STOTSENBURG HOSPITAL, LUZON
APRIL 13, 1945

Olson was out of bed, and with the aid of an orderly and a cane, made his way to General Hoffmeister's office. Olson gingerly sat on a wide-frame chair.

"So how's it feelin'?" Hoffmeister asked.

"I'm smarting, that's for sure, but it doesn't hurt hardly at all down there where it did when I moved it before."

Hoffmeister smiled broadly. "That's exactly the thing I wanted to hear. I'm pleased with the operation. The X-rays looked like we did OK. By the way," he said settling into a chair, "that broadcast of Hubbard's was pretty tough to listen to, wasn't it?"

Olson massaged his lips before responding. He hadn't had an opportunity to discuss it with Hoffmeister since the transcript was brought to him. "It was. There's something really weird about it, though, and I can't put my finger on it."

"Nothin' weird about it at all!" Hoffmeister barked, "They bribed him. That's obvious. They probably gave him a piece of meat or a hunk of bread."

"No... I don't think so..."

"You don't think so? I can see you've never been real hungry kid."

"You're right. I haven't, but I don't want to talk about that. I have to talk to you about something else, Doc."

"What's that?"

"I've been out of action, and I need to get back to work. Any chance I can rent an office someplace from you?"

Hoffmeister paused scratching the grey stubble on his chin. "Oh, I guess I might if you sport me with a Schnapps now and again."

"Smells of extortion to me."

"Take it or leave it."

"I'll take it."

OKINAWA
APRIL 4, 1945

Heavy offshore bombardment from Admiral Spruance and Mitcher's battleship fleet continued pounding the island, while the Marine 77th division and the Army 27th and 96th divisions amassed inland. Curiously, the landing forces met with no resistance from the dug in Japanese. Rusty Atkins took advantage of the absence of hostilities and visited Frank Canali aboard the California.

Canali showed Rusty the teletype. After reading it, Rusty murmured, "That's a strange one. Wonder what he was tryin' to say?"

"What do you mean? He was put up to it. No one knows whether they bribed him or tortured him, but the message is pretty clear."

"So what's the message?"

Canali wiped his forehead peremptorily, and let fall, "Its propaganda. They're just trying to make it look like, to anyone who'll listen, that they don't mistreat prisoners."

"Well, you're wrong. That's not what it's about. I wish I knew how to get in touch with Phil Olson. I'd like to get his take on it. There's more to that than what you think, Frank."

"I can't imagine what it could be, but it'd be a lot easier for Olson to get in touch with you than you getting in touch with him. He knows our corps and division, and the direction we're headed. God knows where *he* is."

Members around the community gathered in Palmer's basement to listen to the record that was sent to the Hubbard family.

Millie rejoiced at his words. When the crowd eventually dispersed, Marshall Reiss, Walter Hubbard, and Royce Palmer remained downstairs.

Palmer exhaled before speaking. "You know your kid a lot better than I do, Walt, but that wasn't a happy message in there. Millie's not getting it."

"I already figured that out, Royce."

"Well, I wouldn't want to tell you about how to run your business, Walt, but I'd think you'd better, as they say 'leave sleeping dogs lie'."

"Royce's right, Walt," Reiss put in. "You'd just better let Millie think what she wants to think."

Walter turned to leave, nodding affirmatively, and murmuring, "Yep."

USS CALIFORNIA
Officer's stateroom
April 13, 1945

Rusty examined the UPI cablegram containing the return address, Washington Post Dispatch, Andrea Vogel, Senior Editor.

"Dear Colonel Atkins," the message began, "I took the liberty of contacting General George Morrison to obtain your whereabouts."

"God! She must be pretty important!" Rusty chirped.

"I feel as I should know you, because Andy, and later on Phil Olson has had so much to say about you. I'm working on the assumption that by now, you've read Andy's broadcast. I don't know if you questioned the contents of that message. In any case, I feel compelled to tell you what it's about."

Andrea explained the code they'd worked out, years back, and how to decipher it. In ending the letter, she explained, "I've wanted to tell Phil all this but I don't know where he is. He went to the Philippines, and I assume he's still there. If you can track him down, let him know that someone's worried about him. If you should ever have time, drop me a line. I would greatly appreciate hearing from you. Andrea Vogel."

UNION STATION
DENVER
MAY 15, 1945

The strapping be-medaled first Lieutenant tripped down the steps of the swanky half-empty Union Pacific Railroad Spirit of San Francisco Pullman car, into the waiting arms of his mother. Surrender papers were signed a week earlier, giving instant freedom to a great multitude of troops serving in the European Theater. Their duties ended when the war ended. Military planners had anticipated that when the armistice came, friendly neighborhoods could accommodate the soldier's presence much more readily than war-torn regions, so they were simply given their separation papers and sent home. Troop trains in large numbers were leaving the harbors of New York, Roanoke and Fort Dix, disgorging servicemen to all parts of the United States. The armed conflict in the Pacific had not yet concluded, so there were no trains from Fort Lewis, San Francisco, or Bremerton heading east. The battle for Okinawa was still raging. The capitulation of Japan would take another three months.

Walter, Mildred, Sam and Ruth headed back across the flat prairie to their farm that warm spring morning. Mildred was guardedly happy, Walter was ecstatic and Ruth was in a swoon. The ride was comfortable in Walter's 1940 Pontiac sedan. Purchasing a car, particularly a late model, was next to impossible, in the war years. The death of an elderly farmer presented the opportunity, so with the help of Millie's school money and the sale of a few cows, the Hubbard family was able to equip themselves with better than decent transportation. The talk was easy and cheerful, and no mention was made about the McCullum property. Walter was saving that for later.

Mildred cooked dinner, and while the conversation was animated, Sam wanted to get out and go over the farm. That was okay with Mildred if the two men intended to spend the afternoon together talking farm, and certainly what Walter had planned, but Ruth let it be known that she wanted to be in on the afternoon. Walter preferred to be alone with his son since some of the conversation wouldn't include her; in fact, some of the conversation shouldn't include her. Sam understood his sister's disappointment and insisted she be along. That was okay with Walter, but adding to the contretemps, he insisted Sam wear his uniform. Sam mildly protested, since he felt wearing his uniform would be awkward. Still Walter insisted. Walter had his reasons.

The first thing for Sam was to see was the tractor, which he mounted and drove, gushing afterward about the magnificence of the machine. Then, in the '37 Chevy pickup, the tour of the farm began, with Ruthie happily sitting in the middle. After they had bounced around the original homestead and the Reiss farm, Walter headed away from the farmhouse. Sam quickly reminded him of that, wherein, Walter merely grinned. Sam quickly realized there was some ruse, commenting, "You're not telling me something."

Ruth glanced up at her father. "Can I tell him, Daddy?"

"You can tell him, Ruthie."

"Royce Palmer got you the McCullum place, Sam."

Sam jerked, eyeing his father. "What?"

"That's sort of right, Sam. You, see, Wilbur changed his mind about sellin' it to MacGregor's kid."

"You made him do that, Daddy!" Ruth blurted.

"Well," Walter admitted, "Yeah. I sorta did."

"That was why I got that reminder of Royce Palmer asking for General Roosevelt's signature! You never told me."

By the time the three drove into the McCullum yard, Sam heard most of the story.

Sam soon realized why his father wanted him to wear his uniform. Both the kindly old farmer and his wife pawned over the striking young officer, genuinely interested in knowing the history behind each ribbon and medal pinned to Sammy's chest. Walter stood back proudly listening.

The two had anticipated Walter and his son's coming to the farm that afternoon. Grace made lemonade and the five sat around the oak table.

"I almost messed up, Sammy, but your dad straightened me out in time," Wilbur explained.

"Sure Sammy," Grace offered. "We're glad you're the one getting it. We didn't even think."

Sam sat at the table, shaking his head. "I just found out about this this afternoon, Wilbur. I was in Germany when I got Mom's letter, and I assumed you had sold it to Cat. I didn't expect any of this."

"Walt told us about you tellin' him about the government's backin' you kids for what you've done. Then Sam Armling called us and said everything was set up with the Federal Land Bank. We're just happy things are workin' out."

"I just hope that the price that Wilbur and me come to suits you, son," Walter put in.

Sam took a deep breath, and studied his father. "A month ago, if someone told me this could be happening, I'd told them they were out of their minds. I can't believe you pulled all this off, Dad."

"You still have to be the one that pays for it."

"I can do that."

"What time in the mornin' we gotta see Royce?" McCullum asked, rising from the table.

"Nine, then Sam and I have to go to Denver and see Armling."

Early the next morning Walter and his son drove into Cottonwood, and once again, Walter insisted Sam wear his uniform. Sam was beginning to understand why his father wanted to marquee his son.

"My!My!My!" Palmer gushed, fingering Sam's collection of ribbons and awards. Normally that sort of sartorial intrusion would be ill-mannered, but Sam didn't mind. Palmer had just done him a gigantic favor—pro bono. Palmer asked several questions about Sam's experiences, following up with specific military and political questions which Sam answered readily and accurately. Walter was agog, but Palmer and Sam, to Walter's astonishment, appeared matter-of-fact about the entire line of discourse.

Four men, Walter, Wilbur, Sam, and Royce sat around a conference table; one giving directions; two signing agreements and contracts, and one witnessing.

"I don't know if your dad told you, Sam, but you have to come back here for me to record the abstract and promissory note in this county."

"I want to tell you, Royce," Sam put in, "I greatly appreciate what you did."

"Don't even think about it, Sam," Palmer offered, "These two farmers will tell you I'd give my left nut if I could to see that that kid didn't get that farm."

Both McCullum and Walter laughed heartily.

Sam stared at the lawyer somewhat startled at his choice of words.

DENVER

Sam was humbled that the head of a large banking institution would heap the praise that he did upon the young lieutenant, but it was sincere and Armling went on to say how pleased he had been that Walter would consider him as a namesake.

"Dad always spoke so well of you, Sir," Sam said, whereupon, Armling recounted meeting Walter a quarter of a century back, and that Walter paid for a truck with money he carried in his boot. The banker said that he had recounted the story many times. Armling also told Sam about the chance meeting with Abner Harper, and that if all Armling's clients were as forthright as Walter Hubbard, his job would have been much easier over the years.

During the spate of pleasantries, the name Royce Palmer surfaced, whereupon Armling remarked, "It looks like you'll be losing your local barrister."

"Why is that?" Walter asked.

"John Metzger is stepping down and the governor has endorsed Palmer."

"I should know who he is. Who is he?" Walter asked.

"The State Attorney General."

"Wow!" Walter declared. "Wonder why the governor wanted Royce?"

"Royce Palmer sticks up for the victim—the disadvantaged—the last in line," Armling explained. "Dunning's that kind of guy himself. That last round Palmer stood up for Sam here against that Smalldones' lawyer. That impressed the governor."

"Can he get elected?"

"You get Grant Dunning's blessing, it's a done deal."

The three parted company, and on the way back to Cottonwood, Sam joked, "I've been in a dull war. I needed to get back out here where the action is."

"Yeah," Walter chortled, "This is the most excitement I've had since someone poked a hole in Jack MacGregor's tractor."

For the first time since Sam came home, Walter heard his son laugh. Sam, who was now driving the Pontiac, glanced over. "Did he ever get it fixed?"

"Naw. Art Young said it's still sittin' in the same spot."

"That's been three years."

"I know."

"He'll be able to buy a new one before long now that the war's going be over."

"You're gonna need one, yourself, Sam."

Both men avoided the one subject that would spoil the afternoon.

Walter and Sam walked into Palmer's office precisely at 4pm. The papers were signed and recorded.

Walter had to know. "Royce, Sam Armling said you might be leavin' us. Anything to that?"

Palmer leaned back. "Word gets around. You're familiar with the parable 'bread cast on the water,' aren't you Walt?"

"Can't be married to Millie and not know that," Walter returned.

"Boy, that's for sure," Sam echoed.

Palmer exhaled a long breath of air. "I've always tried to help the guy who..." He pinched his lip, "maybe couldn't get the help he needed on his own, or deserved it little more than the next guy did. Know what I mean?"

"Sure, I do. I'm one of those," Walter offered.

Palmer was hesitant. Walter had never seen him like this. "Well, I've always been put off by the type who tries to take advantage of another person because he has more money or influence, or just downright greedy. He doesn't do these things because it's right, or he has to do them to survive. He does them because he can. Know what I'm talking about?"

"Sure do."

"I do, too," Sam agreed.

Palmer inhaled again. "A few weeks ago Grant and Elsie Dunning had Margaret and me up the governor's mansion for dinner. I don't know Grant Dunning very well, but I'm an admirer of his, as so many are…"

"I've always voted for him," Walter interjected.

Palmer continued, "He told me he liked these qualities of mine, and asked me if I'd consider running for the office of Attorney General."

"And you said 'Yes'."

"I did. I genuinely hate the thought of leaving Cottonwood. It's been good to me. It's given me my start."

"Aw c'mon, Royce," Walter jibed. "I heard you came from big money back East."

"That isn't so."

"Sure it is! You were drivin' a Cadillac when you first hit this country."

Palmer flashed that roughish smile. "I did have a running start. I won't deny that."

"Well, you'd do a good job," Walter said, adding, "We'll miss you around here, but we'll sure as hell vote for you."

Palmer smiled, extending his hand, "That's the part that counts."

****

August 6, 1945

Sam Hubbard guided the John Deere A down the immaculately straight rows when he sighted a lone figure standing along the fence at the far end of the field. It was three o'clock in the afternoon, and he was finishing cultivating beans.

The summer had been a welcome catharsis for Sam. He loved the open country and the life he was leading. Except for the persistent reminder of his brother's plight, Sam was a happy man.

He identified the figure of his mother.

He shut the engine off and walked up to her. Before he could ask, she said solemnly, "President Truman just announced that we dropped an atom bomb on Hiroshima, Japan, this morning."

"What's an atom bomb?"

"It's apparently a horrible new weapon. President Truman said it is estimated that it killed a hundred thousand people and leveled everything for miles around the blast."

Sam was stunned. "Miles?"

"That's what the radio report said."

"If we've got a bomb like that, this thing should be over quick."

"I hope so, Sam. I just hope Andy's alive and can hold out."

Sam merely nodded. "You know," he began, "I saw a lot of the 'enemy' who wasn't really an enemy at all. They were people just like us. They followed orders." Sam looked down at the soft earth. "God, I felt sorry for those poor people—women, kids and old people, with nothing left of their country. I'll never forget the look of despair on their faces."

Millie embraced her son. "You've come back a very different man, Sam. I'm so very proud of you."

****

AOMORI PRISON CAMP TOKYO
AUGUST 9, 1945

Corporal Ikeya was summoned to the prison commandant's quarters. The corporal bowed stiffly.

"I need to inform you, Ikeya, that another fire bomb has been dropped. This time on our great city of Nagasaki."

Ikeya nodded, apparently not affected by the announcement.

"You should be aware that the end is near for the Imperial Republic of Japan."

Again, he merely nodded.

"I think it would be prudent to be a little less abusive with our prisoners."

Two weeks later, Ozawa summoned Ikeya into his quarters. The atmosphere in and around the compound had progressively become disorganized. Order had become relaxed as had the regimen of work. Prisoners were no longer required to labor in the shipyards, so they hung around languishing in their bunks. It was becoming obvious to all involved that conditions were certain to change. All deliveries were becoming irregular, including food supplies, which affected not only the incarcerated, but the cadre as well.

"Here," the Japanese Major said, handing Ikeya an envelope. Ikeya took it, and gave it a cursory inspection. "It's a letter to Hubbard," Ozawa explained. "I've decided to distribute whatever mail we have to our remaining prisoners. A little kindness at this late hour may save us from being executed. We expect the Americans to be invading our homeland any day now."

Ikeya opened the letter dated May, 1943. "This letter is over two years old," the corporal stopped showing the subservience as was normally expected.

"I know. Just the same I'm having them all distributed."

Ikeya turned to leave. "Oh, Ikeya," The corporal stopped. "You may be aware," Ozawa began carefully, "that I have taken very good care of prisoner Snavely."

"I'm aware," Ikeya responded tersely.

"I don't expect that the Americans will get any careless information that may be used in my disfavor. Do you understand?"

Again Ikeya nodded, bowed, and turned to leave.

"Corporal Ikeya! Did you get my message?"

"Yes," Ikeya said and turned away. Ozawa knew at the moment Ikeya understood, but he, the major, better not rely on any moral support.

Andy was in pitiful condition. He couldn't have gone to work had he been required that morning. His body was horribly emaciated. His eyes bulged from their dry sockets and his joints ached as he moved. He lay in his bunk clasping the silver memento staring absently at the barracks ceiling.

"A letter for you, Hubbard," Ikeya said impassively.

With surprising energy Andy reached for the letter, murmuring, "Thanks."

Without responding, Ikeya turned on his heel and left.

Shakily, Andy fumbled with the letter pinching the keepsake against his thumb and the letter while arranging the missive with his free hand. Unfolding the letter, he felt the annoyance of the censor's habit of blacking out lines. He was aware that they had a job to do, but knew so much elimination of what was said was not necessary to any sort of security.

"March 27, 1943" it read. "Why did it take them so long to get this to me?" he thought.

Dear Andy,
The weather has been warm and pleasant. xxxxxxxxxxxxxxxxxxxxxxxxxxxxxx. Xxxxxxxxxxxxxxxxxxxxxxxxxxxxxx xxxxxxxxxxxxxxxx Maybe we could be in college together. Sam is home. He looks good. Andrea was home last week. We went to the show, and while we were waiting, Chattman drove up in a new convertible with Andrea in the car. xxxxxxxxxxxxxxx xxxxxxxxxxxxxxxxx xxxxxxxxxxxxxxx xxxxxxxxxx xxxxxxxxxxxxxxxxxxxxxxxxxxxxxxxxxx xxxxxxxxx xxxxxxxxxxxxx xxxxxxxxxxxx xxxxxxxxxxx xxxxxxxxxxxxxxxxxxxxxxxx
I love you too, Ruthie"

Andy fell back against the solid bunk. His old feelings of doubt resurfaced in waves. Andrea was the love of his life, keeping him sustained through these unbearable years of prison. Ruthie's letter to Andy confirmed to him that he was not, however, the only love of her life. He felt a token tear slide from his dry eyes and trickle down the side of his face. The silver memento slipped from his defeated hand to the board floor, found a crevice and rolled through to be lost for all time.

Andrew Walter Hubbard was dead.

Mercifully, Ruthie would never know the result of her innocent, caring letter.

CHAPTER 47

TOKYO
August 11, 1945

The Chevrolet troop truck weaved through broken pavement along the desolate dock section in the general direction of the prison compound. Rusty, preparing for the occupation, had studied the Tokyo city map when he was sailing in from Okinawa. Now he was studying it again while riding in the front with the driver. In the bed of the truck, with the canvas removed, two platoons of Marines were jammed together on the benches. Although armed, the complement of liberators didn't expect any resistance. A jeep carrying a photographer and a correspondent followed closely behind the truck. Directly behind the jeep, two Dodge ambulances brought up the rear. The map Rusty held was written in English, so, conveniently, the word AOMORI sprang out before him.

A prison compound is not difficult to identify. If the forbiddingly ugly wire caging and rows of deplorable shacks doesn't give it away, the smell of death will.

As the convoy approached the compound, an animated frenzy of prison guards slinked back toward the rear. Rusty bailed out of the truck striding sharply to the front gate. One prison guard stood resolutely by the entrance. By this time the Marines, all equipped with carbines, were out of the truck and huddled behind their leader, whereupon Rusty made the motion with his arms that the gates be opened. The sentry understood and quickly unlocked the tall mesh-wire gate. Rusty could see figures beginning to move out of the shade of the overhangs into the sun. The retreating guards, becoming intermingled with prisoners splaying out of their confinement, presented a curious dispersion. It wasn't difficult to discern the fed from the ill fed.

Presently a Japanese officer walked quickly across the parched earth toward Rusty, extending his hand.

"Good morning," he said in clipped English. "I'm Major Ozawa. May I be of service?"

Rusty, showing no surprise that the oriental spoke English, avoided the handshake and snarled, "Yeah. You can tell your men what I'm about to tell mine!" Rusty looked at the Marines and barked, "Get in there and get every damn door and gate open and release those men. If anybody gives you any shit, shoot their asses!"

He turned to the major. "Got that?"

The major, visibly alarmed, repeated Rusty's indictment in halting Japanese.

Rusty's men broke for the cages resembling boys let for summer vacation.

Rusty turned to the officer. "Now you can help me. I'm looking for Andy Hubbard. Do you know where I can find him?"

"Ahh... yesss, Prisoner Hubbard..."

The blow of Rusty's backhand knocked Ozawa off balance. "He's not a prisoner, you yellow cocksucker!"

Immediately Ozawa rubbed his cheek, whimpering, "I can take you to a guard who knows where we can find Mr. Hubbard."

Rusty gave an impatient gesture for the officer to move. Ozawa started toward his office with Rusty on his heels. Off to the side, Rusty could see the immediate shuffle of clusters of skinny men making their way out into the open compound.

Presently Ozawa located Ikeya. "We're looking for Mr. Hubbard, Ikeya. Would you take this American Colonel to him?"

Rusty was repulsed by the man, but was amazed at how much he knew about the Americans.

"Do you need anything else of me?" Ozawa asked.

"Not for now, but stay close," Rusty ordered. The officer turned and walked away, leaving the guard and Rusty together.

"Well, let's go! Where is he?"

Ikeya looked down at the powdered earth, and stammered, "Andy's dead."

The gentle guard's soft voice and broken English confused him.

"He..." Rusty caught himself. "What did you say?"

"He's dead, Sir?"

"Do all you people speak English?"

"No, Sir, but Andy and me—we speak..."

At that moment a skinny partially-bald man, approximately Rusty's height, stepped up.

"Rusty?" the man asked.

The collision of events unnerved Rusty. He expelled a volume of air, shaking his head. "Whoa! Who are you?"

"Bob Armstrong."

Rusty swallowed, feeling his throat become dry. He focused on Armstrong, extending his hand. "I haven't seen you since basic."

"You wanted to know about Andy, Rusty. He's dead."

"That's what this guy said," he said swinging an arm toward the guard. "When?"

"Two days ago."

"Just two days?"

Both Armstrong and the guard answered simultaneously, "Yes."

Rusty looked at Armstrong. "Where is he?"

"I don't know now. Do you know, Ikeya?"

The guard looked embarrassed, "He still on pile."

Rusty snapped at the guard, "How the hell can you sonsabitches let him die?"

"Don't get on Ikeya, Rusty," Armstrong defended. "He's been good to us."

At that moment, a chow truck drove into the compound. Out of the corner of his eye, Armstrong saw it, when Rusty said, "Bob. Do you mind coming with me and showing me where Andy is?"

Armstrong hesitated, taking a breath with his skinny chest. "I think I just saw food. Ikeya can show you, Rusty."

Rusty patted him on the shoulder. "Sure, Bob. Go ahead. I'll catch up with you later." Then asked, "Know anything about Snavely, Bob?"

"He got hit in the head on Bataan..."

"I know. I was there."

"He went dingy. That major who runs this joint has been butt-fuckin' him for years. Snavely's fattern' a pig."

"What?"

"Ask Ikeya. He'll tell you all about him."

Armstrong turned to leave, stopping himself. "Rusty?"

"What is it, Bob?"

"If I didn't see the name Atkins on your jacket, I wouldn't have ever known you. You don't at all look like you used to."

Rusty sighed, "You don't either, Bob."

Through a gate, then a narrow passageway they walked. After a short walk around a grove of bushes, the spectacle next to a tin shed caused Rusty to stop short. Seven emaciated bodies were stacked in a pile; Andy Hubbard's corpse lay on top. Shockingly more painful than the sight itself, was the fact that he recognized the extremely-long boned, thick brown haired, bulgy-eyed, open mouth skeleton. He fell against the building in complete disorientation. Rusty had seen death. He had seen swelling bloated corpses, bodies blown to bits, but he had never witnessed the impact of starvation of a real friend.

"In all the tragedy of war that I've witnessed, this is by far and away the worst." He swallowed hard, then murmured trying to keep from crying. "Well, you old bastard, you saved my life, but I couldn't quite pull it off for you. God knows I tried." Rusty began crying unabashedly. "God knows I tried!"

He looked away from his dead friend. His eyes met Ikeya's, who was also tearing. The odd compassion affected Rusty. He would never know that the two had shared similar struggles.

"I'll get his legs. You take his arms. I'll lead the way. I want to put him in an ambulance."

Rusty instructed a corpsman to be certain Andy's body be shipped to the Marine morgue in San Diego. He had two more duties to attend to before clearing the prison; find Bob Snavely, and confront the Japanese officer who had been abusing him. He turned to thank the Japanese guard, but Ikeya was gone.

Ikeya had rushed to Ozawa's quarters to warn the commandant that the American colonel found out about his abusing Snavely and would soon be on his trail. That somehow the prisoner had been a close friend of the colonel's.

Ozawa exploded. "You were given specific orders never to tell!"

"I didn't tell!" Ikeya shouted back, knowing rank no longer mattered.

"How did he know?" Ozawa asked, his tone softening.

"I heard a prisoner tell him."

Ozawa paused, visibly shaken, stammering. "I think you had better go, Ikeya."

Rusty Atkins had witnessed many, many horrifying visions in the course of the war, but none that would cause him to vomit; this one did.

Being a lacky, Snavely would come and go. Work in the garden. Soak in the steam bath. Eat when he was hungry. Sleep when he was tired. Go to the commandant's quarters, sometimes on his own, sometimes when he was called.

Ozawa had been taught as a young Shinto warrior that nothing was more terrifying than western torture. Not risking this certain fate, he took his dagger and performed the ancient ritual of disembowelment. At this moment, Snavely stepped through the doorway, seeing Ozawa in bloody agony crumpling to the floor. Overcome with animal emotion, Snavely rushed forward clutching him and began sobbing uncontrollably. Rusty was close by now, and upon hearing the turmoil, stepped into the small room. Here, he witnessed the visceral bloody embrace. His mind raced to collect his thoughts. He recognized Snavely, even in his corpulent condition, and although he felt compassion for his friend, the scene was too much for him to accept.

Overwhelmed with nausea and revulsion, he stepped outside and vented. The morning was more than Atkins could endure. He walked to his staff car, requesting he be alone. The apparition of WWII had made its final appearance to the innocent waif from Louisiana.

Cottonwood

August 29, 1945

Millie would use Andrea's telephone number, her private line should she ever need it. That morning she drove into town to place a call.

After the usual transfer of operators in person to person calls of the day, Andrea's voice come on the line.

"Andrea Vogel."

"Andrea, this is Mildred Hubbard."

Millie had never announced herself as "Mildred" to Andrea. After an awkward pause, Andrea answered anxiously, "Why are you calling, Millie?"

"We received a Western Union telegram yesterday afternoon form the War Department. Andy's dead."

The abrupt announcement caused Andrea to shriek, then cry out, "When!?"

"There were no details, other than…" Millie broke up. "He's dead."

"Oh, Millie!" Andrea began sobbing. "I had this premonition. I loved him so much!"

"I know you did, Andrea. We all did."

"Millie, you'll have to let me off the phone. Will you let me know when you know more?"

"I will."

****

Rusty Atkins had spent the evening at the Hubbard farm that early September evening, and had been a significant comfort to Millie and the family. Rusty had made arrangements for the body to be shipped to Denver and would have it brought to Cottonwood for the funeral two days from then.

The next morning, Andrea drove to the farm, meeting Rusty in person. Later, she presented the Hubbards with an unusual request; that the body be buried on her acre. The family consented.

"I would like to dig the grave," Rusty offered.

"No. No, you don't have to do that," Walter protested.

"It's the last thing I can do for my friend," Rusty offered.

"Mind if I help?" Sam asked.

"No, I think you should," Rusty answered.

Andrea led the way to the site, followed by Sam and Rusty, in the old Chevy pickup. Talk was an aura of mutual respect.

"I'm aware of your war record," Rusty said.

"It was nothing compared to yours, Colonel," Sam responded.

"Well, it was, and the thing's over with. That's all that matters."

Andrea picked out the spot and the two men took their shovels and went to work. Andrea excused herself and went home.

Mrs. Vogel called upstairs to her daughter who was gathering her personal belongings.

"There's someone here to see you, Andrea."

"Who is it?"

Mrs. Vogel knew who was standing on the porch. "It's Chatman MacGregor."

Andrea had anticipated the moment. "I won't see him, Mother. Can you get rid of him?"

The gentle German lady stepped out the kitchen door, closing it behind her, and stared at the young rancher.

"She won't see you," Sigrid Vogel said with forced authority.

"She knows I'm here?"

"Yes, she does, and she asked me to, in her words, 'get rid of you'."

"I think it would be in your best interests to let me see her."

"You step off my porch or I'm calling Sheriff Young."

MacGregor sauntered toward her, uttering insolently, "You oughta know you shouldn't talk to a MacGregor like that, Sigrid."

The grand insult of the day, of calling an elder by the first name, angered her.

"And you ought to know that your family no longer has any interest in our store, so you can no longer lord it over us! Now get off my porch!"

Chattman was perplexed, overcome by the statement, slowly cowered off the porch. Jack MacGregor never took the time to tell his son of the complicated title issue and statute of limitations.

Ruthie walked to the kitchen window. "Somebody just drove up, Dad," she said.

"Can you tell who it is?" Walter asked.

"Looks like Clete Fossun," she said, brushing the curtain aside.

Walter bolted from his chair and was out in the yard immediately.

MacGregor's trusted cowhand of many years, working earlier for Liam before Jack, opened the door of his pickup.

"No need for you to get out," Walter said invectively.

Old Clete closed the door and rolled down the window.

"Jack wants to know if you'd care if he comes to Andy's funeral."

"You tell the son of a bitch," Walter breathed viciously, "that if I see his face anywhere near there, I'll get my shotgun and fill him so full of holes he won't hold hay!"

"I'll tell him," Clete said, pulling out of the yard.

Rusty and Sam were finishing their job when Lloyd Speer, the bartender at the Tumbleweed drove up.

"Hi, Lloyd," Sam said, wiping his brow.

"They said I could find you here. I came to tell you that there's a guy up at the bar looking for a guy named Rusty." He glanced over at Rusty and grinned. "That might be you."

Rusty smiled and nodded.

"Did he say who he was?" Rusty asked.

"Said he was a reporter of some kind. I gotta get back. Nobody's mindin' the bar. But he's a tall fellow."

"Thanks, Lloyd," Sam offered.

"You have to take me to this bar, Sam," Rusty said, tossing his shovel in the back of the pickup.

Olson was sitting at a weathered round wood table when Sam and Rusty walked in. He forced himself up from the chair and walked up.

"Good god, Phil! You're *walking*!" Rusty exclaimed.

Introductions were made, and the three sat at the rough-hewn table.

"I had an operation," Olson began to explain, "a bone fusion, after I left for the Philippines. I met an old doctor who befriended Andy, incidentally."

"I know. I met him a time or two," Rusty intruded.

"You *did*?"

"Yeah."

"He really did a job on me. It's been a little over four months since the operation, and here I am walking on my own."

Rusty quickly explained to Olson how he knew the doctor, then he suggested Olson do a story on Sam.

"I'd be honored. I find you're quite a hero around here, Sam. How about giving me a story?"

"Not much to tell, but I'll give you what I can," Same responded.

"Don't believe that, Phil," Rusty intruded "His story needs to be told."

Shortly the subject of Andrea surfaced, when Olson gushed. "I *forgot*. She *lives* here. I'd love to see her!"

"I could probably go get her if she's home," Sam offered.

"Would you?" Olson asked. "We'll be right here."

"Andrea! There's some hulk coming on the porch!" Helga chirped.

Andrea stepped to the window. "That's Sam Hubbard." She opened the door.

Before Andrea could speak, Sam said, "Andrea, there's a guy named Phil Olson down at the Tumbleweed. He would like to see you."

She clasped her hands in delight. "Give me just a second, will you, Sam? I'll powder my nose and be right with you."

"You'd better bring your car, Andrea. This looks like it could take a while and I've got to get back to the farm."

"Okay, Sam. I'll be down in a minute. Tell them not to go away."

He smiled. "I don't think there's any chance."

Helga saw the smile and was instantly smitten.

Sam returned to the Tumbleweed. Shortly Andrea entered, whereupon she and the correspondent had an emotional reunion.

"You look older, Phil."

"It's been almost four years, Andrea. But *you* look the same."

The comment brought polite chuckles from Rusty and Sam. Conversation that became warm and easy, was halted abruptly when

Andrea looked menacingly toward the door. Chattman MacGregor stepped in, and upon seeing her with three other men, backed slowly out.

"That would be Chattman," Rusty mused.

Andrea and Sam merely nodded.

The talk continued, mostly about nothing Sam had been a part of. The subject of a hotel was mentioned, and since it was announced that a very elegant old hotel sat hidden just outside the city limits, the three decided to go give it an inspection. Olson announced that Hoffmeister would be flying in from San Diego, Loren Siffering from Los Angeles, and Rusty's wife, Sally, would be coming in from the east. All in the morning. Sam offered to bring in the family Pontiac to take to Denver to pick them up.

Rusty had arranged for the body to be brought from Denver, and since Cottonwood had no mortuary, the fire station would serve as the funeral home. Rusty would drive out to the farm before the hearse arrived in Cottonwood. It was arranged that all meet at the Hubbard farm later in the afternoon. Sam left for the farm to inform the family on the next day's plans.

The gray Navy Packard hearse, followed by a staff car, brought the last of the Hubbards and rolled into Cottonwood that warm Friday afternoon. The remainder of the family, plus Andrea, Phil Olson, Rusty and his wife and General Hoffmeister were there to meet it. Six Marines, in dress blues carried the casket to the bier placed for it. The six servicemen retreated to Buckley Air Station, where the entourage would return again the next afternoon accompanied with a Marine Honor Guard for the funereal.

"Can I see him" Andrea asked nobody in particular.

"I want to see my baby," Mildred Hubbard sobbed.

"Rusty doesn't think it should be opened, so I think we ought to leave it closed," Walter said.

"I want to see him or I'll never really know," Mildred protested.

The women got their way. Rusty had been in charge of the arrangements. Slowly he approached the casket, unlatched it and raised the hood.

Andrea shrieked. Mildred gasped once and fainted into Walter's arm. Walter fought his emotions, trying not to swear. Sam glanced away, tears coming to his eyes. Hoffmeister set his jaw defiantly shaking his head negatively.

As Rusty was closing the lid, Andrea sobbed grievously, "It's him! It's him! He looks just like he did in my dreams!"

Neither Olson nor Sally looked.

The image of her favorite son was engraved indelibly on Mildred's mind, and would bring her out of a sound sleep many times in the years to come. Walter's hate for the MacGregors grew even deeper. Rusty Atkins was right. The casket should have never been opened.

The group drove out to the Hubbard farm and sat around the kitchen table remembering the life of Andy. The recollections of Phil Olson, Doctor Hoffmeister, Loren Siffering and Rusty were most valuable and comforting to Mildred and Walter. A change of the funeral order was made that evening. Walter impulsively asked Rusty to deliver the eulogy. Rusty hesitated, then reluctantly consented. The town minister politely agreed to step aside.

One hundred folding chairs sat before the tent covered gravesite. To the side and front was a rostrum. Cars began filling the area as people came and took their seat in the split rail enclosure. Some one hundred yards away on a slight hill, Jack MacGregor stood hatless in his denim clothes behind a large cottonwood tree.

Four chairs for the Hubbard family were placed beside the casket perpendicular to the large audience. The sun shone brightly that September afternoon. The large fall cottonwoods still had more than half their leaves. Those that fell provided a natural carpet as the ground was covered by the now dead gold petals. A few billowy clouds complemented the dark blue endless sky.

All seats were filled. Many who came to pay homage to the popular young man would have to stand, and many of those standing were curious strangers.

In the front row, the distraught, beautiful Andrea, dressed in black occupied the front seat. Next to Andrea was Philip Olson, Loren Siffering, Sally Atkins, Harold Hoffmeister, Royce Palmer, Marshall and Eleanor Reiss, John Sutton, Felton Caldwell and Forrest Bruenig. Filling the seats behind were farm families, Schatzaeders, Durkees, McCullums, Thurstons, townspeople, school mates and friends. Behind a giant cottonwood, a hatless gnarled rancher silently watched.

Waiting for the services to start, Andrea looked skyward seeing a majestic cloud with its immense columns and plumes. She heard Andy's voice, years before as they lay nude on the sand, "See that big cloud? That's our castle."

Immediate thoughts filled her mind of a young brown haired boy standing at the counter in her father's store, then a tall handsome Marine in his dress blues standing grinning on the porch, the strong supple body making love to her, then the black coupe speeding away in the rainy darkness of the school parking lot. Suddenly, she wept uncontrollably and unashamedly.

A sudden stiff breeze rattled the dry leaves, as an immaculately-uniformed bony cheeked Marine colonel stepped behind the rostrum. On his left as he faced the audience, was a simple farmer dressed in a new blue pinstriped suit. His eyes showed pain as he looked ahead shakily, locking his jaw. The sharp featured woman sat next to him resembling a frightened little girl. She was too tired to cry. She had cried all night. Her red eyes showed sadness as she fought for a reason to live. Just five years earlier, her gray hair was black as the darkest night. Her large blond son, in his military officer's uniform, sat beside her cradling her shoulder in his right arm. His eighteen-year-old sister sat on his left, gripping his hand.

There were no microphones or organ music as Rusty prepared to speak. The audience became still, save the occasional sobs as the most affected relieved themselves of their grief.

"We're here," he began, "to... to say goodbye to a friend."

Rusty scanned the crowd. "But he was more than a friend. He was someone very special. He was first, a very intellectual person. He was an athlete. He was a healer..."

"Yes!" Hoffmeister exulted.

"He was a musician..."

"Amen!" Siffering echoed.

Forrest Bruenig was feeling somewhat embarrassed he didn't say something.

"and, last of all, he was a soldier. He shouldn't have been a soldier, but that sort of thing happens. He shouldn't have been a soldier, because a soldier kills, and kill was the last thing he wanted to do.

"He was a person we all would like to be. Kind, funny, gracious, forgiving, and… innocent. He could look over the hills and see into the valleys. It was all so beautiful to him. But enemies hide in the hills and they hide in the valleys, and he wasn't one who could identify an enemy. He never could. This was not his world. Heaven is his world. Yes, he presides there, and we all should be envious of him because he's doing what he wants. In time, he will summon those he loves. Jesus said 'love your brother as you love yourself.' As I lifted the broken shell of this…"

"Ahh!" Andrea erupted.

"this man and carried him away, a Japanese prison guard assisted me. I saw a tear in his eye. Tragedy is like a loose coat. It never fits, yet we wear it just the same. We wear it because we have no choice."

He looked over at the casket. "Well, Andy, you have shed that tragedy. May you live forever. God forbid it we should ever pass this way again. Goodbye my friend."

Rusty turned and saluted the casket, stepping down. "Reverend Andrews will give the benediction."

Immediately Olson, Siffering, General Hoffmeister and Sam Hubbard stood and saluted.

The military attendants lowered the coffin into the ground. Taps was played. Their responsibility had ended. They left. Some people patronizingly hung around, but eventually, they, too, left. Many gave their sympathies to the Hubbard family, and to Andrea, but soon they were also gone. Andrea was oblivious to life itself as she looked at the wooden red box at the bottom of the grave. She had picked the exact spot they had made love five years ago, where Andy had raised the back seat of the '20 Chevy for the 'winter blanket,' laid it across his future gravesite, and ravished her. Finally, she softly turned and surrendered the last vestige of her love to the earth

The crowd came to Andy's funeral as the grass comes for the spring and those who came to pay their last respects left as surely as the grass cowers to the cold winter. Everyone was gone, his mother, his family, his friends, even Andrea. Andy was finally alone. Suddenly and uncharacteristically, a sharp gust of autumn wind attacked the cottonwood grove tearing the dead leaves away from their pillars. The gust also severed a live green leaf which obediently fluttered downward in a cautious oscillating descent until its gentle vortex spilled it gently, tenderly, on the redwood box that claimed the body of Andrew Walter Hubbard.

MILITARY ACRONYMS

BAR – Browning Automatic Rifle

BOQ – Bachelor Officers' Quarters; office assigning soldiers to living quarters.

CINPAC – Commander in Chief Pacific Fleet Headquarters; the headquarters of Admiral Chester W. Nimitz while he was Commander in Chief of the Pacific Fleet during World War II

CO – Commanding Officer

CQ - Charge of Quarters; the person who stays up all night and keeps an eye on the door, and checks people in and out

DI – Drill Instructor

E-5 – US Marine Sergeant

E-8 – US Marine Master Sergeant or First Sergeant

EM – Enlisted Marine

F4-U – Vought F4-U Corsair; carrier-capable fighter aircraft

G-2 – Army or Marine Corps component intelligence staff officer

KP – Kitchen Police; one who helps the cooks in the kitchen either with food preparation or clean up

LCI – Landing craft Infantry; seagoing amphibious assault ships used to land large numbers of infantry directly onto beaches

LCP – Landing Craft Personnel; a landing craft used to ferry troops from transport ships to attack enemy-held shores

MP – Military Police Officer

P-40 – Curtiss P-40 Warhawk; single-engine, single-seat, all-metal fighter and ground-attack aircraft

PBY – US Navy medium to heavy twin amphibious aircraft used for maritime patrol, water bomber, and search and rescue

PFC – Private First Class

PT – Patrol Torpedo boat; a torpedo-armed fast attack boat valued for its maneuverability and speed

PX – Post Exchange; the shopping center for the military bases

SBD – Douglas SBD Dauntless; naval scout plane and dive bomber

UPI – United Press International

USO – United Service Organization; provides programs, services and live entertainment to United States troops and their families

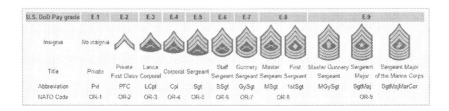

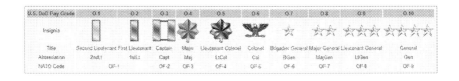

ABOUT THE AUTHOR

Albert Bartlett grew up on a farm in the small town of Deer Trail, Colorado. After serving in the army during the Korean conflict, he attended the University of Colorado. Al spent the first half of his professional career teaching high school English and coaching football and the second half returning to the farming he learned from his father. His oldest brother, Jack, was captured on Corregidor, launching Al's interest and study of World War II. He's currently retired, recently celebrated his fiftieth wedding anniversary with his wife, Nancy, and spends his spare time building birdhouses, which he sells at the local farmer's market.

Printed in the United States
By Bookmasters